I never heard a skid of brakes or a horn either. Something made me turn back, a sixth sense like Flori claims to have or a gust of warm air preceding the silver grill barreling toward me.

Fear blinded me. I glimpsed flashes of red, a dark windshield, and a bright headlight before I turned and leaped to the side into a scrubby patch of ditch and brush. Expecting to feel my body breaking, I clenched, thinking of Celia. How stupid that I would die doing something for my health.

The vehicle sped by in a whirl of wind, dirt, and pebbles that pelted the back of my neck. I fell hard, my palms hitting the ground first, then my elbows and chest. My scream ended in a hiccup as my lungs compressed. Rolling over on my back, I couldn't count the number of places that stung and throbbed, but the pain meant I was alive. For now.

By Ann Myers

BREAD OF THE DEAD
CINCO DE MAYHEM

Cinco de Mayhem

A SANTA FE CAFÉ MYSTERY

ANN MYERS

WILLIAM MORROW
An Imprint of HarperCollins Publishers

This is a work of fiction. Names, characters, places, and incidents are products of the author's imagination or are used fictitiously and are not to be construed as real. Any resemblance to actual events, locales, organizations, or persons, living or dead, is entirely coincidental.

WILLIAM MORROW
An Imprint of HarperCollins*Publishers*
195 Broadway
New York, New York 10007

Copyright © 2016 by Ann Perramond
ISBN 978-0-06-238229-0
www.harpercollins.com

First William Morrow mass market printing: April 2016

William Morrow® and HarperCollins® are registered trademarks of HarperCollins Publishers.

Printed in the United States of America

10 9 8 7 6 5 4 3 2 1

Acknowledgments

I wish to thank all those who helped and supported me in writing this book. Many thanks to my wonderful agent, Christina Hogrebe, and the Jane Rotrosen Agency for believing in the Santa Fe Café Mystery series and finding it such a wonderful home at William Morrow/HarperCollins. To Emily Krump, my fabulous editor, thank you so much for your insight and guidance. I am humbled to have an amazing team from Harper-Collins behind me, including publisher Liate Stehlik, marketing director Shawn Nicholls, Eileen DeWald and Greg Plonowski in production, and publicist Emily Homonoff. Thanks also to the talented Tom Egner for the beautiful cover design.

I am forever grateful to my family, my most enthusiastic and steadfast supporters, and especially to my husband, Eric, for everything. My grandmother, Mary, will always be my model and inspiration.

Rita, Flori, and the crew, as well as Tres Amigas Café and the fighting food carters, are all flights of fiction. Like Rita, however, I am entranced by Santa Fe, a truly special place. Thanks to friends and acquaintances in New Mexico who have made it even more special.

Cinco de Mayhem

Chapter 1

I don't know who came up with the expression "No crying over spilt milk." Does anyone really get that emotional about milk? A fallen soufflé, however, now that's worthy of some weeping. I stared through the glass oven door, helpless as once-glorious pillows of cheesy, eggy delicious-ness sank to the depths of their ceramic dish.

My friend Linda, the soufflé slayer, barely no-ticed. I couldn't help feeling peeved. Linda had seen the dish in the oven. She'd even said, "Oh good, you have the oven on." Right before she jammed in two overstuffed trays of tamales and slammed the door with enough force to bring down my soufflé and any others rising in the greater Santa Fe area. As if for good measure, she stomped her sensibly shoed foot on the Saltillo-tile floor of Tres Amigas Café.

"I hate that man! I hate him!" she said, timing each word to a clomp of her tan loafer.

Such uncharacteristic sentiments from Linda shocked me from my soufflé sulk.

They shocked Linda too. She clamped her hands over her mouth before crossing herself and turning wide eyes to me. "Rita, forgive me. I should never say 'hate' about another human being, especially on a Sunday." Her shoulders quivered and her dark eyes welled with tears.

This was no time to fret about flattened French food. Taking Linda by the arm, I guided her to the main dining room, hoping the exuberant décor would cheer her up. How could it not? My elderly boss, friend, and occasional sleuthing partner, Flori—who was also Linda's mother and an overenthusiastic holiday decorator—had outdone herself for Cinco de Mayo. Garlands of colorful tissue paper cut in intricate patterns crisscrossed the ceiling, interspersed with piñatas, including a sombrero-wearing burro, a rainbow-striped poodle, various ruffled chile peppers, and a turquoise Eiffel Tower. Mexican flags poked from the condiment holders, atop vibrant vinyl tablecloths printed with tropical birds and flowers. Most decorators would have stopped there, if not way before. Not my octogenarian friend. Flori had added a half-dozen mannequins dressed as a mariachi band, complete with instruments and embroidered jackets. I hadn't asked Flori where, or why, she'd acquired the plastic people. I also couldn't tell whether some were male, female, or extraterrestrial. What I did know was that the trumpet player's vacant stare creeped me out.

I caught his unseeing eyes, the black orbs floating in pools of empty white space. Firming up my grip on Linda, I headed for a table by the window. Besides being far from the trumpet player, this spot had a lovely view of our outdoor dining patio, recently reopened for spring. Glancing out, I admired the metal tables with their fresh coat of glossy turquoise paint and the lilac hedge, sagging with blooms of deepest purple.

Linda sank into a chair. Her hair, straighter and darker brown than mine, was salted with silver and skimmed her shoulders in a blunt cut matched by thick bangs. The cut was new, and the bangs, according to Linda, were regretted. She scraped them from her forehead, staring down at the psychedelic tropical forest on the tablecloth.

"It's Napoleon, isn't it?" I asked, adding a hefty dash of sarcasm and eye rolling to the name. I mean, *really*, who changes their name to not only a singular moniker, but one so singularly pompous? Superstar singers, I supposed. Or supermodels, or—

"Yes, Napoleon," Linda said, confirming my guess with a weary sigh.

My eye roll dove into a frown. *Or vain star chefs like Napoleon, née plain old Noel Thomas.* If pompousness could literally inflate, he'd be as puffed as an uppity blowfish. It didn't help that the Food Network recently featured Napoleon's casual French bistro on its "best bites" segment and that the walls of his fine-dining establishment practically sagged with awards. Or, I begrudgingly acknowledged, that his food was so darned good. No, more than good. Napoleon made swoonworthy sauces and appetizers almost too pretty to eat. The trouble was, the big-time chef was also a massive bully.

Napoleon's mean moves were the stuff of legend—and nightmares—among local food workers, who told the tales in hushed tones, nervously glancing over their shoulders. I'd heard various renditions of the time Napoleon bankrolled a friend's restaurant, only to take control and shutter the place. Then there was the head chef he fired for cooking a single steak to well done, and the night he pink-slipped an entire wait staff during the dinner service. Rumor had it that he even booted his own mother from their family's former restaurant. *His own mother!*

In my cooking career, I've misjudged medium-rare. I've dropped soup on customers' laps, rolled burritos onto fancy footwear, and rung up thousand-dollar charges for coffee on my eternal nemesis, the cash register. Mistakes happen in fast-paced, high-pressure restaurant settings. I felt for Napoleon's victims, especially his mother. But what really rankled me was his new food-cart enterprise, Crepe Empire. So far, the empire consisted of a single cart, but that was enough. From its helm, Napoleon was laying siege to Santa Fe's central Plaza, forcing out longtime vendors like Linda, who operated Tía Tamales. Linda was around my age now, in her early forties, when she got into the tamale business. Initially, she sold her homemade goodies from a cooler out of the trunk of her car. She became such a success that her eldest son built her a cart, which has been her main source of income since her husband passed away several years ago.

My hard-working friend swiped at her bangs

again. "I am sorry I got upset, Rita, really I am. It's okay. Everything's okay. No worries."

Had Linda just said "no worries"? Now I *was* worried, and I knew Linda must be too. Of course she was. Worrying was in Linda's nature. She viewed trips to the walk-in fridge as brushes with hypothermia. She murmured prayers before stepping into crosswalks, and fretted that her friends and family faced imminent dangers from the Southwestern droughts, wildfires, and pine beetles, to say nothing of the bubonic plague striking prairie dogs. Usually, I tried to brush off her concerns so as not to heighten them in her and myself. Not this time.

"You don't need to apologize," I assured her. Napoleon was the one who should ask for forgiveness, not that he ever would. Preparing myself for fresh irritation, I asked, "What's he doing now?"

Linda slumped in her chair. Not for long. The wooden seats at Tres Amigas feature hand-carved sunbeams, flowers, and sparrows, all punishers of poor posture.

Shifting upright, away from sparrow beaks, Linda said, "The usual. Napoleon got Crystal's juice stand shut down. He had a food inspector come by and question her permit. And he chased away some nice guy playing his guitar, and that funny man who dresses like an old-timey woodsman. You know, the older gentleman who walks around in the fur hat and the hide cloak?"

I knew the woodsman. I wasn't worried about him. Anyone who wanders around town in old-timey trapper attire had to be pretty thick-skinned. I waited for Linda to go on.

She wrung hands toughened by decades of food work. In a small voice, she said, "Crepe Empire took my spot."

Now I felt like stomping. Everyone knows that Linda's humble yellow cart stands at the south-west corner of the Plaza, diagonally across from the Five and Dime. It's featured in guidebooks and tourism brochures, and visitors and locals alike flock to "Auntie Tamales" for quick, tasty snacks. Even pooches pull their owners to Linda's corner, lured by the free dog biscuits she hands out.

"Why can't he set up somewhere else?" I asked, though I already knew. Because he was a bully, that's why. As a kid, Napoleon probably swiped his classmates' lunch money and stole their desserts.

Linda's shoulders rose and slumped like my soufflé. Her bangs sagged to the middle of her forehead. This time she didn't bother to push them aside.

"It's Sunday," she said. "I don't usually work a full day anyhow, but the weather is so nice, and I like to feed folks getting out of church. Of course, I told Napoleon we could share the corner, but when he set up nearby, all he did was taunt me."

I bit my tongue and the *why would you do that*, threatening to burst out. If Linda had a fault, it was that she was too nice.

She shook her head as if baffled by the out-come of her generosity. "If someone came to my stand, he'd yell mean things about tamales. Hor-rible things. 'Stiff old corn gruel,' he called them. 'Mush in a husk.' I couldn't stay and listen to those awful words, Rita. I told him he wasn't being fair or nice. He laughed. He says he can do what he wants. He says the mayor backs him too. That the city needs modern carts, not my old wooden pull-cart. He says tourists like crepes." Her voice had risen to a panicked pitch. "People do, don't they? They like crepes!"

Guilt made me avoid her stricken gaze. I was one of those people. I liked crepes. Scratch that. I loved crepes and all sorts of French food. Back in my culinary school days, I took special courses on French sauces and pastries, and before moving to Santa Fe, I worked in a Midwest version of a French restaurant. My current culinary loyalty, however, was to the wonderful New Mexican fare we served up at Tres Amigas. And to my friends.

That's why I'd stopped frequenting Napoleon's cart. I'd gone cold turkey. No more delicious buck-wheat galettes oozing melted Gruyère cheese. No more lemon crepe, tart and sweet, sparking with fire-glazed sugar. Or the chocolate-hazelnut delight with whipped cream and a brandied cherry on top. Oh, and the brie and tomato with Dijon mustard and the exquisite duck confit and . . . *No!* I mentally slapped myself. *No more forbidden culinary thoughts!* Supporting my friends meant not supporting a bully.

But other than foregoing French treats, what could I do? Confront Napoleon? I might fantasize about running Napoleon off the Plaza, but in reality, confrontation makes my hands tingle and my voice rise into perky chatter. I fell back to my usual comfort strategy. Food. I offered Linda iced tea and freshly flattened soufflé.

Linda stirred not one, not two, but three teaspoons of sugar into her tea. I watched with increasing concern. My friend was not herself. The Linda I knew avoided sugar, wary of tooth decay, and probably links to climate change and the prairie dog plagues to boot. She glugged her sugar tea, taking down half the glass before trying the soufflé.

"Delicious," she said. "What is it? One of those Spanish tortillas, the omelet kind? Maybe I should make those, like they do at that tapas restaurant you like. Tapas are trendy, aren't they?" Her hopeful look faded. "I'm too old for trendy."

"Sixty isn't old," I chided. Nor was forty-one, as I kept reminding myself, or even eighty-one, as Flori told anyone who dared offer her a senior discount, which she always took after delivering a good chiding about ageism. I continued with my perky pep talk. "And of course you should keep making your tamales. People come to Santa Fe for history and culture and that's all wrapped up in tamales. When we put them on special, we sell out before lunch. I can never guess which will go faster, the green chile and cheese or the red chile pork with black beans."

Linda smiled weakly. "The green chile is my favorite. That's why I love this funny baked omelet of yours."

I admitted I'd been trying for a soufflé, leaving out Linda's part in its flop. Heaven knows she already felt bad enough.

"I'm working on a new recipe for Cinco de Mayo," I said. "Gotta love the holidays!" Perky isn't just my confrontation response, it's my go-to reaction for combating glum too.

"Sure," Linda said, not at all perkily. She took another bite and chewed slowly, assessing. "I see. Mexican and French together in one dish, and the hot chile comes out the winner. Clever, Rita."

I smiled, glad that Linda got my attempt at Cinco de Mayo symbolism. Linda's a native New Mexican, with a family tree growing here for generations and distant roots to Spain and Old Mexico. She understands the regional history and the distinctions among Mexican, New Mexican, and American festivities and foods.

I'll never be considered a true local. I'm originally from Illinois, and my three and a half years here make me a newcomer in the eyes of longtime Santa Feans. That's okay with me. The important thing is that I feel at home, more than anywhere else I've lived. It's hard to explain, especially to my mother. Mom keeps hoping I'll move back to my "real home," Bucks Grove, Illinois, a land of corn and casseroles and flat expanses.

Mom contends there's no reason for me *not* to move back. I can cook anywhere, she points out. Plus, I'm divorced. Less than a year ago I officially reclaimed my maiden name, Lafitte, after splitting from local son and philandering police detective Manny Martin. I usually grant Mom these points because I know she'll then wreck her argument by citing aspects of Santa Fe she dislikes but I love. It's so "different," she'll say, unintentionally repeating Santa Fe's proud nickname, The City Different. Mom also objects to the altitude (high), the weather (dry), and the walls (adobe), which she says make her claustrophobic. And don't even get Mom started on hot chiles and beans for breakfast. I counter with the special light, the gorgeous sunsets, and the fabulous food and art. My winning point, however, is my daughter. I can't rip Celia away from her father and high school, just as I can't tear myself away from my home and friends.

Linda turned her face to the ceiling. "I love Mama's decorating for Cinco de Mayo. I haven't done any special decorations for my cart yet, but I did make chicken *mole* tamales. It's a special black *mole* with five kinds of dried Mexican chiles and dark chocolate and pumpkin and sesame seeds. I started selling them today and people seemed to really like them until . . ."

Until Napoleon chased her off.

Linda continued on the subject of tamales. "I made a few with habaneros, but I decided not to sell them. I worried that someone really sensitive to chile heat might eat one and have trouble breathing. Mama says I worry too much. She says the hotter the better."

I had to smile, imagining my own mother's reaction. Mom claims that mild Anaheim peppers set her throat on fire, and when I told her about our Cinco de Mayo preparations, she snorted in disapproval. Likely she pictured me surrounded by bucket-sized margaritas and mountains of nachos. I can't blame her. I love any excuse to indulge in a tart drink and cheesy chips, and that's how much of the country views the holiday. Flori, however, taught me the true meaning. Cinco de Mayo, or May Fifth, commemorates the day when underdog Mexican forces in the state of Puebla fought off French invaders. Don't ask me the exact date, although I think it was sometime in the mid-nineteenth century.

Flori saw the holiday as a chance to decorate and add some Mexican specials to our New Mexican menu. A few days ago she cooked up a vat of delicious red *mole*, or *mole coloradito*, a Oaxacan recipe with spicy smokiness from dried red chiles and tangy sweetness from raisins, cinnamon, and cloves. We'd serve that this week, along with Baja-style shrimp tacos topped in a zippy lime dressing and a burger stuffed with fiery jalapeños and melty *queso fresco*. I'm the one who thought the holiday provided a fine chance to spice up a French classic.

I closed my eyes to taste-test the would-be soufflé. Texture aside, it was pretty good. Next time I'd add more cheese and a few extra peppers. An intensely flavored base is one of the keys to soufflé success. So are room-temperature eggs, a superclean mixing bowl, and judging the perfect glossy stiff peaks of your egg whites. Needless to say, you shouldn't rock your oven by hurling in casserole dishes.

I opened my eyes and faced soufflé flatness. Thank goodness this was a test run and not my final version. Butterflies swarmed across my stomach as a dire thought struck me. What if the soufflé flop was a sign?

I wasn't honing the recipe as a Cinco de Mayo week special. I was making it to serve to Jake Strong, Santa Fe's hunkiest lawyer, a man of rugged cowboy good looks and twinkling-eye charm. The man who kept asking me out despite my supposed dating moratorium, not to mention my inability to dance, my divorced-mom status, and my penchant for stumbling upon crime and corpses. Over the past several months, Jake and I had progressed from casual coffee meetings, to lunch, and then to happy hours and dinners out. This Friday would be a dating milestone. Dinner at my casita. My tiny kitchen was definitely an intimate setting, and I had no one to blame but myself for the romantic escalation. The dinner invitation fell from my mouth when Jake mentioned missing his mother's home-cooked meals. What woman could resist such sweet sentiment? Not me, clearly. Now, however, the nervous lobe of my brain nagged me to call off home-cooking and call out for Chinese.

I wasn't so worried about kitchen failures under pressure. I'm a café chef, after all, and even a flat soufflé is tasty. It wasn't holiday expectations either, since the fifth fell on the Monday after our date. No, I was more anxious that my relationship with Jake might be moving to another level. Did I want that? Was I ready?

Linda reached across the table and scooped out a chunk of soufflé, making appreciative sounds as she did. "Will you put it on the menu?" she asked. "A soufflé seems risky. Look how this one fell for no reason."

Right, no reason. I helped myself to another bite of golden, cheesy eggs.

"Exactly! Risky!" This exclamation from Flori coincided with a thump on the back of my chair. My shoulders jolted so high, I nearly punched myself out. I swear, Flori has the footsteps of a ghost. I hadn't heard her sneak up behind me, and yet there she was, all five feet barely three inches of her. Inexplicably, at least to me, she wore a karate costume tied with a crocheted sash. Floury fingerprints smudged her Harry Potter–style glasses.

"Rita's making this soufflé for her hot boy-friend," Flori informed Linda, pushing back her spectacles to peer into the blue ceramic dish. "I tell you, Rita, forget the fancy French food and make that man a good, solid green chile stew. He's a true New Mexican. My Bernard says that once he tasted my stew, he had to ask for my hand in marriage. You and your sisters wouldn't be here, Linda, if it wasn't for my stew."

Linda groaned.

I silently seconded her feelings. A proposal was not on my wish list. Plus, as I'd told Flori, I'd already blabbed to Jake about my soufflé plans. My culinary honor would fall flat if I didn't make one.

Flori was still set on getting me an engagement ring. "Linda, your father also wanted to propose after his first bite of my *pastel imposible*, but he held off because he's a gentleman. No man can resist a magic chocoflan. Mark my words, Rita. If you have chocoflan on your date-night menu, that handsome lawyer will be down on one knee before you can clear the dinner dishes."

Linda and I shared an eye-rolling moment. Flori loves to dish out dating advice. Some of her tips are fine, like making a truly magic dessert that transforms into moist chocolate cake on the bottom and a delicate caramel flan on top. Other advice, like pinching hunky men on the tush and excessive eyelash batting, is better left ignored.

Linda was a master at deflecting her mother's romantic suggestions. She claimed to be happy in her widowhood and never wanted to date again.

After my divorce, I'd also instituted a dating moratorium. One year, I'd vowed. Twelve months, at least, to come to terms with my single self. The attentions of Jake Strong had turned those plans topsy-turvy. I did a quick calculation. Here it was, roughly month nine, and I was already fixing an eligible hunk dinner at my house. A romantic French soufflé, no less. Plus some kind of dessert. Magic flan cake is one of the best desserts I've ever eaten, and I've eaten a lot. But was it too forward? The dessert equivalent of a plunging neckline and stilettos? My mind turned to modest fruit salads and old-fashioned berry crumbles. Images of my Aunt Sue's rainbow Jell-O mold with grated carrots and celery chunks flashed through my head. Vegetables in layers of cherry, orange, and lime Jell-O would keep any man at arm's length, especially if I went for Sue's Christmas version in which she added festive mini-marshmallows and cheddar cheese chunks. I put down my fork, feeling slightly queasy, and not only because of questionable gelatin concoctions.

Luckily, Flori didn't notice or she would have given me more romantic tips involving hot chiles and hotter flirting. She'd turned to Linda, asking why she wasn't at work. Linda, in the same fashion as my teenage daughter, muttered an unintelligible response.

Flori employed the time-honored mom move of waiting her out.

After a long silence, Linda relented. "Fine, I'll

tell you. I was out with my cart, but Napoleon
squeezed me from my regular spot. It's okay,
though. I'll serve the rest of my tamales at the soup
kitchen tonight. I'm keeping them warm under
foil. Lucky for me, Rita already had the oven on."

From Flori's frown, I could guess that her
thoughts mirrored mine. *That jerk Napoleon. That
mean, petty, place-stealing bully.* Except, as usual,
Flori went further. She didn't offer Linda more
tea. She slammed her arthritic fist on the table and
declared war.

"That's it! The final straw! That man has to be
stopped. We'll arrange a citywide boycott. We'll
identify his weaknesses and run him out of town,
Old West style. Ha!"

For a moment I felt emboldened by Flori's passion and her karate costume. Then she turned to
me. Her eyes sparkled with determination and
flashes of danger. "Rita, what are you doing this
afternoon?"

I may have felt bold, but I wasn't ready to jump
into one of Flori's frying pans. I delayed answering. Yes, I was technically free. Ever since Flori's
seventieth birthday, Tres Amigas had closed on
weekends, her version of retirement, although we
often came in to prep vats of stews and sauces for
the coming week. I could be prepping or revamp-
ing my soufflé or dozens of other less Old Westy
activities.

I considered how far I'd go in a Napoleon
battle. I could wave a protest sign or join in anti-
Napoleon chanting. I'd happily write irate letters
to the mayor. Knowing Flori, that's not what she
had in mind.

She adjusted her orange and yellow crocheted belt. I hedged, leading with a drawn-out "Well . . ."

"Good, sounds like you have time," Flori declared. "Let's gather the other food vendors and surround his cart. I have pretty new handcuffs. We can chain ourselves to his cart. Well, two of us could latch on, unless we buy some more cuffs."

I looked to Linda for guidance. Fire was in her eyes too, but of another kind.

Linda pushed back her chair, nearly tipping it. "Mama, no! Please! I appreciate your offer, but I can handle this myself. Do *not* get involved."

My teenage daughter, Celia, would have the same look and tone. She'd stomp off just like Linda was doing too, slamming the door behind her. The piñata nearest the entryway, a blue poodle, trembled. If my soufflé hadn't already flopped, it would have fainted.

Flori frowned in the direction of Linda's departing backside.

I offered her some tea. "She says she'll handle the situation," I said, understanding the pain of a daughter's rejection of well-intentioned maternal help.

Flori accepted the tea but didn't drink it. She thumped her index finger on the brightly colored tablecloth. "I have a bad feeling about this, Rita."

I sipped my tea, telling myself that Flori was wrong. Linda was a grown woman, a hardy small-business owner. She could take care of herself.

I should have known better. Flori may offer off-base dating advice, but her bad feelings are always right.

Chapter 2

I should have known something else too. Flori wouldn't stay out of the Napoleon battle. Midway through the breakfast rush the next morning, she announced a strategy of covert warfare.

I admit, I didn't pay proper attention. Otherwise I might have stopped her when she mentioned "striking his soft parts." Another problem was distracting me, namely the conundrum of a cheese-free cheese enchilada, which I was trying to work out with our head griddle guy, Juan.

"The customer requested the same enchilada, just minus the cheese," I said, my voice extra chipper in anticipation of disagreement.

Bilingual grumbles preceded Juan's perfectly reasonable logic. "A cheese enchilada without cheese is not a cheese enchilada. It is the tortilla without cheese."

"What about a tortilla dipped in red chile sauce and rolled up with some nice diced onions or pickled jalapeños on top?" I asked. "Could you do that?"

Of course he could. That, Juan informed me, would make a rolled flour tortilla in *chile colorado*. Not a cheese enchilada. An enchilada encasing rice but no cheese was also no cheese enchilada. Stacked tortillas, northern New Mexican style, minus cheese, similarly fell outside the cheese category. As Juan launched into other cheeseless tortilla configurations, I sensed that we'd entered the territory of unanswerable philosophical questions. Does a falling tree make a sound if no one hears it? Can one hand clap?

"Right. True," I said, mainly to placate Juan, who was recalling another recent mind-bender, a request for vegetarian *carne adovada*. "*Carne*," Juan said, rolling the *r* with extra verve. "*Carne* means meat."

"Yes, I know, I agree, but—" I was about to lie and say the customer was always right. Little did I know, I'd just agreed to Flori's scheme.

"I knew you'd agree!" my elderly friend crowed. "We'll defeat him before he sees the battle coming!"

"Wait! What? Who?" I spun around to question Flori. My questions went unanswered as she hustled toward the dining room loaded down with four platters on her palms and wrists. I marveled at her balancing skills and strength. Most of all, I worried. *What had I just agreed to?*

"Like I said . . ." Flori said, when she returned empty-handed.

Since I didn't know what she'd said, I waited.

Flori addressed Juan. "We'll take the Sun Tzu approach on that mean little man, right, Juan?"

"*Sí,*" Juan replied in the same tone my teenage daughter pairs with "whatever." His spatula hovered over an egg nearing the perfect over medium. Juan was short, but no one would call him little. No one could call him soft either. Juan was a bundle of muscles honed by his maestro moves at the grill. He shrugged his thick shoulders and resumed his philosophical grumblings about cheese.

Flori stood across the kitchen, stirring a vat of chile. Scarlet sauce dripped from the spoon she pointed at me. "You weren't listening, were you, Rita? I was saying, I'm taking tai chi at the Senior Center, and we're reading *The Art of War* to get in the mood."

This news got my attention. Thanks to the well-meaning folks at the Senior Center, Flori and her compatriots knew how to count cards, tread water, and chip flint into arrowheads. Flori had also recently taken a women's self-defense course that taught her the fine arts of well-placed kicks and Taser zapping. I believed in self-defense for women of any age, and treading water, even in a desert, could come in handy. But ancient Chinese war techniques in the hands of Taser-wielding bifocal wearers with access to arrowheads? I sensed danger all around.

"I thought tai chi was about slow movements and breathing and meditation," I said, swaddling crispy bacon, roasted potatoes, and scrambled eggs in a burrito the size and weight of a newborn. I took my bundle of joy over to Flori, who bathed it in red chile sauce. After a sprinkling of shredded Jack cheese and a quick broil, the burrito would be treacherous to deliver and a delight to eat.

"Tai chi is the world's deadliest martial art," my elderly friend said cheerfully. "It's good for arthritis too."

"That's wonderful," I said, focusing on the health benefits for Flori's aching knees and hands.

She, however, was still fixated on war. "Know your enemy. That's what Sun Tzu teaches. Defeat your opponent without fighting."

No fighting sounded good. I heaped praise on Flori's nonconfrontation technique, though I had my doubts. Napoleon would eat nonconfrontation for brunch. Besides, he'd already confronted and won.

Juan grunted. He sounded as impressed with battle-free battle as he was with cheese-free cheese enchiladas. Or maybe he was commentating on the next special order. "Burrito with no tortilla wrapper, coming up," he muttered.

While we waited, Flori enlightened me on her newfound ancient wisdom. "You surely know some of the key points, Rita." She stopped for a beat, likely for effect. "The enemy of my enemy is my friend."

I had heard this. Now I considered it in terms of a food-cart war. "We know a lot of people who don't like Napoleon. Like Crystal. Linda said that Napoleon got Crystal's juice cart shut down. Something about her permit paperwork. She has to be upset about that." I was too. What if Napoleon had run her off for good? How would I get through a southwestern summer without Crystal's cool fruit *aguas frescas* or her *jamaica* tea,

bright red and brewed from hibiscus flowers?
Crystal not only made great drinks, she was kind.
When I first asked for *jamaica* tea, pronouncing it
as an English speaker refers to the island nation,
she didn't scoff at my poor Spanish skills as my
ex would have. She kindly coached me. "Ha-
Mike-ah," she said, adding an affirmation. "And
you're right. The flower is named for the island,
flor de Jamaica." Poor Crystal. Another nice person
Napoleon had bullied.

Flori accepted the enchilada order from Juan. A
rolled tortilla dipped in red chile lay beside little
hills of guacamole, refried pinto beans, and green
and red salsas. I was glad Flori was taking it out.
She could practice her subduing techniques if the
customer got fussy.

"Crystal's a good person and an ally," Flori
said. "We need to befriend Napoleon's powerful
enemies too. Perhaps your hot lawyer boyfriend
knows a judge or commissioner who'd help in exchange for free burritos."

I wasn't ready to think of Jake as my "boyfriend." I also wasn't eager to mess with anyone's
soft spots or burrito-bribe public officials. Besides,
we had a bigger problem, as I delicately reminded
Flori.

"Linda doesn't want our help. She got upset
when we offered yesterday." When Flori offered, I
held back from saying.

"Linda's too nice," her mother countered.
"Always has been. Have I told you about that
time she picked up a stray wolf, thinking it was a
German shepherd? The kids were little then and
buckled in their car seats, right by that wolf. My

daughter frets about everything except the very things she should be worrying about."

Juan uttered some holy names, possibly in regard to wolves or the mound of scrambled eggs, crispy potatoes, and chorizo that composed the wrapperless burrito.

Flori nodded. "Exactly, Juan. Napoleon's much more dangerous than that wolf, which was actually kind of cute. Linda *needs* our help. She just doesn't know it yet." With that, Flori raised her spoon in a tai-chi striking move and gave me marching orders.

I protested, but only slightly. I agreed that Linda could use some help, and I liked my mission. Walking the few blocks to the Plaza, I felt like a kid playing hooky. Birds warbled, new green leaves glittered, and I was off work on a sunny spring morning. I practically skipped. I may have whistled, until the killjoy, list-making side of my brain reminded me I wasn't a carefree school kid.

Here I was, skipping along like Little Red Riding Hood, off to spy on a wolf in French chef's clothing. Not only that, my to-do list was growing to epic length. Groceries, laundry, driving out to chain-store land to stock up on cat supplies, calling my mom, e-mailing my sister, perfecting a Cinco de Mayo soufflé, picking a dessert that said let's take our time . . . *ack!* All these tasks were doable, I assured myself. Even the task I dreaded most, the one that involved sorting, cleaning,

managing teams of movers, and—worst of all—
loads of emotional baggage.

The very thought brought a cloud to my morning. At least Celia and I weren't packing up and
moving, although that hardly cheered me. Nor
did the fact that the person whose home I was to
"streamline" had moved on already. Victor—my
landlord, neighbor, and dear friend—had been
murdered last year, and I'd helped catch his killer.
His younger sister, Teresa, inherited his home and
planned to use it as a vacation retreat for herself
and out-of-town friends. I was relieved the adobe
compound would stay in Victor's family. I was
even more relieved that I could keep renting the
nearby casita. I loved the little cottage's beautiful
wood beams, colorful Mexican tiles, and quiet setting by Victor's gardens and the burbling upper
reach of the Santa Fe River. I'd also been happy
when Teresa offered me the job of caretaker. All I
had to do was watch over the mostly vacant house
in exchange for lower rent. Saving money is what
every single mom and café worker craves. The job
sounded pretty easy too . . . except for one catch.

Teresa wanted me to assist in clearing Victor's
home. Depersonalize it, she said, so that she could
put her own touches on it. Or, rather, her decorator could. The hardest part, Teresa claimed, was
already done: Victor's art collection. A world-
renowned folk artist, Victor had packed his home
with floor-to-ceiling art. Teresa's appraisers and
consultants had tagged and removed the most
valuable pieces, sending them to specialty storage, faraway auction houses, and the Museum of
International Folk Art just over the hill. I was to

deal with the everyday items, like the comfortable furniture, knickknacks, clothes, and the miscellany packing the closets. *The hard part.*

"Clutter," Teresa had said with a wave of her manicured hand.

Victor's life, I thought, and I didn't know where to begin. I hadn't begun, unless wandering his house, feeling overwhelmed, counted.

"Rita? Hey there. Hi!"

A familiar voice jolted me back to the springtime present. I looked up and spotted my best friend Cass a few feet away.

"I was waving like a fool from across the Plaza, trying to get your attention," she said with a grin. "You were in another world. It's the weather, isn't it? Much too nice to stay cooped up inside with a torch, right?"

I agreed, but then I shied away from Cass's torches in any weather. My silversmith friend wields flames attached to giant vats of flammable gases and looks great doing it. Her lemon-yellow dress, lime-green cardigan, and dressy leather boots made her look like she was popping out for an artistic ladies' lunch, not taking a break from melting metals. I get nervous heating the deep fryer and don goggles when making caramel. If I had Cass's work, I'd be decked out in fireproof coveralls and a welder's helmet. Or at least jeans, which is what I had on most days anyway. Today, I had on my "good" jeans, the dark, dressy kind, topped with soft T-shirt with a scalloped neckline. For my outdoor spying mission, I'd added a cotton scarf the color of lemon curd and a spring jacket, olive green with a peach polka dot lining, a coup from my favorite secondhand store. Despite my dating doubts, I'd been paying more attention to my wardrobe since Jake Strong started paying attention to me.

Cass asked what I was doing. I told her about Flori's new Senior Center class and my mission to scope out Napoleon's weak points.

She chuckled. "I love that Flori's practicing deadly tai chi. How exactly are you supposed to be scoping out the enemy, though?"

"That's the best part. I've been ordered to buy a crepe." After weeks of boycotting Napoleon's delicious snacks, I was delighted with this excuse and hoped to make repeat scouting trips.

"Ooo . . . I want in on this," Cass said. "My stomach's rumbling just thinking about that lemon sugar crepe he does."

We approached Crepe Empire from the periphery, as Flori recommended. Flanking, she'd called it, technical terminology she probably picked up at the Senior Center.

"There he is, the man himself," I said. Napoleon stood behind the narrow counter, wearing a white chef's jacket and a hat that reminded me of my prefallen soufflé.

Cass sniffed. "That hat is absurd. Pompous little man."

"He's full of himself," I said. "All bluster." I was bluster too. The spring in my step slowed to a stall. As much as I wanted a crepe, I dreaded ordering from Napoleon. He tolerated no hesitation, no changing of one's mind or requesting special ingredients. Napoleon was happy to let his customers know they were wrong.

"Buckwheat with ham and cheese," I repeated to Cass as we swung into a front approach of Crepe Empire. "Make sure I order that. I freeze up when he glares at me."

My brave, fire-wielding friend made a dismissive *pah*. "Don't let him bother you. He thinks too much of himself. He does make good crepes, though." She strode boldly toward Crepe Empire.

"Hold up," I said, putting a hand on her elbow. "Flori wants me to look for vulnerabilities. Health code violations. Improper food and cash handling. Pigeons, dogs, kids with sticky fingers, anything . . ."

"Looks pretty good to me," Cass said, slowing to strolling pace.

Unfortunately, she was right. Napoleon's cart of polished stainless steel gleamed under a blue and white striped awning. The quavering voice of Edith Piaf, the famous wartime lounge singer, wafted toward us. There wasn't a rat in sight, unless you counted Napoleon.

Cass and I stepped up second in line and inspected the blackboard menu. Flowery cursive script listed six crepes and, in the biggest font, NO SUBSTITUTIONS! I mentally rehearsed my order as Cass asked for lemon with a sugar brûlée.

Too late, I realized that Cass had stepped aside.

"You! Make your order. You're holding up the line!" Napoleon snapped at me. His dark hair swirled like horns up the sides of his towering hat. His lips turned downward, outlined in deep clench lines.

"Order or get out of the way!" he demanded.

"Buckwheat crepe," I stammered. "With egg and ham. Oh, I mean, the fried egg and with cheese."

My request was met with disdain. "Of course with cheese and the fried egg. No substitutions! And I assume you mean the galette. There is no buckwheat crepe."

He spat out the correction as if any fool would know that buckwheat turns a crepe into a galette. I actually had known, but I'd forgotten under pressure. I'd also forgotten to get out my wallet.

"Ten fifty-five," he ordered, making no moves to assemble my crepe until I'd paid.

I forked over a twenty and reluctantly left two dollars in his tip jar. My bank account would be happy when I went back to boycotting this jerk. Still, I was enthralled as he spread the crepe batter into perfect circles of uniform thickness. After flipping my crepe—correction, galette—he added thinly sliced ham and grated cheese to the center. An egg, frying at the side of the griddle, topped off the masterpiece, and Napoleon tucked the four sides of the crepe inward so that only the sunny yolk poked through. Gorgeous. Cass's sweet crepe was just as pretty. The pale yellow batter bubbled into delicate lace that Napoleon sprinkled with sugar, a squeeze of lemon, and a dash of lemon *liqueur*.

I stepped back as the bully chef reached for a blue propane torch. He spotted my retreat and smirked. "Scared of a little fire, ladies?"

Cass snorted. I suppressed a snicker, imagining what she must be thinking. *My torch is bigger than yours, little man.* Napoleon didn't notice our snorts and snickers. He ran a hissing blue flame over the lemon sugar, creating a bubbling caramel. With a few flicks of his wrist and a dusting of powdered sugar, Cass's crepe was folded into a neat triangle. He slid the paper trays across the counter and dismissed us with a wave of his hand. No "thank you" or "please come again."

"Next!" he yelled.

Cass and I found a free bench near the center of the Plaza. She shook her head. "I've heard of this happening, people lining up to be abused for soup or corned beef, but I never thought I'd see it here. Santa Fe's a relaxed, accepting place. You don't come here to be yelled at by some jerk with a fake accent." She took a bite of crepe and moaned. "I do wish his food wasn't so delicious. Maybe we could make crepes at my studio. Do you think my acetylene torch is too powerful?"

"A tad," I said, thinking more of what she'd said about Napoleon's accent. "Fake?" I asked. "I thought he was French."

"Ha!" Cass replied. "He studied cooking in France for a couple years and I think he does have some distant relatives there. Mainly, he's New Mexican, from a suburb of Albuquerque. He should take pride in both sides of his heritage." She paused to enjoy another bite, then said, "A while back he catered a gallery opening for one of my friends and refused to make anything resembling New Mexican food. No green chile crepe. Nothing with cornmeal. Too common, he claimed. Insecure little bully . . ."

I considered this information. Was Napoleon's denial of local ties a point of weakness? Maybe, but then Flori probably already knew more about his family connections than he did. She had a chessmaster's mind when it came to relations and was a grande dame of gossip.

The screech of brakes broke my thoughts. I turned to see Linda's battered white truck pulling up to the northwest corner. Her wooden tamale cart, painted bright yellow with a Zia sun symbol on top and colorful flowers along the edges, rattled behind the pickup.

I panicked. "She can't see us eating these!" I warned Cass. Luckily, Linda didn't notice us gobbling our last bites. She was a one-woman moving machine. She got out, laid down a ramp, jumped back in her truck, and expertly backed her cart up the ramp and onto the Plaza. Hopping out again, she unhooked the tow hitch and pushed the cart into place.

"Wow," Cass said admiringly. "Linda's stronger than she looks."

"You should try arm-wrestling Flori," I said, feeling wimpy.

Linda got back in her truck and sped off to park. Within minutes she was hurrying back and calling out, "Tamales! Fresh, New Mexican tamales! Santa Fe style."

My heart soared for Linda. Good for her! People in Napoleon's line began to drift her way. "Fresh hot tamales!" she yelled again, drawing in customers from all sides.

I couldn't wait to tell Flori. Linda had the situation under control. She didn't need us or Sun Tzu. She could handle Napoleon by herself.

Except that the battle was coming to her. Linda's control of the corner lasted about fifteen minutes, until Napoleon stormed across the Plaza, chef's coat billowing. With one hand, he held down his puffy hat. In the other, he brandished a cell phone, as if ready to throw it. It was his expression that disturbed me the most, though. The glint in his eye and his thin lips twitching in mean glee.

Cass and I jumped to our feet as the petite tyrant passed, followed by a pale, panting man in wool suit too warm for spring and too large for its wearer. I wished I'd had the forethought to trip Napoleon. As it was, I was ready to rush to Linda and help. I took a step forward.

"Hold up," Cass said, putting out an arm to stop me. "Let's let Linda handle this. That's what she wants, right?"

"Right," I said, uncertain that what Linda wanted was the best course of action.

We watched as Napoleon and the man stopped a few yards from Linda's cart.

"Beware that woman's food!" Napoleon bellowed in a voice worthy of the Santa Fe Opera.

"Fresh tamales, homemade tamales! Mexican *mole* for Cinco de Mayo!" Linda called out, similarly operatic.

"Corn mush in old husks," Napoleon chanted, his voice becoming higher pitched the louder he yelled.

Linda countered, offering wholesome tamales at half price. "Tía's best tamales, healthy and delicious. Auntie Linda's freshly steamed tamales!"

Her voice quavered. I glanced at Cass. We nodded in silent agreement and rushed to Linda's side, reaching her at the same time a scream cut through the other voices.

"A cockroach! There's a cockroach in my tamale!" A few steps away a lanky, twenty-something man with a mop of wavy red hair and a redder face spit out a mouthful of tamale. "Bug!" he yelled.

The crowd congealed around him. Exclamations of disgust filled the Plaza as the redhead held the tainted tamale high. I looked away, hating bugs but hating Linda's pain more.

She trembled, whether in rage or shock, I couldn't tell. "No . . . no! That's a fake, Rita. That tamale's not mine. It can't be."

The man in the ill-fitting suit approached Linda. "Health inspector, ma'am. I'll have to shut you down until I can get some samples of your cart and kitchen."

Linda lunged at Napoleon. "You did this! You won't get away with it! I'll show you!"

Cass and I grabbed Linda by her elbows.

"Linda, he's not worth getting upset over," I said.

Linda wrenched her arm from me and for a moment I was afraid she would strike out again.

"Look at her," Napoleon said, giddy in Linda's agony. "The hysterical woman who would feed you roaches."

All eyes turned to Linda. Dear, kind Linda who volunteered at the soup kitchen and rescued stray wolves and maintained—I knew—a spotless kitchen. She wobbled and then ran down the street to her truck. The crowd gawked.

Napoleon sneered as he strode past me and Cass. "Tell your friend it's over," he said.

"It's not over," I sputtered. *Not if I could help it.*

Chapter 3

I understand the agony of embarrassment. I don't mean minor mortifications either, like stomping on a certain handsome lawyer's polished cowboy boots or spilling soup on his pants. No, those kinds of flubs can be brushed—or wiped—off. The worst embarrassment is the social kind. Forgetting a person whom you once had over for dinner, for instance. Or blurting out words in anger. Or throwing a Bloody Mary at your philandering husband in a dive bar in downtown Santa Fe. I've done all of those. The drink-throwing incident, I blame on extreme stress. That and binge-watching *Sex and the City*, although I didn't end up sipping cosmos with my chic, confident girlfriends. Seconds after vodka-spiked tomato juice and a stalk of celery struck Manny's face, I was drowning in humiliation. I still avoid the bar where it happened. Not just the bar, the entire street.

Try explaining such chagrin to an octogenarian who says she's old enough to do as she pleases and practices the world's deadliest martial art.

"Linda's embarrassed," I said, once again. "I'm sure that's why she's lying low."

"Linda should have kicked him in the shin or elsewhere," Flori grumbled, hacking at a pile of tomatillos. The waxy green fruits, tart and destined for salsa, turned to pulp under her knife. They weren't the only victims of Flori's mood. Tomatoes, peppers, and several mangos had already turned to mince as Flori took out her anger on produce.

"She would have felt worse," I said. "Linda felt awful when she simply said she hated Napoleon. Can you imagine if she kicked him?"

From Flori's wicked grin, it seemed she was imagining the joy of kicking rather than its consequences. "A woman has a right to defend her honor," she said, bashing a head of garlic with a cleaver. The garlic collapsed into cloves that Flori smashed again to remove their papery wrappings. "I'm not saying that Linda should do anything extreme, of course," she added, rather primly.

I nodded, keeping one ear pressed to my cell phone. The ringing on the other end stopped and Linda's voice mail kicked in, inviting me to leave a message and have a wonderful day. I pressed End Call. I'd already left Linda two messages.

"Maybe she's out for a walk or taking a nap," I said, as much to reassure myself as Flori. "We should make her a care pack. Ice cream or some muffins."

Flori made a harrumph sound. "Linda doesn't eat ice cream. She's worried it'll give her tooth decay. Says it makes her teeth ache too. That child has always been sensitive. Let me call her. She has to answer for her mother."

I took over the tomatillo salsa preparation, mixing in minced onion, garlic, and cilantro. The tangy salsa paired perfectly with our steak and eggs breakfast plate and was always popular with salty corn tortilla chips. My mouth watered, and I reached for a chip. Someone had to taste-test.

Flori dialed from her rotary phone at the front desk. While the dial turned, she fussed with the mariachi mannequins, dusting them and their instruments with a napkin.

"Linda!" Flori exclaimed. She abandoned her cleaning, leaving the creepy trumpet player's head at an unnatural tilt. His right eye seemed to stare at me from all angles. I turned away, both from him and from Flori, so I wouldn't appear to be eavesdropping. I couldn't help hearing Flori's side of the conversation, though, and her offers to help. I could also guess Linda's responses.

When Flori put the phone back in its cradle, I said, "She says she doesn't want any help?"

Flori's snort confirmed my guess. "She's always been like this. Stubborn. The most stubborn of my three daughters. I don't understand it."

I hid my smile from my stubborn friend. "She needs time," I said, in the tritest of parenting advice. How many times had I heard those words in regard to Celia's tortured hairstyles, gloomy artwork, and sullen moods?

Flori repositioned a few mannequin arms into

tai-chi poses. "We'll have to work behind the scenes," she said. "And keep your phone on. Linda says she's resting but promises she'll call you back. Maybe you can convince her. Kids never listen to their mothers."

I knew that. I kept my phone close, checking it in the grocery store, where I imagined I heard it ring in the deli and again in the chips aisle. I stared at its supposedly smart screen as I waited in my car outside Celia's school. I wished that Linda would call, and that I hadn't shown so much snack-food restraint back at the store. Chips increasingly seemed like a stress-management necessity.

"What's up, Mom? Waiting for your boyfriend to text?" my daughter teased, plopping in the front seat. Black and red paint dotted Celia's once-white T-shirt. Her shoes had enough paint drops to pass as modern art. Then there was her hair. A shock of orange fell across her left cheek, bumping against her nose. This color was no art mishap. The pumpkin orange was semipermanent and an intentional dye-job disaster.

As her mom, I preferred her natural color, a rich espresso brown. I also preferred her silky, straight locks to the chopped, tortured, and tangled style she'd taken up around the time Manny and I separated.

I smiled at my daughter. The "give her time" advisors were probably right, and no matter what, I loved Celia wholeheartedly.

"I'm not waiting to hear from Jake," I said, feeling lucky that Celia had accepted him. His charm and his bulldog, Winston, had won her over. The turning point came when Jake and Winston dropped by for a walk, and Winston allowed Celia's kitten, Hugo, to ride on his back. Since then the dog and kitten have been unlikely pals, as have Celia and Jake.

"And anyway," I said, starting the car. "He's not my 'boyfriend.' We're friends."

"Right, Mom. Sure," Celia said with a devious grin. "Is that why you're kicking me out of the house Friday?"

"I'm not kicking you out," I said. "You already had those plans with Sky and Rosa." Sky, Cass's son, was like an older brother to Celia. They'd been close as twins since they met, and I never worried about them getting into trouble. That is, unless Celia instigated it. Rosa, Linda's granddaughter, was as responsible as Linda, but without her worries. Celia loved staying at her house. However, part of me wished she'd come home, both because I loved my daughter and because I might want chaperone limits on my date night.

I craned over my right shoulder to maneuver the Subaru into a tight three-point turn. That's when I saw Celia wave, a flick of her fingers, followed by a crack in her ennui mask. A boy with orange spikes in his hair and skinny, chain-draped black pants waved back, grinning widely.

"Who's that?" I asked.

Celia dropped her hand as if she'd grabbed a hot pan. "No one."

No one, eh? My maternal warning bells chimed. Did my daughter have a boyfriend? I pondered this for several blocks of car silence.

"Hold my phone?" I asked her when we stopped at a four-way intersection and waited for a herd of camera-wielding tourists to pass. "I *am* waiting for a call. From Linda. If it rings and you see it's her, will you answer?"

My daughter forgot her silent treatment. "Poor Tía Linda. Kids are calling her stand the 'cockroach cart.' I told them to shut up."

Great. If high-schoolers knew about the tainted tamale, the whole town probably did. "Cass and I were there when the bug was supposedly found. We think Linda was set up."

Celia didn't need convincing. "No doubt. You'll help her, right?"

I glanced at Celia, surprised. Her typical response to my sleuthing is a dramatic display of teen embarrassment. Eye-rolling, sighing, shoulder heaving, foot stomping, you name it, voiced over with, "Geez, Mom, leave things alone."

"Bullies are the worst," she muttered. "They shouldn't mess with Tía Linda."

"Absolutely," I said, hopefully with more confidence that I felt. "Flori and I will help. Tía Linda will be fine."

But how could I help? And would Linda let me? The phone remained silent through dinner, my evening walk, and as I nodded over my bedtime reading. At nearly midnight I gave up. Turning off the lamp but not the phone, I vowed to call Linda tomorrow. If she didn't answer, I'd track her down.

Tracking wasn't necessary. When the cell phone's melody rang in the darkness, I initially incorporated it into my dream, an anxiety nightmare involving a packed auditorium and me, partially unclothed and totally unprepared to lecture on Cinco de Mayo cuisine. The nightmare audience included my high school gym class, Jake, Mom, and George Clooney.

Dreamtime me was cowering behind a podium when I realized the ringing was real. I grabbed the phone and answered in automatic maternal worry mode. "Hello? Celia?" I remembered that Celia was presumably sleeping down the hall about the moment I recognized Linda's voice.

"Linda?" I said, resisting the urge to ask, *Do you know what time it is?* I didn't know myself, except that the room was still dark and my eyelids wouldn't fully open.

My grumpiness faded as Linda gushed apologies. "Oh Rita, I'm so sorry. It's not even six and I shouldn't call you and I wouldn't except, oh heaven help me . . ."

Now I was awake, wide-awake. Blood rushed through my head. I sat up and fumbled with the light. "Linda, what's wrong?"

Muffled prayers came from her end, a jumble of English and Spanish.

"Linda!" I practically yelled. "What's happening?"

"Napoleon," she cried out. "He's . . . he's dead."

Good riddance nearly fell from my mouth. Then reality struck me. Dead? Napoleon was a jerk, but a man not that much older than me. How sad and shocking, but how did Linda know? And why call me? The tragic news could have waited for hot coffee and hushed gossip over breakfast.

"My cart," she said in between gulping sobs. "He's under my tamale cart, Rita. Come to the Plaza, please. We have to do something!"

I sped to the Plaza, breaking traffic laws on the empty streets. There would be no helping Napoleon. I saw that right away. His eyes stared blankly heavenward, toward the charcoal dawn sky that would turn into a sunny Santa Fe day. His cheeks puffed as if stuffed. His chest pushed up the front wheels of Linda's cart. One arm extended above his head, the pale underside up, the hand twisted downward. On his wrist, a flashy gold watch was cracked and broken.

Except for Napoleon, Linda and I were alone on the Plaza. I'd parked my car next to her truck, both in illegal spots. A parking ticket was the least of my worries.

"Don't touch him!" I commanded Linda. She knelt near the body, one hand reaching out as though to heal him. At my harsh words, she jerked her hand back.

"What if there's a pulse?" she asked, reaching again. "I couldn't make myself check before."

I took her by both arms and pulled her up gently. "I'll do it," I said, regretting this noble offer the moment I said it. I held my breath and flinched when my hand touched Napoleon's cool wrist. There was no pulse, no movement. I forced myself to look closer. A red stain marred the side of his chef's coat and something viscous had oozed into a crack in the sidewalk. It wasn't red chile. *Blood*. Blood whooshed through my head, and I feared I'd be the next one on the ground. Fainting wouldn't help Linda or Napoleon. I turned my eyes to his twisted hand and the watch. Beneath shattered glass, the gold hands had stopped at eleven-fifty. Is that when the man stopped too?

A few feet away, Linda paced. "I woke up early with a terrible feeling. A panic. I thought it was because the tamale warmer in my cart was still left on. Yesterday I called a friend, Don the hotdog vendor, and asked him to shut it off for me, but when I woke up, I thought, 'What if he didn't? It could start a fire!' Or what if he did turn it off, and someone ate a chicken *mole* tamale that had been sitting out all night? People die from food poisoning . . ."

People die from murder too. Food poisoning hadn't caused the blood. It hadn't rolled a tamale cart over Napoleon's lifeless body either. "Linda," I said gently, "I don't think a bad tamale killed him."

"My cart," Linda said, her voice cracking. "It's a hazard. I think the tank's out of fuel, so the warmer's off and it won't start a fire. It's crushing Napoleon, though. How do I get it off him? What do I do, Rita? Can you help me lift it? If we lift it, maybe he'll be okay . . ."

There was no way Napoleon could be okay. I led her to the green wrought-iron bench where Cass and I had eaten the day before. The last of Napoleon's crepes I'd ever have. Sorrow for their maker struck me, followed by dread. Linda's cart hadn't moved itself, and Napoleon, I was sure, hadn't died a natural death. A man whom Linda publicly fought with and threatened lay dead, murdered. I wished I could whisk her cart away and shield it and her from the scene of the crime.

I couldn't. I'd been married to a cop, and I'd been involved in murder and crime before. I knew what I had to do. Sitting on the chilly bench next to Linda, I dialed 911 and listened for the wail of sirens.

Chapter 4

Yup, he's dead." My ex, Detective Manny Martin, stepped back and scowled down at Napoleon.

I resisted a snarky, *No kidding, Sherlock.* Antagonizing Manny wouldn't do anyone any good, least of all me. Manny already looked grumpy. He doesn't do morning well, unless he's stayed up all night to get there.

Bunny, Manny's body-building partner, yawned and rolled her neck and shoulders.

"One hour," Manny complained. "We were off call in one lousy hour and then this." He glared at me as if I'd found a dead guy simply to wreck his day.

Bunny stretched each elbow across her chest, her eyes scanning the scene.

I practiced an exercise I'd gotten pretty good at in the last year. Ignoring Manny. His sniping still rankled me, though. I'd like to be back in bed too, and it's not like I enjoyed finding corpses in the morning, or any other time of day.

Bunny, limbered up, waved over a waiting crime tech with a camera around his neck. "Shoot it all. Everything," she instructed. "When the medical examiner gets here, tell her I want temperatures of the body, the scene, and those tamales."

The tech, fresh-faced and eager, beamed in anticipation. He looked younger than Celia. I thought about how fast my daughter was growing up. Closing in on seventeen with orange-streaked hair, charcoal eye shadow, and—egad—a driver's license. Plus a boyfriend? I wondered if Manny knew anything about her love life. Sometimes Celia confided in her dad if she thought I'd get upset, and vice versa. In some ways, she was mastering her divorced-kid status a bit too well.

Camera flashes lit up Napoleon's body, and I went to join Linda. She slumped against a tree a few yards away, her fingers rolling across rosary beads and her lips moving in silent prayer. Above, the brilliant rose and lavender hues of sunrise were fading into clear blue skies.

Bunny fell into step beside me. Her warm-up exercises had apparently been for interrogation drills. She peppered Linda with questions.

Linda answered in bursts. "Yes, I found him . . . No, I don't know what happened . . . I didn't see anyone . . . I wanted to get my cart and make sure it was okay and get it home before the Plaza got busy. I ran off yesterday and left it here, which was very irresponsible of me. I'm so sorry. Can I take my cart now? It's in the way of everybody."

Bunny wrote as Linda talked. Her questions

seemed pretty neutral until she asked, "So, Ms. Santiago, why did you fight with the deceased yesterday?"

Linda started to answer. I swung my arm over her shoulder. "Not now. My friend is shaken up," I said to Bunny. "She's in shock," I continued. "I'm taking her home."

"But my cart . . ." Linda said. "I can't leave it here any longer."

Bunny leaned in so that her face was directly in front of Linda's. Enunciating each word, she said, "The fight, Ms. Santiago. Why did you fight with Mister . . ." Bunny consulted her notepad and frowned. ". . . Mr. Napoleon?"

"Napoleon. One name only," I told her, biting back inappropriate sarcasm regarding the dead.

Linda shoved her bangs over her left eyebrow. "I didn't want to fight with anyone. I'm sorry I reacted the way I did."

"Shh . . ." I urged, before Linda said something she regretted. To Bunny, I said, "She'll come in later and give a full statement." I backed away, tugging Linda with me.

Linda was hard to budge. "I'm sorry, Detective," she said, resisting my tug. "I have to go with Rita. She's upset. She touched Napoleon."

Bunny scowled.

"Sorry about that touching," I said, pulling Linda toward my car. We were nearly there when Manny stepped between me and my Subaru.

"Not so fast," he said. He raised his chin, an acknowledgment to Bunny.

"This Napoleon guy appears to have been murdered," Manny said, presumably speaking over our heads to Bunny. "Looks like someone stabbed him in the back before rolling over him with a tamale cart."

Linda gasped.

"Yep, and here you and your friend are, Rita," my ex continued testily. "Messing around with another dead guy." He looped his thumbs over his belt and assumed the stance of a frontier sheriff ready to shoot it out at high noon. Manny works hard on his supercop look and his looks in general. He shaves high to leave a five o'clock shadow, has skin the color of cappuccino, and—according to one of his recent girlfriends—resembles an actor on a popular *telenovela*. I'd yet to Google the actor, although I didn't doubt that Manny could be his fill-in. The man can act, especially when it comes to turning on the charm. He charmed me for years, until I discovered that I wasn't the only one being swept off her feet. An attractive female deputy passed by and Manny's gaze tracked her. *The same old Manny. Good riddance.*

"We're leaving," I said with more resolve.

"*You're* more than welcome to leave, Rita," Manny said, stepping aside so I could get in my car. "Linda's coming with us. She needs to answer some questions."

Linda's politeness instincts kicked in full force. "Of course," she said. "I'm happy to help. You go back home and get some sleep, Rita. I'll go with the police. They'll sort this out."

I looked from Manny to Bunny and feared they were sorting it out. All wrong.

"If Linda's going, I'm going too." I reattached myself to Linda's elbow. She patted my arm as if

I was the one who needed comfort. I left her side only for a minute. She waited in the back of Manny's car while I dialed Jake Strong. I wasn't calling to discuss a dinner date menu. I feared that Linda might need the services of Santa Fe's top criminal defense attorney.

Standing outside the police station, I watched Jake get out of his silver Audi. He looked good. Who was I kidding? He always looked good. This morning, though, he looked good in a way I hadn't seen before. Instead of his usual Western lawyer getup of dark, trim blue jeans, cowboy boots and hat, and finely tailored suit coat, he wore running shorts, a blue windbreaker, and a sweaty T-shirt advertising one of my favorite ice cream shops, Taos Cow. I sighed, both at the handsome man and the thought of ice cream. I wished we were meeting for a road trip to the creamery, up the Rio Grande to the cute, artsy village of Arroyo Seco. I knew what I'd order. Cherry *ristra*, rich cherry ice cream dotted with piñon nuts and dark chocolate chunks. Or maybe the chocolate malt with Oreos. Or anything with salted caramel.

I shook these fantasies away and greeted Jake and the drooling companion who followed him. Winston the bulldog panted up at me. I patted his wrinkly head, causing his entire behind to wag and his head-heavy front half to wobble off balance.

"Sorry to call you so early," I said to Winston's handsome human, taking a line from Linda's politeness handbook. I no longer worried that I'd woken Jake up. Judging from his attire, he'd been up for a while, burning calories. I knew Jake belonged to a club basketball team and I assumed he worked out. I hadn't known he was an early morning runner.

Frankly, I found this a little intimidating. Don't get me wrong. I try to be healthy. I eat fruits and vegetables, and I often walk to work, where I spend my days on my feet lifting weighty burritos. I have weaknesses, though, in the form of cheese, French pastries, salty snacks, and, well, food in general. I'm also a reluctant exerciser. When my gym membership expired in January, I told myself I'd save money and jog. I've yet to jog more than a handful of times, mainly because I'm too tired after work and too lazy in the morning. I eyed Jake, wondering if sportiness was going to be a relationship problem. Let's see, so far I didn't dance, I didn't run, and I wasn't a statuesque blonde like his ex-wife and the women he'd dated before me. Hadn't he noticed by now?

Winston flopped at my feet, all legs splayed outward, his lips draped over my left sandal. Warm doggy drool reached my foot, and Winston sighed in contentment.

"I'll apologize on his behalf," Jake said, frowning down at man's drooliest best friend. "I was taking him for his morning walk after my run when you called. We ran back home and jumped in the car. He's not a runner."

A creature after my own heart. "Good boy," I assured Winston, who groaned as if he understood. I quickly filled Jake in on Napoleon. Once again proving how nice he was, Jake didn't point out my involvement with yet another dead guy.

"Where's Linda, and why are the police so interested in her?" he asked, focusing on the person of immediate concern. He had his serious lawyer face on. As I described Linda's run-in with Napoleon yesterday, his expression turned hard and I glimpsed what his opponents must face in court.

His seriousness heightened my anxiety. "Linda's in a 'conference room,' as Bunny calls it, but it's probably more of an interrogation room. I got Linda to ask for a lawyer, so they shouldn't question her, right? Or maybe they can still talk at her, but hopefully she'll stay quiet? Anyway, it looks bad, with her cart rolled over the body and the fight, but Linda's innocent. Completely innocent."

I would have loved a perky, affirmative response like, "Of course she's innocent! No doubt!"

Jake's expression remained hard. "You were right to call me," he said, his jaw set firm. Then his eyes softened. "Will you do me a favor?"

My mind said, *Of course, anything!* My lips, thankfully, formed a less eager, "Sure."

In one quick movement Jake kissed my cheek and handed me a leash. "I shouldn't be long," he said. "And Winston shouldn't go in. He gets edgy around uniforms. Would you mind watching him?"

I was still blushing and smiling inappropriately when a car sped into the parking lot and double-parked behind a police van. A glimpse of the driver's face wiped away my smile.

"Oh, Brigitte," I said to the statuesque blonde who got out and rushed up the steps two at a time. I knew Brigitte Voll casually. A few months ago we shared a table as judges of a green chile cheeseburger contest. She'd been friendly, and we'd chatted about being outsiders in Santa Fe. I learned that she hailed from Alsace, a storybook-pretty region of France on the border of Germany. She spoke French, German, and dashes of Italian and Spanish, and managed the financial and front-of-house aspects of Napoleon's restaurants. A big and demanding job, but one she seemed up to. Although a decade younger than me, she'd lived in more countries than I'd ever visited, and since coming to the U.S., she'd worked in New York, San Francisco, and Seattle before landing in Santa Fe. To tell the truth, I was daunted by her experience and cool, confident beauty. That's partly why I hadn't called to set up the coffee meeting we said we must do. Everyday routines and work had also gotten the best of my good intentions. Now too much time had passed and we were meeting under awful circumstances.

I told her how sorry I was for her loss. Trite, inadequate words, yet Brigitte embraced me, squeezing hard.

"Detective Brown—Bunny—called me," she said. Her French accent, usually slight, was more pronounced than usual. "Bunny and I are friends from the gym. She knew that Napoleon and I . . ." She swallowed hard before continuing. "She knew how close we are . . . were . . ."

Close as in romantic? Santa Fe's cooking community is a stew of gossip. I knew that Napoleon had gotten around, but I hadn't heard anything about him and Brigitte. On the other hand, I tried not to sniff out gossip that didn't concern me, unlike Flori and her network of elderly informants. You never know what information you'll need, she always contended. Now I wished I knew more.

Winston gazed up at Brigitte through droopy eyelids. She managed a weak smile. "You are a sad-looking creature too." She bent down to ruffle his wrinkles. When she straightened up, she seemed more in control of her emotions.

She took a deep breath. "Okay. I must go. I told Bunny that I need to be sure. I need to see . . . to see Napoleon's . . ."

The word "body" didn't come.

"It's hard to comprehend," I said. "I'm so sorry." I took the hug initiative this time. "Call if there's anything I can do," I told her, feeling both helpless and two-faced.

Just yesterday I'd been spying on Napoleon, seeking out his weaknesses. I'd called him a jerk, in my mind and out loud. He had been a jerk, I rationalized. There was no sin in thinking the truth. But Brigitte didn't need to hear it, and I certainly hadn't wanted him dead.

She thanked me and patted her already perfect hair, cut in a short, angled bob that matched her put-together nature. Her pale blue eyes, though ringed in red, lifted with her attempt at a smile. "You are kind, Rita. I will be fine. There will be some closure soon."

"Closure?" My head snapped up. Winston stopped drooling long enough to whine plaintively.

Brigitte, already halfway through the door, turned. "Bunny told me as a friend. I suppose I can tell you as a friend too. She says they have a good lead on the killer. They are questioning her, in fact."

Now I was the one with stuck words. I gawped at Brigitte. "Her?"

Brigitte shook her head sadly. "The tamale lady. Bunny said she's all but confessing."

Chapter 5

Jake emerged nearly an hour later. A long hour, during which I called Flori and Celia and risked Winston's negative feelings toward uniforms. Flori threatened to mobilize an elderly tai-chi army and storm the police station. I'd talked her down, so far. Celia said she'd get a ride to school with a friend, deemed the murder "sick," and urged me not to worry. "Dad will find who did it," she said, showing a daughter's love—and naiveté—of her father. Winston, indeed, had issues with uniforms. He growled in all directions as I hurried us through the police station lobby and down the hall to a coffee vending machine. The brown liquid burned my fingers through the paper cup and tasted bitter and dank. I gulped it anyway, desperate to clear my head of the fuzzy ache signaling a caffeine-addict headache. The caffeine helped, but I didn't like what I was hearing from Jake.

"There's some good news, I suppose," he said, rubbing his temple. "Linda didn't exactly confess. That's a start."

"Didn't exactly?" So much for headache relief. Tension tapped across my forehead, taking over where the caffeine deficit left off.

Jake shook his head and glanced at Linda, who stood a few yards away staring at a neglected flower bed.

"I'll tell you," Jake said. He kept his voice low, which made it deeper and, I hated to think it at such a time, even more alluring. "I rarely have clients who won't stop talking about how guilty they feel. Mostly, they yell that they're innocent. All this apologizing makes things, well, let's say 'challenging' for a defense attorney."

From what I'd heard, many of Jake's clients *should* be apologizing. I didn't go there. Instead, I said, "Linda's shaken up. Finding Napoleon dead like that, it was a shock. For me too."

Jake's smile warmed me. So did his hand on my arm. His next words, however, sent a chill to my core. "Linda has to understand the situation she's in, Rita. You should as well. As the police say, she has motive, means, and opportunity. She fought with the deceased the day before. Her cart was literally the scene of the crime. She *sounds* guilty. The police will look at her, hard."

I already feared that and told Jake what Brigitte had said. "Bunny basically told Brigitte that they had their suspect."

Jake watched Winston spin in a circle, clumsily chasing a moth. "I got that impression," he said. "If I could have, I'd have lassoed Linda and dragged her out of there, but she kept saying she wanted to stay and help. She has no alibi other than an early bedtime and being nice. She's going to help herself right into a murder conviction."

The coffee roiled through my stomach. Winston lunged at the moth, missing. I handed over his leash to Jake and went to dump the half-full cup of acid brew in the trash. On my way, I collected Linda.

"It's okay," I said, when she apologized again for getting me up early. It was okay that she'd gotten me up. Everything else was not.

Jake offered to drive us. "I'll take you ladies wherever you'd like to go," he said. "Where to? Home?"

I didn't hesitate. "Tres Amigas."

Flori met us at the back door, giving each of us, including Winston, a hug. The warm, inviting kitchen smelled of bacon, roasted chiles, and baked goods. Juan stood at his griddle, overseeing rows of perfectly round pancakes. The cakes were tempting, but I gravitated toward the coffeepot and something else. A buzz, like chattering cicadas, emanated from the dining room. It was nine-fifty on a Tuesday morning, a time when the café was typically pretty empty. People should be at work or school or getting on with their day, not filling up every table.

"What the . . . ?" I blinked, taking in the crowd. "Did a tour bus come by?" That happened sometimes. Juan dreaded tour buses and the crush of urgent and oftentimes menu-modifying orders they involved. Although I loved sharing tourists' excitement about Santa Fe, I wasn't in the mood to explain unfamiliar menu items or New Mexico's official state question, "red, green, or Christmas?" The question refers to chile choice. I used to dither about my answer. Not anymore. Christmas is the way to go. Spicy green chile on one side and smoky, earthy red on the other. Delicious.

"Not a bus, me love. Supporters." These chipper words, in full-on faux British, came from Addie, our part-time waitress and backup cook, the latter in emergency situations only, as Addie can burn just about any substance except water and maybe even that. The British arises from what Addie considers striking similarities between herself and English pop star Adele. She and the real Adele share the same May birth date, although our Addie's younger by several years. Both are fabulous singers, with a love of wigs and belting out bluesy soul music. The similarities end at their figures. Addie consumes double helpings of New Mexican classics, trying to achieve Adelelike curves. To her despair and my envy, she remains as thin as a walking-stick cactus. Her accent isn't exactly going smashingly either, despite studying *Downton Abbey* and chatting up any customers presumed to be British, including a few Australians, Swedes, South Africans, and Canadians.

"See those in the fancy dress?" she said, pointing to a mostly white-haired contingent on the east side of the room. She clasped her hands together, pleased. "Miss Flori had me send out a text to them and they popped right over."

The "they" in question wore bands around their foreheads, like sushi chefs wear, except apparently improvised from our stock of chile pepper napkins.

"Flori's gossip network?" I asked.

Addie giggled. "That's the right name for 'em, isn't it? Informants, that's what she called 'em. Amazing how many of the old dears have smart phones now. The other side, they're supporters too, only different."

"Different?" I asked, but Addie was being summoned to the dining room by an elderly man waving a butter knife and his coffee cup our way.

"Oops!" Addie exclaimed. "I promised coffee and muffins and a side of beans and more syrup and Bob's your uncle! Ta!" She grabbed a coffeepot and was off.

Addie had picked up "Bob's your uncle" from a British skit show. I wasn't sure what the odd idiom meant and kept meaning to ask. Now was not the time, though. There were pancakes to serve and coffees to refill. Maybe. I bent to tie my shoe and by the time I looked up, everyone in the dining rooms was on their feet.

Addie bustled back with two empty coffeepots in her hand.

"What's going on?" I asked. "Are they all leaving?" I wouldn't mind if they did. I craved peace and time to think and eat my own breakfast.

Flori's ninja-attired friends raised their mugs in the air. The other side of the room stood too, clapping loudly.

"No, not leaving," Addie said, smoothing her ruffled apron, a patchwork of English tea towels.

"Jolly rowdy out there, isn't it? Those in the karate costumes, they're from Miss Flori's exercise group and supporting Miss Linda. They mostly think she's innocent. The blokes on the other side . . . well . . ."

I scanned the other side of the room, recognizing the faces of cooks and waiters, dishwashers and a smattering of food cart owners. Some cheered, others whistled. No one appeared to be mourning. They were all, to use Addie's term, jolly.

Addie put my fears into words. "Those over there, some of them think Linda's innocent too. Some others, they think she knocked Napoleon off and are right pleased." She frowned. "Miss Flori didn't say whether the doubting types get free pancakes or not."

The rowdy foodie side of the room began to chant Linda's name. Confusion evident on her face, Linda ventured out among them, lending her shaky hand to high-fives.

"How can anyone think Linda's guilty?" I asked. I said this indignantly and rhetorically. I didn't notice that Flori, in her ninja-silent sneakers, had sneaked up behind me.

"I can see how," she said.

What?" I demanded. I knew I sounded righteous and probably rude, but how could Flori, Linda's mother, say such a thing? I'd never suspect Celia of a crime. Okay, I had accused Celia of drunk driving once. I was wrong, although Celia did have an open beer can in the vehicle. I'd also believed she was responsible for artistic cactus tagging (she was), rogue wall murals (again true), and sneaking out after her curfew (not that a curfew has ever worked with her anyway). But murder? No way. Never. Certainly not an intentional, brutal murder followed by a crushing with a tamale cart. I'd never say or think such a thing about my daughter. I hoped.

Flori raised one arthritic finger after another, ticking off perfectly valid reasons to suspect her eldest daughter. "Linda fought with Napoleon in public. She refuses to flirt and thus lives alone and has no alibi. She has motive. That horrible man, God rest his soul, was trying to destroy her business. He stole her spot on the Plaza. He planted bugs in her tamales." She stopped to shake her finger. "Mark my words, Rita, Napoleon was behind that bug in Linda's tamale. It's a clear frame-up. In any case, he ended up dead under Linda's cart. Very rude of him, although I'd expect nothing else. He called tamales peasant food. He insulted New Mexican chiles. Imagine! He compared *masa* to soggy sawdust and—"

"Okay, okay," I said. "Yes, those are all reasons, but other people had the same or similar motives. What about all of them? The jolly ones?" I pointed to the potential murderers taking cell phone selfies and raising toasts and flashing V for victory signs. The only good thing about their glee was that they were happily throwing down cash, enough to alleviate Addie's worries about stingy tips for free breakfasts.

"We may as well serve 'em more cakes," Addie

said. She called over her shoulder, "Juan, keep flipping."

Juan grunted.

A chill ran through me. "Any one of them could be the killer."

"Then they should tip us extra for Miss Linda's trouble," Addie said. She narrowed her long fake eyelashes and pointed to a table doling out a stack of bills. "Like them over there. They seem happy. Wonder who they are?"

Flori squeezed in between us. "I have all their names," she said, waving a small notepad. She handed me the pad. "I noted which ones seem extra happy and which think my Linda's guilty. Of course, maybe the killer would say that Linda's innocent."

"Ah, as a trick," Addie said, tapping her forehead and inadvertently dislodging her wig.

Or maybe the killer would stay home and not go out for breakfast, free or otherwise. I took the proffered notepad and studied the names. They were all in different handwriting, some with added smiley faces and inspirational statements, like, "You go, Linda!" and "We stand behind you!" and "We understand!"

You had them sign their own names?" I asked, impressed with my friend's boldness.

Flori grinned. "I told them I was keeping a memory book, like old people do. Young folks can be so gullible." She patted my arm. "Not you, of course, dear. You're a keen sleuth. As soon as we get rid of our freeloading friends out there, we can get to work."

"Work?" I asked. Feeding people was our work.

But I didn't need keenness to figure out what Flori was about to say.

"Catching the real killer," she said matter-of-factly.

"Jolly good!" Addie exclaimed, raising her hand for a high five.

I reluctantly raised my hand. Addie slapped it hard as my stomach dropped.

Chapter 6

An hour later most of the pancake eaters had exhausted their rousing speeches and left. Linda
had slipped out the back, heading for solace
at the Cathedral. Juan was taking a well-deserved
break. I would have taken a break too, except
Flori was packing me a tote bag I could have done
without.

"I really don't need all this," I protested. What I
needed was a nap, and possibly a few more pancakes, although I'd already had a short stack with
an over-easy egg, two strips of bacon, and extra
syrup on top.

"Best to be well supplied and strike while the
scene's hot," Flori said. "That's what Sun Tzu
would say."

I reminded myself that a year ago Flori had
taken up fencing, again at the Senior Center. She'd
practiced by striking our flour sacks with a saber
until one day she jabbed too hard and we had an

industrial-sized cleanup on our hands. Tai chi would pass, and maybe the Senior Center would start offering more age-appropriate workshops like scrapbooking or bird-watching.

"Here, to stuff in your pocket or brassiere. The smallest binoculars I have." Flori handed me binoculars fit for a doll. "They're from that New Year's bird count that my friend Miriam insists on. Why she's interested in that, I'll never know. Cold and boring, if you ask me, and we never see more than a few finches and towhees."

"Towhees are beautiful, and didn't you see a whole flock of sandhill cranes once?" I said encouragingly. "How amazing was that?"

Flori acknowledged the beauty of cranes. "I didn't go looking for them, though. I saw them when I was out spying on the postman because Bernard—the old fool—thought he was smuggling counterfeit Hatch chiles."

I recalled the incident. Bernard, Flori's husband and love of her life for sixty-some years, detected the scent of freshly roasted chiles on their mail. This would be perfectly normal in late summer and fall, when New Mexico ships out fresh, frozen, jarred, and dried chiles by the ton. In early spring, however, the scent aroused Bernard's and Flori's suspicions. Tailing the postman revealed that he was uninvolved, except for delivering South American chiles to a restaurant claiming to serve only New Mexico's finest. Flori tipped off a newspaper reporter who publicly exposed the lie. No one passes off fake chile around Flori and gets away with it.

Now she stuffed two brown paper sacks into

the canvas bag embellished with an image of San Pasqual, the kitchen saint.

"What is all this anyway?" I asked.

My friend and boss pushed back her thick round spectacles. "You've had too much sugar, haven't you? You're like my great-granddaughter Rosa. Too much sugar makes her cranky and edgy."

I clamped my mouth shut, realizing that any retort might indeed sound cranky and edgy. Plus, Flori was right. I hadn't simply added extra syrup, I'd made syrup soup of my pancakes. That, on top of the police station coffee and two too many cups at Tres Amigas and touching a dead body, and I was definitely on edge.

Flori thrust the pretty, overstuffed tote at me. "Sleuthing supplies. If you won't take them for Sun Tzu, think of the Girl Scouts."

I recalled my one summer in the Girl Scouts before cookie sales stressed me out. What was the motto? Sell more cookies? No. "Be prepared?"

"Exactly," Flori said. "Just like Sun Tzu said." She handed me the tote.

I lifted the bag a few times. If nothing else, it was useful for weight-training exercise. "What did you pack in here? Melons? Lead?"

"My tactical-force binoculars that'll let you spy on anything, a fresh notepad, bottled water because you should avoid dehydration at high altitudes, a pen, a plastic bag for your cell phone in case it rains, which is unlikely, or if you fall in a hot tub, also unlikely but it does happen, as you know . . ."

I lifted out one of the lunch sacks.

"Be careful with those!" Flori exclaimed.

I dropped the bag as if singed.

"One bag has muffins in it in case you get hungry," Flori explained. "The other's pepper spray. Hot Flash, it's called. The spray button is sensitive. That's why I put it in the bag."

Juan, sitting on a stool by the counter, chuckled. Easy for him to be cheerful. He was tucking into a plate of bacon, eggs, and cheesy *chiles rellenos*. I wouldn't have minded some more bacon. I wouldn't even have minded washing pots, pans, and knives like Addie was doing.

"Jolly fine," Addie said.

I knew why I felt grumpy, and it wasn't just the sugar. I dreaded a return to the murder scene. More than that, I didn't want to get involved in another murder investigation. *No!* I wanted to yell. Let the police handle it. Let Jake, "the Strong Defender," prove Linda innocent.

Then I caught Flori's worried frown and thought of her ticking off the ways in which Linda looked guilty. If Celia were in trouble, I'd want all the help I could get. Besides, Linda was my friend and a good, kind person who had come to my aid in the past.

I took a deep breath and focused on the positive. I was getting another springtime walk to the Plaza. And muffins. I asked Flori about their flavor, mainly to delay some more.

"My health food muffins. To keep up your strength," she said.

This was good news. Flori's health food muffins aren't the no-sugar, all-bran doorstops the name implies. They're rich chocolate with chocolate chips. The healthy, in Flori's mind, comes from using olive oil instead of her usual choices, butter and lard.

I stalled a little longer by rearranging the tote. Grabbing what I hoped was the bag of muffins and not the pepper spray, I moved it to the top. I didn't want smashed muffins. I also didn't want to accidentally Hot Flash myself. Something fluffy came along with the muffin bag. "What's this pink, furry—" I started to say. Then I realized.

"Ack!" I let go of the pink fur in horror.

Addie looked over my shoulder and tittered.

"Handcuffs," Flori said, answering what I'd already figured out. "Cute, aren't they? I found them at a yard sale a few weeks ago. Now don't give me that face, Rita, I ran them through the dishwasher. The key's attached in case you have to use them."

I prayed I wouldn't have to use—or touch—the handcuffs again. And what else had Flori been throwing in the dishwasher? I made a mental note to use the "sterilize" setting from now on.

"You never know when you'll find a criminal," Flori was saying. "Remember, be prepared. Addie, Juan, and I will hold down the café and keep our ears to the gossip front." She thumped me on the back in an obvious "off you go" gesture. When I didn't go, she gave me a little shove.

I reluctantly stepped toward the back door.

Juan waved a slice of bacon.

"Ta!" Addie called after me. "Have a jolly good time!"

set off, not at all jolly. My Grinch mood, however, didn't last. The day was too pretty. Birds were

singing, tulips were blooming, and the open-air
tour buses were rolling by, filled with happy visitors. Once again I thought how lucky I was to live
here.

At the Plaza, I reclaimed the bench where Cass
and I had sat just yesterday. I'd planned to indulge
in a muffin, but my hunger, even for chocolate,
had vanished. I stared toward the bandstand and
the spot outlined in caution tape, visions of Napoleon's body flashing through my head. Swal-
lowing hard, I forced myself to replay the scene.
I recalled Napoleon's open yet unmoving eyes,
his puffed cheeks and pursed mouth. Why had
he looked like that? Had he been eating? His last
meal?

When people pass away on vacation or pursu-
ing some dangerous passion like jumping out of
airplanes or running in front of bulls or golfing in
lightning storms, everyone says they died doing
what they loved. As if this somehow made their
death more palatable. Still, if Napoleon was eating
his last bite, I hoped it was something he loved. In
his case, that likely meant his food and his food
only.

A few onlookers lingered along the outskirts
of the yellow tape bordering the crime scene.
Some pointed. Others snapped photos with their
phones. The police had left, except for two techs.
One, wearing plastic booties, leaned against a
white paneled van. The second, bent nose to the
ground in ostrich fashion, scoured an area enclosed by a white blobby circle. There was no
body outline, but I knew that's what the chalk
blob represented.

Linda's cart stood just outside the white line, festooned like a carnival float in yellow tape. I bet the tape was Manny's work. My ex went overboard with tape in everything from home repair to his police work.

The ostrich tech craned his head to the ground, tipping his cheek parallel to the pavers and gravel and something else. Tweezers followed, and he meticulously plucked and deposited his find in plastic evidence bags. Remembering Flori's binoculars, I dug around the tote and extracted them from underneath the questionable cuffs. The binoculars, small and light, mostly fit in my hand. Trying to act like a casual bird-watcher, I leaned an elbow on the bench. So I wouldn't have to lie, I located a bird, a crow tearing at a paper food wrapper. The crow stepped on the edge of the paper with both feet and ripped the opposite edge with its imposing bill.

Bird-watching cover accomplished, I zoomed in on the tech and his clear plastic bag. The image jiggled each time I breathed. Giving up on discretion, I put both hands on the binoculars and aimed my magnified stare at the tech.

His gloved hands grasped something dull yellow. A clump of dirt? No . . . I ticked through more possibilities, from gum to buttons to potato chips until I could deny it no longer.

Tamale. The tech was bagging fractured chunks of steamed corn-flour dough. Nearby, I spotted the telltale corn husk that's traditionally wrapped around the *masa* dough and the savory or sweet fillings inside. I let the binoculars sink to my lap. I didn't need them to see the tech wave over his van-

leaner colleague. Together they wrapped plastic around the wheels of Linda's cart. I watched as the men lowered a ramp and shoved the yellow cart up and into the van.

The van doors banged shut and indignation rose like bile in my stomach. Of course, I knew the indignation was misplaced. The techs had to take Linda's cart. Its wheels had rolled over a murder victim. But the cart hadn't moved on its own. I recalled helping Linda once. Even loaded with tamales, cooking utensils, hot sauces, warming trays, a cooler, and a chubby propane tank, the cart moved easily with its four thick wheels and lightweight hitch. Linda was no buff, bodybuilder type like Detective Bunny. If she or I could move it, practically anyone could, and the cart hadn't been secured after Linda abandoned it following her run-in with Napoleon and the food inspector.

I wondered about the inspector. Had Napoleon called him to the Plaza as soon as he saw Linda return? And what about the lanky redheaded guy who found the buggy tamale? The timing was too convenient for me to believe in coincidence. I dug out the notepad and started a list. I needed to talk to the inspector and the bug finder.

I looked up and saw someone else I should question. Gathering my tote bag, I headed across the Plaza to interrogate my first potential murderer.

Chapter 7

I wasn't about to whip out the pink handcuffs and pepper spray for my encounter with Don Busco. First, I'd never overpower him, even with Flori's Taser, which I prayed she hadn't packed in with the muffins. Don stood well over six feet, with a few inches added by a black felt Stetson topped with a feather. Second, I'd feel too guilty. Don beamed at me, little knowing that I suspected him of violent crime.

"Rita!" he said jovially, coming out from behind his ketchup-red hot dog cart. When I was within hugging reach, he threw an arm over my shoulder, enveloping me in the scent of campfire smoke. Since Don steamed his hot dogs, I wasn't sure how he managed the campfire perfume, but it went perfectly with his cowboy-cook look.

"Great to see you!" he said from high above my shoulders. "What brings you out to the Plaza on such a fine day? Hankering for a hot dog?"

Suspecting nice people like you of murder. I smiled at Don and assured myself that he had to make the list, if only to be crossed off. Don used to tend bar at Napoleon's chic bistro, OhLaLa. Cass and I went occasionally to enjoy Don's innovative cocktails and tales of his time in the local film industry. New Mexican landscapes, Don informed us, have appeared in not only Westerns, but also Middle Eastern action films, vampire flicks, and even *Indiana Jones* and *Independence Day.* I'd also learned to keep my eye out for famous part-time New Mexico residents including Robert Redford, Gene Hackman, Julia Roberts, and Shirley MacLaine. Don clearly loved film work, but bartending offered steadier pay and he had a talent for adding southwestern flair to cocktail classics.

Cass and I later speculated that the flair might have gotten him fired. No matter how tasty and popular the drinks, Napoleon wouldn't have liked pickled chiles in his French martinis or a *kir royale* composed of champagne sweetened with pink prickly pear syrup.

The "official" reason for Don's firing, however, didn't involve cocktail innovation or tall tales. Napoleon sent an e-mail to elite restaurant owners warning that Don had palmed tips and whole tabs and bottles. The news swept through the food community. At the time, I wondered why Don didn't sue Napoleon for libel. Unless the accusation was true, in which case why didn't Napoleon go to the police? True or not, Napoleon's bad-mouthing swirled like a desert dust devil, essentially blacklisting Don from restaurant work around town. If I were Don and innocent, I'd be bitter. Bitter enough to kill, though? If so, why wait until now, nearly a year after the fact?

Don certainly seemed jolly, to use Addie's term. He gripped my hand and told me how much he missed seeing me and Cass. "You girls should come 'round for hot dogs or *frito* pie. Best in town, right here!" He patted his cart proudly.

Under other circumstances, I would have been tempted by his gourmet dogs. I stood back to admire the menu. "Wow, green chile and cheese dog? *Frito* pie dog? Don, these sound great. If I hadn't already eaten . . ." And if my stomach wasn't rolling from the crime scene. Adding Fritos, chile, cheese, onions, lettuce, and tomato to a hot dog would not be a good choice right now. In my peripheral vision, the crime tape fluttered. I wondered about Don's choice of venue. He often wheeled his cart to the trendy Railyard District or over to the state office buildings to catch the nine-to-five crowd. It seemed rather morbid to sell hot dogs within eyeshot of a murder scene. Was it possible that Don didn't know what happened?

Oh, but he did know. "Yep, that's why I'm here," Don said, in answer to my tentative question. "I owe a lot to that slandering slimeball, Napoleon. If he hadn't fired me, I'd never have started this cart. Best thing I ever did. I'm my own boss now."

"So you obviously heard from someone . . . ?" I prompted.

He repositioned his hat, tugging the brim down to shade his eyes. "Pretty much everybody knows. In fact, I heard you and Flori held a pancake celebration this morning. I do love Flori's pancakes. If I'd known, I'd have hauled myself out of bed early."

"We didn't intend for a celebration," I hastily clarified. "Flori is so worried about Linda because of the fight she had with Napoleon yesterday. It looks bad to the police. Maybe you heard about that too?"

Don massaged the thin line of facial hair connecting his flaring, almost-handlebar mustache to his goatee. In his bartending days he'd worn hip black vests and sported an intentional five o'clock shadow like my ex. Now he wore a denim shirt, jeans, cowboy boots, and a bolo tie. Maybe his days in film had taught him about costuming.

He continued to rub, his thumb and index finger meeting at his chin. "I saw that fight. The tail end only, but I could hear it from blocks away. Linda stood her ground. I like that in a woman. The police are fools to think she's involved, no offense meant to your ex there, Rita. Manny and I are drinking buddies. Next time I see him, I'll tell him what I think."

I told Don that I appreciated his support for Linda. "I already told Manny the same thing," I grumbled. "He won't listen to me."

"Power in numbers," Don said, bobbing his head in affirmation of his own platitude. "We're all gettin' together to help Linda, you tell her that."

"We?" As far as I knew, Don's hot dog cart was a one-cowboy operation.

"Us food carters. We're gonna stick together from now on. No more rogue warriors. All for one and one for all and all that. Ah, here's another one of us now."

A van towing a cart swung in toward the curb.

"A new food cart era is beginning," Don said grandly.

And another suspect is arriving, I thought, recognizing Crystal's juice cart.

Don waved in Crystal as she backed up her van and angled her juice cart next to his. Crystal's dress and sweater matched her juices, bright red and orange. Her long dark hair bounced in loose curls down her back and her makeup was equally bright. She greeted Don with a lipstick-preserving air kiss. I got a wave and a cheerful, "*Hola*, Rita."

Don and I helped her unload her van, lugging out jugs of *agua fresca*, sweet fruit juice lightened with water. For a woman who'd been shut down yesterday, Crystal had prepared a bounty of juice for today. I read the labels as the jugs emerged. Strawberry with mint. Mango sweetened with honey. Pineapple and lime. And, one of my favorites, tamarind. The tamarind wouldn't win any beauty contests with its color of wet adobe, yet thinking of its tart tang made my mouth water. So did the last jug that Crystal retrieved from her passenger seat, a milky white *horchata* made from rice and almonds that had been soaked, blended, and strained. Spiced with cinnamon and nutmeg, the beverage reminded me of my grandmother's rice pudding and could be just the medicine my rolling stomach needed.

Crystal offered me a beverage, free except for more guilt. Here was another nice person for my suspect list. I considered declining to maintain my investigative integrity. On the other hand, I didn't want to tip her off with unusual behavior. I ended up sipping soothing *horchata* and dancing around the question of when Crystal and Don had last seen Napoleon.

Crystal had last seen the crepe bully when he chased her off the Plaza. Her sunny disposition turned dark, and was I imagining it or were tears welling in her eyes? She ducked behind her cart to retrieve some cups. By the time she straightened again, her expression had turned hard. "He was a bad man, that Napoleon. Cruel. Slippery. Deceitful."

Don agreed and said he'd seen Napoleon later on, after the fight with Linda. "Napoleon was strutting around like a rooster," he said. "I thought about setting my dog stand up on another corner of the Plaza, but decided to go somewhere with less aggravation."

Crystal nodded. "He got in everybody's business. I showed him. He thought he could get rid of me? I got my permit settled and now I'm back." She held up a wooden spoon in triumph. Don raised some tongs and they knocked the utensils together.

"So you weren't that worried when Napoleon questioned your permit?" I asked Crystal.

Crystal shrugged. "I sorted out that paperwork right away. A lost form, they said. I bet it got lost on purpose. I told the clerk, 'I have three kids and this cart to run and my husband's working two jobs. I don't have time to waste.'"

Don said, "I hear you."

"I won't say I'm glad a man's dead," Crystal continued. "That would be wrong. But am I happy he and his health inspector won't be bothering me?"

It was a rhetorical question, one Don answered with a robust grunt. "If that inspector comes around, we'll show him what for. You run a spotless cart, Crystal, and so does—did—Linda."

Crystal thanked Don and praised his hot dog

cart. The big man blushed under the slew of compliments from the attractive juice maker.

"About this health inspector," I said, interrupting their compliment fest. "Don't you think it was odd that he was right here when that redheaded guy found the cockroach?"

Don and Crystal agreed. "Too convenient for my liking," Don said. "We know Napoleon's dirty ways, though, don't we, Crystal?"

She sniffed. "Yeah, we sure do. Don's right. Linda ran a clean operation. We know she didn't have bugs. Not such a big bug anyway. You'd notice that putting together a tamale. Imagine you are folding the fillings into the *masa*, you'd see a bug like that." She curled her lip in disgust.

"You'd notice all right," Don said. "Rita, you tell Linda I'd be honored to sell her tamales from my cart if she wants." He grinned, his teeth bright under the shade of his hat. "Tell her I need only tamales as payment. I never did get to try her *mole* special before she ran off yesterday."

I thanked them both and promised I'd tell Linda. "That'll cheer her up. She needs all the support she can get."

Don agreed. "That's why we made this. Might be premature, but if the police are setting their sights on Linda, she'll need a lawyer and a whole mess of money." He reached under his counter and produced a glass jug with a piece of paper taped to it. The paper read, *Free Linda*. A blurry, ink-jet image showed Linda's face. She was smiling and standing among a larger group. Someone, presumably Don, had hand-drawn black vertical bars over her face.

"Aw . . . that's nice, Don. Really nice," Crystal said. She turned to me. "We can make some bumper stickers too, if Linda ends up in real trouble. My nephew runs a screen-printing shop. He can do T-shirts, tank tops, caps, stickers . . ."

I cringed. Linda behind bars was not the image I wanted spread around on bumpers and tank tops. "Linda's not under arrest," I clarified, after reiterating how great their support was. "She only went to the police station this morning to help out and give a witness statement. If there is any trouble, she has Santa Fe's best defense attorney on her side. And, of course, she's innocent."

"Exactly! I believe in her fully," Don said. "That woman is both my friend and the salt of the earth. As innocent as my own *abuela*. Isn't that right, Crystal?"

Crystal twisted her cherry-red lips and said nothing. I doubted she was questioning Don's grandmother.

"Crystal?" I asked. "You *do* believe Linda's innocent, right? She'd never hurt anyone."

Crystal concentrated on polishing her already spot-free counter. "Sometimes, people go a little loco. They get mad and then you don't know what can happen. If that's what happened with Linda, I don't blame her one bit. In fact, I want to help her." She reached over and dropped a dollar in the donation jug.

"Linda wouldn't hurt anyone," I reiterated. I offered up anecdotes about Linda feeding the hungry and rescuing wolves.

Don agreed enthusiastically. "An absolute saint! I tell you, she's like my very own grandmother on my mother's side. My paternal grandmother, well . . ." He shrugged, implying his other granny might be incited to stabbings.

Crystal frowned. "But, Don, my sister called me when I was driving over here and she said she saw Linda at the Cathedral, weeping and begging the priest to let her into a confessional. And you know what?" Crystal lowered her voice and glanced over her shoulders, gossiper's code for about to dish up dirt.

Don leaned in. I gripped my *horchata* cup so hard the plastic crumpled.

"It's not even the regular confessing day," Crystal whispered. She followed this statement with a knowing bob of her head.

"Linda's a pious woman," Don said after a beat. "My *abuela* went to confession every week and hadn't a sin in her life. Not a one."

Crystal appeared not to hear him. "My sister said, Father Joseph, after he came out, he looked sad too. Upset and sad both, and he's a priest!" She shivered.

I could have hugged Don as he held firm about Linda's innocence. "Linda's a kind, God-fearing woman," he assured a skeptical Crystal. "She's surely sad about any death and wanted to talk to the priest about it. He'd be sad too. Priests are like that. Caring and whatnot."

Crystal's doubtful look remained. If I hoped to sway her—not to mention Manny—I needed another suspect. I switched back to the topic of their alibis.

"The police want to know everybody's alibis," I said, exaggerating with "everybody." So far,

Manny and Bunny seemed most interested in Linda's alibi. "I hope you two have people to vouch for you. You do, right?"

"Me?" Crystal punctuated her answer with a scoffing sound. "I was home with my husband and kids, working and making juice." She listed a litany of household chores that made my to-do lists seem like nothing. She'd made four batches of cookies for a school bake sale and all the juices for today. She helped with homework and read bedtime stories and packed lunches for all family members including herself. "Burritos with avocado, rice, beans, and cheese," she said. "Really healthy."

"And your husband was there all night?" I asked.

"What does that mean?" Crystal demanded. "Where else would Chago be?"

One of his two jobs perhaps? I hardly dared ask Crystal, who was getting testier than me on too much maple syrup.

"Chago gets home for the kids' bedtime and reads them books," she said. "He's a *good* man. We have a *good* marriage, stronger than ever. I *love* him."

I sighed, thinking I could have used a good man around the house when I'd been married. I risked getting Don prickly too and asked about his activities.

Don was less clear than Crystal. Actually, he was downright fuzzy. He was, as he put it, "here or there" and "out and about." He tipped back his hat and rubbed his forehead, as if this might scour out some more details. "I'll admit, I rambled around and had a few drinks," he said. "I feel a mite bad. Turns out that Linda had left me a message 'round dinnertime asking me to turn off her warmer tray in her cart if I was down at the Plaza. I didn't check my phone till this morning." He glanced toward the crime scene. "No getting there now. It probably ran out of fuel on its own anyhow."

"So you were on the Plaza?" I asked.

"I was out selling hot dogs until about eight, I'd guess," Don said. "After that, I figured I'd done enough business, so I packed the cart up. Had a few beers with the boys afterward. I'm sorry now I didn't pay attention to my phone. I'm not a phone guy."

Manny had claimed to not be a phone guy too. Funny how he'd become one when he got a smart phone for texting his girlfriends.

I tried again. "We really need a witness to help out Linda," I said, giving up the ruse that the police were the only ones asking. "Maybe you walked by the Plaza and saw something or someone or Napoleon? Anything could help."

Don rubbed his goatee thoughtfully. "Well, can't say that I recall. I chatted with some folks. Didn't see Napoleon, not that he went to the bars I go to these days. I saw your ex, though. We had a beer at the Cantina. I suppose he's my alibi, if that's what you're feeling around for. Ha! A policeman. That's a pretty good alibi, now isn't it?"

Yeah, good for him. Bad for Linda, and for me, since the Cantina was the site of my Bloody-Mary-throwing incident. I wouldn't be going in there or questioning Manny. *Like that would get me anywhere.*

"So who do you think killed Napoleon?" I asked the twosome.

"Lind—" Crystal started to say.

"If it wasn't Linda," I said, cutting her off.

She shrugged, her dark curls tumbling over her shoulders.

"Could have been anyone," Don suggested, also unhelpfully. "A random killer like you see on TV. Some dude, a psycho type, comes by with a knife and that's that."

Crystal said she didn't like that idea.

I didn't either. How could the police locate a random stranger? How could I? But I doubted Don's theory. What were the chances that an unknown murderer came across Napoleon, worked up the ambition to stab him, and then took the extra step of covering his body with a tamale cart? No, this crime suggested a personal grudge. More than that. Intense hatred or a burst of anger.

"What about the health inspector?" I suggested. "The guy who shut down Linda's cart? Do you know anything about him? What if he and Napoleon were involved in dirty business together and the deal went bad?"

Crystal clamped her red lips shut and busied herself rearranging the juices.

Don laid his hand on my shoulder. It felt like a steel baseball mitt. "Rita, I know about you and Flori and your sleuthing. You girls have to be careful. Asking questions about killers and food inspectors—especially that one—is dangerous business. Real dangerous. Linda will be fine. She's innocent." He squeezed my shoulder and then patted the donation jug. "We've got her back."

"Free Linda!" Crystal yelled, raising a wooden spoon high. Heads turned our way.

I turned to go. As I did, Don's iron grip latched onto my arm. "I mean it, Rita," he said in a low voice. His friendly grin was gone and his eyes dark under the brim of his hat. A shiver ran up the side he gripped. "Stay away for your own sake, and for Flori's and Linda's too."

He released me and I hurried off. *Free Linda* rang through my confused head. Was I imagining it, or had I just been threatened by a nice guy?

Chapter 8

By the time I reached the other side of the Plaza, I'd convinced myself—mostly—that Don had issued a friendly caution. What nice guy doesn't warn a single woman to take care around a killer? Or warn a fellow food professional about a potentially dirty health inspector? I probably misread the hard edge in his voice. And his eyes, maybe he was squinting against the sun. Except that his hat shaded his eyes. Maybe my initial impression was right and Don was warning me off his murderous business. Don definitely had the strength to overpower Napoleon. He also had a beef.

But why now, when his hot dog cart was thriving and he claimed to be happy? Had Napoleon sicced the health inspector on Don? Restaurants fell afoul of inspectors all the time. Besides, a failing grade wasn't always bad. Problems could be fixed, and some fanatic foodies even considered infractions a sign of greasy-spoon gems.

Engrossed in these thoughts, I didn't notice the
TV crew until I stepped into their shot.

"Cut!" a man's voice boomed in my ear.

I jumped backward, apologizing.

"Good one, Rita," a grouchier male voice said.
Manny stood a few feet away getting his nose
powdered.

Just what I didn't need, Manny, and in front of
a camera no less. My vain ex would be puffed up
like a law-enforcing prairie chicken.

The woman holding a News 6 microphone waved
off the disruption. "Doesn't matter," she said breez-
ily. "I didn't like my lead in. Let's do it over. This
time, can we get more of that crime scene van in
the background? What if it was open?"

I recognized her from a nightly news program
out of Albuquerque. Her name was Milan Lujan,
and she was as exquisite as I imagined her namesake city to be. Exactly Manny's type. Shorter
than him, with long black hair and dark, almond-
shaped eyes hovering far across her cheekbones,
like a sexy space alien.

Manny turned on his charm. "I'll handle that,"
he said, waving down the lounging crime tech.

I might hate confrontation, but I couldn't stop
myself. I stepped up to my ex. "Manny, you know
Linda's innocent. *Anyone* is innocent until proven
guilty."

Milan stepped away to have her makeup ad-
justed. Manny flashed me his pearly whites.
"Spending too much time with that criminal-
chaser lawyer, are you Rita? I'm sorry about
Linda. I'll miss her tamales, and she's a nice lady.
But even nice ladies can snap."

The crime tech moved the van closer. His partner flung open the back door, revealing the imprisoned cart. I could see the red and orange flowers painted along one side and the word TÍA. Anyone local could fill in the rest, if they hadn't heard already.

Manny was right about one thing. Nice women can snap. I wanted to push him aside and slam the van doors shut. Fortunately, I didn't have a chance to make a newsworthy scene of myself.

The cameraman tugged on my jacket sleeve. "Ready to roll," he announced.

I stepped back, and Milan took her place beside Manny. He adjusted his black leather jacket, unzipping it to show the viewers of New Mexico and southern Colorado his tight black T-shirt printed with the word POLICE.

Milan arched her perfectly shaped eyebrows. "Horror in Santa Fe," she intoned. "As a renowned figure in the culinary world is brutally murdered on the historic Plaza, behind the bandstand which brings joy to so many. The incident was reported early this morning, leaving a community in shock and diners around the world in mourning." She swung her microphone to the side and the camera followed. "I'm here with Officer Martin of the Santa Fe police. Officer, do you have a message for our viewers?"

Manny morphed his face into an expression of grave concern. "Thanks for having me on, Milan," he said. "We're asking anyone who might have been on or near the Plaza last night, particularly around midnight, to come forward. Anything, even something small, that you witnessed could be a vital clue in our investigations."

"Indeed," Milan said, smiling admiringly at Manny. "Are there any leads so far, Officer Martin?"

"We are investigating a person of interest," Manny said, and I bit my lip hard to keep from snapping.

In front of me, the cameraman appeared to zoom in on the van as Manny said that the crime scene techs had been busy gathering evidence.

"We're closing in," Manny said, puffing his chest.

Right, closing in on the wrong person.

Milan stood practically cheek-to-cheek with Manny. "Can you comment on reports of a local food cart war?" she asked.

Manny, his own tone implying great regret, said he could not comment. He did, however, turn to look meaningfully at the van.

Milan filled in the rest. "We at News 6 are working to confirm reports that the victim clashed with another food cart operator on the Plaza yesterday. We'll stay in close touch with Officer Martin and keep you, our viewers, apprised of new developments in this case."

She smiled at Manny before giving a serious nod toward the camera. "Todd, back to you in the newsroom."

"Cut!" the cameraman yelled, and Manny's sympathetic expression lost out to his pearly whites. Manny could star in toothpaste commercials if he hadn't found his calling in law enforcement. He turned his smile on Milan, likely asking for and getting her number.

I made a move on the cameraman, but not for

the same reasons. He was wrapping up his cables,
a toothpick dangling from his lips.

"Hey," I said, lowering my voice to a husky whisper, like I imagined covert informants used. "Tell
Milan the police are mistaken. They're looking at
the wrong person and a killer is getting away."

The camera guy twizzled his toothpick. "Yeah?"
he said, sounding uninterested. "So who did it?"
He was young, with tattoos of New Mexican icons
running up each arm—a roadrunner, a horned
toad, a Zia symbol, a Route 66 sign, and a green
splotch half covered by his shirtsleeve, probably
a green chile. Clearly, camera guy loved his state.
Maybe I could use that to my advantage.

"I can't say yet," I said. "But Napoleon trashed
New Mexican cuisine." My informant voice was
straining my throat. I switched to normal speaking volume. "Linda Santiago makes some of the
best tamales in the state, and she's being framed."

He finished wrapping up his cord and eyed me.
"Yeah? So? What do you want me to do?"

Good question. I knew what I didn't want,
namely the nightly news flashing shots of Linda's
cart and implying her guilt. "I . . . I want Milan to
have the story! Exclusive tips." Making a split—
and possibly terribly wrong—decision, I blurted,
"Tell her to look at the dirty food inspector."

Panic zinged through my body to the tips of my
fingers. Why hadn't I said dirty hot dog man? Because I wasn't sure, that's why, and Don, towering above me with that dark look, had shaken me.
However, I wasn't sure about the food inspector
either, and the last thing I wanted was to get on

an inspector's bad side. Picturing the man shutting down Tres Amigas with made-up health violations, I backtracked. "Others too. I mean, look at all the people Napoleon fired and businesses he ruined." I turned and rushed off.

Camera guy called after me. "Hey, what's your name? Milan might want to interview you."

"Anonymous!" I yelled, reaching the curb. I jogged across Palace Avenue and ducked into a crowd of art lovers viewing Native American jewelry by the Palace of the Governors. The one-story adobe extends the length of the Plaza and recently celebrated its four hundredth birthday. From what I can tell from old photos, the structure hasn't changed much in all that time. Today, as in decades past, vendors sat under the covered walkway, cast in sepia shadows, their jewelry laid out on blankets in front of them. Words from the region's original languages mingled with English, Spanish, and a tour group speaking Mandarin or Cantonese. I fell in behind an English-speaking tour guide who was announcing that the building had four-foot-thick walls and was the oldest continuously occupied public structure in the U.S. The tourists oohed and aahed and patted the smooth adobe surface.

I glanced nervously back toward the Plaza and the modern news crew. The camera guy was talking to Milan. He raised his hands in an I-don't-know gesture. Milan cocked her head, seemingly intrigued. I could read Manny's gestures too. His hands went to his hips. He leaned to one side. He'd be frowning and sighing and hopefully not revealing my name.

Later that afternoon, I sat on a stool in the kitchen of Tres Amigas, under orders from Flori to rest. My feet did appreciate the break. My mind, however, was running laps. I had to confess to my possible café-threatening bluff. I did so when Flori's attention was on a pot of stubborn pinto beans. Three hours, she'd been complaining. The beans had cooked longer than usual and remained mealy rather than creamy. Beans can be fickle, especially at Santa Fe's seven-thousand-foot altitude. So can cakes and breads and soufflés, as I well knew.

A twinge of nerves struck me. I still hadn't decided on a dessert for my dinner date or achieved a soufflé with proper puff and flavor. And what about side dishes? I couldn't feed a man only fluffy soufflé and dessert. I had a recipe for tasty roasted asparagus dressed with French-style mustard vinaigrette. What if I added some Mexican flair with cilantro and lime and topped the dish with spicy, fried tortilla strips and toasted pine nuts? That might work. So could a recipe I'd tried out for Thanksgiving, sweet cherry tomatoes baked with baguette croutons and a sprinkling of Parmesan. If I did that, I'd have the red, white, and green of the Mexican flag. I scribbled down notes, adding to the to-do list that included grocery shopping and interrogations.

Glancing up, I noticed that Flori had stopped stirring. I hurried to apologize. "I'm so sorry! I spoke without thinking to that cameraman. If that food inspector's dirty and comes after us, it'll be my fault!"

Flori spooned up a bean, nibbled it, frowned, and punched another forty-five minutes on the timer.

"Sun Tzu couldn't have done it better, Rita," she said, nodding deliberately, like the long-ago sage might have. "You're flushing out an enemy."

I doubted Mr. Sun ever contemplated the vengeful ways of unethical health inspectors. "I didn't give my name," I said, mostly to comfort myself since Flori seemed more concerned about the beans. "But Manny was there. He might have told the reporter. It was Milan Lujan from News 6. You know, the pretty one with the amazing eyes."

"Ha!" my elderly friend said. "Manny wouldn't admit to a hot reporter that his ex-wife is a better sleuth than he is."

Flori was as wise as Sun Tzu, if not more so. Manny wouldn't say anything about me and my sleuthing, especially if he had any doubt that I might be right. I relaxed a little, yet kept Flori's Girl Scout/Sun Tzu motto in mind. If the food inspector came, Tres Amigas would be prepared.

I spent the afternoon cleaning all surfaces I could reach. I scrubbed the sinks, dusted the shelves, checked every use-by date on every food product, and stocked the bathrooms with loads of sanitizing soaps and paper products. I tested the temperature of our walk-in fridge and ordered some extra-large hairnets for Addie's wig. By the time I was done, the place sparkled, the scent of bleach filled the air, and I was beyond exhausted.

That night, my eyelids drooped long before the ten o'clock news. My head bobbed. Hugo purred on my lap, urging me to sleep.

"Let me sit up. We have to see this," I told the cat. Hugo gave an exaggerated yawn before loping down the hallway to Celia's room, where my daughter was likely plugged into her headphones. Turning to Channel 6, I steeled myself. Would Linda be lead news? Would I, the not-so-anonymous informant, be caught on film scuttling away? But no, Santa Fe's hometown murder didn't make the first few stories. Albuquerque had its own mayhem. A man had driven off with an ATM, dragging it through Old Town before crashing into a wall. Another hapless robber had stolen a tow truck and somehow rammed it into a nail salon. Then there was potentially violent weather to report. A spring storm was approaching and the weatherman urged viewers to stay clear of arroyos, the usually dry creek beds that could transform to raging torrents. My eyelids began drooping again as the weatherman elaborated on temperatures for each corner of the state and southern Colorado. At the announcement of "shocking" news from Santa Fe, however, I jolted upright.

The male anchor, Todd, the one with a great wave of newscaster hair, shook his head sadly. "I ate at Chez Napoleon just last week. A fabulous meal and a once-in-a-lifetime experience, it seems now."

Vanessa, his female counterpart, lamented that she'd never gotten a chance to go to either of Napoleon's restaurants. "A tragedy," she said. "The sudden death of a revered chef. Let's turn to our coverage, recorded earlier on the Santa Fe Plaza."

There was the scene, replayed. Milan Lujan reverently questioning Manny. His concerned face, his blatant nod toward the crime scene van. The cameraman had gotten a great shot, zooming in close to Linda's festively painted cart, zooming out to Manny adjusting his serious crime-fighter scowl.

I let out the breath I hadn't realized I was holding. Milan would now say, "Back to you Todd," and I'd go to bed, foregoing more arroyo warnings and sports scores. Except Milan didn't say that. The frame flashed to her standing outside Chez Napoleon, Napoleon's namesake gourmet restaurant. Milan gave the location, and the cameraman panned across the marble-tiled patio with its tiered fountain. Water poured out the mouth of a weathered stone face straight from a medieval church.

"This murder may not be as easy to solve as the police hope," Milan said. "After our filming on the Plaza, an anonymous informant alerted us to the possibility of deep corruption involving a city official. Government sources refused to comment, as did the chefs and manager here at Chez Napoleon." The camera changed perspective suddenly, and Brigitte Voll came into focus in one of the large paned windows. She must have sensed the camera's shift because she drew back, out of view, into the dark interior of the restaurant.

Poor Brigitte. The last thing she needed was to be hounded by the press. I felt responsible and vowed I'd call her for that coffee. I'd take her some soup. I'd get her some nice flowers or bake her a cake or . . .

Milan's perfect eyebrows were center frame again. "Diners, chefs, and kitchen workers in the City Different won't rest easily until the brutal murderer is brought to justice," she said.

I pulled the bedcovers to my chin. Forget cake and flowers. I'd warn Brigitte to watch her back and tell my friends at Tres Amigas to do the same.

Chapter 9

The food inspector arrived at high noon the next day. He stood in the doorway of Tres Amigas, the bags under his eyes sagging as much as his wrinkled suit, slumped shoulders, and low-hanging jowls, which reminded me of Winston's bulldog flaps. Winston, however, was a whole lot cuter, drool included.

Addie had alerted me to his arrival. "Oy," she'd said, in a bit of misplaced Australian. "That bloke over there's asking for you."

I'd peeked through the pass-through, expecting Milan and her news camera, fearing that Manny had blown my anonymous cover. When I recognized the inspector, I ducked to counter level.

"Did I do the wrong thing?" Addie's fake lashes widened. "He wanted to know who was asking about the health inspector. He says that's him. I remembered you and Miss Flori yesterday saying you wanted to find that inspector, and here he is, right at our doorstep."

"You did the right thing," I assured Addie. "Nothing's wrong." I held back adding *yet*. "Will you go look for Flori?" I asked her. "I think she's in the pantry. And here . . ." I gave up hiding, grabbed a hairnet from the box on the counter, and squished it over Addie's wig. Then I grabbed some more plastic hats for me and Flori and a resistant Juan.

"No hair, see?" Juan patted his head.

This was untrue, I told him. He did have hair, even if it was buzz-cut to near baldness. He also had the shadow of a thin mustache and skinny beard hugging the ridge of his chin, clearly distinguished by a shaving line of laser-cut crispness. I wondered if we had any beard guards. Probably not. Tres Amigas had been all *amigas* until Flori, conceding that she might need extra help, hired Juan and some guys to help with occasional heavy lifting.

Juan was looking mutinous. Could I improvise a beard guard by looping the cap around his prominent ears? I leaned closer, tilting my head as I considered his facial fuzz.

"No!" he said, eyes narrowed, guessing my intent. For added emphasis, he shook a spatula at me. "No way! You put a shower cap on my face, I go home. Addie can grill."

It was a good threat, considering all that Addie could set alight on a grill. I reconsidered Juan's skinny stubble. Maybe the inspector was here by chance, for a simple meal and not hair checks. Maybe he'd heard about our famously fluffy *chiles rellenos* or Flori's legendary blue corn waffles, which were on special today with Cinco de Mayo toppings of chorizo, roasted jalapeños, fresh Mexican farm cheese, and sweet chile maple syrup or savory chorizo gravy.

"The food inspector, he's over there," I whispered to Flori when she came in cradling a jumbo-sized bag of chocolate chips. Her hairnet rested on the rims of her glasses. Addie's perched atop her wig, jauntily tilted in beret fashion.

"How did he know to come here?" I murmured, knowing full well. I'd opened my big mouth and brought trouble on us.

"I called his office and told him to come on over," Flori said, plopping the chocolate chips next to the olive oil, sugar, and cocoa already set out for her so-called healthy muffin.

I gaped at her. Practicing the deadliest and slowest martial art is one thing, but purposefully asking a health inspector over? Flori was brave. Maybe too brave for her own good, not to mention the café's.

"Why?" I demanded. "What'd you say?"

She smiled, sly as a tai-chi-practicing fox. "I told him we had a few questions. Questions about his dealings with Napoleon."

I winced. Flori kept on explaining. "Now, his name's Gerald Jenkins, and my sources say there is indeed talk of him being buyable. Word is, you can pay your way out of bad inspections." She thumped the bag of chocolate. "I'll bet you that he takes bribes the other way too, bribes to cook up violations. That's what I intend to ask him about."

"Isn't this against your *Art of War* practices?" I asked, dreading any encounter with the man in the ill-fitting suit. "I mean, would your guy Sun say to invite the enemy to our café?"

I sneaked another peek. Jenkins was approaching the only empty table, the one overlooked by the mariachi band. He frowned, rightfully so, at the trumpet player. My mind flashed through possible public health and safety violations involving creepy mannequins.

"Piffle," Flori said, straight from Addie's British Empire playbook of scoffing sounds. "The *Art of War* says to gather information on your enemy. 'Those with all the information win,' or something like that. In any case, we don't have time to fool around being coy. It's like flirting. Best to be direct."

She made a tush-pinching gesture, grabbed the coffeepot, and was out the door before I could object. I tugged down my shower cap and followed Flori into battle.

"Mr. Jenkins!" Flori exclaimed. "So good of you to come. Coffee?"

Jenkins straightened to a more upright slouch. He eyed the coffeepot, craning his neck around it as if he had X-ray vision for germs.

"Fine," he said, after perusing the spotless pot. "But I prefer my own cup." From his oversized coat pocket, he produced a plastic bag holding a thermos. He unsealed the bag and removed the top cup, daintily grasping the handle with the tips of his right index finger and thumb. Twisting the thermos top off too, he said, "Refill this while you're at it, and I'll need something sweet. One of those cookies." He pointed to a jar of *bizcochitos*, New Mexico's official state cookie.

Flori poured and took a seat across from him. Making a show of using hygienic tongs, I selected three anise-flavored cookies from the jar and placed them on a clean plate. I pushed the plate in front of Jenkins, pulled a chair close to Flori, and perched on the edge of the seat. No way could I get comfortable by this man.

"Mr. Jenkins, we've heard that you had a certain business arrangement with the recently deceased Chef Napoleon." Flori leaned in, thrusting out her chest. This, I guessed, was not one of her flirting moves. More likely, she had her tiny tape recorder strapped to her brassiere again.

Jenkins sniffed then sipped his coffee. "My business is food establishments and making sure they meet city codes." He took a cookie and looked around Tres Amigas, his gaze lingering on the ceiling and the festival of Cinco de Mayo décor. An orange and pink piñata donkey swayed, seemingly on its own. Horrified, I watched as it stirred up a faint puff of dust, lit by a sunbeam.

Flori leaned in so far that she was practically lying on the table. "That's not what we heard. Tell him, Rita."

Tell him what? That I'd insinuated to Albuquerque's finest news crew that he was dirty and possibly involved in a brutal murder? Flori nodded to me, encouragingly.

"You know," I said, vaguely yet pointedly.

"Yes, we know that you know," Flori added, thumping her fist on the table.

Jenkins tilted his head and I saw that his crown

was thinning. He'd let the remaining hair, a mix
of wiry gray and wispy strawberry blond, grow
long enough to fluff over the bare patch. "Know
what?" he said. "What's wrong with you people?
And what's with all this junk on your ceiling?
This isn't Mexico. It's *New* Mexico, and we have
strict health codes."

"There's nothing about piñatas in our health
code," Flori countered. "And what Rita means is,
we know that you and Napoleon were colluding
to put Tía Tamales out of business. Now tell us
the whole story and maybe we won't go to the
police or the press." She tapped her fingers on the
wooden table and added ominously, "Maybe."

"Maybe I'm due to check out this place." The inspector might be rumpled, but his voice had a sharp
edge. He tugged in the lapels of his shapeless suit
coat. "How about I start right now? Or should I surprise you later?" His watery eyes scanned the room.

What had I missed in my cleaning spree? The
ceiling and mariachi band, that's what. They
hadn't been touched. And what about the salt and
pepper shakers? I glanced at the salt shaker inches
from Jenkins's hand and noticed a fingerprint
smudge. Or maybe it didn't matter. Someone who
could plant an entire cockroach in a wrapped and
steamed tamale probably would have no qualms
about sprinkling around mouse droppings. Did
Jenkins have some on hand, in another plastic bag
stuffed in his pockets?

Flori would not be cowered. "Linda Santiago is
my daughter, Inspector. If you think I'll leave any
tainted tamale unturned, you don't know me."
She thumped the table with her fist.

Goose bumps rose on my arm. Flori was a fierce tigress mother protecting her daughter.

But Gerald Jenkins had a threat of his own. "Ma'am, if you had any evidence of wrongdoing, you wouldn't have asked me here. You'd have gone straight to my boss or the police. Tell you what, if you care so much about your daughter, I can make that bug report go away." He picked up another cookie. "Think about it," he said. "Have your daughter call me. Or you call me. Either way. We may be able to come to a mutually agreeable arrangement, if you understand what I mean."

I understood him. He'd essentially demanded a payoff right here in front of me, Flori, and the mariachi band.

He drank his coffee slowly, siphoning it through his teeth. The liquid in the cup barely diminished with each sip. I willed him to glug it down and leave. He was a disturbing man, slimy under his rumpled suit. But there was something else too.

"You look familiar," I said. Squinting, I tried to figure out what was bugging me.

The left corner of his lip curled up. "You were on the Plaza the other day, weren't you? The day I had to shut down Tía Tamales for violating health codes? I remember you and your friend getting in the way."

"Not just that . . ." I willed my brain to connect the dots.

He shrugged and pushed back a stringy lock of strawberry blond hair. That was it! The red hair. The jowly jaw. "Do you have a son, Mr. Jenkins?"

His frown told me that I was on to something. I turned to Flori. "The young man who 'discovered' the bug in Linda's tamale had red hair too and a striking family resemblance."

"Is that so?" Flori said, narrowing her eyes.

Jenkins siphoned up more coffee. "Yeah. So what? That was my son, Junior. He's got my name, and I guess he picked up my nose for food contamination too."

Flori and I exchanged a knowing glance. Addie, wiping down tables nearby, gasped and hurried back to the kitchen.

"Good to know, Mr. Jenkins," Flori said. "Come on, Rita. We have work to do."

Flori expressed disappointment when Jenkins finally left without paying. "Great job connecting Jenkins to the bug finder," she said to me. "I was hoping he'd be more blatant, though."

"He wasn't blatant enough for you?" I asked. "He basically threatened us."

She patted her chest. "I know. I had my tape running. Too bad he didn't come straight out and ask for cash. Maybe we can provoke him. I'll read ahead in Sun Tzu and see if he has any ideas."

Flori headed for the pantry before I could question Sun Tzu's wisdom in this case. I was thinking of a tactic from Manny's favorite philosophical guide: sports. Defense, that's what we needed. I reached for my bleach bucket and a mop. If Jenkins found anything dirty in Tres Amigas, it would be because he planted it.

An hour later Linda came in, her face ashen except for bloodshot eyes. "The police wanted to talk to me again," she said, rubbing her temples. "They keep asking what I did after I left my cart at the Plaza that day. It's so embarrassing, and Mr. Strong keeps telling me not to say anything unless he's there, but I hate to be rude."

I guided Linda to a cozy table by the window. "What *did* you do?" I asked gently.

Linda avoided my eyes. "I went home."

"Nothing embarrassing in that," I said. I'd have fled home too, right after stopping at the store for several tubs of ice cream.

Linda moaned. "It's worse! I took one of those nerve pills the doctor prescribed me, back from when I had to fly all the way to Florida for a wedding. They knock me out."

I assured her that there was nothing wrong with that either, and probably healthier than ice-cream therapy.

My friend gripped my hand. "I don't like to take drugs of any kind, Rita, and look what happened. I fell asleep and didn't go turn off my own warmer and move my cart. I was irresponsible."

"No you weren't," I said. "I talked to Don Busco. He said you left him a message."

Linda refused to let up on herself. "He didn't get the message in time. Anyway, my cart is my responsibility."

Addie, cleaning tables nearby, chimed in. "A

cup of tea! That's what we all need!" Her chipper tone sounded forced and her need for tea bordering on desperate.

I followed her to the kitchen to help, and to check on her. "Addie? Is something wrong?"

She stuffed a handful of chamomile tea packets into a teapot and dumped a packet of milk chocolate HobNobs—her go-to British cookie—on a platter. Her eyes darted to the dining room, where Linda sat, spinning the salt shaker in her hand.

"I may be cavorting," she whispered.

"Good girl," Flori said, appearing silently behind us. "I've been telling Rita to cavort a little, and to make magic chocoflan."

I rolled my eyes.

Addie gripped a HobNob. "I mean, cavorting with the enemy. Not that *he's* the enemy or that I'm really cavorting." She stuffed the cookie in her mouth and reached for another.

Flori's forehead wrinkled confusion. I took the opportunity to ask for clarification.

"What do you mean, Addie?" I asked.

She swallowed hard. "The guy I've been kinda dating, I think he's the one who found the bug in Miss Linda's tamale! The son of that food inspector. I'd never, ever do anything to hurt Miss Linda, and I'm sure Junior wouldn't either. He's nice and the best guy I've dated in a long time." She shot me a pleading look.

Flori clasped her hands together. "Fabulous! You can be our mole! Find out what your fellow knows about dirty tamales."

"Flori!" I protested. "Addie shouldn't spy on her boyfriend."

"He's not really a boyfriend," Addie mumbled.

"Why do you modern girls keep denying you have boyfriends?" Flori grumbled. "In my day, if a nice man held the door for you, you were practically engaged."

When neither Addie nor I answered, Flori patted Addie on the arm. "Are you sure that we're discussing the same man?"

Addie bobbed her head. "Junior. Junior Jenkins. When that food inspector guy said his name, I knew for sure, but I knew anyway. Like Rita said, there's the family resemblance. But Junior's nice and a lot cuter. He's kind and friendly and he plays the accordion. Sometimes, him and his band invite me to sing *corridos* with them. I have to save my voice for my real act, so I usually say no, but sometimes I can't resist."

"Is that who you sang with last summer on the bandstand?" I asked Addie. "Those songs were beautiful." *Corridos* were folk ballads, many passed down through generations. My rudimentary Spanish didn't let me understand each word, but the emotion needed no translation. I'd gotten teary-eyed listening to Addie croon about lost loves and broken hearts.

Addie shrugged. "They're okay. Kind of old."

"Timeless," Flori corrected. "The tea's probably ready. Let's go keep Linda company."

Addie carried out the tea tray, cups wobbling precariously. Flori and I hung back.

"Addie could be in danger," I said. "Or at least involved with a sketchy guy. Should we warn her to stay away from him?"

Flori produced a paperback copy of the *Art of*

War from her apron pocket. "Keep your enemies close," she intoned.

I thought about Napoleon's unblinking eyes. He'd let an enemy get close. Close enough to stab him in the back.

Chapter 10

After Linda returned home, Flori hustled out our last customers, three cheerful ladies who'd been lingering and chatting over a platter of chips, guacamole, and three salsas: roasted tomato, sweet-savory mango chile, and tart tomatillo with cilantro.

"Come again!" Flori said, handing them bags of what I hoped were muffins and not Hot Flash pepper spray.

She bustled back into the kitchen and tucked a similar brown bag into the tote bag of spying supplies.

I wasn't ready to go anywhere. I ignored the implied "let's get spying" message and dipped my spoon into a minisoufflé, my latest version of my date-night main dish. The soufflé had puffed in golden plumes. I took a bite, savored the cheesy, eggy goodness, and then gasped.

Flori reached for her own spoon. I waved her away. "Hot!" I wheezed.

She took a big bite anyway and declared the soufflé magnificent. "Fiery," she said. "I may have forgotten to tell you. I had extra habaneros so I mixed them with our mild New Mexicans to spice them up." She took another bite. "You'll have a hot date night for sure if you serve this."

Yeah, hot as in a flaming tongue and throat. My eyes watered and my ears rang as I rushed for the walk-in fridge in search of ice cream. All I found was some lemonade frozen into ice cubes. I popped one in my mouth before realizing it was the frozen form of Flori's hot-chile-spiked lemonade.

"The texture is lovely too," Flori said, bravely savoring another bite. "Now, what are you making for dessert?"

I couldn't answer right away. I'd spit out the ice cube, run to the fridge, and was now swirling milk like mouthwash. I swallowed. "Maybe a fruit crisp?" My tongue felt slightly better. My lips still burned. I was trying to dip them in the milk glass when Flori handed me an oozing branch of aloe vera, fresh from a plant by the sink. I pressed the gelatinous end to my lips and found that aloe went terribly with the tastes of milk and remnant hot lemonade.

Flori pursed her lips too, although her distaste was with my dessert idea, which she slammed with faint praise. "Well, warm fruit sounds nice. Healthy. Light. Very, ah, midwestern."

At least my midwestern homey dish wouldn't set mouths aflame. I thanked Flori for the aloe cure and told her that she could take the rest of the soufflés home to Bernard, who shared her love of hot food.

"He'll adore them," she said. "I know who else will like one too. My informant."

"You're planning to torture information out of someone?" I joked.

Flori shoved the tote bag closer to me, shaking her head as she did. "Ida Green hasn't had taste buds for decades. At least, I hope not. Otherwise, there's no explaining that woman's food."

She and Addie left a little later. I headed out too, walking slowly and shifting the heavy tote bag between shoulders. I supposed I should have been glad that Addie had volunteered to accompany Flori to Ida Green's notorious bail bonds/diner on the south side of town. Out of the two-dozen restaurant owners Flori had called, only Ida would admit a run-in with the health inspector. Others had hung up (suspicious), said they never heard of Jenkins (also suspicious), or warned Flori never to utter his name (very suspicious). Ida, however, was more than happy to dish on Jenkins. She'd invited Flori to tea, a scary prospect, as Ida's cooking is riskier than her high-interest bonds. The joke goes that Ida's tortillas can serve as prison shanks and her tamales as blunt-force weapons. Her green chile stew ranks among the infamous, gray and gelatinous as if made with a gravy of old shoes.

On the other hand, Flori's information-gathering was out in the open. I was off to secretly interrogate a would-be friend. For support, I stopped by to see a true friend first.

I found Cass in the soldering studio at the back of her shop. "I'm a bad person," I told her, leaning against the door frame.

Cass turned off her torch and lifted her goggles. The flame gulped for air, popped, and disappeared.

"I'm sure that's not true at all," she said. Using copper tongs, she picked up a ring, black from the flames, and dropped it in a chemical bath called "pickle." The name, she once told me, came from real pickle brine, an old-fashioned, all-natural way to remove fire char from metal. Chemical pickle worked best when warm, and Cass simmered hers in a mini Crock-Pot. I reminded myself yet again to never borrow any of her Crock-Pots, tongs, or pickles.

"Oh, it is true," I said, going over to peek into the miniature cauldron. "I'm pretending to be a supportive friend to a woman in mourning, but really I'm pumping her for information."

"There's worse stuff going around," Cass pointed out. "Murder. Running over dead guys with tamale carts. Cockroaches. That kind of stuff." She fished a different ring from her pickle vat and held it up. A single raised ridge snaked around the wide band. A man's ring, I guessed, or a ring for a bold woman. I glanced at my unadorned fingers. Cass had volunteered to outfit my fingers, but since my divorce, I hadn't wanted rings of any sort. I wouldn't, however, mind one of her gorgeous necklaces. I picked up a pendant from the nearby table. Using a saw blade slimmer than angel hair pasta, Cass had sliced the outline of a crow into the center of the metal. Her work was so intricate that she'd captured an open-beak caw and hooked feet.

Cass rubbed the ring with a buffing cloth. "So, I'm guessing you're on your way to see Brigitte?"

"Yes. I want to ask her about Napoleon's dealings with a dirty health inspector and our old bartender pal, Don Busco." I filled Cass in on our main suspects so far. "And I have to consider Brigitte a suspect too," I said, trying to laugh off this last part. "Colleagues and the closest people to the victim, you know."

Cass snorted. "Well, if you're feeling guilty, I can help. You don't have to worry that Brigitte killed that awful little man, although I can see why anyone might want to. I can alibi her."

"You?" I asked, about to add, *That's great!*

Cass frowned and buffed the ring harder, revealing the deep shimmer of silver. "That night, the one when Napoleon died? We were both at a benefit dinner. It lasted forever," she said with a groan.

I stifled a smile. My glamorous friend, blessed with charm and beauty, poise and bravery, and more dating offers than she can rebuff, becomes a cowering introverted wimp at parties.

"We were both stuck there until midnight!" she exclaimed, making it sound like the partygoers had been held hostage. "I wanted to leave after dinner, but I'd foolishly let Salvatore accompany me. There was a band he wanted to see that didn't start playing until eleven, and people began dancing. Of course, Sal insisted on staying for that." My single friend managed a smile, which

I thought completely reasonable. Salvatore is an amazing woodworker and a gorgeous man who has the confidence to knit in public. I've seen him knit, and if he can make that sexy, he's probably causes swooning on the dance floor.

Cass shrugged. "Sal *is* a good dancer. I told him, though, at midnight I turn into a wicked witch. We left at 11:59 sharp. Brigitte did too. I remember because we were all collecting our coats, and she got her English wrong and said she'd turn into a squash."

If only I had an exotic French accent to blame when I mixed up words. A natural propensity to dance would be nice too. However, if Cass could fill me in on Brigitte's alibi, one of my wishes would come true. I could cross Brigitte off the suspect list and drop by as a supportive friend trying to solve her boss's murder. I asked Cass about the benefit.

"It was for art in public schools," she said. "It's a wonderful cause, although we had to listen to endless boring speeches. The speeches went on over dinner, and I sat at a table with a view of Brigitte, so I know she suffered through them all."

She grimaced, looking like she wanted to tell me something more.

"And . . . ?" I asked. Was it the food? Had Ida Green catered with her bail-bonds fare? Were the speeches that bad?

"Then there was a silent art auction," Cass continued. "Brigitte was there. She and Salvatore joked about a piece of art glass they both bid on. She won." She shrugged. "Just as well, I told Salvatore. Glass is not his style. Too fragile and transparent."

"Okay," I said, seeing why Cass had been exhausted by the evening. "So, she's there for dinner, the auction, and then there was dancing?"

Cass shook her head. "I know, right? Way too much! I'd have paid double to stay home." She put the ring aside and picked up an amoeba-shaped bit of silver, likely on its way to becoming a pendant. Using a round-headed hammer, she tapped gently around the sides of the pendant, curving the metal as she created a ripple of dimples.

I raised my voice to be heard over the hammering. "And you saw her dancing and then leaving around the same time you did?"

Cass nodded, tight-lipped. So what was the problem? She couldn't still be grumpy about socializing past her witching hour. I used a Flori technique and waited, staring at her in silence.

"Okay!" Cass said after a minute. She stopped hammering. "Here's the thing . . . Jake was there."

"Okay," I said. Repeating what the other person said is another one of Flori's interrogation techniques, acquired from a Senior Center class on boardroom success.

"Don't worry," Cass said quickly. "He was there with a business date. Not a date, date. A client. He was with Georgio Andre the art thief."

"Alleged art thief," I said automatically and with a wry smile. "Jake got him acquitted in time for Christmas last year. I hear he's facing new charges, though?" My smile came easier now that I could see Jake enduring dinner speeches with Georgio, a tall, dark, and flashy art collector who favored suits the colors of eggplants and was rumored to acquire some of his pieces in not-so-legal ways.

Cass shivered. "Honestly, I get crawly skin if that man slithers within ten feet of me." She waved her hammer as if fending off Georgio. "I'm sure he was involved with that latest break-in on Canyon Road. Not far from your house, Rita! And he's rich enough to buy his own art, so he must be a crazy kleptomaniac or thrill seeker. I don't know how Jake does his job sometimes. If I had to stand up for people I knew were guilty and try to get them free . . ."

"Some must be innocent," I said, to reassure myself as much as Cass. "Like Linda."

"True," Cass said. "Others aren't so innocent." She looked me in the eye. "Like Brigitte Voll, who spent the night flirting up your Mr. Strong. There! That's what I didn't want to tell you! That's why I kept an eye on her the whole evening!"

"Flirting up?" I asked over my quickening heartbeat.

"Definitely flirting. And dancing," Cass replied darkly. "Lots of dancing."

Chapter 11

When I divorced Manny, I instituted a dating moratorium for perfectly reasonable reasons. One was to fend off the pressures like the un-asked-for advice that everyone from grandmas to supermarket checkers feels free to give: "Get on Match.com or Hookup or Tinder," or other such cringe-inducing online dating site. "Everybody's doing it!" This command is usually followed by anecdotes like, "That's how so-and-so's cousin met her fifth husband and look at them!"

I could be happy for so-and-so's cousin. I just couldn't imagine myself posting my photo and chatting and emoticon winking or electronic poking or flirting. And then actually going out to meet strangers? No way.

Another reason I fended off dating was one I wouldn't admit to anyone but Cass. Emotions. Namely, I was sick of them. I wanted none of the ups and downs I'd had with Manny. The arguments and accusations, the blind love and make-up bliss followed by the nagging worries and sorrows. I also feared reverting to my teenage anxieties, although those needed an update as much as my dating wardrobe. In high school, Mom had screened my sister's and my landline calls. The thought of hovering by my cell phone or waiting at my computer keyboard seemed somehow worse. Plus, I had no call screener, although Flori had volunteered. Imagining Flori's over-the-top flirting as my call screener made me smile. I summoned my adult sensibilities and assured Cass that I wasn't upset in the least.

"*Brigitte* was the one doing all the flirting!" she clarified, hammer raised. "Jake was merely seated beside her. We had assigned seats." She waved the hammer. "Anyway, I thought you should know. But you have no need to worry. He'll be smitten more than ever after you feed him that green chile cheese soufflé. This Friday, right?"

I knew Cass was trying to make me feel better. Little did she know of my soufflé flops and dessert dithers and relationship anxieties. "Yeah, Friday," I said, mentally confirming that this was really Wednesday afternoon. I wished I had another week . . . or more. "Jake can dance with whomever he wants," I said, hoping I sounded more resolute than I felt.

Cass, a single mom who vows to remain unencumbered by marriage and any relationship prompting a registry or paperwork, would have said the very same thing. Hearing me say it, she narrowed her eyes to imply, *Who are you and what have you done with my friend Rita?*

"Really!" I said, now sounding on the edge of psychotically perky.

"Okay," Cass said, still eyeing me skeptically. "That's a good, healthy attitude."

Healthy, I reminded myself, after letting Cass get back to her work of firing up metal. I was walking—a healthy activity—toward my original destination, OhLaLa Bistro, where I hoped to find Brigitte. Well, "hoped" was the wrong word. I still dreaded meeting her, although at least now I didn't have to accuse her of murder. I chided myself once again. I'd meant what I said to Cass. Brigitte was free to flirt. Jake was free to dance. We hadn't expressed love or promises. We were friends. Except when my friends gave me a peck on the cheek, I didn't tingle down to my toes.

I walked another block, swinging the over-loaded tote and forcing myself to focus on positives. The weather was certainly one. It was another gorgeous spring afternoon with a sky the color of turquoise. As I turned the corner, I spotted Brigitte stepping into OhLaLa. I'd correctly guessed that the statuesque blonde wouldn't face grief like me, lodging myself on the sofa and sniffling through reruns of *Law and Order* or rereading *Wuthering Heights*. No, she'd grab ahold of work and routine. At this time of day that meant OhLaLa, which, unlike Napoleon's fancy flagship, opened for lunch.

The French bistro occupied an adobe house

with square-edged walls, a deep covered porch, and a line of brick trim along the roofline. A rustic picket fence, painted a muted gray-blue, enclosed a brick patio set with metal café tables. In the herb garden lining the fence, daffodils and tulips turned their faces to the sun and the soil smelled cool and damp.

Diners already occupied a few of the tables. I let myself in the front gate and couldn't resist glancing at their plates. My stomach rumbled at the sight of a *croque-madame*, a French wonder of ham and cheese. Open-faced, the sandwich was draped in creamy béchamel sauce, broiled to bubbling deliciousness, and topped with a fried egg. I slowed to gawk at the dish.

"They're open," the lucky lady with the *croque-madame* told me, mistaking my gaze as one of surprise that the bistro had opened its doors. "They're carrying on to honor Napoleon." She raised a fork toward the heavens.

I murmured some thanks and made my way to the front porch. Brigitte had her back to me. Her sleek short hair fell perfectly into place and she wore trendy tight-hipped black slacks, a black shimmery top, and wedge capri sandals that would have me tripping into the tulips. The server who hurried by also wore black, so I couldn't necessarily attribute either of their looks to mourning. Brigitte certainly wasn't weeping at the moment. She was chewing out a red-faced waitress.

"No, no, no! *Croque-monsieur* with a *q*, DeeDee. "*Mon dieu!* Now of all the times, I cannot tolerate your spelling mistakes. Fix this at once before anyone sees it!"

Before I could catch her attention, she disappeared into the building.

"Sorry. So sorry!" the hapless DeeDee cried after her. When she saw me, she blocked the blackboard with her body. She was in her twenties, I guessed, and prettily curvy in a way Addie would kill for.

I smiled at her. "Tough day," I said, hoping to glean some information before me and my emotions faced Brigitte. "I'm sorry about your boss."

DeeDee ran a hand through her curly hazel hair, revealing a tattoo of a whisk pricked into her soft underarm. "I can't believe he's gone. He was so big for such a small guy."

A big bully, which is probably what got him killed.

DeeDee, thankfully, couldn't read my thoughts.

"Ms. Voll says we have to stay strong in Mr. Napoleon's memory," she said. "He'd want it that way. He'd want everything perfect. He always wanted things perfect . . ." She glanced down at the sign, spelling desperation evident.

"I work at a café too," I told her. "The pace can be frantic sometimes. Hard to be perfect."

She shot me a then-you-understand look. "The last time he spoke to me, it was the day before yesterday and he was mad that I was three minutes late. He demanded punctuality. Then today, I already dropped a plate and spilled a water pitcher and I can't spell the stupid sandwich right. Mr. Napoleon would yell that I'm stupid. I can't disappoint Ms. Voll. She's working really hard to keep the place going." She sniffled.

"Here," I said, feeling for her. "Let me see that blackboard. I think I can help." I'm no spelling-bee champ, that's for sure. In fact, since computerized spell-check entered my life, I've lost much of my spelling ability. Still, I knew a glaring food error when I saw one. *Croak Monsieur Napoleon,* the chalkboard read in lovely cursive script. A shiver ran through me. Monsieur had indeed croaked.

I set down my tote and fixed the spelling. DeeDee thumped her forehead with her palm. "Stupid," she muttered. "That's where the Q goes."

I knew I didn't have much time with DeeDee before a customer or Brigitte demanded her attention. "How did the staff get along with Napoleon?" I asked.

She stopped abusing her forehead. "We all got on fine," she replied quickly. "It's an honor to work here. He is—was—a great chef. We're honored."

She sounded brainwashed. Or scared. I tried to assure her that she could tell me if anyone had a grudge. "Someone killed your boss," I said. "Murdered him. If you can think of anyone here . . ." I let the idea hang, hoping she'd catch on.

She did, almost too much. Her eyes widened with fear and I was afraid she was about to bolt. "Oh my gosh! No! You think someone here . . . ?"

I nodded, and her eyes darted toward the kitchen, where several sous-chefs labored. "He fired a bunch of people," she said. "Henri and Vickie. Val . . . Oscar . . . that guy who did the dishes whose name I never got. Mr. Napoleon threatened Estevan and Lila the other day for kissing by the Dumpster, but they had to know they had that coming." She ticked off several more names, a lot of people fired, threatened with firing, yelled at, or otherwise abused. Midway through the list I reached for the notebook in my tote.

"Can you think of anyone who was particularly upset?" I asked, pen poised.

DeeDee squished her face into deep thought. "No . . . well . . . Ivan, one of the dishwashers, he was real upset and waved around a knife, but that was months ago and, anyway, he's in jail for violating parole for domestic violence or something."

Part of me hoped that Ivan had broken out of jail with one of Ida Green's tortilla shanks. I wouldn't feel guilty fingering a suspect with a domestic violence conviction.

As I pondered Ivan, DeeDee clamped her hand to her heart, relief washing over her face. "Oh! All this talk of killers made me forget. I'm an idiot! I *am* stupid! I already know who killed Mr. Napoleon!"

I stopped breathing. My body tensed in case the murderer appeared and I had to whip out the handcuffs or pepper spray.

DeeDee's head bobbed. "Yeah, yeah, everybody knows. The tamale lady. The sweet older lady who runs Tía Tamales. It's a shame. I love her tamales. My mom's real upset. We get all our Christmas tamales from Tía's. The best are her sweet ones with the dates and prunes and the *piloncillo*, you know that dark cane sugar that's shaped like a cone and tastes kinda like molasses? It won't be Christmas without those tamales."

It wouldn't be Christmas without Linda either. Before I could give DeeDee my Linda-is-innocent speech, she was scooting off to a customer waving from the far side of the patio. "Sorry!" she called to me as she left.

So was I. I could delay no longer. Time to face

Brigitte. I stepped inside and smack into Brigitte. She dodged me with poise.

"Inside or out?" she asked automatically, before recognizing me and grabbing me in another bone-crushing hug. Mid-hug, right about when my back felt about to crack, I resolved to tone up. I'd renew my gym membership and sweat and lift weights. I'd do more than walk to work. I'd jog. I'd take up yoga. Right. The last time I tried yoga, I threw out my neck. Maybe I'd start by buying a mat and getting a yoga book from the library. I'd jog to the library.

Brigitte released me. "So good of you to come by, Rita!"

"I wanted to check on you," I said. Yeah, check on her alibi and her flirting, I thought before reining in my teenage emotions.

She grabbed my hand. "I am the one who should be checking on you. What a shock you had too. I can't thank you enough for trying to help Napoleon. Such a shock for everyone . . . to think he's gone. You must think me awful to keep the restaurant open."

I didn't, I assured her. "Staying busy is good in times of grief, that's what my mother always says." Mom also claims that adobe walls abet burglars and that I'll eventually be lured home by an intense longing for her tuna-noodle hot dish. In other words, Mom does not always base her opinions in reality. However, Mom was probably right about staying busy to combat grief.

"My mother says the same," Brigitte said. "Most of all, I am here because it is what Napoleon would want." She waved for stressed DeeDee to take over the hostess station. "That girl," she complained as we walked through the dining room. "I will have to make some changes around here."

Poor DeeDee. Had she dodged Napoleon's firings only to be guillotined by Brigitte? Brigitte stopped to shift a table a microscopic distance, and I took in the bistro. The plaster walls and viga ceiling beams were pure New Mexico. The décor was subtly French, with marble-topped tables and wicker chairs sporting cushions in Provençal patterns. Edith Piaf again quavered on the sound system, softy crooning a mournful tune. A bartender in a white shirt and black vest polished wineglasses behind an ornate, dark-wood bar stocked with exotic liquors. Before his cowpoke hot dog attire, Don Busco had stood right there. I recalled a moment from a happy hour about a year ago. Don had chatted with me and Cass about dream jobs. We pretty much had ours, we'd said. We were lucky. He'd gestured to the bar and said, "I definitely have mine." Not soon after, he'd been fired and publicly maligned by Napoleon. Did he resent his former boss enough to kill? Had his anger been seething and simmering for months?

Brigitte suggested that we have coffee in her office. We passed through the kitchen, where she made us two mugs from an espresso machine the size of a small refrigerator. "Back here," she said, leading the way through swinging double doors. Walking through a dark hallway, we passed a small room filled with the usual restaurant backroom paraphernalia of excess linens and utensils. Brigitte announced that the next office was hers.

While she unlocked her door, I peeked in the half-open doorway of the room across the hall, expecting more supplies. What I saw brought me to a gawking halt.

"Oh," fell out of my mouth. I blinked and added a hopefully tactful, "Wow ... that's ... ah ... impressive."

Brigitte stepped across the hall and opened the door wider. "*Oui*. Napoleon's office. It is, how do you say? Pure him."

You could say that. Pure arrogance pretty much summed up the man himself. The recently deceased's office was decorated in dark wood trim and leather chairs. But those weren't what stopped me. It was the life-size portrait of Napoleon Bonaparte in his famous hand-in-jacket pose.

"Yeah, pure him," I agreed. I craned my head around the door to take in the wall-sized portrait. The other walls featured framed culinary awards and photographs of Napoleon with famous people. There was Napoleon shaking hands with the President, Napoleon serving the governor a crowned rib roast, Napoleon posing with Jay Leno in a cranberry red vintage truck, and Napoleon presenting a basket of golden croissants to the cast of *Breaking Bad*. I was peering at what I thought was Napoleon cheek-kissing celebrity chef Giada De Laurentiis when Brigitte called to me.

I crossed the hall to her closet-sized headquarters. Spreadsheets covered her desk. She tidied some into neat piles and placed them on the floor, apologizing as she did. "I handle all the accounting for all of Napoleon's enterprises. Bookkeeping is never done. You must excuse my mess."

"You haven't shared a mess until you've lived in a tiny house with a teenager," I joked. We sat in chairs made of molded, modern plastic. I was surprised to find that they felt great, the butt- and back-hugging opposites of Flori's carved-wood punishers. For a few minutes we sipped our coffees, which were dark and strong and just what I needed. In other circumstances I would have felt the need to fill the void with small talk, but with Brigitte, the silence seemed as comfortable as the chairs. She gazed beyond me, toward Napoleon's office door. I wondered what she was thinking and what I should say. *Petty prospects flashed through my mind. So . . . tell me about your handsome dancing alibi for the time of Napoleon's murder. Did you take your alibi home with you? No. I didn't want* to know. I was here to investigate a murder.

I placed my mug on the white glossy table that served as her desk. "The night of Napoleon's . . . demise—" I started to say.

She jolted upright and gasped. "Napoleon?"

I knew I should have started with small talk, not words that sent Brigitte bolting from the room.

Chapter 12

Once again I smacked into Brigitte, this time her back. She'd stopped short in the doorway to Napoleon's office.

"*Mon dieu*, I thought . . ." Her voice trembled. So did her back, filling the half-open door to Napoleon's office.

I pushed the door open wide. A figure in a black chef's coat and a puffy-topped chef's hat was ducking under Napoleon's desk. For a second I thought, as Brigitte must have, that I'd seen a ghost.

She, however, quickly recovered her senses. "You are not Napoleon! What are you doing here?"

The figure gave up trying to hide under the office furniture. As he rose, his puffy hat toppled, revealing a receding line of strawberry red hair.

"Gerald Jenkins!" I exclaimed. To Brigitte, I said, "Have you met our city health inspector?" I jammed my fists into my hips.

Brigitte wrinkled her nose. Oozing scorn, she said that she had not had the pleasure.

"I have every right to inspect," Jenkins sputtered. "I don't have to notify the restaurant beforehand." He stepped on the hat, crushing it to fallen-soufflé flatness. "I'm done in here. I'll be leaving now." He picked up a paper shopping bag and headed our way. Neither Brigitte nor I moved from the doorway.

"Why are you in disguise?" I demanded. "I saw him earlier this morning," I told Brigitte. "He came to Tres Amigas to threaten us and he wasn't dressed like this."

Brigitte stepped into the room. "Why indeed?" she demanded.

Jenkins backed up and nearly into the oil painting of the original Napoleon. Under the portrait, the inspector seemed small and inconsequential. Had I really been scared of him? Surely Napoleon hadn't been, but had that been a deadly mistake?

"I'm . . ." Jenkins drew out the word, hedging for time. "I'm undercover. Common practice and none of your business. Anyway, your own waitress showed me back here. Chubby girl with some stutter name. DaDa. FooFoo, Mimi?"

"DeeDee!" Brigitte fumed.

Brigitte seemed to be losing focus on our true problem. I nudged her. "Brigitte, let's see what he has in that bag. There's no food preparation or storage going on in this office, right? That means he's here snooping in Napoleon's business."

Brigitte uttered one of the few words I remembered from high school French. A curse. The bag ripped as she tore it from Jenkins's hand, and a manila envelope fell out.

Jenkins grabbed at the envelope but Brigitte was faster. "Let us see what is in here, *oui*?" she said, a hard edge to her fluid French accent. We peeked inside to find a wad of fifty dollar bills.

"Caught, bare-handed!" Brigitte announced. "Rita, we shall call the police, *maintenant*."

"Red-handed," I corrected automatically, although I was all for calling the police *toute suite*. My phone was in Flori's tote bag of crime fighting tools, across the hall in Brigitte's office. I imagined slapping the pink fluffy handcuffs on Jenkins and hauling him into the police station. In this fantasy, Bunny booked him for burglary and murder. Case closed. Linda would be freed. Then I'd be free too, back to my own mundane problems, like working on Victor's house, detecting whether my daughter was dating, and determining a perfect date menu. Jenkins held up his wrists, mockingly. Ready for cuffs, if only I had them.

His thin lips opened to a sneer. "Call the police if you want. I'll tell them you're stealing my money. See my name on the envelope? It's mine, for consulting services. Napoleon owed me, and he's not about to write me a check from the morgue, is he? I came to collect it myself."

Brigitte held the money behind her back. "What 'consulting' services?" she asked. "I have never heard of this, and I am the general manager and the accountant of Monsieur Napoleon's restaurants."

"Ha!" Jenkins laughed, and not in a happy way. "Like he'd tell the 'accountant' everything. I sent Napoleon my bill. If he didn't get it to you, that's not my problem."

I willed Brigitte to call the police. She continued to fuss about finances. "Consulting on what? Where would I enter this charge?"

"I do private consulting," he said with a mean snicker. "I help clients meet their restaurant health inspection needs."

Needs like staying open and avoiding public shame. My resolve wavered. Here I was, antagonizing Jenkins again. He'd set his sights on Tres Amigas for sure. *What would Flori do?* She wouldn't shrink away and hide. She'd invited Jenkins over! Plus, I wasn't stepping up to protect Napoleon's office or even for Brigitte. No, I was doing it for Linda. Gerald Jenkins had just snooped his way to the top of my suspect list.

"What kind of consulting were you doing for Napoleon?" I asked. "Planting cockroaches in Linda Santiago's tamales? Losing the permit paperwork for Crystal's juice cart? Or was he paying you off for a made-up health infraction at OhLaLa? Did he resist? Say he'd call the police? Is that why you killed him?"

Brigitte and I, as one, stepped toward Jenkins. Slippery as he was slimy, Jenkins scooted around Napoleon's desk.

"You can't threaten me!" he sputtered.

"It is no threat," Brigitte declared with all the boldness of Flori. "Napoleon had friends in high places, and as manager of his legacy, so do I. I have spoken to Napoleon's financial backer in Dallas. He gave me temporary control over managerial decisions and I am making one now. About you, Mr. Jenkins. I will not let you make a mess of me or my friends." She threw her arm around my shoulder, gripping with such strength I had to hold back a wince. I wasn't about to correct her English.

Jenkins's smirk turned upside down. He glared in the direction of the envelope full of cash, now held loosely at Brigitte's side. For a second I thought he might grab at it.

Brigitte must have sensed it as well. She stuffed the envelope in her back pocket. "If this is a legitimate payment, send me a detailed invoice and I shall consider it," she said, shaking an accusatory finger at Jenkins. "But if I suspect anything, how do you say, fishlike? Then I shall call the police and IRS and your supervisor too."

My fantasies of hauling off the slimy health inspector fell flat. With an indignant huff, he pushed past me, departing with another version of his earlier threat. "You'll be sorry you messed with me," he snarled as he slunk past.

Brigitte and I stepped out into the hall to make sure he left.

"This is horrible," she said as the swinging doors swung closed on his departing form.

I agreed and was about to say so, until she continued.

"How do I account for this cash? What line do I put it under?"

"Bribes?" I suggested glumly.

Back in Brigitte's office, a puddle of cream floated on my coffee. I sipped the tepid brew anyway, wondering how to restart the conversation I'd barely begun. Brigitte, meanwhile, shuffled through the stack of spreadsheets on the floor. *Priorities!* I yearned to yell. *Your boss has been murdered. The killer might have just been here. Feet away! Forget the accounting!*

I let Brigitte sift and mumble for a minute or two longer. "Brigitte," I said, after she hoisted a stack of sheets to desk level. "I'll come right out and say it. I'm investigating Napoleon's murder because I know that Linda is innocent. She's too kind to hurt anyone. She volunteers at the homeless shelter and gives away soup and rescues stray animals. Wolves, dogs, I've even seen her save a spider. We were driving to a tamale contest in Rio Rancho and there was this gigantic tarantula crossing the street and Linda drove practically into a ditch so we wouldn't hit it. See how she is? She's completely nonviolent. You might not believe me yet, but—"

"Maybe I do," she murmured, eyes following her index finger across a row of numbers.

"You do?" I asked, surprised despite myself. What had convinced her? The soup? The wolf? Not the tarantula, which raised hairs on my arms merely thinking of it. Frankly, I'd expected more resistance since Bunny and Manny had basically told Brigitte that Linda was the culprit.

She looked up. "I talked to Don Busco earlier. He called me to invite me to join the food carts on the Plaza. It is kind of him, *non*? I liked him when he was bartender here. He knows that I have always wanted to cook. Don, he says that with my French heritage, I'm destined to be a crepe natural."

"Great news!" I exclaimed, glad to have something to honestly cheer. I'd definitely welcome the return of crepes. Still, I didn't get the connection to Linda's innocence until Brigitte continued.

"Don also told me that Linda must be innocent," she explained. "He said that Linda is a kind and saintly person like his beloved grandmother. He has theories about the killer. A vagrant, he says. Or that man Ivan who Napoleon fired a while back." She shrugged. "In any case, Don says that the killer must be someone else. He says I must be very careful."

Yeah, right. Someone else. Like Don himself. Or Jenkins. Or . . . who? I couldn't be sure without more evidence.

Brigitte tapped the sheets of numbers. "Honestly, I did not believe Don. I believed the police." She hesitated, as if debating whether to tell me. After a few beats, she said, "It is probably unrelated. I overheard Napoleon in his office last week, yelling into the telephone. Though, he often yelled. It could be nothing."

"Yelling?" I prompted. "About what?"

She pursed her lips and exhaled in a quintessentially French fashion. "I wish I had heard more. As I told the police, I thought he was upset about a building he wished to acquire, a difficult real estate transaction. He turned agitated, so much so that I was concerned and listened. I think he said, 'I will not pay you. You don't frighten me.' And now, I find this. Look." She turned a sheet toward me, her finger underlining a row of numbers. I commanded myself to focus but my eyes and mind glazed over.

Brigitte explained. "This row, it represents withdrawals from Napoleon's business account. *D'accord?* I found the statements on his desk this morning. I wondered what the withdrawals were for. Not supplies or tax or payroll. Look at these, several large withdrawals of cash. One matches the amount here on the envelope with Jenkins's name." She patted the envelope. "Others? I do not know. Personal items, but what? He had little personal. Napoleon, he was all work."

"Absolutely. Jenkins is suspicious," I said, eager to place blame on the inspector. "Brigitte, I know Napoleon was your friend and boss, but what if he paid Jenkins to shut down competing food carts for health violations? Like Linda with that cockroach. There's no way she put that in her own tamale by mistake."

Brigitte shook her head slowly. "I hate to agree, but he may have. Napoleon, he considered Linda his biggest competitor among the food carts. Once he set his mind to something, he could be ruthless." She gazed at me with the scrutiny she had been applying to the spreadsheets. "It could mean something else, Rita. Say Napoleon did what you suggest. Why would Jenkins wish to harm Napoleon, his money source? And Jenkins, he could not then blackmail Napoleon without exposing his own wrongdoing. Perhaps there is someone else involved. I must look into these numbers more closely. Maybe we can find the truth in them. Numbers are the key."

I didn't know about the numbers, but I liked where she was headed. "Brigitte, my friend Flori and I have gotten involved in investigations in the past. We've helped solve crimes by digging up information. We always say that information is the key."

Brigitte raised her eyes and assessed me with a steady gaze. I half expected her to dismiss my amateur sleuthing. Instead, she nodded seriously. "It is like forensic accounting, then," she said, her eyes returning to the pages of numbers. "Unfortunately, I do not see much hope of finding information the police have not. They were very thorough in their questions."

They sure were thorough in questions regarding Linda. I stopped myself mid-snort as Brigitte continued.

"I only wish I'd been with Napoleon that night," she said, tearing her eyes from the pages. "To think, I was out having fun." Her voice caught.

My stomach tightened. She'd given me the perfect opener, right where I dreaded to start. "Oh? Where were you?" I asked, already feeling deceitful. I knew full well where she was, and I was checking up on her for more reasons than Napoleon's alibi. Could she see straight through me? Brigitte, however, hovered over her numbers, frowning as she scanned the pages. She took a minute or two to answer, during which time I scanned the white walls of her office. No photos of family. No postcards or paintings from all the places she'd lived before. She was either unsentimental or a strict declutterer or both. I wished I could borrow either of those traits for my depersonalizing task at Victor's old place.

When Brigitte did reply, she sounded distracted. "A benefit . . ." she said, eyes still glued to the numbers. "For kid art." She looked up briefly and sighed. "Napoleon was supposed to go. Actually, he was the invited guest. I was to accompany him to handle the financial donation, ensure that it was deductible from taxes. He shouldn't have been on the Plaza that night."

I got out my notebook for this new information. "Why didn't he go?"

Brigitte flipped a page. "Work," she replied with a shrug. "What else? He said I could handle the event by myself. I wish, now, that I'd insisted he join me. What might have happened if he'd joined me?"

I knew the torment of "what ifs." I asked Brigitte what he was working on.

She didn't know. "He always had so many business ideas. Maybe it was his food carts." She smiled briefly. "That was his current obsession. He wanted several carts. A true Crepe Empire."

And he'd want his competitors out of the way. Competitors like Linda, but also Don and Crystal, who had their own grudges. I pointed this out to Brigitte. "So other food cart operators could have been upset too. Actually, I heard that he and Don Busco had a beef."

"Beef?" she asked, wrinkling her brow. "Le boeuf?"

I apologized and explained.

"Ah, I see. The restaurant business is very demanding. Napoleon had to fire people who failed to meet his high standards. It could not be helped. So, oui, Don Busco had the beef, but it was not unusual or important."

Not important, except that Don lost his dream

job, just like Linda was about to lose hers, as well as her freedom. I followed up with what I thought was a routine question. "When did you last talk to Napoleon?"

Brigitte's answer—or rather, its precision—surprised me. "Fifty-eight minutes before his death." She gave a sad smile. "I know because my phone records the time of calls, and the police tell me that they know the exact time of his demise. Eleven fifty-one. Napoleon's watch was always exact, like him."

"Where was he when he called?" I asked. "What did you talk about?"

Brigitte exhaled loudly. "He did not say where he was, and we spoke only of business. He had an idea, he said, to put Crepe Empire carts on every corner of the Plaza. I suggested other locations, the courthouse or the Railyard or near the schools, but he was adamant. He wanted me to run numbers of costs. I wish now that we'd spoken of something more meaningful, more personal."

I did too, like who was skulking around in the darkness waiting to kill him. And what was Napoleon doing out and calling Brigitte so late at night? Flori often rousted me out of bed early in the morning, but she'd never call past ten.

When I asked Brigitte, she said that Napoleon called at all times. "He barely slept. He assumed no one else did either, or if they did, that their sleep did not matter. If he got excited about an idea or a deal, he called. That he was out is no surprise either. He had so much energy at night, and he liked to walk when he was planning his big ideas."

"You said the other day that you were close?" I asked, and then tentatively added, "Romantically?"

Now she looked up, her smile wry and a blush on her cheeks. "Me? *Non.* I am too tall, a French giraffe, Napoleon called me. We were close as business colleagues." She sniffed, and I quickly changed the subject back to the one I dreaded.

"After he called, you stayed at the benefit?"

"I did. There was a band and ballroom dancing. I do love to dance and I had a fabulous dance partner. I stayed until midnight, and then my dancing man drove me home. Little did I know, Napoleon was already gone."

Drove her home and then what? I said, "How nice," all the while thinking how un-nice it was for me. Brigitte was tall and blond, like Jake's ex-wife. She could also ballroom dance, whereas I stomped on toes in line, swing, ballroom, free-form, and any other type of dancing.

Brigitte's phone rang, jolting me out of my haze. "Oh! There's my dancing alibi now!" she announced. "I should get this and thank him again."

I propelled myself out of my modern plastic chair, nearly knocking it over. "I'll get out of your way."

Brigitte was already talking. "Jake, how kind of you to call . . . Yes, I thought I lost an earring in your car . . . No? Okay . . . Oh, yes, I'm doing the best I can."

I waved. Brigitte waggled her fingers in response and mouthed *Sorry* and what I thought was *Call me.*

I didn't know if I'd call. I definitely knew that

I didn't want to listen in on her call. I was gently shutting the door when she called to me. "Rita, you forgot your bag. Oh! *Oh la la!* What is this? Pink handcuffs? Rita, *mon ami*, do not forget these!"

My face blazing, I rushed in, grabbed the tote, and fled. This time I yanked the door shut, but not before I heard Brigitte saying, "*Pardon*, it was my friend, she forgot her bag of naughty goodies. You are *très*, *très* kind, Jake. So kind to follow me home the other night and to ask how I'm doing . . ."

I hurried through the dining room, past DeeDee and chatting diners, and out through the pretty garden. When I reached the street, I breathed in the cool, head-clearing air. Yes, Brigitte certainly had an alibi. A strong one. Jake Strong.

Chapter 13

I speed-walked past the Georgia O'Keeffe Museum and shops I usually paused to gaze into. I cut broad diagonals across streets. I ignored traffic lights and specials boards posted outside favorite restaurants, and even a baker friend inviting me in for fresh-from-the-oven chocolate cookies. All I wanted was to get to my car and then home, where I planned to hug my cat and talk myself down from eating too much ice cream. I lost steam as I neared Tres Amigas, wishing I'd snagged some of those cookies and trying to remember if I'd already polished off our ice cream supply. Should I detour to the store? A little ice cream wouldn't hurt. I had to have something to talk myself out of comfort-bingeing on, and stale crackers and soggy celery wouldn't cut it.

I was unlocking my car and thinking I'd dash into Kaune's Neighborhood Market, a family-owned grocery with indulgent imported wine,

cheese, and ice cream offerings, when a horn
beeped. I ignored it, still pondering ice cream.
Salted caramel or chocolate chunk brownie? Or
an exotic flavor like fig or sweet tarragon? No,
for comfort I needed swirls of caramel and rich,
fudgy brownies and peanut butter cups. Lots of
peanut butter cups.

The horn sounded again, grating at my already
touchy nerves. Even more irritating, the flashy
sports car making the racket blocked my way out
of the parking lot. I got in my Subaru and maneuvered it to within inches of the high-end jerk.
Through a clenched smile, I waved and mimed
that I wanted to turn right. Manny would have
used other hand gestures. Unlike my ex, however,
I had no badge to shield against road rage.

The sports car didn't move. Instead, the passenger side window slid down revealing Georgio
Andre, Jake's alleged art thief client, and his reptilian smile.

Reluctantly, I opened my own window and
craned my head out. "Hi, Georgio. Car trouble?"

My move-out-of-my-way hint had no effect.
Georgio leaned across a cream leather seat and
said, "Ah, the lovely Ms. Lafitte! I thought that
was you. What a lovely coincidence."

What a pain. I struggled to maintain my tight
smile and perky tone. "Yep, well, nice to see you!
I've gotta get going . . . I'm on my way home . . .
long day . . ."

Georgio's jacket matched his car, a dark egg-
plant purple, bordering on black. The car emitted
a throaty rumble. Its driver continued smiling, and
I saw Cass's point. The man radiated creepy vibes.

"I'll just scoot past, then," I said, trying again. If he didn't move, I was prepared to go overland. I had four-wheel drive, and I could probably weave between the ornamental grasses planted by the sidewalk. I looked both ways, checking for pedestrians and most of all Manny, who'd love to write me a ticket.

Georgio was talking again. I shook my head, trying to replay his previous words, which I must have misunderstood. Did he just say that he'd see me back at my casita?

"Sorry, what was that?" I asked.

"I said, *perfecto*! You are returning home. Exactly where I hoped to find you. *Ciao, bellissima*. We will reunite within minutes."

"But—"

"Do not worry. I know the way."

The dark tinted window glided up, the engine growled, and the aubergine sports car sped off, leaving me with grit on my windshield and nagging questions. Should I still stop for ice cream? And what would an "alleged" art thief want with me?

I pulled out, bumping a tire over the curb. The jolt dislodged a more worrisome thought. What if Georgio wasn't seeking me, but instead some of the artwork still in Victor's house? I channeled Flori's driving skills and stomped the gas.

On the way, I assessed what I knew of Georgio Andre. Not much. He was an infrequent cus-

tomer at Tres Amigas, where he selected healthy
menu items like yogurt and granola. He was
Jake's client, and the two were seemingly friendly
enough to attend art benefits together. Either that
or Georgio needed a criminal defense lawyer on
hand whenever he got near art. He creeped out
Cass, and according to her, dabbled in cat bur-
gling and black-market art dealing. And now he
was in my driveway, parked in Victor's old spot.

Georgio leaned against his vehicle, his hands, in
butterscotch leather gloves, folded neatly in front
of trim Eurotrendy black pants.

I pulled in closer to my casita and got out. The
logo on the back of his car read MASERATI. Art
dealing, legal or otherwise, must pay an awful lot
more than cooking.

"A beautiful afternoon with even more beautiful company," Georgio said.

I like compliments as much as the next person.
I didn't believe them, though. Catching my reflec-
tion in his darkened windows, I cringed at the
glare of my shiny forehead and my hair, lopsided
and mostly falling out of its ponytail.

"Why do you want to see me?" I asked. I would
have worried about sounding rude, but the man
had kept me from a date with gourmet ice cream.

He grinned, or rather leered, in the direction of
my chest.

Self-conscious, I followed his gaze. The tote bag
that earlier embarrassed me at Brigitte's was now
tugging down my shirt to reveal the top of my
bra, the lacy black one I only wore when I'd run
out of fresh laundry.

Georgio's lips flicked in a crocodile's grin. As

I yanked my shirt into place, he said, "I would enjoy seeing more of you. But first, business. You are the caretaker of Victor Zamora's estate." It was a statement, not a question.

"Yes," I said, drawing out the word. Seeing his crocodile gaze turn to Victor's house, I tried to change the focus. "I'm the caretaker. Mostly I arrange for specialists to come in when needed. Like gardeners. There are some heirloom apple trees on the property. I need a good horticultural-ist and landscaper. Do you know anyone?"

"I have no interest in plants," Georgio said. "Art, that is my passion."

As I'd feared. "Well, I don't know much about the art. That's why my landlady hired consultants. Yep, all the good stuff has been inventoried and is safe and sound in museums or specialty storage."

Georgio turned back to me and winked, slow and reptilian. "All the good stuff except the piece I desire."

I fumbled with the lock to my front door. Recently, the lock had been sticking, particularly in damp weather. Or when I most wanted to get inside, like now. I wasn't about to waltz into Victor's house and hand over the painting Georgio claimed to have a hold on. I wanted to call Teresa and con-firm that she'd agreed to sell it, and I was going to do that in private. Inside, behind a locked door. If I could get inside.

"Problem?" Georgio asked as I tugged and twisted.

"No problem."

A gloved hand slid over mine.

"Let me help," Georgio said. I had no time to protest. He took the key, wiggled it gently, and the door swung open as if it had never been locked.

"Oil, that is what you need," Georgio said, his hand still on the key. "Leave this to me. I shall help. I have a kit in my car. Your lock will be smooth as satin."

"That's okay," I stammered. "I need to call a locksmith anyway." I snatched the key, squeezed in, and shut the door—and Georgio's chuckling—behind me.

"Geez," I whispered to Hugo, who wound around my feet. I gave him more than his usual allotment of tuna-flavored treats and let him stand on the forbidden kitchen table while I waited for Teresa's secretary to get her on the line.

"Rita!" Teresa exclaimed, interrupting the second repetition of electronic pan flute hold music. "You're just the woman I've been meaning to call."

"Me?" Somehow I didn't like the sound of this. I liked it even less when Teresa continued.

"I've changed my travel dates. I've been meaning to tell you. I'll be in Santa Fe a week early! Don't worry about the house. I have a new idea. Forget streamlining. Let's clear the place out. It'll be easier! Just leave a bed and a few bits of silverware, and then my decorator can take over. She's thinking Scandinavian meets Southwest? I don't care as long as someone else does it." She laughed.

I tried to imagine Victor's historic adobe home, with its eclectic clutter of art and warm colors transformed to Nordic sparseness.

"Great!" Teresa said. "Glad you agree."

Had I said something? I may have groaned, or perhaps she heard Hugo's low yowl aimed at a squirrel outside the window.

"Er . . ." I said, still at a loss for words. I found my tongue again when she asked me why I'd called.

"There's something I need to ask you." I told her about Georgio.

"Ah, I forgot that too!" Teresa said. "Where's my mind? It's that time of year." She went on to regale me with the multitasking required of her job and the complexities of fiscal calendars. As my brain glazed over, I thought about how Brigitte would delight in the talk of finances and balances. All about the numbers, Brigitte had said. If only life could be figured out so easily.

"So, in short, yes," Teresa said.

I blinked and refocused. "Okay," I said. "Just to be clear . . ."

"Yes, by all means, have that sexy Italian—or do you think he's Greek?—whatever he is, have him look at that painting. He told me he wanted it months ago. I've never liked it, but if he does, have him send me his offer in writing. We can do the deal when I'm in town. See you soon!" she said cheerily and hung up.

Steeling myself, I went back outside, ready to relay Teresa's message to the sexy but slimy Italian. Georgio, however, was nowhere to be seen.

I followed a scent trail of cigarette smoke and eucalyptus-scented cologne to Victor's open front door. *Who did he think he was? He broke in? The nerve!*

"Ah, Rita, I was becoming bored so I decided to

start the search." Georgio greeted me in Victor's living room as if he owned the place.

"How did you get in?" I demanded.

His shoulders rolled ever so slightly. "Old locks. Your employer should consider having them changed, although all locks have their vulnerabilities."

I decided I'd go out later, both to acquire multiple pints of ice cream and to buy a chain lock for my own door.

Georgio scanned the room. "Folk art," he said with a sniff. "I suppose it appeals to some."

Yeah, some like me and Victor. My landlord had built up a massive collection, and a lot of pieces remained, deemed less important by Teresa's consultants. I looked around, my irritation turning to packing panic mingled with sorrow. How could I box up all of Victor's beloved belongings? Removing everything hardly seemed easier. I ran my hand over a green velvet love seat. Surely Teresa's decorator could work with this and some of the other pretty items.

"Bellissima," Georgio said, slinking across the room to me. "Do not look so sad. This art, it is nice. Primitive but fine. Very fine."

"It's not that," I muttered, feeling a sting of welling tears. I pinched my arm to try to distract my emotions.

"Tell Georgio," he said, swinging an arm around my shoulders.

I pinched myself harder. "Allergies," I lied through a sniff.

His tilted head and *"bellissima"* let me know that he didn't believe me.

I wiped my eyes, feeling like an idiot. I was

tired, I reasoned. I'd started off the week by touching a dead guy and just had listened to a beautiful blonde flirt with my dinner date, and now *this*.

Succumbing to Georgio's version of puppy dog eyes, I admitted, "Teresa wants all of this stuff gone. The furniture, the art." I waved my hand. "Rugs, side tables, the kitchen table, everything. I think some should stay. That was our initial plan. A little bit of Victor's character left in the house. A few special items for her decorator to work from."

Georgio pulled me to his chest. "I can help with that too."

Two hours later the room looked like one of Flori's piñatas had exploded out sticky notes. Green, the sparsest color, marked items to keep, including the love seat, a Navajo rug, and a sideboard that Georgio deemed rustic but sublime. Pink meant artwork that could fill in any remaining space in the specialty storage facility. Yellow indicated items for the regular storage units Teresa had reserved. Blue was for donation.

"I can't believe how much we've done," I said, coming out of the kitchen.

Silence greeted me in the living room. Georgio had once again slipped away. I found him in Victor's bedroom, standing nose-to-brushstroke with a gilt-framed painting above Victor's nightstand.

"Ah . . ." he exhaled in apparent bliss. "Worth the wait, the tease. Of course, I find it here, in the room of seduction."

Loath to join him in a room of seduction, I squinted at the painting from the doorway. An angel, I guessed the Archangel Michael, stood above a writhing serpent, sword raised. Cherub heads ringed the scene. One reminded me of Flori's creepy mariachi mannequin.

"So that's it?" I asked. "Teresa said if the painting looks okay, send her your offer." I stepped closer, wondering what made the work special.

"More than okay," Georgio said, reaching over to grab my arm and pull me closer. He looped our elbows and leaned in. My eyes watered again, this time from Georgio's cough-syrupy cologne. I stiffened and tried to inch away, but he leaned closer. "The brush strokes, they express the passion of the artist, the intensity. Do you see?"

I didn't. I was wondering how to politely extricate myself when a noise made me jump. Still stuck to Georgio, I twisted to find Celia standing in the doorway, scowling.

"Mom," she said, her voice dripping disgust. "What's going on?"

I wrenched myself free. "Honey, this is Jake's client Mr. Andre. He's hoping to buy this . . . er . . . lovely painting."

My daughter snorted. "I didn't mean with *him* or *that*. What's with the living room? What are all those sticky notes by Victor's stuff? You're not dumping more of his things, are you?"

"We're not dumping," I said. "A lot's destined for storage. Teresa's arriving sooner than I thought, and she wants a neutral look."

Celia was already stomping down the hallway. "Neutral sucks!"

"Pizza night?" I called after her. The stomps stopped, and for a moment I thought my lure had worked. I caught up with Celia at the front door.

She twisted a lock of already tangled hair. "Yeah, about tonight, I'm meeting some friends for an art thing. Can I stay at Dad's after? It's closer."

It was, also, less regulated in terms of Celia's curfew. I hesitated. "What friends? And aren't you at your Dad's this weekend?"

A look darker than thunder clouds over the desert brewed on Celia's face. "The art thing's at *school*, Mom. All sorts of people will be there."

I caved. If clearing out Victor's house was traumatic for me, it was even more so for Celia, for whom Victor was both a friend and artistic mentor. She needed some space. "Okay, honey. Text me when you get to your dad's, though, and let him know you're coming. I'll be working here for a while."

Her glare focused over my shoulder. From the wave of cough-syrup cologne, I could guess who she was looking at. "Yeah, right. Have fun with that, Mom."

"Kids," Georgio said, coming to stand beside me after Celia had banged out the door. "They do not handle changes well." He took me by both arms and kissed my cheeks before I had a chance to evade. "Take good care of my painting, Ms. Lafitte."

I stood on Victor's porch, watching until Georgio roared out of sight. Kids weren't the only ones who hated change. I didn't like it either.

Chapter 14

After Georgio left, I went back inside and wandered among the sticky notes. The guy had creeped me out, but he'd been company. By myself, the house felt too lonely. There was something else too. I kept checking behind me and peering out the windows, feeling that someone was there, that I was being watched. My New Age neighbor Dalia would say that Victor's spirit lingered. But Victor's spirit would have been a calming, friendly force, not an unsettling one. As the sun sank and the garden outside dipped into shade, I locked up Victor's place and headed for my cozy casita.

Hugo flopped at my feet when I stepped inside. "I know, what a day," I told him, not caring that I was the type of woman who vented to felines. I not only vented, I carried on whole conversations with Hugo. He rolled onto his back, curling his paws and daring me to touch his yellow-spotted belly fur. I couldn't resist, even though I knew needle-sharp claws would grab my hand.

"Yeah, I wish Celia was home to play with you." I carefully extracted my hand, wishing that Celia was home to eat dinner with me too.

Sometimes I revel in time alone. I lounge around the house in sweatpants, flipping through cookbooks and sipping wine or hot cocoa, depending on the season, time of day, and level of decadence. I make meals of cheese and crackers. Any cheese will do, although only when I'm alone will I secretly dip into Celia's stock of jarred nacho cheese dip. I felt the siren's call of nacho cheese, but I didn't feel like reveling.

I checked the freezer and confirmed my earlier fear. No ice cream. The fridge was similarly disappointing since I'd been holding off shopping until I settled on my date menu. I pushed around jars of condiments, hoping to find a lost pudding cup. The shuffling only unearthed older condiment options. How could two females and a cat possess five types of mustard? The hydrator similarly brought no joy. Limp carrots lay next to a mushy lime and the half an acorn squash I meant to do something with. I was a shame to my profession, I thought, throwing out the lime. The squash again failed to speak to me.

"No treats, Hugo," I informed my feline friend, who was again showing me his round belly. "Time for both of us to get on an exercise regime."

Hugo mewed and ran off down the hallway, tail puffed in feigned terror. I agreed. The thought was enough to send me running for pizza. I retrieved the bowl of dough from the fridge, where it had

risen slowly during the day and now strained
against the plastic wrap covering.

Pizza didn't have to be unhealthy. All a tasty
pie needed was a simple sauce, some leaves from
the spindly potted basil in my window, and a few
rounds of mozzarella. Preheating the pizza stone
for an hour seemed like too much effort. I could,
however, make a personal-sized pizza in my cast
iron frying pan. I'd heat the pan to smoking, slap
down the dough and toppings, cook until the
bottom was crispy, and then finish the pie off
under the broiler for bubbly toppings.

I opened the pantry and eyed the cast iron skil-
let, buried under a pasta pot and several casserole
dishes. Retrieving the pan seemed like too much
work. The truth was, I didn't want pizza for one.
Not tonight. Cass, I knew, was busy this week fin-
ishing a commission, personalized necklaces for
a gaggle of bridesmaids. And Jake? I considered
proposing a night out for preholiday margaritas
and loaded nachos. Then I thought about his earlier call to Brigitte. What if he already had plans?
Chickening out, I dialed a number that involved
no romantic anxiety.

Flori answered on the first ring and compli-
mented my sixth sense. "You knew I was about to
call you, didn't you?"

"Ah, yeah, right," I said, hating to discourage
her sixth sense.

"Good, because I'm inviting you to dinner."

A dinner invitation was exactly what I'd hoped
for. Still, I hesitated. Mom's rules of etiquette,
drilled into me since childhood, demanded that
any invitation be met with an "Oh no, I couldn't

possibly impose" kind of refusal. The method came with risk, namely that the inviter followed similar rules, apologized for being a bother, and withdrew the offer. That was highly unlikely with Flori, but I wasn't about to take any chances.

I thanked her, adding, "This will be great. I'm all alone tonight. Celia's out with friends and wants to stay at her dad's later."

"I know," my elderly friend said, making me again wonder if she was indeed clairvoyant. Or if she had me bugged. She had surveillance equipment and knew how to use it.

She interrupted my paranoid ponderings. "Bernard picked me up from tai chi earlier and we cruised past the Plaza. Celia was down there with some skateboarders. I always thought I'd like skateboarding. In my day, girls didn't do that. I wonder if it's scary?"

I wasn't thinking of skateboarding. I was wondering if Celia had lied about her plans.

"Did you see a boy with orange hair?" I asked Flori.

"All sorts of hair colors in that group. I missed that trend too. I suppose I could be a blue-haired lady if I wanted."

"Sure," I said, my mind on Celia. "That'd be great," I added just as absently. Should I call Celia and check in? She'd grumble that I didn't trust her. I did trust her . . . mostly.

Flori probably didn't need clairvoyance to read my thoughts. "Oh, she was just having fun, Rita. They were eating *frito* pies and hanging out like kids do. Don't worry and don't turn an old lady down. Come to dinner."

Flori rarely played the "old lady" card. She must

really want company. I did too. I told her I'd be right over.

Flori met me at the door of her quaint adobe home and ushered me inside.

"I'm so glad you came," she said. "We have work to do after we eat." She nodded toward the dining table. Her Taser sat next to a bowl of salsa. Binoculars rested in a basket that should have held chips.

Bernard waved to me from his recliner throne in the living room. I went in to say hi. On the muted TV, investigative reporter Milan Lujan once again stood on the Plaza.

"Mind if we turn up the volume?" I asked Bernard.

"Happy to," he said with a chuckle. "That Milan's cute as a button." He aimed a remote at the TV. The ancient remote was the size of my shoe and held together with electrical tape. The image on the small, old curved screen wavered, but I could see Milan clearly enough.

She looked straight into the camera and said, "More on our investigation into the death of the famed chef whose single name summed up his singular greatness: Napoleon. I'm here live tonight with Don Busco, an organizer trying to rebuild the food cart community. Mr. Busco, tell us about your efforts."

Don towered over the reporter. He tipped his hat back and looped his thumbs under the front of his denim apron. "Well, Milan, we're making a real effort to work together now. Look over yonder. Just this evening, we got a bunch of folks together."

"For a memorial?" Milan asked.

Don's happy-campfire-cook composure wavered into vexation before being replaced by a wide smile. "For renewed life in our food cart community," he said smoothly.

The camera panned out, showing the Plaza, golden in the light of the setting sun. Crystal was there, waving to the camera from her juice stand. There was a guy I didn't recognize selling tacos, the lady who made gourmet popcorn, and a familiar sleek silver cart with a blue-and-white awning. Crepe Empire.

"Looks fun," Bernard commented from his recliner.

It did look fun, until the camera zoomed in on Crepe Empire. "Is that Brigitte?" I asked, sure that the blurry old TV was playing tricks with my eyes.

Flori, using her silent walking, had come up behind me. "That's her all right," she said. "Oh dear . . ." The camera zoomed in as Brigitte attempted to flip a crepe as thick as a bloated pancake. The top part, underdone, splattered and part folded under the burned underside.

The cameraman, likely recognizing a culinary catastrophe, refocused on Milan's perfectly made-up face.

"Santa Fe police tell us that new details are emerging in the murder case," Milan said. I wished that the camera would show Don. Would he have the nervous tics of a guilty man? Beads of sweat? Shaking hands? But no, when the picture included him a few moments later, he was nodding seriously and explaining the donation jar.

Ketchup, in a blood-splatter pattern, dotted the homemade sign proclaiming *Free Linda!*

Bernard, Flori, and I groaned.

"One of our own is being unduly accused," Don said, patting the jar.

"Our martyr!" Crystal yelled merrily, waving to the camera from her juice stand.

Don continued, "We all stand behind Linda Santiago of Tía Tamales, who has been unduly persecuted for her brave act of discovering Napoleon's body under her cart. An outsider, a random killer, that's who we believe is responsible," Don said, speaking over the "Some of us!" correction lobbed over by Crystal.

"And why do you suspect an outsider?" Milan asked.

Don answered evasively. "I have my reasons," he said. "The owner of that killer tamale cart, she's a good woman. Once she's cleared of health infractions, I'll proudly serve her tamales. All proceeds will go to clearing her name."

"Free Linda!" Crystal exclaimed. A general chorus followed. "Free Linda! *Viva* Linda!"

Milan's smooth brow wrinkled in concern. "Passionate yet uncertain times here in the City Different. Was Chef Napoleon's killer a stranger, a colleague, or, as an anonymous source suggested yesterday, a person in a position of power in Santa Fe's own city government? We at News 6 at six will continue to probe this complicated story. Back to you in the newsroom, Todd."

Todd turned to Isotopes baseball stats.

I turned to Flori. "Poor Linda. All this attention isn't helping her. What can we do?"

Flori didn't use her silent walk. She stomped back to the kitchen. "Find the real killer," she said. "But first, we eat."

Flori served up a feast of cilantro rice, pinto beans, and corn and piñon nut tamales, with salsas and sour cream on the side. I indulged in a second plump tamale, justifying it as vegetarian and thus healthy. Besides, my exercise regime started tomorrow. I needed the energy.

"I'm running tomorrow," I announced, to make myself accountable.

"Running for what?" Bernard asked, befuddlement clear on his broad face. "From what?"

"She's in love, my dear," Flori explained. "That's what young people do these days."

"That's lovely, Rita," Bernard said, still looking confused.

"I'm not in love," I said. "I'm getting in better shape, that's all."

"Rita heard that that tall, blond hottie Brigitte Voll was out dancing with Jake Strong the night of Napoleon's murder," Flori said to her husband. To me, she said, "Yes, I heard all about that. I had to double-check her alibi, didn't I? All sorts of people said they saw her. Said she's quite a dancer." Flori patted my hand. "Now, Rita, you have nothing to worry about. We all saw it right on News 6: the woman obviously can't cook and that's the way to a good man's heart. You might want to step up the romance a smidgen, though, dear. Bat your eyes when you serve that magic chocoflan."

"That'll do it," Bernard affirmed. He leaned up to kiss Flori on her wrinkled cheek. I couldn't help myself. I sighed. Theirs was the kind of romance I wanted. Sweet, forever, no worries, no jealousy.

I let them flirt while I thought about date-appropriate desserts. Chocoflan still seemed too brazen. Rich chocolate cake topped with flan *and* caramel? Maybe I could make just the cake part. Or the flan. But both? No, I decided. I didn't want to come off as desperate.

"Did you learn anything else about Gerald Jenkins Senior and Junior?" I asked Flori when she stopped making eyes at Bernard.

She'd heard all sorts of things, which she described as I helped her clear the table. None of them, not Gerald Senior's medal in high school archery or Junior's volunteering on an archeological expedition, tied directly into Napoleon's murder.

Flori produced a flan, minus the cake, from the refrigerator. "But I did learn something else sweet," she said.

I waited as she soaked the bottom of the fluted pan in warm water to loosen the caramel, and then performed the delicate operation of turning the flan upside down. The custard slipped out, beautifully molded in a sunflower shape and draped in rich caramel sauce. She took the platter to the table.

"Don Busco was on the Plaza around the time of Napoleon's murder," she proclaimed, setting the flan down with a flourish.

"Aha!" Bernard exclaimed, whether about the flan or Don, I couldn't tell. Bernard took charge of doling out the jiggling custard, kindly ladling extra caramel sauce on my serving.

I considered Flori's information. Don had already told me he was out and about that night. He'd even offered up Manny as one of his alibis, as I reminded Flori.

Flori pointed toward the end of the table where her spying equipment occupied two place settings. "Not merely nearby," she clarified. "Joe Toya told Milly Schultz, who told Bill Hoffman's granddaughter, who told Bill that Don was lurking by the bandstand late Monday night."

My head spun, trying to connect the gossip dots. As always, they connected to Bill Hoffman, the keystone of Flori's elder informant network. Bill, in his nineties, hasn't slept longer than two hours straight in decades, or so he claims. To while away the time, he tunes into the police scanner and chats on shortwave radio. His shortwave pals in the Maldives and Siberia probably knew more news from Santa Fe than I did.

Flori said that she'd called Joe to confirm. "He said he couldn't be sure of the exact time, except it was late. He was absolutely sure it was Don. I promised him five free breakfasts," she said. "The code is 'Informant Five.'"

"Great," I muttered, knowing I'd forget this, as I did so many of Flori's coded freebies.

Flori, meanwhile, had moved on to the meat of her gossip. "Joe said that Don was standing by a tree in a dark spot a bit away from where Linda's cart was parked. Joe thought that Don might be feeling wobbly after too much beer, so he didn't go over." She made a tsk-tsk sound that was seconded by Bernard. "When Joe saw all the police tape the next day, he thought about it some more. He speculated that maybe Don was hiding behind that tree, lurking, waiting."

I thought about it too. "Don claimed he didn't get Linda's message asking him to check on her cart until the next morning. But what if he did? What if he went to the Plaza and—"

Flori jumped in. "And he found Napoleon there, messing with Linda's property. He'd step in."

"Self-defense," Bernard said. "Or cart-defense."

There hadn't been any obvious damage to Linda's cart, though, and our scenario depended on supposition and coincidence. "I hope this Joe guy tells the police more than he told you and Milly Whatshername."

Flori and Bernard exchanged a look.

Bernard explained. "Joe won't be talking to the police. They don't get along."

Flori added, "Joe's a nice man but he tends to steal cars. Can't help himself. He steals other things too. ATVs, fire trucks—"

"Mules," Bernard said with a chuckle. "Remember that one he 'acquired' out in Glorieta? And that riding mower he drove all the way to Española and the incident with the mechanical bull from the rodeo? Pretty much anything that moves, Joe will 'borrow' it."

"He has a problem," Flori said. "Besides, Joe's a second cousin to Don. He wouldn't say anything against a relative. His mistake was telling Milly. That girl is such a gossip."

Flori, queen of local gossip, started clearing the table. I rose to help her, my head anything but clear.

"If he is the killer, how do we catch him?" I muttered.

"Spying." Flori held up a worn copy of the *Art of War*. She nodded to the end of the table and the surveillance paraphernalia. "Pick your spy weapon, Rita."

Chapter 15

The next morning as I gasped for air, I wished I hadn't eaten second helpings of tamale and flan. I also wished I'd listened to Hugo. He'd meowed sorrowfully when I rose before dawn and donned exercise clothes, telling myself it was the perfect morning for a jog. It was. The tender spring leaves wore jewels of dew. The air smelled fresh, and the sky promised another sunny day. Perfect for running, or for snoozing under a quilt and a feline, as Hugo had tried to tell me. Puffing down scenic Upper Canyon Road, I thought of Hugo and my warm, soft bed. I mostly thought about my coffeepot. How could I have run off without caffeine?

As bad as I felt physically, though, I was pretty darned pleased with myself. Brigitte had nothing on me. Well, except her tall, blond, Frenchness and command of numbers and dancing. I upped my pace down Canyon Road, panting past art galleries and bronze statues. My route was lovely. Historic, artistic . . . and all downhill.

I realized the error in my downhill ways when I reached the loop road around Santa Fe's core, Paseo de Peralta. My return route would be all uphill. A slight grade, but definitely up.

I panted beside Peralta, considering my options. Hugo was fed. Celia was at Manny's. I could continue on to Tres Amigas. I kept a spare set of clothes in the storeroom in case of emergencies, like oil splatters or waitressing mishaps.

I hefted my foot onto a nearby stone wall. Stretching seemed like the real-runner thing to do and a good excuse to catch my breath. I was craning my head toward my knee, thinking that stretching was a literal pain, when a van and trailer bumped to a stop at the intersection. I recognized the cart immediately. Crepe Empire. Brigitte Voll rolled down the passenger window and leaned across. Her sunny *bonjour* squashed my initial flash of pettiness.

"*Bonjour,*" I replied. Sometime during the stretch, my leg had stiffened. I hoisted it off the wall and hobbled, peg-leg fashion, over to Brigitte's van.

"*Bravo!*" Brigitte exclaimed, as if crippling myself was a praiseworthy accomplishment. "I did not know you were a runner, Rita. We must train together someday. If I did not have the crepe cart, I would join you immediately."

I silently thanked the cart and told Brigitte I was a newbie jogger, lest she get any wrong ideas. "I'm afraid I got a little too enthusiastic today," I admitted. "I'll stick to my part of Upper Canyon Road next time. Where are you going so early?"

She was headed to the Plaza, she told me. "I want to claim my spot. I practiced making crepes for hours last night. I am ready! Don was so kind to invite me."

Was Don being kind, or was he putting on a show of niceness to cover his tracks, like with his Free Linda campaign? I thought of the picture Flori's informant had painted. Don, at the scene the night of the murder. Lurking in the dark. Or taking a tipsy break by a tree. Should I warn Brigitte? She was chatting enthusiastically about crepes and how she had *absolutely known* she had an innate cooking skill in her. How she'd spoken with Napoleon's out-of-state business partner and he'd agreed to let her try her hand at running the crepe cart. How delighted she was.

She seemed so happy and excited. I hated to get her down. I also had no firm evidence.

"Just be careful," I said. "There's still a murderer on the loose."

She nodded, serious now. "You be careful too. Running alone can be dangerous. You should always carry a phone and maybe the chile spray."

I didn't have pepper spray, a Taser, or, thankfully, pink handcuffs on me today. I did have my cell phone, strapped heavily to my arm, and my library card on my key chain. If I ended up in a ditch, Manny could identify my body and any overdue books.

Brigitte reiterated that we must have coffee.

"Sure, yeah," I said, ashamed that my enthusiasm was much less than before I knew of her dancing and flirting talents.

"We must talk of clues as well," she said. "I seek

more receipts and financial records. Today, I plan
to search Napoleon's office with the comb. If I find
anything, shall I call you?"

"Absolutely," I said, more enthusiastically. "Definitely, call me."

After a pleasant adieu, I justified my self-
interested enthusiasm. I wanted more information on Napoleon's dirty business dealings. Flori,
in her *Art of War* mode, would approve. She'd say
we needed to know Napoleon to know who killed
him. She'd also say to keep one's enemy—or romantic nemesis—close.

I sighed, disappointed in my emotions. I needed
to get them, not to mention my dinner date menu,
under control by tomorrow. Any thoughts of jogging back home had been replaced with a desire
to sprint to Tres Amigas, especially when I remembered the breakfast special.

Chilaquiles, part of Flori's Mexican specials for
Cinco de Mayo, are basically breakfast nachos, a
revelation to my Midwest worldview. My family
back in Bucks Grove eats cereal for breakfast.
Plain, healthy, whole-grain cereal in low-fat milk.
On weekends or holidays, we might indulge
in pancakes (a very short stack) or French toast
(made from wholesome wheat bread). My mother
would never, ever condone tortilla chips in chile
sauce for breakfast, no matter how delicious.

Flori makes her *chilaquiles* with day-old tortillas,
which she panfries until golden brown, crispy on
the outside with some chew on the inside. She
then coats the chips in red chile sauce and tops
them with a fried egg, a dollop of sour cream,

roasted green peppers, and a sprinkling of *cotija* cheese. Extras can include bacon, guacamole, and pickled jalapeños, all of which sounded like just rewards for my morning exercise.

Waiting at an intersection, daydreaming about a nachos breakfast of champions, I barely registered the WALK sign flashing on the other side or the silver Audi pulling up beside me.

"Need a ride?" Jake rolled down his window. Wrinkled bulldog lips flopped out and Winston woofed.

Startled, I resorted to instinct, namely Mom's polite refusals. "No, no thanks, I'm too hot," I blurted out. My face flared red. Flori's knack for unintentional innuendos was rubbing off on me. She, however, can claim age and general brazenness. The worst thing was, I was in no way "hot." My leggings, intended for yoga that never happened, revealed all the curves I meant to tone. My sweatshirt, oversized and advertising a long-ago police softball tournament, had been Manny's and I should have tossed it ages ago.

Jake's laugh lines crinkled attractively at the corners of his steel-blue eyes. "Yep, looking hot," he said. "All the more reason to give you a ride." He directed his next words at Winston. "Time for you to get in the back, buddy."

I launched into more polite refusals. "No, I couldn't. You really don't want me in the car. I'm probably sweaty."

Jake ignored me, put on his blinkers and started to get out of the car. "I insist," he said.

I'd already refused twice, thus fulfilling Mom's

etiquette rules. I decided I could now accept a ride. What I wouldn't do was dislodge Winston, sitting proudly on a tartan-print blanket.

"I'll hop in the back," I said, prompting protests from Jake.

"It's a mess back there," he said. "Files everywhere. I have a bear of a case."

I lived with a teenage daughter who collects more hair dye and art supplies than one casita can comfortably hold. I wasn't worried about stray filing. Otherwise, Jake's car was spotless with a perpetual new-car smell laced with a dash of manly cologne and a touch of bulldog.

"Where to, *madame*?" Jake asked, tipping an imaginary chauffeur's hat.

"Tres Amigas, *s'il vous plaît*," I said with a grin, forgetting my dating doubts. "We have *chilaquiles* on special this morning . . ." If that wasn't a flirtation, I didn't know what was.

"Yee-haw," Jake exclaimed. Winston let out a howl, and we sped through the yellow light in the direction of Tres Amigas.

The file folders fanned across the seat beside me. I could read a partial name on one: *rgio Andre*. Filling in the hidden letters was easy. Georgio Andre.

"So, Georgio," I said, restacking the folders. "I heard that you two had a date the other night."

"I heard that *you* saw Georgio yesterday," Jake said slowly. In the rearview mirror, a frown crossed his face. "About Georgio, watch out for—" he started to say and then stopped. A wry smile replaced the frown. "Georgio *loves* art. Remember that if you ever leave him alone in Victor's old place. And, if you were referring to our 'date' at

the art benefit up on Museum Hill, he bought the
tickets. If I'd bought 'em, I would have invited a
more attractive date."

Did he mean me? Or Brigitte? I couldn't tell
and got no hint from Jake, who was concentrat-
ing on avoiding a street sweeper brushing down
the middle of the road. "Ah," I said, buying time
as my mind spun for ways to change the subject.
I forced a laugh. "Guess Georgio can't be Napoleon's killer, then."

"Guess not," Jake agreed. Then he added in a
dry tone, "Guess I'm all sorts of people's alibi for
that night."

I was determined not to ask about Brigitte. Instead, I focused on Linda. "I wish Linda had been
at that benefit." I wouldn't have minded if she'd
danced the night away with Jake, far from the
scene of the crime.

Jake agreed. "Her early-to-bed routine isn't
much of an alibi, that's for sure, although I've seen
worse."

Surely he had. An idea occurred to me. "You
haven't heard anything about shakedowns at the
health inspector's office, have you?" I asked, mon-
itoring his reaction in the rearview mirror.

His eyebrows wrinkled into a frown. "No . . ."
he said slowly.

"What about Don Busco? Do you know him? I
mean . . . well . . . professionally?"

"You mean, in my side professions of mixing
drinks and fixing gourmet hot dogs?" he joked.
"Or do you want to know if he was a client?"

"Client," I said, worried that I'd set myself up for
a cross-examination of motives.

"You know I can't discuss clients, even if I wanted to," Jake said, turning into the back parking lot of Tres Amigas. "Of course, I can say that Don's never been a client of mine." His next words verged on suspicious. "Why do you ask, Rita?"

Winston saved me from having to plead the fifth. He let out a howl that echoed through the Audi. I looked out to see a man in a UPS uniform walking two wolfhounds.

"Uniforms," Jake said over the baying bulldog. "His most hated thing, along with any dog taller than him and bicycles and squirrels and certain statues . . ."

"Good boy," I told Winston, and jumped out of the car.

Well, well!" Flori said happily and a tad suggestively, when Jake, Winston, and I came in through the back door of Tres Amigas.

I quickly explained so she wouldn't get the wrong idea about my early morning male companionship. "I went running," I reminded her. "I jogged down Canyon Road and Jake happened by and gave me a ride."

Disappointment flashed behind Flori's spectacles. She recovered by offering Winston a biscuit from the dog-treats cookie jar. The bulldog turned in clumsy circles until the bone-shaped cookie reached his floppy lips. To Jake, she offered an even better treat: taste-tester of the daily special.

"Into the dining room now, both of you," Flori

said to the man and his dog. Jake settled in and
took out his cell phone. Winston laid down,
stretching his front and back legs out in what Jake
once called his Superman flying pose.

"That's one chivalrous man," Flori said to me.
"Always showing up just when you need him, and
an early riser too, a good feature." She frowned
at my attire, suggesting I could step up my fashion if I was going to run into hunks first thing in
the morning. I went to change into my backup
clothes. When I returned, in faded jeans and a
black T-shirt, Flori handed me a plate.

"Here, deliver this hot plate to your hot friend,
and here's one for you as well." Flori winked.
"There's nothing like a warm breakfast to grab a
man's heart."

I rolled my eyes and took the two plates. I had
a good grasp until she added two mugs of coffee.
Jake saw me coming, a jiggly eggs, scorching
coffee, and hot chile disaster waiting to happen.
He quickly put away his phone and cleared the
table. From unfortunate past experience, Jake
knows that I'm a waitressing hazard.

"Lovely," he said once I had safely landed our
breakfast plates.

It was lovely. The café wouldn't open for another
half hour so we had the dining room to ourselves.
Our own private breakfast. A beam of sunlight
cut a bright line across the tile floor and set the
colorful ceiling decorations aglow. Flori, in the
kitchen, sang along to New Mexican folk music
on the radio. She always said that this was her favorite time of day. Early morning before anyone
else was up, when she could listen to her music

and plan the day's food. I could see why she liked it.

Jake and I chatted easily about one of my favorite topics: food. Jake recounted a trip to Mexico City, where his hotel had served memorable red chile and green chile versions of *chilaquiles*. I admitted that I'd never had them until a visit to New Mexico with Manny. It had been love at the first taste.

"I know what you mean," Jake said. "I do adore Mexican, and Tex-Mex too. Of course they can't hold a candle to *New* Mexican cuisine and I surely look forward to your French feast."

I studied the chip-fragment remains of my *chilaquiles*, suddenly feeling nervous. That French feast could be a flopped soufflé. And what if the date was a flop too? I sipped my coffee and told myself to grow up. When I wasn't quizzing Jake about awkward topics like murder suspects and alibis, we had a great time together.

Jake finished off a last bite of spicy tortilla and pushed back his chair. "I hate to eat and run," he said, "but I have a packed schedule today. That's why Winston's with me. I'll be lucky to get home before dark." He gave me a smile that could melt chocolate and my heart. "I want to clear my desk so I won't be late for dinner tomorrow night."

And I needed to shop for dinner ingredients and commit to my menu, oh and find a killer along the way. I told Jake that I'd be busy as well.

"With sleuthing?" His laugh lines flattened to steely.

I didn't answer directly. "Looking into some things."

I couldn't fool Santa Fe's best defense lawyer. Jake reached out as if to grab my hand. Then he pulled back. "Rita, I wish you wouldn't . . ."

"Wouldn't what?" I asked, too sharply. Under the table, Winston groaned.

His owner drew a deep breath. "I only mean, I worry. I know you've been asking around about Napoleon's death. I know you visited Brigitte and quizzed her about Napoleon's enemies. I understand that you and Flori are worried about Linda, but there's a murderer out there. Someone *stabbed* Napoleon and rolled a cart over him. I only hope you'll be careful." He smiled now. "Plus, I want that soufflé you promised me. Can't have anything happening to you."

I smiled, already regretting my defensive tone. "Flori knows martial arts," I said with a forced laugh. "We'll be fine."

"I bet she's deadly," Jake said. He grinned. "And you're carrying around handcuffs, I hear. Dangerous indeed."

My face must have blazed redder than the chile. Jake was putting on his jacket when his cell phone buzzed. I glanced down as the caller ID flashed across the screen. *B. Voll.* Jake looked at the screen, frowned, and silenced the ring.

"Just be careful, Rita," he said, before leaving me with a warm kiss on my forehead and a pit in my stomach.

Chapter 16

ater that morning I stood near the entrance to the Five and Dime, surveying the Plaza. Flori hadn't exactly kicked me out of Tres Amigas, but she had enthusiastically encouraged me to leave. She argued that I should go shopping for soufflé supplies. This was true. She also noted that I had way too much nervous energy. This from a woman who had pulverized every tomato, tomatillo, and chile in sight, all while studying the *Art of War* and practicing accelerated tai-chi moves. I knew my elderly friend was worried too. That's why I'd stopped by the Plaza again before heading to the grocery. I hoped to spy on Don and discover clues or murderous vibes.

So far I'd seen only happy people. Tourists flowed in and out of the Five and Dime, which sold souvenirs and necessities like Band-Aids and aspirin. Another necessity, if you asked me, was *frito* pie, a delicacy consisting of individual bags of Fritos smothered in steaming chili, shredded cheese, chopped onions, and pickled jalapeños. Some locals claim this snack was invented right here at the Five and Dime—then a Woolworth's—back in the 1960s. Texans give origin credit to San Antonio. Still others say the recipe came from a man raising money to return home to Mexico, or, less romantically, that it emerged from corporate test kitchens. A young couple stepped out of the store, heads down, plastic forks burrowing into bulging Fritos bags. They wouldn't care where the idea came from, just that it was a good one.

I watched them cross the street and pass by Crepe Empire. The slick cart stood at the spot Napoleon had stolen from Linda. Its rolling metal shutter was pulled down, and a paper fluttered on it. I went to investigate. The note in slanted cursive read *Back soon!* but gave no indication of when the writer—presumably Brigitte—had left.

I felt relieved, yet knew I couldn't avoid her forever. The town and food community were both too small for that. If I saw her return, I'd stop by and try one of her pancake crepes. Or maybe I'd have another kind of treat. With Napoleon gone, food carts flourished. On the southwest corner, little Mexico had popped up. Mouthwatering scents of grilled meat wafted from stands selling fajitas, tacos, and *tortas*, hearty sandwiches stuffed with grilled meats, guacamole, salsas, and even refried beans. On the far corner of the Plaza, I could see the red and white colors of the gourmet popcorn lady. Then, of course, there were the king and queen of food cart collegiality. Don and Crystal had pulled their carts to the very center of the Plaza, adjacent to the veterans' memorial. A guy in a sombrero and sandwich board circled the stone obelisk, yelling, "Hot dogs! Cold drinks!"

I considered my next move. A dozing man occupied my usual spying bench, which was too close to Don's cart anyway. Officer Bunny's direct approach came to mind. I could boldly stride over and inform Don that he'd been spotted at the crime scene. I, however, was not Bunny. I lacked her muscles, authority, and bravery. I did not want to tip my hand to a possible murderer.

I fell in step behind a group of sixty-somethings in flashy turquoise jewelry and leather fringe coats. The group, chatting loudly, headed to the taco cart and debated what *tacos al pastor* contained. I bit my tongue in order to blend in. Usually I'd have jumped in and recommended the dish of tender pork marinated in spices and pineapple before grilling. The pineapple, I'd learned from Flori, contains an enzyme that tenderizes the meat. Chemistry was never my favorite subject in school, but I knew delicious food alchemy when I tasted it.

I let them move on to the question *adovada* and acted like a customer patiently waiting her turn. In actuality, I was watching Don out of the corner of my eye, waiting for some clue. I got nothing except a stomach calling for the *adovada*, pork simmered in red chile sauce.

Don, meanwhile, was acting like any hot dog entrepreneur. He dished up dogs. He laughed with customers. He dropped some change into the Save Linda jug. The group in front of me decided on chicken-lime tacos, a safe yet tasty choice. I

had to choose too. Find another place to blend in?
Confront Don? Order a taco? I let my eyes wander
to the menu. Luckily for my health-food regime,
a skateboarder bumped my elbow just as I was
justifying *adovada* as a light afternoon pick-me-up.

"Hey!" I said to the teen's departing slouched
shoulders. His jeans sagged down his butt, and
his hair was inky black and spiky like Celia's. I
cringed as he barely missed crashing into a baby
carriage and a trembling Chihuahua. Maternal righteousness filled me. My daughter would
never be so rude. Anyway, she was in school right
now, diligent about her studies.

Wasn't she?

Skateboard kid jumped his board off the curb
and came to a floundering halt by a picnic bench,
where similarly attired teens lounged. The half-
dozen heads featured the same black, spiky hair,
except for one orange and another streaked with
orange. Could that be Celia and the mystery guy
she'd waved to? *No. I was imagining things.* All
the same, I gave up my spot in the taco line and
started toward the picnic table.

"Lady!" a male voice exclaimed. "Watch out!"

I stumbled backward, realizing that I'd stepped
blindly into the street and traffic. A horn blared
and a truck the size of a brontosaurus roared by.

"Thanks," I called to the man who'd saved me
from another brush with vehicular crushing. I
couldn't tell if he heard me. He was heading up the
sidewalk toward the center of the Plaza. Toward
Don, I realized, but that's not what sent the jolt
up my spine. My savior was tall and gangly with
wavy red hair. Gerald Jenkins Junior, the guy who

found the cockroach in Linda's tamale, and who was either nice, according to Addie, or corrupt like his father, as I suspected.

I started to follow him before I remembered the teens. Which did I want to know more? What Junior was up to, or whether my daughter was ditching school? I chose, as always, Celia. Turning away from Junior, I moved behind a tree. The teens were decamping from the picnic table in a tight but disorganized cluster. I held my breath when I realized they were moving my way. What if Celia was among them and caught me spying? I would still be the one in the right, I reassured myself. Or I could fake bird-watching again. I peeked out from behind my tree post. The teens were bad-mouthing each other in a way they seemed to enjoy but would have mortified me at their age. Skateboard guy passed. So did the orange-hair kid I recognized as the guy I'd seen outside Celia's school. He didn't look my way, being occupied teasing a girl with nose piercings. None of them seemed to notice me, and none—to my relief—was Celia.

I took a deep breath and felt guilty for letting my suspicions slip into my family life. I owed Celia a treat. An afternoon at the movies or a night out for pizza. I could still hear the teens' harsh laughter as I turned back to Junior Jenkins. Him, I didn't feel bad suspecting.

Junior stepped into line at Don's hot dog cart. He shifted from sneaker to sneaker, hands stuffed deep in baggy cargo pants pockets, shoulders twitchy.

Who's that nervous about buying a hot dog? He had to have other motives. My heartbeat sped up as I got in line behind him. Lacking a disguise, I got out my cell phone, let my hair fall over my eyes, and pretended to text.

"Next dog fan, step right up!" Don boomed. "What'll it be, pardner?"

"Whatever," Junior mumbled.

"Yes, sir, *frito* pie fiesta, coming right up! Special of the day! Extra hot sauce!" Don responded, as if Junior had placed an actual order.

I dared glance up. Junior, like his dad, wore clothes a little too large. He tugged up a baggy shirt, dug in his back pockets, and extracted a folded manila envelope. Don handed over the dog, piled high with Fritos, chopped onions, and chili con carne. Junior, instead of paying, thrust the envelope at Don, dropped the hot dog back on the counter, and hurried away.

Don shoved the envelope under his counter and pushed the hot dog to the side. "Up next, what'll it be young lady? Hot dogs for a hot—" He looked up, recognized me, and frowned before quickly recovering. "Ah, Rita, my favorite Midwest cowgirl. What can I get for you? Dog on the range? Chile-charged challenge?"

Junior was moving fast. He was almost to the other side of the Plaza. I didn't have time to wait for a dog, and I certainly didn't have time to eat one.

"Oh, darn it," I said, patting my pockets. "I forgot my wallet." I started to go.

"No trouble," Don said. "Not for one of my favorite customers. I'll spot you. Pay me in one of Flori's famous chocolate muffins. Here, have some Fritos while you wait." He tossed a packet of corn chips at me.

"Ah . . . I ah . . ." I stuttered, grasping for an excuse. I went with my real excuse. "Gotta go," I said, leaving the chips by the Free Linda jar. I took off at a near jog, fearful of looking back.

Don's voice followed at my heels. "Devil dogs! Who wants to dance with the devil?"

I'm no professional spy, by any means, and it's not like I've had tons of experience tailing people. However, in my humble opinion, Santa Fe has to rank among America's top tailing towns. There are always lots of tourists, for one thing. Tourists mill around, often in big, slow-moving groups. They stop to gaze in windows and consult maps. Around here, a lot of visitors and locals alike also sport big hats of the sun-blocking and Western varieties, good for hiding behind. Better yet, Santa Fe is literally plastered with adobe. Adobe walls with decorative nooks and buttresses make fabulous covert stops. So do the covered walkways, or *portales*, attached to buildings ringing the central Plaza.

All in all, I felt pretty good about my ability to tail Addie's friend Junior. He took the route I'd chosen when fleeing the News 6 cameraman, straight to the shaded walkway along the Palace of the Governors. At the corner, he slowed, stuck in a small crowd gathering around an elderly lady selling piñon nuts. I hovered behind the other on-lookers, momentarily distracted. Piñons were on my shopping list. The woman was saying that she harvested on land of her Pueblo ancestors, shaking the nuts from the cones of the squat pines that dotted the hills. *I'd love to buy some piñons from a local collector.* She held up a dark-colored nut, explaining that for each pinkie-nail-sized prize, she removed the hard outer shell by hand. Now I understood why the local nuts cost so much. I moved closer, tempted to buy a packet. Then I noticed that Junior was on the move, jaywalking across Washington Avenue.

I gave up on pine nuts and jogged across the street. Junior had stopped up the block to check his phone, so I slipped behind a display of chile *ristras* outside a gift shop. Flori once told me how her grandmother strung dozens of *ristras* in the fall, enough to cover the family's chile needs until the next harvest. The general rule was that each person would eat his or her height in the spicy staple. Flori laughed, saying her family loved chiles so much, they had to double or triple that figure.

Peeking through a round pepper wreath, I saw that Junior was on the move again and heading toward a place I considered my territory: the public library. Was he meeting someone else? Another handoff? Despite Addie's nice words for Junior, I'd already judged him and guessed he wasn't stopping by for a new book. I slowed, confident that I'd find him outside. But Junior wasn't out front. He also wasn't waiting at the nearby light or heading to the gelato shop across the street. I hustled back to the library and went inside, panting too loudly.

Once in the main foyer, I took a deep breath. The library always calmed me. I liked visiting the closet-sized space where volunteers sold used books for a dollar. I loved the surprises in the new acquisitions section and flipping through old favorites in the grand reading room that housed the New Mexican and Southwestern collection. The reading room was the stuff of my library fantasies, from its dark wood ceiling and tables to the glass cabinets filled with bibliotreasures. It's where I found Junior, taking a seat at one of the sturdy wooden tables. High above, chandeliers made of punched and painted tin—better than any crystal bobbles—hung from carved wooden beams. Desk lamps with dark metal shades stood on each table. Junior switched his on and, to my chagrin, opened a book.

Quiet readers and laptop users claimed most of the other seats. I approached Junior's table and made an *Is this seat taken?* gesture. He smiled and nodded. Nice, but I wouldn't withdraw my negative judgment simply because he had good library manners. I recalled him maligning Linda, brandishing the tainted tamale for all to see.

As I sat, I realized that I had no book. I resisted the urge to peruse the shelves. I wasn't here for pleasure, unlike Junior, who seemed engrossed in a book about New Mexican petroglyphs.

"Neat stuff," I whispered, nodding toward his book.

Junior's head remained buried behind the book.

His eyes lifted long enough for him to grunt an affirmation.

I couldn't blame him. I wouldn't want some stranger bugging me in the library. A more direct approach was needed.

"You're Junior Jenkins, right?" I asked. Taking his frown as affirmation, I continued. "I know about your dad's 'business' and that you planted that cockroach in Linda Santiago's tamale."

The petroglyph tome was lowered. Junior's cheeks burned as red as his hair. Was he mad or shy? I settled on ashamed, which he should be. He'd helped shut down Linda's business and position her as a murder suspect.

"I don't handle Dad's so-called business," he said. "You have a problem, take it up with him."

Ah, now this was something. "No, you tell me. Who's your father blackmailing? Tell me or I'll call the police." I was bluffing. I had nothing.

"Leave me alone, lady," he said, and not in a whisper. "This is a library!"

A woman at the next table scowled from behind purple horn-rimmed glasses. "The library!" she whispered for emphasis.

Junior, sensing support, added, "Yeah, stop harassing me!"

Horn-rimmed woman made a huffy sound, and other heads bobbed in affirmation. My attempt at a friendly smile worked on neither the woman nor Junior, who pointedly raised his book to block me out. The back cover featured the outline of a hand, one of the common symbols carved and painted by ancient peoples throughout the Southwest.

Risking further reading-room ire, I whispered,

"I know you took part, Junior. You and your father were in cahoots with Napoleon and now he's dead. Murdered! What do you know about that?"

Junior jerked his head back. "*I* didn't have anything to do with that! You work with Addie, don't you? Well ask her about me. She'll tell you. I'm a musician and an archeologist." His outburst faltered. "Or I will be, soon as I get through school."

A librarian walked by the doorway, eyes scanning the room. I fell silent, waiting for her to leave before I resumed my questioning. "I saw you hand that envelope to Don Busco. What was in there? Is your dad blackmailing Don? Junior, if you have evidence that can clear Linda, you *have* to take it to the police. Addie will say the same thing."

He slammed his book down. "Leave me alone!" he cried, his voice echoing across the cavernous room. "And don't bad-mouth me to Addie! I mean it!"

Heads turned. The lady in the horn rims stood. "I'm getting security," she announced.

"No—" I started to say, but she was already marching to the door with Junior close behind her. I jumped to my feet, causing my chair to tip into a man working on his computer.

"Careful!" he snarled.

Suddenly the silent reading room became of cacophony of chastisement. "Take it outside lady!" "Stop bothering people." "Shhhhh!"

I fled more than followed Junior, and ran when I saw reading-room lady pointing me out to a bulky security guard. Bolting out the back exit, I hid behind an SUV in the parking lot. My heart thumped and a truly terrifying prospect struck me. What if I'd become a wanted person in one of my favorite places? I pictured myself sneaking into the stacks wearing sunglasses and one of Addie's wigs. It was a dismal thought. I slumped against the SUV, feeling defeated, but only for a moment. My touch triggered the behemoth vehicle's alarm. Lights flashed, the horn blared, and a siren screamed. I ran as fast as my jogging-sore legs allowed to the nearest gelato shop.

Chapter 17

I slunk back to Tres Amigas a little after the lunch rush and volunteered for hazard duty as penance for missing work and disrupting the library. Deseeding Flori's extra-hot chiles required gloves. I added a plastic apron and wished I had a pair of Cass's goggles. My eyes watered from spicy pepper fumes, a dangerous situation because I kept catching my chile-contaminated hands reaching to wipe them. After preparing more than enough peppers for the hot chile cheeseburgers and salsas, I stepped outside for fresh air. That's when I spotted the official vehicle coming our way.

"Heath inspector!" I yelled, rushing back into the kitchen. "Jenkins Senior! All hands on deck. I mean, all hairnets on!"

I adjusted my own net, strung one as a beard covering on grumbling Juan, and doubled up the plastic coverings on Addie's wig. By the time Jenkins Senior slouched in, we in the kitchen looked more like crazed surgeons than cooks.

"Inspector," Flori said, holding up her gloved hands as if preparing to operate on a plate of enchiladas. "What can we do for you?"

He snapped on his own gloves and smirked. "Time for your inspection."

He's taking a magnifying glass to our salt shakers," I reported, spying from the kitchen. "He swabbed the mariachi players." Most of our customers had left, opting for doggy bags when they saw the gloved man combing over the café. A few others had relocated to the patio.

Flori, her face hovering over a pot of posole, made tsk-tsk sounds. "Silly man. He's making a show, that's all."

A show we'd have on video if he tried to plant anything. I'd instructed Addie to follow him with her cell phone set to video. She was currently shooting from a crouched position, seemingly getting an artsy, edgy shot.

"That's it!" I heard her say. "Nice! Good angle. You want, we can stop and powder your shiny forehead? What about that red nose? No?"

"Not good," Juan said. He sat on a stool sucking red juice through a straw, his protective beard and hair coverings scrunched in a puffy ring around his forehead.

"Not good at all," I agreed. I could have used a drink. A margarita would do, but it was way too

early. "Is that one of Crystal's juices? What flavor?"
I asked Juan.

"Raspberry mint," he said. "Free like yesterday,
except then I got strawberry."

My first thought was that Crystal was awfully
nice. My next thought was that she wanted something. "Free? Like Flori gives away free food for
information?"

Juan's broad shoulder rose and fell a few mil-
limeters. "She only asked if Flori and you were
looking for the murderer."

I raised my eyebrows, silently encouraging Juan
to reveal what happened next.

"I said, '*Sí*,'" he said. "What else could I say?"

True. Any local like Crystal would know of Flori's reputation for sleuthing. And despite my intentions to stay far away from crime and conflict,
I was building the same reputation.

"How did Crystal react?" I asked Juan as he
loudly extracted the last drops of juice from the
ice chips.

He rattled the ice and thought. "She said that
Napoleon tricked everyone. She said that she bets
his death will too. I don't know what she means,
but she asked me to keep her informed." His lips
twitched in the hint of a conspiratorial smile.
"You want me to tell her something special, you
let me know."

Jenkins reached the end of his swabbing and
analyzing about forty minutes later, wiping his

brow. His face was paler than usual, yet sweating. He slumped into a seat by the window, retrieved his thermos and a laptop from a satchel the size of a small suitcase, and began pecking at the keyboard with his index fingers.

"You want me to keep filming that bloke?" Addie whispered when I came out to the dining room, wearing a fresh apron and bearing a bleached menu.

I told her to save her battery, for now. "But sit behind him. If he reaches for his pockets or gets up, that's when he could plant something."

"Jolly good, guv'ner," Addie said. Having triple-watched all available episodes of *Downton Abby*, she'd started in on British crime dramas. Flori thought this was a great idea and had given Addie an entire Agatha Christie DVD set for Christmas.

Jenkins looked up as I approached his table. "Lots to write about," he said, tapping away.

About how spotless Tres Amigas was? About how the air smelled of lemon bleach and baked goods? I forced a smile and asked if he'd like anything from the menu. "We're known for our green chile stew," I said as pleasantly as I could muster. "Customers rave about our healthy muffins. We have some Mexican specials too, for Cinco de Mayo. Shrimp tacos?"

The inspector clutched his stomach and made a sound of disgust. "Shrimp?" He tapped a few words while I waited, wondering if seafood so far from the sea was some sort of infraction. "Fine," he said, looking up. "So you'll leave me alone. Get me a bowl of chile stew. Flour tortillas on the side and a muffin for later. This is on the house, I assume?"

"Of course," I said through my frozen smile. "Any coffee with that? Tea?"

He reached for his thermos. "No drinks. Just bring me that soup. Make sure it's hot. Then get me the owner of this place and we'll talk."

His attitude made me think that we wouldn't be chatting about the A+ rating we were about to receive. I glanced at Addie and she gave me a thumbs-up with one hand. In her other hand she aimed her cell phone at Jenkins.

Back in the kitchen, Flori threatened to add habaneros to Jenkins's bowl of green chile stew. "That'd fix him," she chuckled.

"That's all we need, more for him to write up. He seems to disapprove of shrimp, and he says that he wants to talk to you."

Flori ladled out a bowl of stew, a flavorful mix of green chiles, tender lamb, and creamy potatoes. "He can have stew, but no payoffs." She placed the bowl on a tray and tightened the sash around her karate top. My elderly boss was dressed for battle, from her orange sneakers to the karate-style band wrapped around her hairnet.

I delivered the food along with a shiny spoon, a falsely perky "Enjoy," and a failed attempt to read over Jenkins's shoulder. He snapped the laptop closed and held the spoon up to the light. I was glad I'd repolished it and that Addie was filming.

Jenkins peered up at me through narrowed, watery eyes. "You want to stand here and stare at me while I eat? Your funny friend already has a recording."

"Funny? Who are you calling funny, you . . . you . . ." At a loss for Britishisms, Addie muttered a few choice words of Spanish. "Don't worry, Rita love," she said to me. "I'll bleep that bit out of the film."

I took a seat by Addie and watched Jenkins slowly sip soup.

His son's nothing like that shifty one," Addie whispered, keeping her eyes on Jenkins Senior. "Junior's a good lad. I asked him about his dad and he told me to stay clear. I said, 'not if he's messing with me friends, I won't.' "

Worry jolted me from the monotony of Jenkins's sipping. "Addie, please be careful," I said, aware how prickly I'd felt when Jake said the very same thing to me. Addie was young, though, and trusting.

She also wasn't deterred. "I told Junior, I said someone hid that cockroach in Miss Linda's tamale and set you up to find it. He was kinda angry that I knew, but he agreed that that's what must have happened. Not that he knew firsthand."

"That's one possibility," I said. Telling a friend that her boyfriend is a jerk, or a potential accomplice to murder and cockroach treachery, rarely works out well. I squeezed Addie's free hand. "Promise me you won't trust anyone," I said.

Her eyes widened. "Even Miss Flori and Linda?"

"No, no. I mean anyone who could be a suspect or close to a suspect, okay?"

"Right. Just like with Miss Marple," Addie said, seriously. "Anyone could be the killer. Too bad we don't have a butler to pin it on."

We had a shifty food inspector, a question-able hot dog guy, and a generous juice lady. That seemed like more than enough suspects to me. The door chimed, announcing new customers. I got up, ready to seat them as far from Jenkins as possible. Maybe they'd choose the patio. Out of habit, as I passed Jenkins's table, I asked if he was doing okay. I seemed to have interrupted a sip. He gurgled, then coughed. Sweat beaded on his pasty face.

"You okay?" I asked with real concern. "Would you like a drink? More water?"

"No. No drink," he stuttered, his voice raspy. "What did you put in this?"

Addie had come up beside me, her cell phone held low to her side.

"Did you get a hot pepper?" she asked. "They give some people the sweats, they do."

Jenkins's head bobbed and wobbled until a final backward fling that sent him toppling from his chair. Addie and I grabbed his arms and sat him upright against the table. His breathing came in ragged jags interspersed with groans.

"Water, Addie!" I commanded. "And get Flori!"

One of the new customers, a slight man in a leather-fringed jacket, appeared at my side. "I'm a doctor," he said, lifting Jenkins's head and peering into his rapidly blinking eyes. His words calmed me, until he added, "Call 911! This man needs to get to the hospital, fast!"

Chapter 18

Flori's green chile stew recipe has been called heart-stopping, soul expanding, a heavenly experience. Never, however, has it brought a diner so close to the other side. I called the hospital the next morning while waiting for Celia to draw on her eye makeup.

"You a relative?" the receptionist asked.

"I . . . er . . . I was there when he passed out," I said, unwilling to tempt additional bad fortune by lying to strangers.

Silence on the other end was followed by, "Rita? Is that you? It's Ana-Grace, Addie's cousin. I recognized your *er*."

I admitted to being noneloquent me. "You probably heard, then. He was eating our green chile stew and . . ." I stopped before adding another *er*.

Ana-Grace had heard. "Yeah, everyone's heard. Weird, huh? Addie said he was eating and she was filming and then he got as sick as a cow on jimson weed." She lowered her voice. "I shouldn't be saying, but that's what the doctors are looking into. They're running tests."

Cows? Jimson weed? I had to ask for clarification.

"Poison," Ana-Grace said, sending shivers up my arms. "The docs don't know what type yet. Possibly a nasty plant like jimson or a bad mushroom got into his food by mistake."

Or not *by mistake.* I gripped the phone.

Ana-Grace said, "Oops. My switchboard's lighting up. Gotta go. Be careful what you eat, okay?"

D o you know anything about jimson weed?" I asked Celia as she settled into the passenger's seat. I was driving us both today. Celia often carpooled with a friend and the friend's teacher mom. This morning, however, she had to go in early to set up a theater backdrop she'd helped paint. I, meanwhile, was running late. So much for my noble vows of walking or running to work. I'd left an apologetic message on the café's answering machine for Flori. I could blame the long wait on the hospital switchboard. More truthfully, I'd overslept. My dreams had been a repeating reel of nightmare images featuring Jenkins as a walking-dead zombie inspector and ghostly Napoleon berating me for not solving his murder. Dream Napoleon had called me an idiot and thrown crepes at me, and then we'd gotten on a roller coaster with Flori's mariachi band and I couldn't find my purse. Only near morning—and unfortunately after I'd shut off my snooze button—did I fall into a more peaceful sleep.

Celia stopped messing with her cell phone and looked up. "Jimson? Is that what the health inspector guy ate? It's supposed to make you high. Really messed up."

I clamped my lips shut before *Don't do drugs!* fell out. Instead, I asked what she knew.

"You know that famous flower painting by Georgia O'Keeffe?" my daughter said. "Okay, I know, she did tons of them, but it's a white flower, really up close? The one that sold a while back for like forty-four million? That's datura. Jimson weed. You've seen it. There's some in Victor's garden down in a sunny spot by the creek."

"Kind of like a big morning glory?" I asked.

"Yeah," my daughter confirmed. "But they have spiny fruits that kind of look like prickly pears, and they're poisonous, even to touch but especially if you eat the fruits and seeds. Some kids from my school ate a bunch of datura." Celia shook her dyed head. "Stupid. They ended up getting their stomachs pumped."

Definitely stupid, I agreed. I felt better about Celia, if not the ailing food inspector. "Honey," I ventured, since my daughter seemed to be in a sharing mood, "are you hanging out with some new friends lately?"

She shot me a frown. "Yeah, some. It's no big deal."

No big deal unless her new friends were a bad influence. I took a deep breath and launched into my stay safe and smart speech. I wrapped up with, "As you said, drugs are really stupid, like skipping out of class. You wouldn't want friends like that, right?"

Celia lowered her mascara-coated eyelids. "Geez, Mom, what's going on? I thought we were just talking about jimson poison and now you're getting all intense. I have a new friend or two. It doesn't mean I've ditched school or my old friends. Things change, isn't that what you told me? Look at you and Dad, and you kicking out Dad."

Okay, she had me, although I didn't kick Manny out. I'm the one who left. He kept the house and garage, where a bunch of my stuff still languished in storage boxes. Anyway, he was the one who cheated.

"Relationships *do* change," I said, diplomatically.

"Right!" Celia exclaimed as if I'd just affirmed her teenage worldview. She inspected her clumps of mascara in the visor mirror. "Like you and your new boyfriends."

I caught the stressed plural on "boyfriends," as Celia had intended.

"What?" I asked my daughter. "I don't have an actual 'boyfriend' let alone a bunch of them."

"How about that guy Georgio?" Celia teased. "He gave me a ride downtown last night. We talked about art, and he said he wanted to stop by and see you again."

I blinked and tried my best to appear calm. "Celia, I'm sorry, I should have given you a ride yesterday or let you take the car. Please don't accept rides from Mr. Andre again."

"Why? Because he's an art thief?"

I gaped at my daughter. *How did she know about that?*

Celia laughed. "Don't worry, Mom. I didn't grill

him about crimes like you and Flori would have. I've read about him in the paper. He sure knows a lot about art. He told me all about that painting he wants to buy." She fiddled with her cell phone. "He said that even if Victor's art goes into storage for a while, it's okay. When it comes out, it'll be like it's brand new, a surprise again, like that painting he wants. I don't get why he likes that one so much, though."

Celia raised her earbuds. Before she plugged in, she said, "Anyway, it's your big date night tonight, right? When I stopped by Tres Amigas last weekend, Flori said I should tell you to make chocoflan. She's right, you know. That's the most awesome cake ever."

"Flori has some extreme dating ideas," I told my daughter, who snorted in laughter.

We swung by Celia's school. She got out, still plugged into her headphones. Before she shut the door, she gave me a wink. "Good luck tonight, Mom!"

I had a feeling I'd need luck, and not only tonight.

My feeling was confirmed when I reached Tres Amigas.

The CLOSED sign dangled in the front door. A few would-be customers waited outside, checking their watches and cell phones. I checked my watch too, although I knew it was already past opening time.

"You're closed?" one of the women asked, recognizing me. Her brow wrinkled in worry and incomprehension. "You're never closed on Fridays. This is Friday, right? I didn't miss a day?"

Oh, it was Friday, all right. I'd double- and quadruple-checked that myself. I was starting to worry when Flori opened the door a crack and handed out a paper bag.

"Muffins on the house," she said to the ladies. To me, she said, "We have a small problem in the kitchen, Rita dear."

I feared I knew the problem. What I wasn't prepared for was who was delivering the bad news.

Manny posed in front of the mannequin band, flashing a smile as he snapped a selfie. When he saw me, he stuffed the phone in his pocket and put on his cop-business face. "Shutting you down here, Rita. You almost killed a man. It's unlike you. Usually you only stumble on the bodies."

"Can he do this?" I asked Flori.

My elderly friend wore a fluffy red cardigan over her tai-chi attire. For a moment she seemed frail to me. Then she straightened to her full petite height.

"He can't, but we'll take the day off for propriety's sake." She raised her voice and said, pointedly, "And so we have time to investigate who actually poisoned that dirty man."

"Some would say *you* poisoned him." Manny flashed his toothpaste-model smile at us. "In fact, that's what Mr. Jenkins himself says. The doctors are thinking poison mushrooms. Did you slip some in his chile stew?"

Flori's frown suggested confusion mixed with a

hint of disgust. "Mushrooms? No one puts mushrooms in green chile stew."

Jenkins knew he didn't eat mushrooms here, I was sure of that. The man was a liar. Besides, he'd seemed feverish before taking a single sip of stew. I described his preexisting symptoms to my ex, ending with, "If you don't believe us, Addie has it all on video."

"And why exactly is that?" Manny asked in over-the-top exasperation.

"So he couldn't plant another cockroach," Flori said, as if this should be obvious. She waved a finger at Manny. "You should be investigating health inspector Jenkins. He and Napoleon were wrapped up in dirty business together."

Manny snorted. "I'll be investigating here first. I need to see your frozen food."

It figured that Manny would be checking the freezer. My ex's cooking skills were limited to microwaving TV dinners and opening cans of soup. He had little interest in food in general. Other than New Mexican, Tex-Mex, and Mexican, he steered clear of regional and ethnic foods, and when it came to green vegetables, he had the culinary range of a fussy toddler. In retrospect, I should have taken Manny's eating habits as a sign of our incompatibility. Love is blind, though, and sometimes lacking taste buds too.

Bunny emerged from the kitchen, followed by Juan. "I've bagged everything that looks like a mushroom," she said. "Your turn to check the freezer, Manny."

Manny left, grumbling. Bunny gave a rare smile. "We drew straws for the frozen duty," she said.

"I'm glad you won, dear," Flori said, and offered her some coffee. "Unless you're scared of our food," she added.

Bunny, who lifts weights for fun, flexed broad shoulders. "You don't scare me, and I sure wouldn't mind one of your health muffins. But first I have something to show you ladies. We're not only here for that sick inspector. We're still investigating a murder. Do either of you recognize this knife?"

I caught Juan's widened eyes. He shook his head ever so slightly side to side.

Bunny drew a clear plastic evidence bag from her inner jacket pocket and held it up for us to see.

"Juan here denied recognizing any knives," Bunny said. "Even the one he was chopping onions with. This knife, it was found in some mulch by a tree a few feet from Napoleon's body."

Standing behind Bunny, Juan shook his head more vigorously and mouthed what I thought was *No*.

I recognized the knife and I knew that Flori did too. So would Juan. The blade was common enough, about seven inches long and what my culinary school instructors would have termed a general utility knife. The handle, however, was one of a kind. I stared at the familiar carving on the worn obsidian, an outline of an owl done in a Native American style. Linda had used this knife for as long as I'd known her and probably much longer than that. She kept it in her cart and used it for mundane tasks like opening packaging and cutting the corn husk ties around her tamales. I let Flori answer.

"That's Linda's," she said without hesitation.
"It's the murder weapon," Bunny said.

Bunny had a search warrant allowing her to look for more than mushrooms. She wanted access to our personal lockers, where we kept changes of clothes and, in Addie's case, extra wigs. Manny, meanwhile, was acting needy in the walk-in fridge and freezer. The man did not know his food.

"What's this?" he asked, petulantly, with each package he pulled.

Juan excelled at stoic, one-word answers. Leaving him to deal with Manny, I was about to step out to the patio when my phone buzzed. I wrenched it from my pocket a ring before its cutoff for voice mail.

Jake's name flashed up on the caller ID. "Rita," he said abruptly. "Have you seen Manny?"

I'd seen more than enough of Manny. "He and Bunny are here at Tres Amigas searching for poison mushrooms." I inhaled deeply and exhaled bad news. "They have a knife, Jake. Linda's knife. Bunny said it's the murder weapon."

"Yep," Jake replied. "I heard. Manny called me. Said I have an hour to find Linda and bring her to the police station or else they'll put out an APB on her. I'd rather save her the embarrassment. Thing is, I can't find her. I've been by her house. I've called her and Flori's cell and the café number. No one's answering, and the café phone says you're closed?"

"I'll ask Flori and call you right back," I said. Poor Linda. It's what we'd all expected, but the reality still shocked me.

"Wait, Rita," Jake said. "I forgot to say good morning."

"Oh, that's okay—"

"And how much I'm looking forward to tonight." He hung up.

"Your cheeks are as red as a chile," Flori said with a chuckle. "Was that about your date tonight? Did you make magic chocoflan? You know it's best to let it sit a few hours or overnight for the flan to set and the cake to get all nice and moist from the caramel."

I had made flan last night, without any chocolate cake attached. Scouring my cookbooks and online recipe sites had been a fun distraction. Thinking of my French-Mexican theme, I'd hedged between a recipe for Parisian flan and the caramel-draped Mexican classic. The Parisian variety is firmer, set in a buttery shortcrust and baked to golden brown on top. A great advantage is that no flipping is involved and thus less chance for mishaps. The classic local flan resembles a Midwest egg custard, although better because it bakes in a caramel sauce. If all goes right, the caramel forms a pretty topping, and I had fresh strawberries and whipped cream on hand to cover any flipping flaws.

"That's not why Jake called," I said, breaking into her talk of the romantic potential of chocoflan. "He said that the police plan to arrest Linda." My throat tightened. "He needs to find her and get her to the police station. Do you know where she is?"

Juan, sitting at the counter nearby, uttered some holy names.

Flori took the news with the calmness of a tai-chi master. "I expected that," she said. "Tell Jake to try the Cathedral. At this hour, if Linda's not home and not here, that's where she'll be."

"It'll be okay," I said, reaching for my phone. "She's innocent and Jake will help her."

"We will too," Flori said, but her voice cracked.

I caught Juan's eye and guessed his thoughts. *What if we couldn't help her?*

Chapter 19

I arrived panting at the Cathedral, having jogged-walked the several blocks from Tres Amigas. Jake waited by the massive front doors. He hefted one open and we entered to the front gift shop where the Cathedral sold books and art.

"Did Flori say where Linda might be?" he asked. He held his hat respectfully in his hand. His boots made a clogging sound against the wood floor.

"No, she suggested we try the main area or Conquistadora's chapel first."

In the grand, main space a few tourists snapped photos of the high arches, soaring heavenward and painted in intricate patterns of red, green, and gold over creamy white. Sun beaming through the stained-glass windows cast rainbows across the floor and pews, and the air smelled of candle wax and lilies.

I nodded toward a figure hunched in prayer. Jake and I approached, but as we got closer, I

knew it wasn't Linda. Linda also wasn't pray-
ing to Our Lady of Peace, a seventeenth-century
wooden statue of the Virgin Mary, also known as
La Conquistadora.

"Back rooms?" I asked, but neither of us knew
how to access them.

"I'll look for someone official to ask," Jake said.
"Maybe you can peek in that silent prayer room."

I lingered, gazing up at La Conquistadora's
placid face and her resplendent blue velvet robe.
Jake's footsteps sounded up the aisle and then a
familiar voice wrecked the tranquility. Manny
greeted Jake in a fake chummy tone.

"Ah, Rita," my ex said when I returned to
the main chapel. "When you ran off from Tres
Amigas, I figured you were going somewhere important. I should thank you. You got me out of my
freezer duties." He laughed as if I would find this
amusing too.

A young policeman in uniform pushed through
the double doors. His eyes rose to the ceiling and
even I, a terrible lip-reader, understood his silent
mouthing of *Wow* as he took in the beauty.

Manny snorted. "Newcomer. We're here to
work, deputy, not sightsee. Our suspect is an older
woman. Gray hair—"

"More like deep black hair with lovely silver
highlights and cute bangs," I corrected. "And six-
ties are not old."

"About five-foot-five and possibly armed,"
Manny continued. "Wanted for murder."

The deputy's eyes widened. Gripping the butt of
his gun, he headed down the aisle, peeking under
pews as he went.

"Oh come on," I said in exasperation. "You know that Linda's not dangerous, Manny."

My ex shrugged. "She owns a gun, Rita. Not to mention knives. I know it's hard to accept, but face facts. Her fingerprints are all over the murder weapon." He instructed the deputy to head left while he took the right side of the building.

"Of course her fingerprints are on the knife," I said, knowing I'd have better luck conversing with one of the deceased archbishops entombed nearby. "It's her knife!"

"Sure is. Her own mother acknowledged that," Manny said, aiming this jibe at Jake.

My dinner date leaned against a pew, boots crossed, thumbs looped in the pockets of his dark jeans. "I'm sure my client will readily identify her knife," he said coolly. "And will remind the police that said knife was left in an unsecured, public location overnight for the actual murderer to steal."

"Whatever," Manny said, adopting a favorite line from our teenage daughter. "Let's find your client, shall we?" He headed for the altar and massive pipe organ. Jake chose the confessionals, tapping lightly on each door before peeking inside.

I used to love hide-and-seek. Not this version. Where should I look? The gift shop? Behind a stand of flickering votive candles in red glass containers? The bishop's lounge? As it turned out, I didn't have to go anywhere. I was lingering by the baptismal font, admiring the peaceful pool and wondering if the church had any secret passages or hidden restrooms, when Linda came up beside me.

"Rita? What are you doing here?"

"Linda!" I exclaimed, loud enough to send the

patrolman spinning. Manny, who had been tapping a drum set by the choir box, tensed into his supercop stance, feet apart and knees flexed. The look suggested he was ready to shoot to kill, or return a tennis serve.

"Hands in the air!" Manny commanded, his hand resting on his service holster.

Without thinking, I stepped in front of a gasping Linda. "Manny Martin, stop that right now!" I said in the voice I once used on misbehaving kids at Celia's elementary school summer camp.

Linda put a steady hand on my shoulder. "I'm sorry," she said. "You were all looking for me?"

If there's such a thing as having a too-nice syndrome, Linda has it, and there's no curing her. She continued to apologize for causing everyone trouble.

"Linda, please don't apologize. He shouldn't talk to you like that," I said, adding, "Especially not in church." My jibe lobbed over Manny's head. He did, however, break from his melodramatic stance. He and Jake converged in front of us as Linda apologized profusely.

"Oh, I should apologize to you all. I hope you weren't looking for me too long. I was in the back, mending a dress. I'm on the committee to help preserve La Conquistadora's wardrobe. We have to get ready. We're exhibiting her outfits and jewelry for her Procession this summer."

"Neat," the young deputy said, earning a frown from Manny.

It was neat. I'd seen La Conquistadora parade across town last summer, along with a thousand or so of her fans, many dressed in seventeenth-century costumes. The event had given me goose bumps, and I would have loved to view her sacred closet. Devotees present her with fine, hand-sewn outfits that the Cathedral carefully preserves and only rarely displays. I couldn't beg Linda for a peek now, though.

"Linda," I said. "You know why we're here? Why the police wanted to find you?"

She patted me comfortingly on the arm. "Of course. They think I killed Napoleon. I am so very sorry for fighting with him. I've already gone to confession and apologized."

No! I wanted to yell at her. *Stop apologizing and saying "confess"!* I raised my eyebrows in a frantic "do something" gesture to Jake.

He already was. Taking Linda by the elbow, he said to Manny, "Ms. Santiago will ride to the station with me. If I'm not mistaken, Detective, I still have time in our 'gentleman's' agreement to escort my client to your office."

I appreciated the edge Jake landed on "gentleman" and his polite gestures. He held the door. I stepped through to find Bunny in the lobby bookshop, along with two priests, a gaggle of gift shop ladies, and several neck-craning tourists.

"We got our suspect," Manny's voice boomed behind us. A few of the tourists held camera phones high to take pictures. The gift shop ladies gasped, their fingers dancing on rosary beads.

"Head high, Linda," Jake said softly.

Outside, I blinked at the brightness. Jake offered me his other arm, but I declined, telling him to help Linda. I probably should have accepted. Linda was fine and fit, whereas I not only had watery eyes but also achy legs, thanks to yesterday's overambitious jog. I could see enough to spot an irritation, though.

Slips of paper fluttered under the wiper of Jake's car. "Really, Manny?" I said to my ex, who was bounding happily down the front steps. "*Two* parking tickets?"

Manny feigned innocence. "What can I do, Rita? This car's illegally parked. In front of a church." He grinned at Bunny, who didn't reciprocate. Catching my eye, she shrugged slightly. I could guess who'd written the citations.

Jake collected the tickets without complaint and helped Linda into his car. She scrunched down low in the front seat. While Jake was being the chivalrous chauffeur, I noticed another assault on his otherwise spotless car: a tow-notice sticker, bright pink, slapped on the driver's side window. This time I didn't bother with verbal sarcasm. I rolled my eyes and head theatrically. I needn't have bothered. My ex didn't see my performance. His eyes were on his favorite subject. Pretty women.

Brigitte and Crystal, minus their crepe and juice carts, rushed up San Francisco Street. Crystal's skirt, as bright red as her hibiscus tea and taut as mango skin, edged up her thighs as she trotted to keep up with Brigitte. Brigitte, taking long strides, wore her usual outfit of all black, except for an apron splattered in crepe batter.

Manny stepped forward to meet them. I followed, worried that their flushed faces meant more bad news.

"Hello there," Manny said, voice as smooth and

sticky sweet as molasses. "Is there some trouble, ladies?"

"Yes, trouble," Brigitte replied as Crystal caught her breath. "We hear you are making an arrest of an innocent woman and we protest."

"Free Linda!" Crystal gasped.

Manny's glee morphed into distaste. He'd likely expected adoration for the hero cop making an arrest. "Why do you ladies want a murderess to go free?" he asked.

"Because Rita and I are hunting the actual killer," Brigitte said, and Manny's expression turned downright sour. She looped her arm around mine and tugged me close.

"Because Napoleon could drive a saintly woman to despair and beyond," Crystal added, dramatically and unhelpfully. "If Linda killed him, she deserves a medal. A medal!" She leaned around me and Brigitte and waved in the direction of Jake's car, where only the top of Linda's head was visible.

Brigitte, still firmly attached to my elbow, turned us as one to wave to Jake. "*Bonjour*, counselor," she called out, gesturing for him to join us.

Feeling decidedly short and unfashionable next to Brigitte, I wished I could scrunch down and hide like Linda. Jake, standing by his car door, hesitated before pulling his Stetson low over his forehead and coming to join us. "Ladies," he murmured politely to Crystal and Brigitte, who gave twinkling smiles in return.

"You will want to interview us, Monsieur Strong?" Brigitte asked. "Regarding Napoleon's character and finances?"

Crystal added, "We can tell you a thing or two about that man."

"I'm the one you should be talking to," Manny grumbled. "In fact, both of you have already been interviewed. Have you thought of something else to report? Did you withhold evidence?"

"Perhaps we find new evidence," Brigitte said with a French pout and shrug.

I shifted slightly away, a move that prompted her to grasp me tighter.

"What evidence?" Manny demanded.

"Ambiguities in Napoleon's financial records, specifically the outgoing payments column of miscellaneous accounts and unrecorded withdrawals and receivables. Numbers, they tell everything," Brigitte said as Manny's eyes glazed over. Attributing a crime to a wronged woman in a rage was much more his style than forensic accounting.

"Passion," Manny said. "That's what spurred this murder. Extreme emotion. Not someone who got mad about some missing withdrawals."

"But I am passionate about numbers," said Brigitte in her French accent that could make talk of numbers sound sexy.

My ex perked up. "I bet you are passionate in many ways," he said with a lascivious grin.

Try as I might, I couldn't stop a groan from escaping my lips.

Brigitte replied seriously, "I am. It is true." She turned to Jake. "I am passionate, Mr. Strong, and I wish to help solve the numeric mystery. We shall discuss the financial ambiguities over dinner, say tonight? Or do you prefer dancing?"

I was halfway thankful that Brigitte still had

my arm, otherwise I might have withered away. Would Jake forget our date? Ditch me for a tall, passionate, dancer? I studied the sidewalk, fixing on an ant struggling to carry off a potato chip triple its size.

"Well, that's a mighty kind offer," Jake replied smoothly as the ant dropped the chip and my heart sank. "But I have dinner plans with a special lady tonight. Rita here is making me a Cinco de Mayo soufflé."

"Oh," Brigitte said. She dropped my arm and twisted my shoulders into an embrace. "Rita, you sly girl, I thought we were friends and yet you do not tell me you're fixing a French feast? A soufflé? *Très romantique! Très difficile, non?* Me, I would be in the kitchen already, making preparations."

I felt all eyes on me and my cheeks burning. I focused on the friends part. "Of course we're friends, Brigitte!" I said. "And I've tested the soufflé recipe a couple of times. It's pretty good, except the one that fell and the one that burned my tongue and . . ." I stopped talking.

Brigitte patted my arm. "So many soufflés to taste. No wonder you are jogging."

"Yep, more jogging tomorrow," I said, feeling a sting of French shaming. "First thing tomorrow morning."

Manny, for once, came to my rescue, albeit unintentionally.

"We'd all love to hear more about your dating and exercise attempts, Rita," he said, sarcasm oozing. "But Bunny and I have a murder suspect to book. Strong, we'll follow your car."

Jake tipped his hat to me, Linda, and Crystal before returning to Linda.

"Ah, now there's a man," Crystal sighed. "I bet he wouldn't use a good woman and toss her away like that beast, Napoleon."

She stomped off, heading back toward the Plaza, but not before I'd seen tears welling in her eyes.

Brigitte saw them too. She nudged me in the ribs. "Now it is clear."

Was it? I asked Brigitte what she meant.

She kept her eyes on Crystal's departing form. "Yes, clear. I said to myself when Napoleon shut down Crystal's juice cart, why does he do this? Juice, it is no competitor to his crepes or restaurants. But, what if Crystal and Napoleon fought for other reasons? What if they had a tryst, a relationship that went poorly?" She turned to me. "I asked the kitchen staff, the gossipers. The stupid girl, DeeDee, she reported seeing Napoleon and Crystal together in his office at OhLaLa. Several times, after hours. Then, one night, yelling and weeping." She shrugged. "It is not unexpected. Napoleon, he . . . what is the phrase? Destroyed his romantic bridges?"

"Burned his bridges," I said, still processing the main part of Brigitte's message. Crystal's tears and bitter words did suggest a more personal pain than food cart clashes. What would she see in him in the first place? Power? Mean charisma? Infatuation with crepes?

"Crystal's married with three kids," I pointed out, knowing full well from my philandering ex that marriage vows presented no barrier to trysting.

"Exactly what Napoleon preferred," Brigitte said. "Napoleon, he wanted what others had, and he wanted no romantic commitment. Crystal is exactly his type. Petite, pretty, married, sweet . . . gullible."

As I walked back to Tres Amigas, I thought about Crystal's tears and Manny's words. I hated to admit it, but my ex could be right. Maybe Napoleon's death wasn't about finance or food inspections. Maybe it was a crime of passion.

Chapter 20

B y late afternoon I'd run out of preparations for my home-cooked meal. I'd grated cheese, separated eggs, and twice checked my roasted chiles to ensure that they weren't firebombs in disguise. The soufflé required only simmering and assembling the cheese sauce, whipping the egg whites, and folding everything together. Oh, and saying a prayer to San Pasqual the kitchen saint that the soufflé would rise and stay risen. I once again rehearsed my culinary game plan. While putting together the soufflé, I'd roast fresh spring asparagus to golden brown. When it was done, I'd pop in the soufflé, along with a gratin of sweet cherry tomatoes tossed with garlic, olive oil, Parmesan, and crusty baguette cubes. Right before the soufflé came out, I'd drizzle the asparagus with a French-Mex vinaigrette of lime, cilantro, and Dijon and top it with crispy tortilla strips and toasted pine nuts. Then, *voilà*, as Brigitte would say. Dinner would be ready to serve.

I looked around the small living room, wondering what I'd forgotten. I'd already tried on half my wardrobe and settled on a soft charcoal gray dress that felt like a T-shirt and yet looked dressy casual with black tights and a new yellow belt that Celia claimed made the outfit "pop." I'd removed cat fur and magazines from the sofa, brushed Hugo, sipped calming tea, and paced not so calmly. There was one big problem. I still had no word from Linda or from Jake.

I checked my watch for the millionth time. How long did getting arrested take? Would Linda have to stay in jail?

It was my own fault that I knew little of arrest procedures. I'd been married to a cop for fifteen-some years. Why hadn't I learned more about Manny's work? I'd always asked him about his day. "Fine," he'd usually say. Sometimes I tried to dig deeper, but truth be told, I hardly wanted to know. For most of Celia's childhood, we'd lived in a leafy suburb of Chicago. Manny, however, worked in urban neighborhoods that too often made the nightly news, and not in a good way. He'd told me some about the gangs he dealt with and sad tales of neglected kids and senseless deaths. I sympathized and still did, even if Manny and I didn't see eye-to-eye. Being a cop anywhere can be tough, dangerous, and scary. To a lesser extent, so is being a cop's spouse.

Readjusting the oven rack to soufflé height, an image of Linda behind bars flashed before me. I pictured her in an orange prison jumpsuit, languishing in a dingy cell, eating awful slop from a tray. No, that wouldn't be Linda. Linda would set up a literacy program and teach other inmates to make wholesome slop. She'd be calm and helpful, like I wished I could be. I picked up a mewing Hugo and paced. Maybe Flori had heard something and forgotten to call. I doubted this, but with Hugo purring in one ear, I dialed Flori's number. Her daughters bought her a cell phone last year, insisting she carry it for safety. She carried it, but the phone faced the most danger. Flori tended to drop it into stew pots, and just last week she'd nearly roasted it with a pork shoulder.

To my surprise, she picked up after the second ring, answering with a "Shhhh" followed by rustling.

I automatically whispered back, "Flori, what's going on? Are you in the library?"

"Rita? Is that you?" she said, voice still low. "I thought I was quieting the ringer, not answering."

"Thanks a lot," I grumbled.

"Now, now," my friend chuckled. "I intended to call you later. Any news from your handsome Mr. Strong?"

"None! I hate waiting! I want to do something." More rustling ensued on Flori's side of the line. "What are *you* doing?"

"Spying, of course," she replied. "I couldn't sit around waiting either. I didn't invite you along because you have a hot date tonight. Did you come to your senses and make chocoflan?"

I had half a mind to cancel the date. How could I think of fun, let alone romance and soufflés, if Linda was in jail? I pushed aside these thoughts and focused on a more immediate concern. "Spying on whom?" Her target couldn't be Jenkins. He was probably still in the hospital and low on our suspect list, unless he'd poisoned himself on purpose or accident. My stomach flipped, dreading what I knew Flori was about to say.

"Don Busco. I'm hiding behind some *chamisa* along the side of his house. He really should prune them so he gets better blooms."

I wasn't worried about Don's shrubbery maintenance. *Chamisa*, or rabbitbrush, was hardy. It grew in wild pastures and along roadsides, erupting in gorgeous yellow blooms and sage-green feathery leaves. "Flori, what if Don is the killer?" Another thought struck me. "What if he's a poisoner too? That would mean he's escalating, like the psychokiller he keeps trying to pin the crime on. You should get out of there now and—"

My octogenarian pal cut off my protests. "I'm just fine. Don's sitting at his computer with his back to the window and doesn't know I'm here. If he weren't so big shouldered, I could get a view of what he's so interested in on that machine."

Short of driving over to Don's and abducting Flori, there was no way to dissuade her. Still, I gave it one last try. "What if he does look out and see you, Flori? You should get out of there."

Her *"pah"* expressed what she thought of that. "I have my pepper spray and handcuffs and police whistle and this phone you girls insist I carry. I'm fine. I'm sitting near an ant mound, that's my only problem. Ants everywhere." Slapping sounds ensued and Flori hung up.

When the phone rang again, I expected Flori and an update on ants or a murderer. Instead, Jake's name flashed across the caller ID.

My relief spilled out. "Jake! Are you two free? I mean, is Linda free? How is she?"

His drawn out, "Well . . ." sent my excitement level plummeting.

"Well?"

"We're going to be stuck here awhile longer," he said slowly. "I'm cautiously optimistic that I can get her out on bail, or maybe even on her own reconnaissance. I'm waiting on a judge who's been delayed. I'm so sorry, Rita. About tonight—"

Getting Linda out was all I wanted to hear. I cut off Jake's apologies. "Of course! We should postpone in any case. Linda's all that matters. Can I bring you anything? Food? Walk Winston? Anything?"

He said a neighbor kid was entertaining Winston. He also declined food. "I wouldn't waste your fine home-cooking on this dismal place. I am sorry. I was truly looking forward to this evening."

So was I, I realized when I hung up. "Oh well," I said glumly to Hugo. "You and me, buddy." He purred as if this was the best news since his last tuna treat.

I texted Celia, telling her to be safe and have fun with her friend Rosa tonight.

Linda? She texted right back.

In a message she'd usually laugh off as too long,

a "mom text," I explained that Jake was still working to get her out.

Her *SORRY* came with a glum-faced emoticon.

Yeah, I was sorry too, most of all for Linda. I
slumped on the couch, Hugo still latched onto my
shoulder, and turned on the TV. I was flipping
through my dozen free-access channels, half of
which were in Spanish, when a horn beeped in
the driveway. Hugo launched himself off me, all
claws out, and sped down the hall.

The beeping sounded happy. Could Jake have
sprung Linda early?

The female voice and British accent dashed that
idea. So did the old panel van airbrushed with
images of the Union Jack, the Queen, and corgis.
Addie waved from the vehicle she called the
Queen Mum. " 'Ello, Rita! I've come to collect you
for a wee bit of spying!"

M iss Flori heard from Mr. Strong," Addie said
after I'd apologized to Hugo, changed, and
locked up. Anything was better than sitting
around waiting, I'd rationalized. Well, almost
anything. Addie turned on an Adele CD and
pumped the gas.

"The Mum's a bit temperamental in springtime,"
she informed me, right before letting up the clutch
and punching the accelerator. We barreled up the
driveway and sped across town. "Miss Flori told
me to hurry and collect you. I left her out in the
shrubbery. No place for a lady."

That was for sure. I hoped that ants were still the worst of Flori's problems. When we turned onto Don's street, a few blocks west of downtown, we found Flori standing in the street waving her arms.

"Just in time!" she said, sliding open the side door and climbing in. "He left a minute ago, heading thataway, toward Guadalupe Street, I'd bet."

"Right'o! Buckle up!" Addie declared, and we zoomed off thataway.

Despite the jerks and jolts of Addie's driving, I relaxed in her tartan-covered passenger seat, confident that we'd lost Don Busco. Yes, I'd wanted action, but not the risk of chasing a suspect. When Flori and Addie accepted that we'd lost him, we could go out for pizza or crumpets and discuss our next move. I reclined my seat a few inches and watched adobe and brick storefronts go by. Barbecue at Whole Hog would be fun. Or Fire and Hops, which served local brews and tasty nibbles, although Flori gets rowdy on even a thimbleful of beer. If we did go out, I planned to call Cass to see if she could join us. With all the activity of this week, I hadn't seen much of my best friend.

"There he is! The red truck at high noon!" Flori crowed from the backseat.

"Tallyho!" Addie declared, stomping on the gas and crushing my hopes for BBQ.

The Queen Mum isn't a subtle spy van. Its base color is royal blue, which could blend with the turquoise New Mexican sky. Its embellishments, however, make it stand out, to say the least. Addie's cousin Jesús, a true master of automotive airbrushing, had gone wild on the Mum. Queen Elizabeth waves from the hood, ringed by fluffy-hatted Royal Guards. The side panels feature corgis, the Queen's favorite dog, romping with sheep and bagpipers over fields of heather. Union Jacks grace the roof and rearview mirrors. Only on its back doors does the Queen Mum slightly blend in with the landscape and other painted vehicles. There, Jesús painted a southwestern scene of red buttes and blue skies, above which floated Addie's name in flowery cursive script.

"We should stay far back. We're easily identifiable," I said, pointing out the obvious. Don barreled up the entrance ramp for the freeway, headed toward the pretty village of Tesuque and the world-famous Santa Fe Opera.

Addie stayed several cars behind. We passed the opera house, an amazing, open-air structure tucked amidst rolling hills. Cass had gotten tickets one summer and we'd gone on a warm August night to see *Carmen*. I'd been as entranced by the lightning flashing over the distant Sangre de Cristo Mountains as by the flamboyant costumes and booming voices.

"Never did understand opera," Addie remarked. "But those girls do belt it out. I like that."

"What will we do if we catch up with Don?" I asked, changing the subject back to the tailing at hand.

Rustling in the backseat suggested that Flori had come prepared. "We'll observe first. I have my zoom lens," she said. "In case he meets up with a co-conspirator."

Who would he be meeting out here? We were near some reservation lands, and farther north, the turnoff to Los Alamos. The government laboratory town, perched high on the Pajarito Plateau, had remained shrouded in secrecy during World War II as its scientists worked to develop the atomic bomb. If a whole town and the deadliest of weapons could be kept secret, what hope did we have in figuring out a dead man's secrets? Or Don's?

"Heads up," Flori said from the backseat. "Our target is turning right . . . right into our hands."

Chapter 21

Addie swung into the parking lot of the Golden Owl Casino and Resort, and I had a flashback to a Thanksgiving about seven years ago. This was before Manny and I moved permanently to Santa Fe, and we'd come to visit his family. Manny, however, soon tired of family festivities and decided we needed to do something "fun." He'd settled on a boxing match out here at the Owl. Boxing will never be my idea of fun, especially when I could be blissing out on Thanksgiving leftovers. Seeing the two-story owl outlined in flashing gold lights, I remembered my disgust midway through the first round or bout or whatever the initial flurry of punching was called. I'd slipped away to the Owl's museum, a fascinating collection that included ancient Pueblo cooking pots and utensils. I'd enjoyed that, although Manny grumbled all the way home that I didn't support his interests.

"Oooo," Addie said as the Mum jolted into

lower gear. "It's Friday, isn't it? They have heavy metal cover bands here on Fridays. They're a hoot. I saw a group doing KISS a few weekends ago."

"Ha!" Flori said. "A hoot! Good one, Addie. The Owl's buffet is something special too. Before I put my foot down about gambling, Bernard used to drive us out here for the weekend buffets. They had crab legs by the bucket."

I felt that I should say something nice too, so I made a pitch for the Owl's museum.

"We'll come back, let's promise," Addie said. "And we'll bring Junior and Jake and Bernard and Cass and play no more than five dollars each in the machines." She slowed, hesitating as Don parked by the entrance.

"How about over there, behind that tour bus by the putting green?" Flori suggested. We pulled up between a towering bus with Texas plates and the edge of the golf course. Don shrugged on a leather jacket with so much fringe it reminded me of Flori's donkey piñata. He added a matching buckskin cowboy hat and headed for the casino.

Flori got out first. "Okay girls," she said. "Let's blend in."

Blending wasn't necessary in the main room. No one gave us a second, or even first, look. There was so much else to look at, like the flashing machines and disco ball chandeliers and chaotically patterned carpet. Flori, Addie, and I stopped in a rare empty spot amidst the machines.

"Do either of you see him?" I asked. A big man in a cowboy hat would typically be easy to spot. Not here. At least a dozen men, probably some of the tour-bus Texans, sported similar outfits.

"There!" Addie said, pointing to doors on the far end of the room. "He just went through those doors. I recognized his fringe."

We wove through the slot machines to gilt-framed doors. A young man with an owl embroidered on his suit jacket stood in front of the doors.

Flori stepped up. "Thank you for getting that door for us, dear," she said, playing her grandmotherly card.

The doorman didn't move except to say, "This is the members-only Golden Feather poker lounge. Are you Gold Owl Supreme Club members?"

"Yes, that's us, supreme owls," Flori said before I had time to worry about lying. "Addie, Rita, did you bring our owl cards?"

"There are no cards," the man said, backing up against the door handle.

Flori took this setback in stride. "Silly me," she said. "Well, no matter. We need to get inside. Addie's husband needs her at the card table for good luck."

Addie nodded vigorously. "Yep, me husband. I'm a lucky charm, I am!" she exclaimed, sounding more faux Irish than her usual British.

The door guy—rightfully so—looked unconvinced. Luckily for us, four men in slick suits had stepped up, along with one guy in torn jeans and an Isotopes baseball cap. Door guy sprang into action. "Mr. Robbins," he said, bumping me aside as he swung the gold door open wide. I expected one of the suits to step forward. Instead, the kid in grungy jeans slouched by with a tip of his chin to the doorman.

"We're with him," Flori said, and we and the businessmen piled through.

Once inside, I silently thanked the grungy guy. If he hadn't been there, I could have won the worst-dressed prize. Following behind him, I looked straight ahead, trying to pretend I knew what I was doing. This worked until the kid reached a velvet-topped table, where he was once again welcomed effusively.

"Time for us to find Don," I said to Flori.

"We already have," she said, nodding to the next table over. Don, seated, would have been looking right at us if he wasn't staring at the cards in his hand. I instinctively shrunk back. Addie and Flori, however, were already approaching Don's table.

"You guys," I whispered, catching up with them next to a rock column. "What are you doing? He'll see us, and none of us have the money to gamble. I overheard a guy back there saying the chips are a hundred dollars, minimum."

Flori was undeterred. "We'll get behind him. He's not looking."

Skirting wide around Don's table, I saw him shove forward and promptly lose a stack of chips. His face crumpled. Had he really just blown four hundred dollars? Hot dogs must pay a lot more than café tips. Either that or he had a side business, one involving Gerald Jenkins, perhaps?

Don reached into his jacket pocket, and I grabbed Flori by her sleeve. "Look! That's the envelope! The one that Junior passed to Don. I'm

sure of it." Don extracted a wad of cash and exchanged it for more chips.

Flori reached for her bag. "Gotcha," she said,
raising her camera and snapping a bunch of
photos.

Except we were the ones gotten. The security
guard stomping toward us was big, bald, and out-
fitted in all black, right down to the earpiece bulging from his left ear.

"No pictures in the poker room," he said, reaching for Flori's camera. He didn't add please to his
request or his expression.

"Sorry!" I said, mortified for all our sakes.
"We're leaving, right ladies?"

"Not until you delete your photos," the big guy
said. He touched his earpiece, which was probably demanding the same thing, or confiscation
of Flori's camera.

Flori sniffed loudly. "Terrible customer service.
We'll be telling our entire tour group to avoid
this room. In fact, we'll go to Apache Nugget or
Buffalo Thunder next time." She moved to step
around the big man, whose bald head glowed in a
threatening shade of red.

Mom hadn't taught me casino manners, but I
suspected that bringing up rival casinos was a big
faux pas. "Shh . . . don't upset him," I urged Flori.
To the big guy, I said, "We weren't taking photos
of the casino or cards. They're of a guy. That guy."
I pointed with my right index finger, hiding the
gesture behind the palm of my left hand.

His look informed me that no technicalities were
allowed in the Owl's photo policy. He reached for
Flori's camera. She raised her other hand in tai-

chi striking pose, a move that confused the guard long enough for Flori to slip the camera to me. "Go!" she whispered.

I went, dodging the guys in suits and out the gilt doors. When I looked back, I was glad to see Addie and Flori hurrying toward me. My relief, however, was short-lived.

The guard, frowning, had a finger pressed to his ear. His expression suggested trouble, but I saw worse trouble. Don Busco had stood up and was staring straight at me.

I froze as Don's stare morphed into a glare. Unable to pretend I didn't see him, I raised my hand in a friendly little wave that wasn't returned. Don picked up his remaining chips and headed my way.

"Hurry, hurry, he's spotted us," I said to Addie and Flori when they reached the door.

"I'll get the Mum." Addie sprinted off, showing speed I didn't know she possessed. I stayed with Flori, who'd probably moved like a roadrunner in her twenties but not in her eighties. We'd made it across the psychedelic carpet and to the front doors when Don caught up with us.

"Rita," he said, his voice chummy with a frosty edge. "What a surprise to see you and Flori here."

"Girls night out," I stammered.

Flori, a much better lie improviser than me, added, "We were looking for the buffet. The one with the crab legs and shrimp cocktails. Have you seen it?"

Don snorted. "Right, sure you were out lookin' for a buffet. I know you're meddling and why you're doing it: Linda. I *will* take care of her. You stay out of this."

Take care of her? I didn't like the sound of that. "Stay out of what?" I dared ask. "Poisoning the health inspector? Murdering Napoleon?" My bluster was cut off by the belching backfires of the Queen Mum. Addie careened around the curved drive, winging a lamp pole as she did. We all jumped back as the Mum's front wheel bounced over the curb. Seeing two security men heading our way, I yanked open the passenger door, helped Flori inside, and crawled over her to the backseat.

Don grabbed the door before Flori could close it. "I mean it! For all your sakes. Don't dig any deeper or you'll get hurt."

"Sir?" the guards called to him. "What's going on here?"

"Gun it, Addie!" Flori commanded. Addie did, and the Mum roared out of the lot and down the highway toward the distant glow of Santa Fe.

My cell phone rang as we were rolling past the opera.

"Done," Jake said, exhaling the word. "We're leaving the police station now. We got lucky. Judge Alvarez knows Linda and decided that she's no flight risk or danger to the public so she's free to go."

"That's wonderful!" I relayed the good news to Flori and Addie.

"You're all together?" Jake asked. He sounded a bit suspicious.

"Er . . . girls' time," I said.

I had no hope of tricking Santa Fe's most successful defense attorney. "Right," he said, echoing Don's word of skepticism. "Where should I take Linda? She says home, but I'm reluctant to leave her on her own."

I made a split-second decision. "How about my place, if she agrees? Celia's out tonight and I could use the company."

Jake's sigh made my heart do flip-flops. "Yeah, me too . . . okay, I'll bring her by."

Addie broke speed limits, but when we reached my casita, Jake was already there, sitting on my porch bench with Linda beside him.

Flori, Addie, and I gathered Linda in a group hug.

"Thank you!" I said to Jake.

"Don't thank me yet," he said. He pointed to the Queen Mum. "What happened to your side mirror, Addie? It's dangling by a wire. What *have* you ladies been up to?"

Addie gasped at her mangled mirror and said that Jesús would be angry. Jesús, her airbrushing cousin, I hoped is whom she meant.

"We went out for a drive to see the lovely sunset," Flori said, tricking neither Jake nor Linda.

"Mama," Linda cried. "You've been out snooping and corrupting Addie and Rita again. I've told you, I'm fine. Look how it all worked out tonight."

I caught Jake's eye and the slight shake of his head. Linda wasn't fine, not with the law and maybe not with a murderer too. Don's warning buzzed through my mind. *Linda. I'll take care of her. Don't dig any deeper or you'll get hurt.*

Chapter 22

That night, Linda and I polished off half of my
would-be date-night flan and talked about
our children and never mentioned prison
or murder or poisonings. We sipped peach-
chamomile tea and went to bed before eleven,
Linda tucked in with Hugo in Celia's bedroom.
I hoped they both slept more peacefully than me.
My dreams again swirled into nightmares, this
time of Don chasing Linda, Flori, Addie, and me,
and, inexplicably, Celia, Cass, and Hugo. All of
us were crammed in the Queen Mum, careening
down a hill that got steeper and steeper until we
were falling through space.

By the time my alarm went off, my head spun
and my legs wouldn't lie still. I remembered my
vow to jog. A nice little jaunt up to the bird sanc-
tuary would fix me up, I lied to myself. Stepping
outside in a windbreaker and spandex, I doubted
my decision. A brisk north wind whooshed down

the little valley. Coffee would clear my head with a lot less effort. So would a trip to the French bakery to pick up pastry for my houseguest. Visions of croissants, *pain au chocolat*, and custard buns filled my head until replaced by a picture of svelte, athletic Brigitte. She wouldn't let a breeze and a few gray clouds hold her back. And she probably ate muesli or fruit for breakfast. I tightened my shoelaces, stuffed my phone in the armband I'd borrowed from Celia, and plugged myself into peppy eighties pop music. One heavy foot after the other, I made my way up Upper Canyon Road.

If my Midwest relatives were plopped down in the middle of Upper Canyon, they might mistake it for countryside, rather than a millionaire's row. The road is as narrow as a one-lane path in places, boxed in by protruding adobe walls and massive cottonwoods buckling the berm with their roots. Earthen-toned homes lie behind high adobe walls or, like Victor's, blend in with nature-mimicking gardens of rock and native plants with names like Apache plume, bear grass, soap weed, and soft-leaf yucca. As I jogged, I admired my surroundings and again felt lucky to have snagged such a desirable address. Passing a real estate sign, I reminded myself that I was grateful to Teresa too. My new landlady could be selling her inherited estate for a bundle instead of simply depersonalizing it. A bundle as in well over a million dollars, most likely. I wanted to stay in my little casita, and I wanted Victor's home to stay in his family.

Thoughts of my depersonalizing responsibilities distracted me from my lung-sucking agony. I'd call the art movers to take away some of the remaining items. Then I'd deal with the excess furniture. If the movers worked fast, I'd still have a few weeks to clean and have Teresa's decorator come in for a look. Easy, if only I didn't have a job, a teenager, and an off-the-books murder investigation to deal with too.

I turned up the music, letting ABBA pump up my legs. Panting and internally singing along to "Dancing Queen," I never heard the vehicle coming. I never heard a skid of brakes or a horn either. Something made me turn back, a sixth sense like Flori claims to have or a gust of warm air preceding the silver grill barreling toward me.

Fear blinded me. I glimpsed flashes of red, a dark windshield, and a bulging headlight before I turned and leaped to the side, into a scrubby patch of ditch and brush. Expecting to feel my body breaking, I clenched, thinking of Celia. How stupid that I would die doing something for my health.

The vehicle sped by in a whirl of wind, dirt, and pebbles that pelted the back of my neck. I fell hard, my palms hitting the ground first, then my elbows and chest. My scream ended in a hiccup as my lungs compressed. Rolling over on my back, I couldn't count the number of places that stung and throbbed, but the pain meant I was alive. For now.

Would the vehicle return? I scrambled deeper into the undergrowth, pulling my headphones and phone with me. A bit of perky pop music filtered through the now dangling headphones, and my phone flashed its address book as if inviting me to call a friend. For a second I thought of calling Cass, who would surely be sleeping. Or the police. Then I imagined Manny telling me I'd overreacted. I pressed the button to mute the phone's sound and listened.

In the distance, on the other side of the gentle valley of the trickling Santa Fe River, I heard a vehicle. The truck—I thought it was a truck— must be taking the higher dirt road back to town. I dared sit up and take stock of my injuries. It was not a pretty sight. A tear in my jogging tights showed gravel-burned skin, raw, filthy, and painful. I could handle scrapes. It was needles I couldn't stand.

Blood whooshed through my head as I forced myself to take stock of the cactus spines protruding from my skin. I'd rolled onto a cholla, sometimes called a walking-stick cactus because of its hard, straight latticework skeleton. If you ask me, the plant looks more like an assemblage of vicious cucumbers, armed with spines and ready to dislodge into flesh at the slightest provocation. Two chubby cholla arms impaled my elbow. Almost worse, barely visible silken slivers carpeted my arms and knees and, I feared, my forehead.

Cringing, I grabbed a chunk of cholla with my nails and yanked. The cactus attacker released my elbow but shot a spine into my hand. Several minutes of unseemly cursing and plucking later, I had removed most of the biggest spines. The small, nearly invisible ones would have to wait until I got home. I wished they'd magically disappear. If magic was on the table, I wished that I was home, still in bed, about to awake to fresh croissants and a steaming pot of French roast.

No magic cure or fairy godmother bearing coffee appeared. I stood with a wobble and struggled out of the brush. The nearest house was a walled estate that had been for sale for nearly a year. I hadn't seen the owners in ages and suspected that they'd moved out. Even if someone was there, they were unlikely to open the door to a queasy, bleeding stranger covered in cactus quills. On the road, I looked both ways. I kept my headphones off and I didn't jog. I ran as fast as I could.

I let myself inside just as Linda stepped out of the kitchen. Her hair was wrapped in a towel and Hugo trailed her, tail raised and puffed.

"What happened?" she asked. "Are you okay? You're bleeding!"

"Cactus," I said, panting. "A cholla and maybe some other spiny stuff."

Linda gasped. "Jogging is dangerous. Did you trip?"

"A truck came too close and I jumped off the road," I admitted. "I shouldn't have been running with headphones."

Linda shook her head. I expected her to cite a news story about oblivious, music-loving joggers getting smooshed. Instead, she looked concerned the way Flori looks concerned. That is, mad. "What is *wrong* with people?" Linda fumed. "Was the driver texting? Too many people text and drive."

I admitted that I hadn't seen the driver. "They came really fast."

"And didn't stop?" Linda asked. "Did they slow down?"

"They seemed to speed up," I admitted. "But,

like you said, they might not have seen me. Probably texting." I tried to laugh but instead shuddered.

Linda frowned. "Let's get you fixed up," she said, changing the subject. "I've had lots of experience with cactus spines, working at the homeless shelter. You're lucky."

I didn't feel lucky, but I was certainly glad Linda was here. I trudged down the hall and, at Linda's urging, stepped into the tub and ran warm water over my arms. The water felt nice and washed away grit. Yet when I ran a finger over my elbow, dozens of tiny pains prickled through my arm and jolted my nerves.

Linda held my arm gently and inspected the damage. "The tiny ones are the worst. I know a secret, though. Dad taught me. Tape."

Tape sounded like a first-aid trick Manny would like. Although doubtful, I brought Linda some duct tape and bit my lip as she stuck it on and ripped it off along with spines and arm hair.

"Mmmm . . . did it work?" Linda asked. She peered at my ravaged arm.

"Thanks, it's just great," I said through clenched teeth, trying to keep things positive. I still felt spines or the pinprick holes they'd left.

"No," Linda said, shaking her head. "Still some there. We can't leave them. You could get an infection. Glue. That's what we need. That's the trick."

I was even more doubtful of this approach, although if nothing else, the white glue reminded me of icing, always a sweet thing, and the scent returned me to Celia's grade-school days.

Hugo leaned on my ankle and purred. I reached

down to pet him with my glue-free hand, and he hopped in the tub to bat at the drip of water.

"Blow on your arm," Linda said, and I saw again what a saint she must be to needy souls at the shelter. Linda, who could scare herself silly crossing a street, was rock solid in the face of other people's troubles.

After a few minutes, she inspected my glue. "Just about right. It has to be dry enough to rip off in one piece but not so dry it'll stick to your skin forever. Never, ever use a superglue. I've seen that before and it's an awful mess."

I sat on the edge of the tub, dutifully blowing on the glue and feeling pretty content despite the pain and spines. Near death will do that to you. So will a happy cat batting at water and a little pampering by a good friend.

The doorbell shattered my warm feelings. I jumped.

Linda did too. "Are you expecting someone?"

I wasn't. I made a *shhh* gesture, hoping the visitor would go away. The ringing, however, turned to pounding.

"I'll look. You stay here," Linda said, getting up.

Her kindness propelled me to action. "No!" I said. "Please, Linda. I'll see who it is."

"I'm coming with you," she said, grabbing a toilet plunger.

We tiptoed down the hall and I lifted a slat of the front wooden blinds. Heart racing, I peeked out, expecting to see . . . who? Don brandishing a knife? The murderous vehicle, driverless, revving and aimed at my door?

What I saw was a silver Audi idling in the driveway. A bulldog drooled on my doormat, next to long legs in dark jeans and scuffed cowboy boots. Fear fled, followed by embarrassment. Jake! I had an unfortunate habit of answering the door looking like a mess. The last time he'd dropped by unannounced, I'd just suffered a blender eruption and was covered in a Spanish garlic soup.

He must have spotted the movement of the blinds or felt the wave of embarrassment. "Rita? Are you okay?"

I opened the door a crack, thinking perhaps I could make the excuse of not being fully dressed. Winston didn't allow that. He rammed his massive head through the crack. His handsome owner peeked around the door.

"What the—" Jake started.

"Cholla," Linda answered matter-of-factly. "And Rita won't say so directly, but someone tried to run her over."

Chapter 23

Who did this?" Jake demanded. In a Bugs Bunny cartoon, steam would be puffing out his cowboy hat. His boots would grow spurs, and a roadrunner would zoom by. I stifled an inappropriate giggle, thinking I might be giddy or possibly concussed. I was definitely shaken, although I didn't want to show it.

"It was probably an accident," I said. "You know how distracted drivers are these days."

"I know something else about these days," Jake said. "You and your friends are investigating a murder."

What could I say? He was right.

Jake's expression softened. "Are you hurt?"

"I'm fine. Really. Linda treated me with glue." I looked around for Linda. She'd slipped away. From the kitchen, I heard the coffeepot sputter to a start.

"I see," Jake said, his eyes on a spot above my eyebrow. "And tape?"

Wincing, I yanked a stray bit of tape from my elbow.

"Coffee!" Linda called. She came out, wiping her hands on her pants. "You two talk. I'll walk over to Mom's."

Before I could protest, she said, "I need some exercise and time to think. Don't worry, I'll look out for cars. I always do." She nipped down the hall and returned with a box of Band-Aids and her coat already buttoned. Handing Jake the box, she said, "Take good care of her. There are tweezers in here too, along with some disinfectant."

Lovely. Instead of impressing Jake with a stunning soufflé, I was a disheveled patient.

Jake stepped outside to consult with Linda. Winston woofed happily and barreled down the hallway, Hugo literally on his stubby tail. While the dog and cat duo played, I poured two cups of coffee. Black, the way Jake liked his, and real cream for me because I felt sorry for myself.

The caffeine jump-started my brain, and a question brewed. I sprung it on Jake as soon as he stepped back inside. "Why are you here?" Okay, so this wasn't exactly my best hostess line, but why *was* he here and pounding on my door early in the morning?

"Let's sit," Jake said.

He held out a kitchen chair for me and laid the box of Band-Aids on the table. Then he sat, moving his chair so close to mine that our knees nearly touched. He leaned in. For a second I expected a kiss. I closed my eyes and waited. Instead of a tender kiss, pain seared through my right temple. I opened my eyes to see Jake wielding the tweezers.

"Got it!" he said, holding up a cactus spike as thick as a toothpick.

I groaned. "I'm a mess."

"You aren't looking your best, I'll admit that." He winked to let me know he was teasing. "And, I'm here because *you* called me."

I did?

Jake leaned in, again within kissing distance. I caught a whiff of manly cologne as he held the tweezers near my forehead. "Hold still, I see a patch of tiny spines. What'd you do? Tangle with half the cactus in Santa Fe County?"

"*I* called you?" I asked, still trying to work that out.

"You did," he said. "Or at least your phone did. I heard 'Dancing Queen' and a scream and the line went dead. I tried to call back, but no one answered. Winston and I were mighty concerned."

Some people butt dial. I arm-dialed while diving into cactus. I closed my eyes again as Jake worked acupuncturist's magic with tweezers. "Just one more . . ." he murmured. "There." A spine left my forehead, followed by a gentle kiss.

"All better?" he asked.

"Much," I managed to say. He lowered his face to mine. I leaned in and was nearly barreled over. Not from romance but from fifty pounds of speeding bulldog.

"Hey!" Jake protested as man's best friend thundered through the kitchen, chased by a blur of buff-colored fur. Jake sighed and scooted his chair back, the moment broken.

"Rita, why did someone try to run you over?"

he asked in a tone that suggested he already knew the answer.

"Flori, Addie, and I followed Don Busco last night," I admitted. "He caught us at it and got kind of angry." Since no more kissing seemed in the works, I stood and searched the cupboards. For someone who works in food, I had shamefully slim pickings, other than the half-eaten flan. "Homemade granola?" I offered. "It's a bit old, but it's peanut butter."

Jake had a better idea. "How about I take you out for breakfast? Clafoutis or Tune-Up or do you have a new favorite? It won't make up for that fine, home-cooked meal I missed, but . . ."

The man knew my breakfast favorites and my weaknesses. Clafoutis was the domain of buttery French croissants made by bona fide French pastry chefs. Tune-Up offered New Mexican fare with an El Salvadoran twist. Rationalizing that the fat and calories of flaky, buttery pastry don't count after a near-death experience, I chose Clafoutis and hurried to change into something that was not torn spandex.

Okay," Jake said, after we'd ordered coffee and pastries. "You were about to tell me why you all were out tailing Don."

I tore a flaky corner from my ham and cheese croissant. "We think he was involved in Napoleon's death. A guy Flori knows saw Don by the bandstand around the time of the murder. Don

might be the killer, or know who is. Plus, yesterday on the Plaza, I saw the health inspector's son
pass Don an envelope stuffed with cash. Fishy!"

"The health inspector that got poisoned?" Jake
asked with a raised eyebrow.

"Yeah, that one," I said glumly. "He's up to something. The other day, when I was at OhLaLa, Brigitte and I discovered him searching Napoleon's
office. First he claimed he was inspecting. When
we put pressure on him, he said he was looking
for cash that Napoleon owed him." I raised the
remains of my croissant for emphasis. "We think
either Napoleon was paying Jenkins for a good inspection or so that someone else—say a rival food
cart operator—would fail theirs."

Jake's steel-blue eyes had a mischievous twin-
kle. "I'm still imagining you and Brigitte putting
pressure on that inspector. Did I understand correctly that pink handcuffs were involved?"

I blushed and tried to hide behind my coffee,
which was unfortunately a tiny double espresso
cup, not a giant bowl of cappuccino. "Those were
Flori's cuffs. Anyway, Brigitte's been searching
through Napoleon's financial records. She thinks
she's found irregularities. It's all about the numbers, she says. That's the key." I felt my blush rise
again, this time for another reason. "She's . . ." I
struggled to find words that wouldn't reveal my
jealousy. "She's very persistent."

Jake snorted. "You can say that again."

I took note of his tone. "Oh?"

"Yeah," he said, and I thought I saw a blush rise
on his chiseled cheeks. "You may have noticed,
Brigitte Voll has been calling me an awful lot

since I met her at that art benefit." He fiddled with his cup.

Was I imagining it, or did the tough defense attorney seem anxious?

He sighed. "I had to come out and tell her that I'm seeing you, so she wouldn't get the wrong idea. I hope you won't think that's too forward."

I tried not to beam. Cool and collected, that's how Brigitte would react. On the other hand, Jake Strong was sitting here with me, not Brigitte. "Not at all," I told the slightly pink-cheeked lawyer.

He grinned bashfully and changed the subject back to crime. "So if Don's the killer, why'd he do it?"

"Napoleon blacklisted Don from his beloved bartending jobs," I said.

Jake wasn't impressed. "Hardly seems like something you'd kill a guy over long after the fact. Besides, Don seems pretty happy with that hot dog business of his."

"Well then, what if Napoleon was going after Don's hot dog business, like he did with Linda's cart? That could have set Don off. Maybe he snapped."

Jake accepted a refill of coffee from our harried waitress. "I can see that. Don's a big guy. Easy enough for him to stab Napoleon and pull Linda's tamale cart over him, although why he'd get someone else's cart involved is beyond me."

We sat in silence for a few beats before I suggested possible answers. "Linda probably told you that she left a message for Don, asking him to check on her cart. Suppose Don spotted Napoleon messing with Linda's cart and went mad with rage. He stabbed Napoleon and pulled the cart over him to make a point. That might explain why he keeps saying he'll help Linda. Once he came to his senses, he felt bad for involving her."

Jake sipped his coffee. "Possible. He'd help her more if he told the truth. You said someone saw Don out by the bandstand that night? Has this witness spoken to the police?"

"No," I said with a sigh. "According to Flori, this man won't go near the police. He's a chronic thief and somehow related to Don. What's worse is that Don claims he has an alibi. It's Manny, of all people. They were out at a bar that night."

Jake appeared to mull over this information. "Okay. Good to know. However, none of this explains you getting run off the road this morning."

I had a flashback of the silver grill barreling toward me. "I can't be sure who it was, and I didn't get a good look at the vehicle. I think it was a truck." I shivered, involuntarily. "Red like the truck Don drives."

For a man holding a custard-filled raisin bun, Jake did not look happy. "Rita," he said. "You should—" He stopped. "I can't tell you what you should do, but I sure hope you'll be careful. Someone killed Napoleon. Got close enough to stick that knife of Linda's in his back and right through to his heart."

His words sent a chill through me. I clutched my now-empty coffee cup. "I know. But if Don's the killer and getting worried—trying to scare me—maybe he'll make a mistake. Or maybe we can convince that witness to come forward or talk to you. That would help Linda, wouldn't it?"

Jake took his time before answering. "It might

help muddy the waters in a jury's mind. But suppositions aren't evidence. Don won't be the one on trial. Linda will be, assuming I can't get the case thrown out."

"Can you?" I asked.

Jake studied the packed dining room. A young waitress scurried among tables, refilling coffees, taking orders, and delivering food. I hoped Tres Amigas would be open and filled with customers again on Monday.

When Jake spoke, he seemed to choose his words carefully. "I don't know, honestly. Usually I have a feeling about a case, one way or the other, but this one?" He gazed toward the ceiling with its pale, whitewashed beams. "It's tricky. There's the murder weapon, Linda's knife, with her fingerprints all over it."

"But anyone could have stolen her knife from her cart."

Jake recrossed his legs and leaned back in his seat. "That's what I'll argue. The public fight with Napoleon doesn't help her one bit. There's something else too, for your ears only." He leaned across the table. I leaned in too, recalling the earlier kiss. "Napoleon died eating his last meal, and you know what that was?"

I recalled the crime tech picking up chunks of tamale. "Oh no . . ."

Jake leaned back. "Yep, afraid so. Tamale. Found at the scene and in the mouth of the deceased. The lab has to confirm it, but it appears to be Linda's tamale. Chicken *mole*, the kind she had on special."

Suddenly my croissant wasn't sitting so well.

"There could be lots of explanations for that," I said, though I could hardly think of any good ones.

Jake agreed. "I try to think like the prosecutor. Know what he'll most likely say? That it was Linda who was there that night. Napoleon tried her tamale and insulted her and that was that . . . she went wild with anger and killed him. In that case, at least it wouldn't be first-degree murder. The crime wasn't premeditated."

As theories went, it was more straightforward. Unless you knew Linda. "And then rolled her cart over his dead body?" I said grouchily and too loudly. A young couple at the next table looked over at us. I tried to lower my voice and emotions a notch. "Linda would never do that."

Jake reached out and took my hand. His firm grasp was calming, even if his words were not. "You and I think that. A jury may not. Rita, there's something else too. Linda's record."

Chapter 24

The couple next to us glanced up warily from their eggs Florentines. Okay, I'd yelled, "Linda has a record?" louder than I intended. Now I prayed that our table neighbors weren't gossipy locals or potential jurors or news reporters. A group walking past gaped at me. Too late, I recognized one of the women as a member of Linda's choir group.

Jake outlined the bare details, basically all he knew. "You can do me a favor, actually," he said as I considered stress-ordering, and consuming on the spot, a dozen chocolate madeleines. "I have the records, the official paperwork, but Linda says she doesn't want to talk about the past. I need to know the full story in case those convictions are brought up in court proceedings. Typically, they couldn't be, but a crafty prosecutor might worm them in."

I could imagine Linda's refusal to speak. She'd

happily reminisce about friends and relatives and past holiday feasts, but when it came to talking about herself or her now-deceased husband, she clammed up.

"I need to know if I should be a little or a whole mess of worried," Jake said. "Flori will tell you, won't she?"

I hoped so. My mind was still whirling, and this time it wasn't from my tumble in the cactus. I couldn't believe that Linda had a record. And not just *a* record. Jake was saying that she had multiple arrests and was named in a handful of domestic disturbance reports. I knew that her deceased husband, Santos, had been no saint. Far from it. Santos was a bully and a mean drunk. The domestic disturbances made me both sad and mad. Mostly mad. But the arrests? I repeated my bafflement several times on the drive back to my casita.

We stepped inside to find Winston flopped on the cool tiles, tongue out and panting. Hugo purred contentedly on the back of the sofa.

"Did Hugo wear you out, sweetie?" I asked, patting the bulldog's hot, wrinkled brow.

Still, Winston whined when Jake put on his leash. "Gotta catch up on work, buddy," Jake said to the dog. Jake paused on the porch. He reached out and gently touched my scuffed forehead before cupping my chin and drawing me in for a kiss.

My knees wobbled. "Oops, too much running," I said, trying to cover.

He smiled down at me. "Too much jumping into cacti. Promise me something?"

I crossed my fingers, prepared to fib and say I'd give up investigating.

"No more early morning jogging, okay? At least until we find out who did this."

That I could promise.

Jake left me in a jumble of emotions. Selfishly, I was still aglow over the romantic French breakfast and kiss. On the other hand, I had nearly been run over and *Linda had a record?*

I called Flori before driving over to her house.

She met me at the door. "Linda just left. On her way to church again." Flori narrowed her eyes at my scuffs and bandages. "She told me what happened to you. It's darkest before the storm, I told her, although that's hardly a pick-you-up, is it?"

It was about to get darker. I suggested to Flori that we sit on her lovely back sunporch with her cat Zozo. Once the portly orange feline had jumped on her lap and started kneading, I brought up the subject of Linda's arrests.

"Yes," Flori said simply. "My eldest daughter has a record, but it's not what you might think."

I wasn't thinking anything. My mind still couldn't wrap itself around even the idea. "For what?" I asked, wishing I had a chubby cat to cuddle.

My elderly friend screwed up the side of her mouth. "A misdemeanor for disorderly conduct," she said. "She and a dozen others got kicked out of a city council meeting years ago for protesting a nuclear waste dump."

Okay, this wasn't bad. I relaxed and enjoyed

the view of tiny yellow finches flitting among similarly bright forsythia flowers. Flori explained young Linda's noble efforts to secure clean drinking water and keep us all safe from radioactivity and cancer. I felt better. If the prosecutor brought this up, Linda would look like the saint she was.

Relieved, I'm afraid I drifted off in thoughts of breakfast and kissing.

Flori's next words, however, snapped me back to reality. "Then there's the battery of a police officer charge. That's probably what has Jake worried."

I gaped at Flori. Outside, the finches flew away in a cacophony of high-pitched chirps.

Flori petted a purring Zozo. "The assault was a load of . . . well . . . rotten eggs. So long ago too. My dear girl was only in her early twenties then and passionate about civil rights and environmental issues. She was at a big protest in Albuquerque that got out of hand. You know how Albuquerque can be. You know young people too. So headstrong and stubborn."

Celia was headstrong and stubborn. My mind reeled through a horror flick of Celia building a rap sheet.

"But Linda?" I asked. "Assault?"

Flori had her eyes on the garden and a puffy gray cat stalking through a patch of ornamental grass. The feline prowled across the patio, then looked our way. I held its wide-eyed gaze for a moment before it crouched and slunk back under the forsythia.

"Mrs. Baca's cat, Sir Dennis," Flori said with a smile. "He's all bluster. Dennis never catches anything. About Linda, there was a lot of shoving. An officer claimed that protesters shoved him, when really the police were backing them into a corner. It was a trumped-up charge and everybody knew it. Linda did some community service. I told Linda, there are ways to get that off your record, but she said she didn't care. Said it doesn't matter, she was proud of her efforts." Flori turned to me. "It matters now, doesn't it?"

I tried to summon Linda's calm confidence in the face of another's pain. "We'll clear her. I'm not scared of Don Busco." I lied. I was scared of the big man, but I feared more for Linda.

"Good," Flori said. "Because I know how we can spy on him."

Flori's idea was a good one, except for my guilt. Later that morning, I stepped up to Crepe Empire, ready to infiltrate the food carters. I was a mole, a deceiver, a false friend, and I'd have felt a lot better if Brigitte hadn't been so delighted to see me.

"But what has happened to you?" she asked, frowning at my many bandages and scrapes. "You were in an accident?"

No accident, I thought, glancing toward Don's hot dog cart. He was busy ladling chili over hot dogs and chatting to customers. Was he regaling them with cowboy folksiness or a story from his time in the film industry? I remembered liking Don's tales during his bartending days. He'd always seemed so friendly. Not now.

"I had a run-in with a vehicle while jogging," I

told Brigitte, my hand reaching for my forehead. "I look worse than I feel, and it's probably good if I keep up and moving. I'll understand if you don't want me around, though. I might scare away your customers." I halfway hoped she would shoo me off. I'd called her earlier, saying that I had the day off and would love to help her with her crepes. Salvage her crepes would be the more accurate term, but I already felt too much like a false friend to say that.

"*Non, non*, I am delighted! You give me hope. Together, we will conquer the crepe." She came around the front of the sleek cart and gave me a painful squeeze. Lowering her voice, she said, "I will tell you and only you, Rita. I do not know what the problem is. My crepes, they flop when they flip and they splatter and people give them back and want a return of their money. I was starting to think that Napoleon may have been correct about my poor cooking abilities. But with you here, Crepe Empire will again be the best on the Plaza."

And I could spy on Don without being accused of snooping. Tying an apron around my waist, I stepped behind the round griddle and surveyed the setup. The little cart was better equipped than some kitchens. Brigitte turned on the sound system to soft French café tunes. I stirred a speckled buckwheat batter, my mood perking up as I anticipated crepe delicacies.

I started feeling better about my outdoor spying too. It was a sunny Saturday. Petunias and pansies bloomed in planter baskets, robins prowled the grass, and the Cathedral bells rang out, announcing a quarter to eleven. We still had time for some crepe instruction before the main lunchtime rush.

"Okay, first thing, your batter is a little thick," I said. I stirred the batter, which fell in clumpy globs when I raised the spoon. "This is more like an American pancake batter. You want a thinner consistency for crepes." Under my instruction, Brigitte whisked in more water.

"Now, a nice coating of oil on the griddle."

Brigitte added oil and reached for her ladle.

"Wait." I held out a hand. "You want the oil almost smoking, otherwise the crepes might stick and they'll be hard to turn. Now, when the grill's ready, spread the batter quickly but evenly and monitor the bubbles and edges. The batter will turn from glossy to firm and set on the sides. That's when you flip."

I demonstrated how to spread out the batter using a T-shaped wooden tool designed for just that purpose. We waited a minute, and then Brigitte attempted to flip the lacy circle.

"It tore," she said with a pout. "I want perfect."

"Practice will make perfect," I said, resorting to platitudes to cover my distraction. Don was bent over, rummaging in his cart. When he emerged, he held a bag of buns. No cash or smoking gun. Was this a waste of time? No. If nothing else, maybe Brigitte could learn to make an acceptable crepe. The next crepe flipped perfectly, and we filled the golden shell with grated Gruyère cheese, paper-thin slices of smoked ham, creamy horse-radish sauce, and a sprinkling of emerald chives.

Two hours later we'd served a lot of crepes,

many of which our customers, and even Brigitte, labeled as perfect.

"Rita, this is fantastic," she gushed. *"Magnifique! You are the best of teachers and friends."*

I blushed at her heaping praise.

"But why do you keep admiring Don Busco?" she asked, punching me in the arm in a way she probably meant as girlfriendly. "Are you interested in him too? He is handsome in his cowboy outfit, but not as handsome as your Mr. Strong. And that mustache, it is no good."

I covertly massaged my arm where her punch had landed on a patch of cactus-spine holes. "Oh, I'm just checking out your competition . . ." I said.

I'm a terrible liar. Some people would say that's a good thing. Not Flori, who periodically threatens to send me to fibbing camp.

Brigitte narrowed her eyes, scanning from Crystal's juice cart to Don's hot dog stand. "Rita, you are investigating, yes? Is that why you work at Crepe Empire today? If so, you must let me help. I can tell you that the food cart operators are edgy, talking of murder and poisoning. Look at Crystal. She hides behind her juice and avoids us." Brigitte leaned close to me, practically cheek-to-cheek. We both eyed Crystal, or rather the perfectly bouncy curls on the back of Crystal's head.

"See?" Brigitte said. "She cannot look at us, and I think I know why."

Obligingly, I asked, "Why?"

Brigitte tossed a crepe with such vigor that it flipped twice before landing. "Guilt," she proclaimed.

I waited, sensing that Brigitte would go on.

She did. "Yesterday morning, guess who visited Crystal's cart? The health inspector."

"Jenkins Senior? Did he drink anything?"

Brigitte looked over both shoulders before answering in a triumphant whisper. "Yes! She gave him juice. I do not know what kind. It was brown."

And poisonous? I supposed I could imagine Crystal—or anyone—acting under extreme emotion. I couldn't see the perky mother of three undertaking premeditated poisoning in broad daylight.

Don's booming laugh floated our way and sent a chill down my arms. "Hot dogs!" he yelled. "Red hot chili dogs straight off the flames! Come and get 'em if you dare!"

"Or there is him," Brigitte said.

I made a decision and admitted what I was up to, starting with my jogging mishap.

"But you did not see the driver?" Brigitte interjected midway through the story.

"No. It happened too fast. I think the vehicle was red. Don owns a red truck. I want to keep an eye on him. That's why I'm here." I added quickly, "And I love crepes."

"What do you see when you keep your eyes on him?" Brigitte asked.

So far I'd seen hot dogs, a lot of hot dogs.

Brigitte poured more crepe batter. "I understand your suspicion," she said. "However, we must consider the numbers and the food inspector, Monsieur Jenkins. He says he received payments from Napoleon. But for what? What if he is a, how do you say, a black . . . ?"

"Blackmailer," I said.

"*Oui!* Blackmail. He was carried away to the

hospital yesterday, but what if he only pretends to be ill to throw off your suspicion? It is not so difficult, I imagine, to pretend?"

According to Addie's cousin at the hospital, Jenkins's poisoning had been real and potentially deadly. I told Brigitte so, adding, "Maybe he ate a bad mushroom by accident or the person preparing the dish messed up. My friend Flori has a saying, 'There are bold mushroom hunters and old mushroom hunters, but no old and bold mushroom hunters.'"

"How foolish," Brigitte said, presumably about mushroom mistakes. "I tell you, Rita, it is the finances that will reveal all. That inspector, he is the one. I am sure of it."

He'd have to be pretty devious—and incredibly bold or stupid—to poison himself. I sneaked a glance at Don. "There's more," I said, and told her about seeing Junior pass the envelope of cash to Don.

"Mmm . . . that is interesting. This Junior man is the son of the food inspector? Is he clever? Good with knives or numbers?"

All I knew was that he liked music, archeology, and Addie. I wanted to know more. On the other hand, there were only so many suspects we could juggle. "We have to focus on the main suspects," I told Brigitte. "We're under the gun."

Brigitte's chin snapped up. "Gun? There is a gun too?"

"Just an expression. Not an actual gun. We're under time pressure, is what I mean. The prosecutor will be back in his office next week, and he'll push Linda's case forward. Then, for all practical purposes, the police will stop investigating other suspects. Even if she's not convicted, the trail will go cold. We must find something that convinces the police of her innocence." Saying this out loud brought home the urgency. My eye began to tic, especially after Brigitte repeated my earlier mantra about Linda being beyond reproach.

Brigitte sounded so hopeful, so sure. I decided to tell her. "Linda has an arrest record for a felony assault. A very old one, nearly forty years ago, probably, but it adds to the police's case."

Brigitte shook her head. "That many years ago? How incredible that the record remains. The American justice system is very strange to me. Your Mr. Strong will see that she is set free."

My eye tic picked up tempo as I explained that even Jake Strong was worried.

"Then, as you say, you must identify the guilty party," Brigitte said. "Why do you wait and hesitate? Why do we not search Don's home and find the truth?"

Because it was illegal? Because Flori had scoped out his house and reported that he had digital door locks that her amateur lock-picking set couldn't touch? I was starting to explain our inability to get in when a flash of purple caught my eye. I looked up and straight into the reptilian smile of Georgio Andre. An idea struck me. I acted on it before I could think rationally and chicken out.

"Georgio," I said, batting my eyelids as Flori always instructed. I hoped the move came off as flirty rather than a nervous twitch. In either case, it seemed to work.

Georgio sidled up to the counter. "Ah, Ms. Lafitte, my lovely finder of fine art, can I be of help?"

Chapter 25

That night, the sun was setting in a kaleidoscope of tangerine orange and purple flashes when I stopped by Cass's studio. Fire glowed in her studio too, a tight blue flame roaring from her torch. I waited until she turned off the gas and the flame sputtered out.

Pushing back her goggles, she assessed my outfit. "I rarely see you wear all black. Are you going out for cocktails with Jake to make up for that missed date, or . . . ?" Her *or* implied that she could guess my nonromantic intentions.

"I shouldn't say," I said.

Cass cocked her head and raised an eyebrow. "So not a date with a handsome man?"

A handsome, albeit slimy man was involved. Georgio Andre had met Brigitte and me in the parking lot behind OhLaLa, where he'd handed off a lock-picking device while flirting unabashedly. Luckily, Brigitte had handled the flirting.

"Hypothetically," I said to Cass, "if I went to prison, would you help Manny take care of Celia? She'd need a noncriminal maternal figure."

"Rita," my friend said, waving her torch in my direction. "What are you hypothetically up to?"

"Best you don't know." I felt rude, but truly rude would be involving my friend in a crime. I had told Flori, who'd informed Addie, as they were both involved. Addie was following Don to downtown bars, and Flori was keeping her ear to the gossip lines. At Addie's last text-message check-in, Don was watching football at a sports bar with more large-screen TVs than menu items. It was, Addie summarized, beyond boring, and the barkeeper refused to switch even one of the many TVs to BBC America.

Cass grumbled that she didn't like this—whatever "this" was—one bit. "But of course. Celia can spend time with me and Sky. He'll be thrilled. He's been trying to catch up with her lately, but they keep missing each other."

Sky, Cass's son, is a combination big brother and best friend to Celia. They share a love of art and are usually as close as twins. I vowed, yet again, to sit down my daughter and force a conversation on her new crowd and activities.

"Friendships are always in flux, I told Sky," Cass was saying.

Not ours. I hoped.

Cass grinned. "Don't worry. I'll come visit you in jail if it comes to that. I'll bring you some of Ida Green's tortillas so you can break out. We'll go Thelma and Louise, except no driving over cliffs."

Georgio's lock-pick device, although light and

slender, felt like a crowbar weighing down my pocket. I checked my watch, realizing I was about to be late. "I've got to go," I said, suddenly feeling dizzy, either from the scent of acetylene in the air or my impending criminal activity. I wobbled to my feet.

Cass eyed me with concern. "Will you at least tell me where you're going? You know, so I can call in Officer Bunny if you go missing?"

Calling in Bunny was the last thing I wanted. She'd arrest me, while Manny chastised me, or maybe vice versa.

"I'll be fine. I have my phone." I gave Cass a quick hug and stepped outside. I'd have to rush across the street to the Cathedral steps, where I'd arranged to meet Brigitte. At the curb, I bounced anxiously on the balls of my feet as I waited for a car to pass. The black sedan slowed, the side window descended, and Brigitte waved.

"*Parfait*," she said. "Perfect timing. You are ready?"

As ready as I'd ever be. I got in just as Cass came to her front door, waving for us to wait.

"Do you need help? I'll come too," she called out.

Part of me wanted to yell *Yes!* but I knew I shouldn't. My hurried thanks were shut down as Brigitte rolled up the tinted windows with her master controls.

"We need no one else," she said briskly. "You and me. We are an investigative team, Rita."

In the side mirror I saw Cass wave, then drop her hand and go inside. We sped off, my heart heavy and beating hard.

Brigitte drove in silence and just above the speed limit. Like me, she wore all black. Unlike me, she could wear her cat-burglar attire straight out to cocktails and dancing. My outfit included black slacks from my Midwest French café days, topped with a stretchy black top I'd bought as long underwear for a snowshoe trip. The shirt was warm but built up shocking amounts of static. I'd already electrified several doorknobs and a tree.

"This is his block," Brigitte announced, slowing the car to a crawl. I knew this neighborhood pretty well. Manny's house was a few blocks south. He'd inherited it from his grandparents, and we'd all lived together there for about three years. I'd walked here many times and hauled casseroles to a nearby cousin-in-law's house for family meals. I missed the cousins and wished we'd kept better in touch. If I didn't end up in jail, I vowed to reach out to them again.

"New Mexico architecture all looks the same," Brigitte complained.

I smiled, thinking of my mother, who said the same thing. Mom also worried that adobe would dissolve in rain and that the presence of so many walls encouraged misbehavior. Given that I was about to burgle, I couldn't argue with the latter. I did love the nuances in Santa Fe's amazing earthen buildings, though. And, thanks to Flori, I could distinguish a few architectural types, like the straight-lined territorial style and the more fanciful curves of Pueblo revival. I could even sniff out real, solid adobe from the spray-on coating that Flori disdained as "faux'dobe," although I thought both could be beautiful.

"Flori said that Don's house is a territorial-style cottage," I told Brigitte, who snorted as if this information was of no help.

"Numbers," she said again. "That is the key. Look for house numbers."

We spotted Don's number on a stucco-coated mailbox. His home sat on a corner, enclosed by a high wall. My heart sank. What good was Georgio's lock-picking equipment if we couldn't get over the wall? Past snooping endeavors with Flori have proven that I am no good at hoisting myself over walls. Such experience has also taught me that interior gardens can contain hazards ranging from guard dogs and drug labs to trippy burglar alarms. However, when Brigitte turned the corner, my wall excuse vanished. The gate to Don's driveway stood wide open, as if inviting us in.

I checked my phone for any updates. Addie said she'd text if Don left the bar. There was no message. No excuse there either. Reminding myself that this was for Linda, I followed Brigitte down the dark driveway to Don's back door.

"It is easy, *non*? That is what Georgio says?" Brigitte whispered.

Easy for a professional art thief and cat burglar, perhaps. The lock-pick looked too simple, like a thin, miniature pry bar. If it turned up in my drawer of kitchen tools, I might mistake it for a spatula missing its silicon end or a device to free stubborn cakes from their pans. Simply insert behind the side of the lock, yank down, and pull, Georgio had said. He'd even brought a dummy lock to demonstrate on and a cell-phone video of himself using the device at an international lock-picking-aficionados convention. Amateur enthusiasts, he'd said with a wink. All on the up and up.

I'd practiced a few times, and it had seemed simple. In the practice sessions, however, my hands weren't shaking, and I wasn't standing in the dark, about to undertake an actual crime. I fumbled to insert the device, fearing the blare of alarms at any moment. Don't be silly, I told myself. Home alarms were often silent. The first thing I'd hear would be Manny, ordering me to freeze.

"Ease it down . . ." Brigitte whispered over my shoulder.

I eased and something clicked.

Brigitte reached across and opened the door.

"Wow!" I said, momentarily thrilled. Then reality sank in, and I imagined Milan Lujan describing me on the six o'clock news. *Single mom and former policeman's wife in a dramatic fall from grace tonight, breaking into a culinary competitor's home.*

Brigitte was already inside and flipping on light switches. An array of ceiling lamps illuminated a bachelor pad of bulky leather furniture, an oversized TV, and a jumble of pizza boxes and electronics, all under lovely Santa Fe architectural details. The ceiling was crossed by tree-trunk beams. The floor was Saltillo tile interspersed with small tiles of brilliant blue. Take away the single-male clutter and the house was a gem, but I didn't come to gawk at real estate. In fact I didn't want to see any details if that meant we could be seen too.

"Ack! Brigitte, turn off the lights!" I reached to flip the switch.

My co-burglar batted my hand away. "But how will we see? No, this way we look less guilty."

There was no way of looking less guilty. We had a lock-picking device, acquired from a well-known yet nonconvicted criminal/international lock-picking champ, who would disavow giving it to us. We were dressed in black and were rifling through a man's private papers. Or, rather, Brigitte was rifling through the magazines and mail on his coffee table. I was pretty much frozen. What had seemed like a bold move to secure Linda's freedom now seemed a futile if not foolish endeavor.

"Rita, where are you?"

Brigitte's voice jolted me from my thoughts. She wasn't in the living room anymore. I turned off the lights and followed the sounds of rustling down a hall to a small room overlooking Don's driveway and side yard.

"*Voilà*," Brigitte said. She waved her hands to encompass a room decorated in movie star photos and piles of paper and electronics.

I didn't see anything *voilà* worthy. I saw a home office that needed a good dusting and thorough decluttering, although the photos were cool. I recognized Santa Fe residents George R.R. Martin, the writer of *Game of Thrones*, and Robert Redford, whom I'd once literally bumped into with my shopping cart at Whole Foods. As usual in the presence of a hunky man, I'd stammered the first nonsensical thing that came to mind. I told him that I wished he'd make salad dressing like Paul Newman. Then I'd blushed furiously and run for the cover of the cheese display.

I tore my eyes from the walls and studied the shelves of stuff. Old sound equipment, I guessed, along with cameras and other electronics. Remembrances from Don's glory days. I felt a smidgen sorry for the presumed murderer. There was nothing wrong with a hot dog cart, but Don used to rub shoulders with Hollywood royalty. Now what did he have? Hot dogs and stacks of old cameras and recorders and stuff.

"*Oui*. We hit the jackpot of financial papers," Brigitte said in the same pleased tone. "Figures. Numbers. Bank statements. Now we will find the truth."

I left the spreadsheets to her and thought about what Flori would be interested in. She'd snoop in the refrigerator to get a sense of his character. Or his medicine cabinet or nightstand. I decided to get the nightstand over with first. It seemed most personal and thus most wrong. Leaving Brigitte to her numbers, I found a room filled with boxes across the hall, reminding me of my own moving boxes, still languishing in Manny's garage. Next door was Don's bedroom.

The bed was unmade and more clothes lay on an armchair, the floor, and the bed than hung in the cramped closet. Don was a messy bachelor, which was not a crime, although it must be a put-off to dates. I hadn't seen Jake's bedroom or his closet. I imagined, however, they were smooth and put-together, like the handsome lawyer himself. Thinking of Jake made my heart race and not entirely from a romantic thrill. What did it matter if I whipped up a perfect Cinco de Mayo soufflé? If Jake got wind that I was breaking and entering with his client's lock-pick, I wouldn't have to worry about dinner dates.

From my search I learned that Don liked men's magazines, neglected to match up his socks, and had an incredibly hard bed pillow. I patted the pillow again, resisting the urge to tip Don off by fluffing it. The pillow made a crackly sound, as though stuffed like one of Flori's candy-heavy piñatas. I peeled back the dingy pillowcase. It wasn't candy inside. It was something sweeter.

"Cash!" I crowed, carrying my find to Brigitte, who was pawing through what looked like a box of old cell phones.

"*Et voilà!*" she said, clapping her hands.

This time I agreed. There was only one problem. What to do about the discovery?

"Is it like the envelope you saw the food inspector's son deliver?" Brigitte asked, turning a manila envelope over in her hands. She quickly counted the cash inside. "Nearly three thousand dollars. Quite a bit to sleep on each night."

"It's a different color envelope," I said, studying the plain manila paper. "Sure is a lot of cash to keep on hand, and not ones, fives, or tens that customers would pay with at the hot dog stand." Using my cell phone, I snapped a few photos.

"It is a clue." Brigitte started to tuck the envelope into her back pocket.

I'd broken in but I couldn't stoop to actual stealing. "We have to leave it here," I said, hoping she'd see my point. "Don will become too suspicious otherwise, and plus, if we can get the police here, the evidence needs to seem untainted."

To my relief, Brigitte agreed. "This is why you are the detective, Rita," she said. "Me? I find nothing. Only that Don Busco collects too much electronic garbage." She fiddled with a device that looked like a handheld speaker. "Testing," she said. Her voice came out the other side sounding like a ghoul in a horror movie. She reared her head back and then puffed her lips in French disdain. "A grown man and he plays with such toys."

I was feeling pretty proud of my sleuthing abilities. I should have known better. Mom always instilled midwestern modesty in my sister and me. Pride, she warned, never worked out well. In this case, Mom was right.

My cell phone buzzed. Addie had peppered her text message with emoticons in various expressions of anxiety and horror. The message alone was enough to terrify me. *LOST DON IN LOO. TRUCK GONE!!!*

"We have to get out!" I said, grabbing Brigitte by the arm and stuffing my phone in my back pocket. "Quick, turn off the lights and let's go."

Outside, the throaty sputter of a diesel engine approached. Was it Don? I wasn't waiting to find out. Brigitte and I ran through the dark hall to the back door we'd broken into earlier.

"How does it lock?" she asked.

Automatically, I hoped. If not, I prayed that Don wouldn't notice or would blame his own forgetfulness.

We slipped outside and pressed our backs to
Don's house, the adobe still holding some of the
sun's heat. Across the street, Brigitte's black sedan
was in plain sight. "Not yet," I said, holding her
back. "If he drives in the driveway, we're toast.
Quick, let's hide in the bushes along the side."

Scrambling into Don's bushes, I thought of Flori.
This is where she'd hidden to spy on his office.
Indeed, we had a clear view, which would have
been even clearer if Don pruned his shrubbery. In
the room I had been saving for last to search, the
kitchen, a light went on. I held my breath for as
long as I could. Beside me, Brigitte seemed calm
and composed even as more lights came on, suggesting that Don was moving through his home
quickly.

Did he suspect that someone had been inside?
Had we forgotten to shut a door or left handprints
on some dusty end table? The lights in the office
came on last. Through the sheer curtains, I could
make out Don's wide shoulders stooped over the
desk that Brigitte and I had just searched. Then, to
my horror, Don drew back the curtain. He had a
phone in his hand and leaned against the window
frame as he dialed.

"We must go," Brigitte whispered, grabbing my
arm.

"He'll see our movement . . ." Freezing was my
action of choice in such situations.

"Not if we stay behind these bushes and along
the wall." Brigitte was already tugging through
branches. A dog barked at a nearby house and a
porch light came on across the street.

When we reached the sidewalk, Brigitte brushed

a few leaves off her outfit. "There," she said. "All safe." She strolled across the street to the car. I tried to follow her calm lead, all the while tensed, expecting Don to run after us.

When we got to her car, I slid low in the passenger seat and reached for my phone, eager to tell Addie we were in the clear. I patted my pockets, absently at first, then frantically. Where was my phone? I'd had it. I'd gotten Addie's text and put the phone back in my pocket. Or had I? I patted myself again, every pocket and even my bra. It was no use. My phone was gone.

Chapter 26

I didn't dare tell Brigitte that I may have dropped my phone in Don's office or hallway or, best-case-scenario, his side garden. She was so happy in what she thought of as our sleuthing progress.

"We shall go out for a drink and celebrate," she declared. "It is not even ten. Early."

I hesitated only to be polite before declining. "I should get home," I said. "I've had a long day, and I'm pretty stiff from my accident this morning."

Brigitte made consoling noises. "Of course you are! You will not be jogging tomorrow morning, I hope?"

"I promised Jake that I'd avoid dangerous exercise," I said with a forced chuckle. "I'm going home to relax in a bubble bath." I doubted, however, that I'd do much relaxation even if surrounded by bubbles. What if my phone was inside Don's home? He had so many electronics, he might not notice it. Unless someone called. I tried to remember if I had the ringer off. I was pretty sure I'd muted it as part of break-and-entering preparations. I tried to picture my last known moments with the phone. I'd shoved it in my pocket. I was pretty sure of that. It had probably fallen out when we scrambled through the bushes. I hoped.

"Which way?" Brigitte asked at an intersection of Canyon Road. She fiddled with the heat and stereo dials while we waited our turn at the light. "This is Napoleon's car," she said, twisting a dial that turned on the back windshield wiper. "He left his vehicles in the parking lot and spare keys in the office, so I say to myself, why not use one? It is discreet for our spying."

I agreed that this was a good idea, although little about our spying seemed good right now. *If Don found that phone* . . . But what if he did? He already knew I suspected him. That was no secret. And if he was the killer, would he go to the police? Likely not. I squirmed in my seat, feeling phantom cactus thorns prickle my skin. Who was I kidding? I was desperate to retrieve the phone, the evidence of my snooping.

Brigitte dropped me off at the top of the driveway. She waved and bid me adieu and waited until I reached my door.

I expected to find only Hugo at home. To my surprise, Celia sat at the kitchen table, sketching in fast, bold strokes on a drawing pad and plugged into her headphones. Hugo lounged on the chair across from her, meticulously cleaning a claw.

"Honey?" I said loudly, hoping not to startle her.

She stopped shading in a dark storm cloud long enough to say, "Hey."

I gestured for her to take out an earphone. "I'm glad you're home," I said, wondering how to delicately ask why she was back.

She shrugged. "Dad's got a date. I didn't want to get in the way."

"My good luck, then," I said. Something told me that Manny's dating wasn't the main issue. Celia got on fine with Manny's girlfriends, many of whom were closer to Celia's age than his. "Is there anything else going on? How are your friends?"

Celia shaded her storm clouds more aggressively. She'd drawn a desert landscape populated by spindly cactus and the wide-eyed fairy girls that were her artistic trademark. As usual, the fairy girls were in foul moods. These fairies, however, seemed particularly angry. "I'm not hanging out with those guys anymore," Celia muttered. "They're lame. All they do is sit around downtown and do stupid stuff."

"You're okay?"

Celia's steely look wavered. "Of course. I'm fine," she said.

Her defiant, surly tone came as a relief to me. So did her next words.

"I called Sky. Hope you don't mind. He's staying at his Mom's this weekend and bored, and I thought we could watch a movie or something. I mean, it's a weekend, right?"

I thought this was a great idea and also a good moment for my "you can tell me anything" speech.

My daughter stopped drawing. "It's nothing *bad*, Mom. I thought this one guy was cool but his friends are jerks, and he does anything they say. I've got my own friends." She stopped shading and looked up. "You know, if you and Cass want to join us for the movie too, that's cool."

Cass was a night owl, like our teens, and snacks and good company would keep me awake for at least the opening credits. There was one thing I needed to do, though, before I dug out the pop-corn and cocoa. "Can I borrow your phone?" I asked Celia.

The next morning, I berated myself as I drove to Flori's house. Sure, it was her idea to meet at five o'clock, before the sun, and hopefully Don, were up. But it was my fault for losing the phone in the first place, and staying up late.

"I'm an idiot," I said through a yawn, when I picked up Flori and her tote bag of spy materials up at her house. "Sun Tzu would say so too."

Flori got in, flipped on the heated seat, and brushed off my self-deprecation. "Master Sun would be proud of you, sneaking into the enemy's lair to gather information. I bet we'll find that phone right where you dropped it in those over-grown shrubs." Flori, a morning person, was as bright as the sun that wasn't yet up. She informed me that she'd packed cookies, "for later," and a thermos of coffee in case we had to stake out Don's house for a while.

"He'll surely still be sleeping," I said, mainly to reassure myself. I dreaded returning to Don's but I didn't have much choice. Like a fool, or a consci-entious mom setting a good example, I'd taped an address sticker on the back of the phone, a convenient way for any good Samaritans or potential murderers to find me.

Flori was fiddling with her own phone. "You're right. He's one of those up-late people. Addie called last night when she couldn't get ahold of you. Said she spotted Don at the Kiva Lounge and would tail him."

"She shouldn't do that," I said with a groan. Who was I to talk? I drove slowly so as not to break any other laws.

"Addie promised to call if anything went wrong. Otherwise, she said she'd text if it was past my bedtime." Flori punched the screen of her cell phone. "Now how do I get to texts? Aha! Okay, here's her report."

I was nearing Don's street. I parked a few houses away from his and listened as Flori read from the tiny screen, held inches from her nose.

"Don, drinking with mates," she read out loud.

"More drinking.

"Blarmy! Boring."

Flori summarized a few more "borings!" and "blokes and beers" and then held the screen out at arm's length. "Mmm . . . I thought I was reading that incorrectly," she said. "Addie says that Don met with Gerald Jenkins Senior. Jenkins must be feeling better, if he's out at the bars."

"Or he and his co-conspirator are getting nervous," I said, trying to calm my own nerves.

"Exactly," Flori said. She handed me the phone, and I read the series of texts myself. *Alert!! Junior's old man is here! Meeting Don. Looks sick. Drinking a wee pot o tea. Arguing? See photo.* I scrolled down the screen and squinted at the image of what appeared to be mostly Addie's knee in fishnet stockings and a red frilly ruffle. Beyond the ruffle, two blurry men stood by a high bar table. The shorter of the two—Gerald Jenkins Senior, I assumed—held a cup in one hand and appeared to jab his finger at the taller one, Don. I interpreted the scene as a blurry argument.

"Interesting," Flori said, tapping her foot on the floorboards. "Very interesting. I wonder if Jenkins thinks Don tried to poison him? He must know that we didn't do it, regardless of what he told the police."

I thought about this. "Even if I were a blackmailer, if I knew who had tried to kill me I'd go to the police and take my chances. Better jail than dead."

"This is why we're not criminals, dear," Flori said. "They have different values than you and me." With that virtuous declaration, she produced two black hats, hand-knit and perfect for coordinating with any burglar's attire. She handed one to me.

"We *are* criminals," I pointed out. "I've broken and entered. We're about to trespass, and is that Taser you're carrying even legal?" I stuffed the hat in my coat pocket. I didn't want to dress like a crook.

Flori smoothed hers over her silver bun. She didn't deny the criminal accusation or defend her Taser. "All for the good, though," she said.

True, but Manny wouldn't buy that argument. I gave Flori back her phone, not trusting myself with it, and we got out. All noises sounded amplified to me, the thump of the car doors, the crunch of our footsteps on gravel, the baleful howl of a distant dog. The streetlamp in front of Don's house was out, and his and his neighbors' houses were dark. Almost too dark. I worried about Flori. I searched for the right words to keep her safely on the sidewalk.

"Will you be our lookout, Flori? We need a wide view of the house. If you see any lights come on or someone walking by . . ." This is where my plan broke down. Should she bellow my name? Blow her police whistle?

"Then you'll hear my turkey call. If you do, hide," my elderly friend said. She held what looked like a wooden whistle to her lips and gobbles filled the air. I was too surprised to worry about the noise.

Flori patted her heart. "Bernard thought of sending it along. He's a smart one sometimes, and thoughtful. That's why I married him." She agreed to stand lookout at the end of the driveway, back against an elm tree so that she'd be out of sight in case someone drove by on the street.

"I'll retrace my steps," I whispered, my heart thudding so hard I could barely hear myself. "Brigitte and I went into the bushes over there, after sneaking out Don's door. When I get over there, try calling my phone. The screen lights up when a call comes in."

"Ten four," Flori said. "Good luck." She patted me on the back in a kind, grandmotherly off-you-go-to-trespass gesture.

With every step, I cringed at the racket of gravel crunching underfoot. I kept to the edge of the drive near the shrubbery, glad for the predawn darkness. Some light, however, would be helpful. I dared turn on the penlight on my key chain. The narrow beam lit up gravel, dried branches, and the flash of metal. I aimed the beam at the metal. Don's truck and hot dog cart blocked the middle of the driveway. Skirting around the shrubbery side of the truck, I kept my eyes on the bushes. Nothing. Where was that phone? Had Flori tried calling yet? I risked flashing my face with the penlight, making a call-me gesture in Flori's direction. A soft gobble let me know she understood.

Still no flash of light appeared. No buzzing or ringing. No phone. I stooped and peered under the truck, again finding nothing. What if I *had* dropped the phone in the house? I tiptoed around the front of the truck and peeked through the open blinds of Don's office. My stomach bounced off my feet. Under Don's desk a cell phone lit up, showing familiar red and green icons. I flashed the light on myself again and made frantic throat-cutting gestures, hoping that Flori would interpret these as hang up now.

Did I dare break in again? No way. Not when Don was in there. I'd wait until he left for work and hope that he didn't pick this morning to vacuum his office. Maybe I could lure him out early by calling in a hot dog emergency or have Brigitte summon him for a food-cart meeting or . . . I hurried down the driveway, my mind whirling, my feet in automatic escape mode. I didn't dare turn on the light and I wasn't looking down anyway. That's why I didn't see the lump that caught my right foot. I tripped hard, the sickening feeling of falling overcoming me before I could stop myself.

I threw out my hands. One landed on sharp gravel. The other on something soft and rounded. Soft like clothes? Lumpy like a shoulder? I scrambled backward, not wanting to believe my initial impression. I was halfway tempted to gather up Flori and run, but I knew I couldn't. Shaking, I turned on my flashlight.

Don Busco lay in front of me. His arms were outstretched over his head. His eyes shut but not from sleep.

Flori appeared at my side. She assessed Don. "Is he . . . drunk?" she asked, her tone hopeful.

I wanted to believe he was passed out from a late night on the town, but once again I found myself touching a cold, pulseless wrist.

"He's dead," I said shakily.

Her hand danced through the sign of the cross. She murmured prayers. I seconded her "Amen," and I felt awful for adding, "My phone is in his office."

Chapter 27

Flori and I stood over Don. His wrist had been cold, too cold to hope that CPR or EMTs might help. "You'll have to call the police," I said to Flori, resigned that my phone would soon be found in the home of a dead guy. Bagged and tagged as evidence, and then I'd have to explain how it got there.

Flori reached into her tote bag. Instead of her phone, she brought out a headlamp. "First let's look around while we have the chance. Mr. Busco, God rest his soul, won't get any more dead." Her light lit up Don and most of the driveway. A few houses away another dog barked, sharp and urgent. I tensed, fearful that any moment someone would spot us and call the police. I could imagine what they'd describe. Two people, dressed in black, hovering over a body.

Flori aimed her forehead and lamp up the driveway. "Look, are those deep tire marks in the gravel? See how they stop about a foot away? The way he's lying, arms out, do you think someone could have hit him with a car?"

I shuddered. Poor Don. He'd tried to help Linda. He touted her innocence all along.

I forced myself to study Don and his surroundings. "But how?" I asked. "He's lying about even with his hot dog cart. If a car or truck hit him, wouldn't it have struck the cart too?" The cart appeared to be undamaged except for a few dings, likely from normal use.

Flori switched off her light and we stood in silence. Above, the sky was turning a steely gray. A new day that Don would never see. I felt a pang of sorrow.

"Maybe he wasn't standing right here," Flori said quietly. "Maybe he was hit and thrown backward. That's why the tire marks stop up there and the cart's okay."

I closed my eyes and imagined the scene, except it wasn't Don I saw. It was the red truck speeding toward me. I'd been on a narrow, curved street and wearing headphones. Manny would have deemed my death a hit and run. But to speed down a driveway, to strike a big man with enough force to kill him? That couldn't be called anything but murder.

When I opened my eyes, Flori had disappeared. I whispered her name. A soft turkey call sounded, which I traced to Don's back door.

"Look, the door's been left unlocked," Flori said. "You say your phone's inside? Why don't you run and get it while I call the police. I'll call the non-emergency number to give you some time." She handed me something soft. "Gloves. You didn't leave fingerprints before, did you?"

Brigitte and I had worn gloves, black latex. Georgio had insisted on that. I donned Flori's fuzzy knit gloves and reached for the doorknob, trying to talk down my fear. Don wasn't about to jump out and confront me. And the murderer was likely long gone. I heard Flori greeting the police station operator. She seemed to be establishing that they were related through some distant aunt and great-niece-twice-removed manner. Pretty soon the operator would give up on deciphering the genealogy and send police cars barreling our way. I took a deep breath and stepped inside.

I knew my way down the hallway. This time I didn't linger or peek in other rooms. I went straight to Don's office and grabbed my phone, clutching it in a white-knuckle grip so it wouldn't get away from me again. I was about to hurry back when I noticed something odd with the room. Was it neater? Papers that once covered the desk in the random scatter of autumn leaves now stood in loose stacks. A clean spot on an otherwise dusty shelf suggested that Don's printer had been moved.

I counted myself lucky that Don—or his killer—hadn't found my phone.

The sun lit up the morning sky in pink streaks by the time the first patrol car arrived. More

followed, along with a grumpy Manny, his partner Bunny, and various dog walkers and gawking neighbors. Flori and I waited at the end of the
driveway, as instructed by Manny.

"What are you doing here?" was the first thing
my ex had asked, or rather, demanded. He'd stood
close and I'd detected a whiff of perfume. Manny's date night must have gone well. No wonder
he was grumpy to get pulled out of bed. Plus,
Manny was never a morning guy. We did have
that in common.

"Rita and I were out for a Sunday morning
walk," Flori said. "My headlamp lit him up. We
called right away, and I had the nicest chat with
my grand-niece-twice-removed who works your
phones."

Manny, of course, didn't buy Flori's story. He
stomped off to supervise the crime scene and
search the house.

The next man to show up didn't believe us
either, but at least he was a lot nicer about it. Jake
pulled in behind the silent ambulance. Flori had
called him while we were waiting for the police
to arrive.

"Do I even want to know what you two were
doing?" Jake asked. I suspected that he'd hurried
over. He lacked both his hat and his dog and was
wearing jeans, a faded sweatshirt, and running
shoes.

"No," I said, staring at my shoes. I felt bad that
I'd gotten so many people out of bed early on a
Sunday morning. "You don't want to know. But
we didn't do that." I nodded toward the white
sheet covering Don.

He smiled. "I didn't think you had. Someone sure did, though. Kill him, I mean, and here you ladies are, right in the midst of it . . . again."

My head hurt. I needed caffeine, a nap, and a normal life. I didn't know what to say so I let Flori fill in the conversation with flirtatious small talk. She told Jake that he looked good, which was like telling the sun it was bright.

He tipped his chin in a bashful expression that only added to his good looks. "I doubt that. I didn't have time to shave or have coffee, but thank you, Flori, all the same. You ladies are looking fine, as always." He smiled and for a moment I fantasized about another breakfast date. His smile, however, quickly morphed into his lawyer face. "Please tell me that Linda was in no way involved in whatever you were doing."

I exchanged a look with Flori. I would have pleaded the fifth.

Flori said, "Not directly. Of course, you know that we suspected Don of trying to run over Rita, and he threatened us. Or so we thought."

Jake raised his eyebrows. "So, you came here before daylight to do what?"

I expected Flori to issue an evasive or flirtatious change of subject. Instead, my elderly friend dropped the whole truth. "We were looking for Rita's cell phone. She dropped it in Don's house when she broke in yesterday. Using professional door-entering equipment, mind you. Rita wouldn't actually break anything. And she took along a friend for backup. No need to worry."

Jake was rubbing his temple and saying, "Don't tell me this."

My faced burned. "Hypothetically broke in, she means, with a hypothetical lock-pick from a . . . er . . . lock enthusiast."

"No, no," Flori corrected. "For real she broke in. Rita and her colleague—who we can't name— found a hidden stash of cash. An important clue, which she left where she found it." Over Jake's groan, she said, "And there's more. Our associate, Addie, snapped a fine photograph of Don meeting with Gerald Jenkins Senior at a bar last night. Jenkins is the one the police should be looking at."

I chimed in, eager to shift attention away from me and my crimes. "Addie will have more details, but it looked like Don and Jenkins were arguing."

Jake held up a silencing finger and then used it to rub his brow. "Okay. Unofficial legal advice: don't repeat what you just said. You can tell the police about the argument. Show them the picture and ask Addie to explain. But, please, let them find that cash on their own. Whatever you do, do *not* tell them you were breaking and entering and trespassing and any other illegal activities that I should not hear about if I am ever called as a witness." He held my gaze. Then he lowered those gorgeous steel-blue eyes and leaned in close to my ear. "I still want that soufflé dinner you promised me, and it won't happen if you're in jail or my perpetual client. Lawyerly ethics and all."

Jake left a few minutes later. He had appointments with coffee and then an early practice with his club basketball league.

Flori and I watched him stride to his car and drive away.

"I suppose I should apologize," Flori said.

I was busy worrying in general and regretting the missed dinner date in particular. "For what?" I asked absentmindedly.

"You were right. Jake Strong is a man sensitive and confident enough to love a Cinco de Mayo soufflé," Flori said with an appreciative chuckle. "Now, if you add in my chocoflan, that hot lawyer will be butter in your hands, Rita."

Flori and I waited around for a long half hour before we could give brief statements to Bunny.

"And you were out simply walking?" Bunny said, disbelief obvious. "Before sunrise? Dressed in black, in a neighborhood where neither of you live?"

"Gets the blood flowing," Flori said.

Bunny scowled. Manny reinforced her skepticism.

He leaned against the corner of Don's house a few feet away. "Meddling, that's what those two were up to."

My ex had clearly gotten up on the wrong side of the bed. I might have felt sorry for him if he wasn't being so petulant. Besides, I had myself to feel sorry for. I sure wasn't having a great morning, although I had only myself to blame. If only I hadn't dropped my phone. Or broken in to begin with. I felt that guilt was written across my face. Guilty of blaming a murdered man. Guilty of breaking and rebreaking into his house. Still, I didn't believe that Don was entirely innocent.

I told Bunny about Gerald Jenkins Senior meeting with Don last night. "Jenkins nearly dies from poisoning. Then he gets out of the hospital and—still looking sick—goes to meet Don at a bar straightaway? And they argue? It's suspicious, don't you think? Our friend sent us a photo."

Flori, after a few false starts with her cell phone, brought up the photo and handed the phone to Bunny.

Bunny tilted her head. "Is that a margarita and someone's knee?"

I feared she was missing the blurriest but most important part of the photo. "No, there, those two shapes. They're men arguing."

Bunny returned Flori's phone. "We'll ask Mr. Jenkins about his activities, but there's nothing illegal about visiting a bar."

"Yeah, Rita," Manny said petulantly. The long nights he spent at his favorite bars had sparked arguments during our marriage, especially after I'd spent long days with our infant daughter. I didn't have the energy to argue with him. Luckily, his attention was back on the news van. Milan Lujan stepped out in a sky blue dress, looking freshly powdered and ready for action. Manny straightened his jacket.

Bunny puffed air out her bottom lip. "Why don't you two come in and give formal statements later? Maybe you'll hear more about Mr. Busco's and Mr. Jenkins's activities. Or something else relevant will come to mind, like what you were actually doing here."

"Will do," I said in my peppiest cheerleader voice, ignoring Bunny's jibe. I grabbed Flori by the arm. "Time to go."

We were nearly to my car when I heard a man's voice. "Milan, it's your anonymous informant. *Hey!* You two by the Subaru, wait up. Milan wants to interview you!"

I was glad Jake wasn't around to hear my tires squeal.

Flori praised my driving. "Well done," she said as we peeled down side streets. Once I was sure we were safe, I drove her home so she could change her burglar wear for church clothes. "We're closer than ever," she said.

I thought about this as I drove home. We were closer only because one of our main suspects was dead. I let myself in the casita, expecting Celia to still be asleep. She stood in the living room, wearing skull-printed pajamas. Hugo, perched on her shoulder, attacked a piece of her already spiky hair.

"Dad just called," she said, her words stretched out with a yawn. "He says there're some reporters who want to talk to you."

Chapter 28

Later that morning I tried to take my mind off dead bodies by heading over to Victor's place. I assessed the array of colorful sticky notes and hoped I was making the right choices . . . about everything. Three times in the last hour an unidentified caller had tried to reach my cell phone. Had Manny given Milan Lujan or her cameraman my number? Someone had. When I checked the messages, Milan, in perfect newscaster enunciation, asked to interview me. Off the record, she said. Or on the record, if I wanted some publicity for Linda's cause. I silenced the ringer the fourth time she called and was ready to turn the phone off completely the next time it lit up. Then I noticed Linda's name and number.

She started with an apology for calling and interrupting me. "Mama told me how you found poor Mr. Busco. He was such a nice man. Kind. We helped each other out, and he believed in my tamales. I'm so sorry he's dead and that you found him, Rita. I hope you don't get in any trouble. You have Celia to think of. You and Mama should be more careful."

I reminded Linda that she also had children and grandchildren who needed her. "Don's death is terrible, awful, so please don't take this wrong, but maybe it'll help you, Linda. The police will investigate new leads, which will hopefully take them away from you. They'll find who *really* killed Napoleon, and the same person likely killed Don too."

Linda murmured a prayer in Spanish. "I still feel sorry I got in that fight with Napoleon," she said again.

"No one who truly knows you can think you had anything to do with his death," I said. Except half the people who showed up for Flori's free pancake breakfast, as well as Crystal, although was she pointing blame toward Linda to take suspicion off herself?

Linda, for once, was thinking of the positive. "People *are* being so nice to me. Brigitte Voll invited me to an event on the Plaza this afternoon. The food cart operators are holding a rally to show they're standing together and not afraid." Silence filled the air waves. Then Linda said, "That's why I called. I know you're busy, but could you go with me? I don't want to go on my own, and I'm afraid if I invite Mama, she'll make trouble."

I told Linda I'd pick her up. Celia surprised me by wanting to come along. Although I tried to keep a neutral expression, I must have raised an eyebrow or widened an eyelid or exhibited some other hint of maternal amazement.

My daughter shrugged. "Yeah, whatever, I want to support Tía Linda."

Linda was delighted to see Celia. "This is so nice of both of you!" she reiterated as I maneuvered into a parking spot a few blocks from the Plaza. "Brigitte told me that the rally will be small and quiet, but you never know. Look at that pancake breakfast Mama held. The one side of the room was pretty rowdy."

Flori's pancake breakfast, however, was no match for the crowd we found on the Plaza.

"Whoa," Celia said as we rounded the corner and took in the throngs of people and carts. "Look at all the 'Free Linda' demonstrators over there and the food carts. Awesome!"

"Oh dear," Linda said, scraping back her bangs nervously.

"It's like a festival," said Celia. She led the way. Linda and I followed, awed by the food-cart take-over of the Plaza. The carts encircled the veterans' memorial and were offering up goodies from gourmet popcorn to tacos, fajitas, and hand pies. There was even a lady selling tamales.

"This way," I said, hoping that Linda didn't notice the tamales.

She already had. "Tamales," she said wistfully. "How nice. Do you think we should try them? Look, she has a sweet one with dates and brown sugar like I make for Christmas."

"Maybe later," I said. "Look."

I pointed toward the raised bandstand, where Crystal, poured into a strawberry-red dress, tested a microphone. Behind her an all-female mariachi band tuned their instruments. The musicians'

long black skirts skimmed the floor of the bandstand, weighted down with the signature silver
buttons up their sides. Flori, when setting up her
creepy mariachi mannequins, had explained that
the traditional cropped jackets and silver- and
embroidery-embellished costumes originated in
the *charro* cowboy tradition in Mexico.

The crowd moved toward the bandstand.
Linda, Celia, and I hung back, listening as Crystal tapped the microphone. With each "Test, test,
test," she increased the volume, until her voice
boomed across the Plaza. A man with a video
camera clambered up onto the stage. I recognized
him as the News 6 camera guy. Milan Lujan had
to be nearby. "Can I borrow your sunglasses?" I
asked Celia, who was standing just in front of me.
She handed them back without question.

Onstage, Crystal waved and yelled, *"Hola,"* her
voice echoing off the buildings to the south. "We
are here to remember our friend and colleague,
Don Busco, brutally murdered." She patted the
black band on her right arm. "We remember him
and call for the police to find his killer!" The mariachi band stepped up behind her and struck
somber discordant chords.

The crowd applauded and Crystal continued,
raising her voice even louder. "A killer is after
us. A poisoner, too, targeting our food family."
She paused, looking out across the crowd. "That
person, he—or *she*—could be here among us
now."

A few people looked our way, and I heard Linda's name murmured. She edged closer to me. Celia's shoulders stiffened.

The mariachi band strummed a few stanzas in the minor key. Mariachi bands often give me chills, in a good way. I have similar responses to bagpipers and really amazing orchestras. Now I had goose bumps on top of creepy chills. The killer *would* be here. I was almost sure of it. He—or she, as Crystal said—was bold.

Crystal stepped up to the microphone again. "One of our own, Linda Santiago, has been accused of the murder of Napoleon, a man who made many of us mad enough to kill." She looked out over the crowd and then waved our way. "Hello, Linda!" Linda ducked behind me, and Celia scooted back to help buffer her from staring eyes.

Raising her fist in the air, Crystal declared, "Don Busco believed in Linda, and now so do I! Linda had reason to kill Napoleon, but never Don. Now I know that Don was right. The police have made a mistake to focus on a good woman."

One of the mariachi singers held up a sign. FREE LINDA!

Supporters in the crowd called out Linda's name. I felt a nudge behind me and figured it was my chagrined friend. When I turned, however, I saw Brigitte.

"This is amazing," she said. "Linda, you have so much support."

Linda seemed to be shriveling before my eyes. "It's okay, Linda," I said comfortingly. "Crystal's getting off the stage. Just nice mariachi music now."

Except Crystal hadn't relinquished her microphone yet. She was sticking it in front of the person I least wanted to hear from: Manny.

"Officer," Crystal cooed. "We asked you here because we food carters are scared. Two of our own are dead. The food inspector has been poisoned. Is there a psychopath after us, like Don said? What can you tell us? Can you comfort us?"

I imagined that Manny would be more than happy to comfort pretty Crystal. He bestowed his sympathetic look on her and stepped up onto the stage, where he greeted the cute cello player by name.

"Citizens and food carters of Santa Fe," Manny said, in a voice worthy of soap-opera drama. "We are narrowing in on our suspect right now. The vicious and cowardly perpetrator will be punished." He repeated this in Spanish.

The Spanish was a nice touch, I gave him that. It seemed to impress the crowd, including Celia, who gazed at her dad with rapt attention.

"Hear that, Tía Linda?" Celia said, nudging Linda.

Linda, who had been staring at her feet, looked up long enough to smile at Celia.

Manny was going on about processing evidence, about the important role citizens had in reporting any evidence and in letting the police do their work. "Amateurs should not try to gather evidence or jump to faulty conclusions," he said pointedly.

"*Pah,*" Brigitte said. She whispered to me, "You and me, Rita, we discovered the money trail that the police will say they found. The killer will be the food inspector Jenkins, *n'est-ce pas?*" She pointed to a far corner of the Plaza. Jenkins stood off by himself. Even from this distance, he looked unhealthy. I wished we could yell to Manny, *There he is! There's your man!* Manny would love to make a dramatic arrest in front of Milan and her action news camera. He wouldn't love that it was my idea, though.

"Patience," Brigitte said, as if guessing my thoughts. "All in good time." She wished Linda good luck and hurried back to her crepe cart to get ready for the hungry crowd.

Manny was fielding questions now and deflecting most of them. He couldn't comment, he said, on whether the two murders and poisoning were related. He wouldn't comment on wild theories, including those involving a scary traveling clown and marijuana cookie smugglers from Colorado. I could tell that Manny was getting testy. "I can't comment anymore," he said, thrusting the microphone at the lead mariachi singer.

She launched into "El Rey," a song so famous that even a non-native southwesterner like me could recognize it. Flori had helped me translate the lyrics once. "El Rey" told of a man who thought himself a king. Rich or poor, he could do what he wanted, his word was law. I listened, trying to pick out phrases I knew. Napoleon definitely had a king complex. Only one line didn't fit. *You'll weep when I die.* Except for Brigitte's sniffles, I'd seen no weeping. People were scared, though.

Linda, Celia, and I strolled along the line of food vendors, and I overheard the popcorn and fajita cart owners arguing about who was to blame.

"A psychopath," the popcorn lady contended. "I've read they're everywhere. In boardrooms and lurking where you least think they'll be. He's probably here right now, watching us from the bushes."

"What bushes?" the fajita guy countered. He pushed back the bandanna wound around his forehead and waved across the shrubbery-free Plaza.

"You know what I mean. Behind a tree, then. Or over in that van. Or just walking around, or any-where . . ." Popcorn lady shuddered. The fajita guy looked up, saw us, and his eyes widened.

"Hi, Xavier," Linda said timidly. The stout man backed away and pretended to attend to an empty cooler. The popcorn lady offered us a bag of caramel corn, whispering to Linda, "Don't let Xavier upset you. I don't think you did it. Most of us don't, and we want you back. Xavier believes all the craziest stories, like UFOs and Bigfoot and *chupacabras*. Seriously, ask him about Bigfoot. You'll never hear the end of it."

At the end of the row of carts, Celia was holding free popcorn, hand pies, lemonade, and a tamale, all from Linda's supporters. Others in the food cart line had given us dirty looks or avoided eye contact.

When we reached Crepe Empire, Brigitte shook her head. "You have your hands full. You must be hungry."

"All from Linda's supporters," I said, emphasiz-ing the positive.

"The others think I did it," Linda added qui-etly. "They think I killed those men. I can never come back to work. I'm a pariah. A black sheep." Her voice faltered. "No one will miss my tama-les anyhow. Look, there's already another tamale cart. A modern cart. Napoleon said my cart was old. He was right."

"Never!" Brigitte said with French gusto. "Napoleon, he would never tell you, but he declared your *mole* tamale delectable, Linda. A huge compliment."

Celia jumped in. "She's right, Tía Linda. Your tamales are the best! And this one, it's no good." She covered the remains of the free rival tamale with a napkin. A few moments earlier I'd seen her eating it with relish. "It's, ah . . . it's too sweet, and who wants chocolate chips and banana in a tamale anyway?"

Me? Celia? Melted chocolate, banana, and brown sugar in a tender tamale sounded delicious.

Instead, I said, "They're right. People miss you. Didn't you hear the popcorn lady? And Xavier's own mother begged you to come back in time for Fourth of July and summer picnics."

Linda smiled weakly. "I do hope I'll be back."

"You will be!" Celia said. "Fight for yourself, isn't that what you say, Mom?"

"*Oui, oui,*" Brigitte said. "You must fight. Your own self is all that matters."

Inspiring words. I wanted to gather us all in for a group hug, although that would have mortified Celia and spilled her popcorn. "Soon it'll all be over," I assured Linda. "It's like Manny said up on the stage. The police are narrowing in."

"We sure are." Manny's voice made me jump.

"Dad!" Celia said. "Want some popcorn? It's chile lime. The lady sells cheese and caramel too, like we used to get back in Chicago."

Manny accepted a handful. There was something in his expression I didn't like. He looked a little too pleased, and not simply because Chicago-style popcorn was one of the few things he loved about the Midwest. Had he just snagged a date with Milan Lujan? She was weaving our way, her cameraman in tow. Bunny and the young, wide-eyed policeman I met at the Cathedral were pushing through the crowd as well.

Adrenaline surged through me. Manny knew. He figured out that I broke into Don's, and he was here to arrest me in front of our daughter, News 6, and a mariachi band. No, he couldn't be that mean. Our divorce had been contentious and we still argued, but he wouldn't publicly shame me. Would he?

"Sorry, Rita," my ex had the decency—or gall—to say. He squeezed Celia's arm support-ively. "Sorry, kid. This has to be done."

Bunny stepped up. I took my hands out of my pockets, prepared to hold out my wrists. At least these handcuffs wouldn't be pink, fluffy embar-rassments. Bunny didn't touch me, but her words nearly bowled me over. "Linda Santiago, I am ar-resting you for the murder of Don Busco."

Chapter 29

I stood outside the police station experiencing a bitter taste of déjà vu and watching Winston sniff a flagpole. The bulldog circled the pole before moving on to investigate a tree. At the other end of the leash, I followed. What else did I have to do? Jake had said that he'd be a while. He'd warned me of something else too. This time, Linda might not come out with him.

I'd called Jake from the Plaza, midway through Bunny's recitation of Miranda warnings, right after the News 6 cameraman shoved by me for an action shot. Jake had been taking Winston for a relaxing stroll.

"So much for relaxing, eh, buddy?" I said to Winston. The bulky bulldog kept his nose and jowls to the ground. He did look up and wiggle his stubby tail when Flori emerged through the double glass doors of the station. My heart ached to see her looking so small and frail. I'd called her after getting off the phone with Jake and worried how to break the bad news. As it turned out, I didn't have to. She'd already heard through her high-speed gossip network. At least three people had called her nearly simultaneously, all witnesses to Linda's arrest.

"Well?" I asked, trying to sound upbeat.

She shook her head slightly and bent to pat Winston, who drooled up at her with adoring eyes. "Jake's not optimistic," she said. "The head prosecutor's back, and Jake says he's a bulldog. Not the nice kind like you, Winston."

Winston moaned. I wanted to as well. "What's that mean?" I asked.

It meant that Linda was being charged with Don's murder, in addition to Napoleon's death and possibly the poisoning of Gerald Jenkins Senior.

"Absurd!" I fumed. "How could they think Linda would hurt Don? She had no reason. No motive. No means—"

Flori cut in. "Motive and opportunity. That's what the bulldog prosecutor is saying. The police found paint on the wall by Don's driveway. White paint, matching Linda's truck, and a big scratch on its side. Jake said that Linda doesn't contest she left the paint. She helped Don haul his hot dog cart back home a few weeks ago. She scraped his wall trying to back out of the driveway."

I've dinged and scraped a few walls in my time in Santa Fe. A wall mishap seemed like a perfectly reasonable explanation. It would to Manny too, although he'd say it happened while a panicked Linda was fleeing the scene of her crime.

"Jake says he'll get his own laboratory analysis

done," Flori was saying. "Maybe there's some fancy scientific way to tell how long the paint's been on that wall. He says there might also be ways to . . . well . . . match the marks on Mr. Busco's body."

I tried to stay upbeat for both our sakes. "When can we bail Linda out? I'll go with you to Ida Green's bail bonds café if we can take Winston along, or we can drop him off at my place. Celia's there, and he loves playing with her and Hugo."

Flori kept petting Winston's wrinkles. "Ida can't help, unless her tortillas really can break jail locks. Jake doesn't think Linda's getting out, Rita. Not yet, at least." My elderly friend looked up at me, her expression as mournful as Winston's. "We have to help her, but how?"

I'd never heard Flori express such uncertainty.

"We'll figure out a way," I said. "We have to."

The next morning, Tres Amigas was open as usual. Our clientele, however, was anything but usual.

I nibbled nervously at a slice of extra-crispy bacon, scanning the dining room for our Monday regulars. Except for the elderly men who gathered for gossip and the pancake special, most of our usual customers were missing. The ladies who knit while downing burritos as big as their yarn skeins were no-shows. Same with the legal aides from the courthouse and the woman from the baby boutique down the street and the nice florist and the retired professors.

I reached for another slice of bacon, only to be blocked by Juan, who was hair- and beard-net free. I supposed it didn't matter. No one was around to see our spotless café.

"Where is everyone?" I asked. "Today's Cinco de Mayo, right? Doesn't anyone want *chilaquiles*? What about the piñata party Flori had planned for the preschoolers? Are they coming?"

Juan shook his head. "The preschoolers cancelled," he said with a shrug.

I didn't have to ask why. People were avoiding us and our festive piñatas. Some would believe the news and the stories of poisonings and murder. Others wouldn't know what to say to Flori. After all, there's no Hallmark card for "sorry your daughter's in jail for a double homicide and possible poisoning."

Even strangers knew. A few minutes earlier, a group of cheerful tourists had come and ordered bacon, eggs, and blue-corn waffles. Then one picked up the paper and read it, his good mood changing to visible panic. After a hurried consultation, the group slapped down cash for their coffees and left. They'd tried to tell me that they had a train to catch, but I knew the train schedule and a polite fib when I heard it. I only wondered which story had spooked them. The one about the food inspector claiming he'd been poisoned at Tres Amigas, or the one naming the café in connection with two brutal murders?

Things were bad when people abandoned bacon and piñatas. That didn't mean the bacon should go to waste. When Juan went to the walk-in fridge to put away the waffle batter, I stole another slice and wandered out to the dining room. What worried me most of all was Flori's absence. She'd left an hour ago, saying she needed to run to the grocery store for chiles. It was clearly a lie. We had mounds of chiles, fresh, frozen, powdered, and jarred. That was disturbing as well. Flori was usually a much better liar.

By the time she returned, Juan and I had served a few customers who either didn't read the paper or liked to dine dangerously.

Flori assessed the situation. "No outstanding orders to bother with, then," she said. "Good."

Juan confirmed this, not as happily. "No orders of *chilaquiles*, no tamales, no *chiles rellenos*." Seemingly resigned, he handed me the rack of bacon. I snagged several slices in case he changed his mind.

"No matter," Flori said. "Juan, as soon as the men's coffee klatch leaves, you take the rest of the day off, full pay. Go home and put your feet up."

Juan stared at Flori. "We're closing early?"

"Taking a Cinco de Mayo holiday," Flori said. "Rita, you too, consider this a holiday. A sleuthing holiday. Now let's get you out of that hairnet. We're taking Addie and her beau out to breakfast."

Addie and Junior were already seated at my favorite corner booth at Tune-Up. She waved to us. Junior glowered.

"You're the lady who bugged me in the library," he said sulkily.

Addie patted his arm. "Chin up, love. Rita's just trying to help Miss Linda, like I told you." Her chipper tone sounded strained.

Flori and I took the bench seat across from Addie and Junior, and we all studied the menu in awkward silence.

"I always get the *huevos el Salvadoreños*," Flori said. "There's something so comforting about scrambled eggs."

The Salvadoran version came with scallions and tomatoes alongside pan-fried bananas, refried beans, and a homemade corn tortilla that Flori acknowledged was as good as hers.

Addie ordered the same thing. She nudged Junior. "Give 'em a try, why don't you?"

I'd already had scrambled eggs with Celia. I'd then eaten more than a month's supply of bacon and other nibbles at the café. Reluctantly, I tore my eyes from my favorite—the yummy steak and eggs with crispy, cheesy hash browns—and ordered yogurt with fruit.

Flori led the small talk about Junior's interest in archeology until our plates arrived.

"So," she said, "they make lovely tamales here too, wrapped in banana leaves. You know a thing or two about tamales, don't you, Junior?"

His face turned as red as his hair.

"Go on," urged Addie. "We agreed. It's important. Important to me."

Junior muttered something I didn't catch. "What did you say?" I demanded.

He kept his eyes on his plate. "I knew that cockroach was a plant. The one in your friend's tamale. We got a tamale from the store, and Dad stuffed a bug in it and wrapped it back up. He had a deal going with Napoleon. Napoleon called us when the tamale lady came back to the Plaza that morning and we acted out our parts."

Addie prodded him with her elbow. "Go on, tell 'em more. Say why you did it."

Junior shoved his eggs around his plate, creating pathways through his beans. "I didn't want to, but my college tuition's late." He reached out and gripped Addie's hand. "I'm really sorry."

Flori, if she hadn't gone into food, would have made a great interrogator. Presently, she was playing good cop or sweet, grandmotherly cop. "We understand, don't we, ladies?"

Addie didn't look so sure about that. I wasn't either. I'd seen Junior on the Plaza, holding the tamale high, yelling about filth and bugs and pointing to Linda.

"That's what started all of this," I muttered.

"I know!" Junior said. His voice rose to a squeaky pitch. "Dad's ready to leave town. He says there's a killer out there. Says he might be next. Or me!"

Addie made comforting sounds, which I didn't think Junior deserved.

Flori puffed out her chest and likely the tape recorder attached to it. "Then your father must not think the killer's Linda, since she's locked up. I bet he doesn't truly think we poisoned him either."

Junior nodded.

"What's that?" Flori said in the direction of her brassiere.

"No," Junior admitted. "He doesn't know who did, except it's not you." He looked up, defiant now. "At least, he thinks it's probably not you."

"Poppycock," Addie said. "Junior, you *know* that my friends would never hurt anyone."

I decided to be bad cop. It wasn't hard because I was still mad at both Jenkinses, Junior and Senior. "Someone is hurting people," I said. "Killing them. Your dad could have died, and it's true, the killer might go after him again. Tell us who else he messed with."

Junior slumped so far his chin was nearly level with his uneaten meal. "Okay, this is between us, right?"

Us and Flori's recorder, but I told him to go on.

"You know that woman who sells juice, Crystal? She and Napoleon had some kind of affair that turned nasty. Napoleon wanted her off the Plaza. He told Dad to mess with her permit paperwork, but she got it fixed too quick. Then there was this restaurant Napoleon wanted to buy. He paid Dad to give it a bunch of bad inspections so the price would go lower." His voice turned whiny. "But Dad didn't just play lackey to Napoleon."

"Meaning he had his own dirty business enterprises too? Like threatening Tres Amigas with a failed inspection?"

Addie clicked her tongue disapprovingly.

"Yeah. Okay," Junior admitted. "He did that. But sometimes he helped places out by overlooking infractions." A defiant look crossed his thin face. "He helped people stay in business. That's good!"

I hoped Junior had to take ethics as part of his college curriculum. Something still puzzled me too. "I saw you hand an envelope of cash to Don Busco. Why? Was he part of your dad's scams? Was that Don's cut you handed over?"

Junior sniffed and said with misplaced righteousness, "Don? No way. He was shaking down Dad. Don was nothing but a filthy blackmailer and a gambler."

"Don knew about your father and Napoleon taking down competitors?" I prompted.

"Yeah. After Napoleon died, Don told Dad that he'd send the police sniffing around unless Dad paid him. Dad gave him five hundred and told him that was all he was getting."

Flori asked the question on the tip of my tongue. "How did Don know?"

Junior shoved beans around his plate. "He was a bartender before the hot dogs. Bartenders hear everything, you know? He must have kept the habit. He was smart. He watched people."

Addie agreed with this. "It's true. I know bartenders who soak up almost as much gossip as you, Miss Flori. Oops, I mean, information, not gossip."

Junior pushed away his plate. I still didn't trust him, and not only because he was pushing away a delicious breakfast. I was half tempted to steal his bananas, fried to caramel sweetness. "I think you've just given us more reason to suspect your father of Don's murder. Don't blackmailers keep asking for more and more money?"

Junior grinned. "You fixed that problem, didn't you? You and that Brigitte woman. Once you caught Dad messing around in Napoleon's office, the police went and interviewed him. Dad convinced them he was consulting on restaurant sanitation. He was about to go give Don Busco a *surprise* inspection to get his money back."

Flori muttered about grubby business, and I agreed. I felt dirty simply hearing about the deceit. The yogurt helped. I took a bite of cleansing fruit and considered our living suspects, among which I counted Gerald Jenkins Senior. The man knew food. He could have sickened himself to eliminate suspicion. And what about Don? I no longer thought he murdered Napoleon, but he must have known who the killer was. He'd gambled, both at the casinos and with his life.

I tried a new angle of questioning with Junior. "Where did your father go the morning he was poisoned? Before visiting Tres Amigas?"

Junior moved his eggs around some more. "Who poisoned him, you mean? He thinks Don did it. Or maybe Crystal or one of those taco guys? Pretty extreme, huh?"

Brigitte had already told me that Jenkins Senior had gotten juice from Crystal. I wondered what else he'd consumed. I asked his son.

Junior admitted that his father liked to get freebies, offerings made to butter him up. "A perk of his job, as long as he knew the place was really clean," Junior said. He then went on to list menu items from pretty much every cart on the Plaza.

"Who does he *think* did it?" Flori asked.

Junior's slumped shoulders rose a fraction before falling again. "Crystal? She got snippy with him. Told him not to mess with her again. Plus, he said her tamarind juice was way sour."

"It's supposed to be sour," I said through an exasperated sigh.

Junior sat up a bit straighter. "Yeah, well, she was mad. So was one of the taco guys when Dad cited him for not using gloves. Dad got bagged chips from him, so I guess they weren't poisoned. Don Busco was really ticked. Dad didn't even eat at Don's, thinking Don might spit on his hot dog or something gross."

"So Don couldn't have poisoned him either," Flori said.

Junior perked up. "Wrong!" he said smugly. "Think about it. The police would check places he ate, right? They'd think Don was in the clear. Thing is, Dad's got a bad shoulder, so he left his heavy satchel on a bench when he was inspecting some carts. Dad's theory is that Don sneaked over and put poison in his coffee thermos. After he got out of the hospital, he confronted Don. Don warned him to drop it. Said he was handling things and leave it alone."

Some handling. Don was dead, Linda was in jail, and I feared the killer would strike again.

Chapter 30

After breakfast, Addie wanted a "wee private chitchat" with Junior. Flori and I went to the Plaza, the scene of the original crime.

"I don't like Addie's boyfriend," I said.

Flori was less concerned. "That girl has zero intuition when it comes to cooking. With people, though, she's pretty good."

"Mmm . . . I still don't like him."

Flori stopped and took in the view over the historic Plaza. She reached over and squeezed my hand. "We don't always like who our children or friends date, do we?"

That was for sure. I felt I'd dodged a bullet—hopefully—with Celia and the orange-haired skater kid. Another thought hit me. "You *do* like Jake, don't you?"

She chuckled. "Rita, if I were forty years younger and not forever in love with that old fool Bernard, I'd be vying with you for that man. You keep after him. Don't let that dinner date get away from you."

We walked toward the bandstand. Flower petals lay scattered on the stage. In the middle of the petals stood Don's hot dog cart, draped in black ribbons and white carnations.

Brigitte and Crystal had set up their carts at the nearby corner, facing the Palace of the Governors. Crystal turned away when she saw us. Brigitte waved.

I noticed that the Free Linda donation bucket was no longer on Crystal's cart. Crystal wasn't offering us any free juice either.

"Don't involve me in this anymore," she said after Flori and I stepped in front of her counter. "I stood up and supported Linda at the rally. I did my part. Then I got to thinking, look what happened to Don."

Crystal opened the freezer chest on the side of her cart, chipping noisily at the ice with a metal scooper.

While she was occupied, Brigitte sidled next to me and whispered, "I am watching her extremely closely." She bobbed her head toward Crystal. "I have the day off from OhLaLa so I come here to observe and make crepes. It is, as you Americans say, all good."

Crystal straightened, holding a cup half full with ice, which she rattled nervously. "I'm not saying Linda's guilty, but the police did arrest her. Let them handle it. They know what they're doing. That's their job!"

Beside me, I could sense Flori bristling.

"Sorry, Flori," Crystal murmured. Louder, she

said, "I am really, truly sorry. Look, Don's dead. So's Napoleon. And that food inspector got poisoned, and Rita, weren't you run over?"

I touched the bandage on my elbow and tried to turn the conversation around. "Who brought Don's cart over here? Wasn't it evidence?"

Crystal and Brigitte exchanged weak smiles. "We both did," Brigitte said. "We drove by to pay respects, and his cart, it was outside the yellow boundary tape and it looked so . . ." She seemed to struggle for the right word.

"Lonely. Sad," Crystal offered. "Tragic, like its owner was murdered in cold blood. Besides, Don would want to be here. It's Cinco de Mayo. A big day for people drinking and wanting hot dogs. So sad."

I glanced at the sad cart and reminded myself that its owner was a blackmailer. Did Crystal know that firsthand? If she had an affair with Napoleon, maybe Don picked up on it and was blackmailing her like he had Jenkins. She wouldn't want anyone, especially her husband, to know. I couldn't very well ask her here. She hummed "El Rey" and polished her juice containers. For someone claiming fear and sadness, she seemed in a pretty good mood.

I made excuses to leave, saying that Flori and I wanted to pay respects to Don's cart.

"There's an autograph book," Crystal called after us. "Be sure to sign!"

The spiral notebook lay open on the counter where Don had dished up his hot dogs and entertaining tales. Flori flipped through the pages. "Cute cart," she said.

"Don was pretty proud of this cart," I said, stepping behind the counter. No wonder he had liked working here. Fresh air, nice views, happy people . . . mostly. I recalled Junior storming up and thrusting the envelope at Don, not even keeping the offered hot dog. Don hadn't tucked the envelope in his pocket. He'd seemingly slipped it into his cart.

"Cover me," I said to Flori. "Do something normal and boring like checking your phone."

Flori took her cover a step further, holding her phone to her ear while complaining loudly about how people were so glued to their phones these days. "It used to be, you left the house and people who wanted to get in touch with you simply had to wait. My grandmother never had a phone. If people needed to say something, they had to walk over in person. That cut down on needless chatter."

During Flori's monologue, I checked the steamer compartment, a drawer containing bagged buns, and another filled with tongs. I felt under the counter and scanned the wheels. Nothing. I was replacing a bag of buns when I felt something hard. I squished them again before stuffing the whole bag inside my jacket and telling Flori it was time to go.

We sat at a picnic bench near the corner where Tía Tamales should be. I hid the bag under the table and felt through the soft rolls to the objects at the bottom.

"A phone," I said, bringing it out. "And something else."

Flori and I inspected the other device. It was about the size of a TV remote. Flori, who claims to have no use for newfangled electronics, identified it as a voice recorder.

"Not as nice as mine," she said. "That would never fit in our brassieres."

I looked around. Among the people strolling and taking photos, none seemed interested in us. Flori and I put our ears to the device and pushed the On button. I expected Don's voice. The sound made me shiver.

"Like a horror movie ghoul," I said. I told Flori about the voice modifier Brigitte had found in Don's office.

"He did love working on all those movie and TV sets," Flori said, shaking her head. "He fell pretty far, poor man."

The poor man on the tape, if it was Don, was issuing a threat. "I know what you did and have photos to prove it," the ghoul voice said. "Leave five thousand dollars, cash, under the first pew in La Conquistadora's Chapel by ten A.M. tomorrow. Or else."

I listened again. "Why record this?"

"Stage fright?" Flori suggested. "Forgetful? When my Bernard has to change our answering machine, it takes him at least four or five tries and then he still forgets to say our names."

I turned to the phone next. It was a small flip phone, the type that used to be cutting edge before large, smooth screens came into fashion. Cautiously, I turned it on and learned that it had most of its battery charge left. Punching the arrow buttons eventually brought up the recently called list. Three numbers, unlabeled, filled the tiny screen.

Flori urged me to call. "Go ahead. See who answers. Then we've got him, the killer."

"Or he has us," I said with a shudder. "Thanks to the TV news and Crystal's big rally, everyone knows Don is dead. Why would they pick up?"

We sat a minute in silence before Flori said, "The killer knows that Don—a blackmailer—is dead. What would you do if a dead man called you?"

"Not pick up," I said.

Flori had a bright-eyed gleam, the very opposite of my dismal feelings. "No, no, Rita. If you're innocent, you'd answer. You'd be curious. But, what if you're guilty, and you killed Don because he was blackmailing you? If Don's phone called you, you'd worry that he had a partner or someone he told. You'd want to know who you had to kill next."

I dropped the phone on the picnic table as if it was a radioactive hot potato. "All the more reason not to call!" Crystal's fear and admonishment seemed perfectly reasonable. *Let the police handle it.*

Flori, however, had grabbed the phone and was pressing redial on the third number. I made a halfhearted attempt to stop her. She batted me away. Resigned, I scooted closer to her and we listened as the phone rang and rang.

"Don't say anything if someone answers," I warned Flori.

"No one's answering to say anything to," she said. "Look over there, though. Was Crystal just checking her phone? My bifocals don't see that far."

Crystal, half turned to us, was tucking some-thing into her pocket. Flori hung up and dug her miniature binoculars out of her tote bag. She aimed them at Crystal and asked me to hit redial again.

The phone rang a dozen times, during which Crystal chatted with a customer.

At Flori's urging, I tried the second number. To my horror, the recipient answered immediately.

"Santa Fe Health Inspector's office, Amanda speaking, how may I direct your call?"

I hung up on Amanda.

Flori nodded knowingly. "Figures," she said. "It's not surprising he called Jenkins. Let's try the last one. Three's the charm."

Or the killer. I took a deep breath, hit Call, and we both plastered our ears to the phone. The phone again rang with no answer.

"Could you look up the number?" Flori asked. "Can't your fancy phone do that?"

My Google searching came up empty. So did calling information and even Flori's friend who worked in bill collection and could usually trace anybody. Our best lead so far looked like another dead end.

I ran my hand through my hair, tugging it back. "Maybe I should pretend we never found this and trick Manny into discovering it. His tech people can trace the unanswered numbers."

"Mmm," Flori said, absently. She nudged me. "Pat down your hair, dear. Hot lawyer at high noon."

Jake, deep in conversation with Georgio Andre, might not have seen us if Flori hadn't waved both arms as if guiding in an aircraft carrier. The men came our way. Both smiled, Jake pleasantly, Georgio slimily. Flori and I got up to greet them.

"Ladies," Georgio said. He threw an arm around me, saying to Jake as he did, "Excuse us, Rita and I must have a private chat about art and other important matters."

"We can stay here and chat," I said.

Georgio, however, was practically dragging me off. I caught Jake's eye and the hint of a frown. Georgio stopped a few feet away by a tree. "So, your lock-picking, it went well?"

"We got in," I said grudgingly. Then I added, "Thanks. Truly. I have your lock-pick. I'll get it back to you—"

"Keep it," Georgio said smoothly. "I do not need it. Now, with the murder and the tiresome trumped-up thievery charges against me, it is best if I do not have it, I think."

It was best if I didn't have it either. Still, I thanked Georgio again. His alleged criminal ways had come in handy.

He tried, and failed, to look bashful. "All my knowledge is from books. I am an avid reader."

So was I. I read lots of mysteries. That didn't mean I'd become a criminal. Well, except for the breaking and entering. A thought occurred to me. "Georgio, say you wanted to blackmail someone using a phone like this." I held up the little clamshell phone.

His lizard lips parted. "Ah, a topic I have read about. Of course, I would never do something unlawful. In books, however, you would use a burner phone, like the one you hold."

He held out his hand and I gave him the phone. "Yes," he said. "Ideal. This type of phone, you can purchase at the store with no contract or record. You are well on your way to extortion, Rita."

I ignored the extortion part and pointed to the two unknown numbers. "These are unlisted. We've tried looking them up and asked a bill-tracer friend of Flori's. No luck. How can I find out who they belong to?"

Georgio pondered this, standing too close as he did. I sneaked a glance over my shoulder and saw Flori entertaining Jake with cookies. I was grateful that she had packed snacks in her tote bag of spying goodies.

Waving a slender finger in the air, Georgio signaled that he had an answer. "Perhaps you cannot."

"I can't?" I asked, demoralized.

Georgio's smile stretched. "I propose a beautiful scenario. Say you want no record of owning this phone." He held the clamshell aloft and moved so close our hips bumped. "Say also you want no record of the other person receiving your call? It is easy and elegant. Use two disposable phones."

"So you assume the person you're calling has a spare phone and they willingly give you the number?"

He held up his empty hands. "Feel your pockets. Or allow me . . ."

I stepped back and grabbed at my pockets. There was the phone in my jacket pocket. Georgio had accomplished a sleight of hand right in front of me.

He smiled, pleased with himself and the subject. "Yes, how surprising for the receiver. How frightening, to have a strange phone ring in their pocket and on the other line a demand for cash. I like this idea very much. There are many applications."

Great, I'd inspired new deceit in Georgio. Wouldn't Jake be pleased? He already looked vexed, despite holding a cookie. With Georgio following, I returned to the picnic bench.

"Double chocolate with cayenne pepper," Flori was saying. "I like my cookies hot, don't you, Mr. Strong?"

Jake raised an eyebrow at me and Georgio. "Quite the chat you two were having."

Georgio, surely a natural liar, answered for us. "Rita has contacted her landlady about the painting I desire to purchase. Soon it will be mine." He grabbed my hands in his. "Rita, I shall take you to dinner to celebrate when the transaction is complete."

"That's okay," I said, slipping my hands away and moving behind Flori and the protection of her tai chi and cookies.

Jake tapped his watch. "We have to get going." He gave Flori a little hug and told her to keep up hope for Linda. My hug lasted longer, and included a whisper in my ear. "Please be careful, Rita."

Chapter 31

Back at Tres Amigas the smell of singed baked goods filled the air. Addie popped her head out of the kitchen to greet Flori and me. "I'm making Junior some sweet biscuits to pick up his spirits."

A wisp of smoke rose from the tray she held. Flori praised her good sentiments and suggested less time in the oven. "About ten minutes less for those cookies, Addie. Try ten minutes total, tops."

Addie popped back into the kitchen to burn more cookies. Flori and I took seats by the mariachi mannequins, and I relayed Georgio's theory of untraceable phones and blackmail.

She nodded agreeably. "If he's right, then the only way we can identify the receiver is to keep calling and hope someone answers."

Just what I dreaded. "What if they *do* answer this time? If we keep quiet, they can't recognize us, but we can't lure them out. We can't very well say, 'Hey, you're the murderer. Want to come over for tea and cookies and confess?' "

"That sounds like a right nice plan," Addie said, flouncing in, hairnet delicately balanced on her wig. She held out a tray of mostly unburned cookies.

"Sugar cookies," she said proudly. "With extra salt. Salted everything's popular, isn't it? Salted caramel, salted chocolate . . . so I doubled up the amount. What do you think?"

I settled on "Mmmm" to avoid bad manners and because the salinity had dried out my tongue.

"These will be lovely with big pots of tea," Flori said. "Addie, why don't you join us? We might have a little acting job for you, dear."

A while later Addie clutched Don's blackmailing phone with one hand and a bag of hard cinnamon candies in the other. "Okay, let me practice once or twice." She popped a handful of candies in her mouth and said in a low, garbled voice I barely recognized, "I know what you did. Ha, ha, ha."

"Perfect," Flori said.

"Amazing," I agreed. "But instead of 'Ha, ha,' tell them where we want to meet. The bandstand at eight P.M. tonight."

"Cinco de Mayo," Flori said. "A day of battle. Perfect, and the killer won't have much time to prepare."

Neither would we.

Addie crunched some of her candies. Cinnamon and anxiety filled the air.

"It's okay," I said, to myself as well as Addie. "You're calling the city health department first. Ask the receptionist for Gerald Jenkins. When he picks up, give him your lines, and remember to do the different accent so you won't be recognized."

Our plan counted on the killer actually answering and us luring him or her out, without giving ourselves away in the process.

Addie shifted her candies from cheek to puffing cheek. "Okay, got it. Here it goes." She asked for Jenkins in her candy-garbled voice.

My heartbeat increased as his line began to ring. I halfway hoped he wouldn't pick up, but he did.

"Oh!" Addie said, before switching into a gravely New Jersey mobster voice. "Hey! I know what youz did. Meet at the bandstand, tomorrow at midnight, or you'll swim with the fishes. Ha, ha, ha." She hung up. "Oops. I said 'Ha' and messed up the day and time, didn't I?"

I let Flori do the reassuring. "It's fine," she said. "For the best. Tomorrow gives us more time to get ready. All we have to do now is call the two other numbers and, if someone answers, say the very same thing, okay Addie? Think of that as a practice run."

The second number rang fifteen times before we all agreed that Addie should hang up. For the last number, I counted a dozen rings. Flori murmured prayers and crossed her fingers. Then the ringing stopped.

"Oy!" Addie said in a burst of Australian. "I know what you did, mate. Be at the bandstand, midnight tonight! We make a deal, or I'm calling the cops."

She hung up, hands shaking. "Shoot! I messed up big-time. I said tonight, didn't I? Midnight! That's late, isn't it? I got scared." Before Flori or I could ask, she said, "All I heard was breathing. There was someone there, listening. I can't believe I said tonight. You're not really going to meet them, are you? I could call back and cancel or re-schedule."

Flori was getting up, one hand on the particularly arthritic knee that gave her trouble when bad weather approached. "Visiting hours at the jail," she said, pointing to the wall clock.

There would be no calling back to cancel. Addie knew that too. "Well then, I'm jolly well coming with you tonight," she said.

Setting an appointment with a killer has some major drawbacks. There's the waiting, which I hate. Of course, there's the part about meeting with a murderer too. I spent some of the time with Celia, taking her out to Andiamo, our favorite Italian place. Over dinners of lasagna and butternut ravioli, I got a bit emotional. "Celia, if anything ever happens to me, you know I love you," I said. "More than anything."

Celia stabbed a ravioli. "Sure, okay, Mom."

"And your father's a good man. He made a mistake about Linda, that's all." And about all his philandering and fussy food preferences, although even in my emotional state I wouldn't bring those up.

"Okay . . ." Celia said, frowning. "What's going on, Mom?"

I wasn't about to involve my daughter. I glossed over the murderer part. "I have a late appointment tonight. No big deal. Something with Flori. Would you like to stay overnight with your dad?"

"I'm not a kid, Mom. I think that Hugo and I can fend for ourselves." She snagged a bite of my lasagna. "But sure, if you want."

I stopped myself from blathering on about what she should do and know if I never returned. Instead, I chipped away at the delicious charred cheese on the side of my lasagna dish and chided my nerves. Flori would be there, armed with her Taser and tape recorder. I'd be wearing my own tape recorder. Addie would be there too, and she said she'd bring her cousin Jesús, the airbrusher. Jesús was also a wrestler, specifically a minor superstar of the local *lucha libre* circuit. He wore a mask and spandex pants, had a signature move of smashing prop guitars on opponents, and worked under the stage name El Macho.

"He has a running gig at the Golden Owl," Addie had told us. "He's not all that big, but he's good at hitting stuff, and with his mask and all his makeup, he's kind of scary." She'd shivered and added, "What's really scary was that person breathing on the phone. That was terrifying."

Jake called when I got home from dropping Celia off in front of Manny's place. "Care for a margarita?" he asked. "It is Cinco de Mayo . . ."

Yes! I wanted to yell. "Ummm . . ." I said instead. "Flori and I have this thing tonight." I couldn't go tipsy to a blackmail meeting, and I didn't want Jake to know what I was planning. I suspected that he wouldn't approve of fake extortion of a real extortionist/murderer at midnight.

"Girls night out again?" Jake said, his tone suggesting skepticism.

"Right," I said, through guilt pangs.

"Rita," he said. "If you're tailing someone—"

"We're not! No tailing," I said, and realized how snippy that sounded. "I mean . . ." We weren't tailing. We were luring a murderer, which was worse, since we didn't know who to expect.

A long silence on the other end made my stomach flop.

"How about tomorrow night?" I asked. "There'll be fewer people out."

He had a work dinner tomorrow. "We keep missing each other, don't we?" he said, and my heart sank. Maybe the new point in our relationship wasn't one going forward. Maybe we'd realize that we didn't mesh. Jake had another call coming in. "I'll call you again later," he said, and I hoped he meant it.

Flori, Addie, and I met at eleven thirty across the street from the bandstand, under the covered walkway of the Palace of the Governors. A nearby streetlamp flickered, casting shadows down the brick walkway. We moved to the shelter of the

deep inset doorway of the Palace. Addie had
come straight from a singing gig and shivered
in her black cocktail dress and fluffy shawl. Flori
wore her black karate suit and a trench coat with
bulging pockets. She handed me a tape recorder
and offered me my choice of Taser, knife, or gun.

"It's Linda's," she said of the gun. "I always told
her she shouldn't have such a thing."

I feared guns. I'd likely drop it and shoot my own
foot before defending myself. Same with the Taser.
The one time I'd tried it, I accidentally zapped a
parking meter out of commission. I considered a
knife. Knives I could handle. On the other hand,
I could never imagine sticking another human. I
declined. "I have my phone and the tape recorder
in my pocket. You two are my backup. Text if you
see someone suspicious coming."

Addie's brow wrinkled. "Jesús called and said
he can't make it. He has a special Cinco de Mayo
match."

"No worries," I lied, thinking how great it
would be to have El Macho in his mask as backup.
I repressed a nervous giggle, imagining a pro-
wrestling scenario. I *was* worried. The throngs of
young people who'd been out celebrating earlier
were nearly gone. A single man wobbled across
the Plaza. Over by the closed Five and Dime, a
group of guys laughed drunkenly.

We took up our positions. Addie went around
the corner to a side door of the Palace, where she
could watch the streets to my north and west.
Flori took cover in her car, which she'd parked
near the southwest corner of the Plaza. From there
she could see most of the Plaza, or at least as much

as her bifocals and binoculars allowed. I went to the back side of the bandstand, standing near but not on the spot where Napoleon was killed. From my vantage point, Flori's white whale of a Cadillac glowed under the streetlight. All I could see of her was an occasional flash from her binoculars.

I kept in the shadows with my back to the bandstand so that no one could sneak up behind me. Or so I thought. A few minutes later a whispered "Hey" nearly knocked me over. I righted myself and fumbled to turn on the tape recorder in my jacket pocket.

What I recorded was my best friend apologizing. "Sorry!" Cass said from the bandstand stage. Although the stage was only a few feet off the ground, she seemed to tower above me. I felt foolish and very glad it was her.

Cass looked down with concern. "What are you doing?"

I avoided her question by asking my own. "What are *you* doing? How did you know I was here?"

"I didn't. I was walking home from another dreadful late event, and I spotted Flori with her binoculars. She said you were over here. She told me to sneak up and see if you were 'aware' of your full perimeter. What's she mean?"

"Ancient Chinese war tactics," I said, checking my watch. It was ten minutes to midnight, and I didn't want our mystery prey spooked. I quickly explained to Cass what we were doing. Then, as much as I hated to do it, I told my best friend to leave.

"Rita, this is insane!" she said. "No! I'm not going."

"Will you wait with Flori? She shouldn't be

alone. I'm okay. Addie's watching from over there." I pointed toward the dark corner of the Palace, where I hoped Addie was okay too.

Cass hesitated, warned me to be "aware," and then left, walking quickly toward Flori's car. I resumed my scanning of the Plaza, vowing to up my awareness. At a few minutes to midnight, movement caught my eye. The silhouette of a woman, petite with long, bouncy curls, passed by a streetlamp down the block on Palace Avenue. Was that Crystal? My heartbeat sped up and my phone vibrated. I glanced down and saw that Addie had sent a text, warning me about the woman, who was now looking around as if lost or indecisive. What was she doing? Was she getting up her nerve? I was about to lose mine. I inched a few steps around the bandstand, trying to get a better view. I was so fixated on the figure that I forgot to watch my back.

"Rita? Is it you?"

This time I jumped so far I banged my already bruised elbow on the bandstand railing. So much for enhanced awareness.

"Oh, Brigitte!" I said, vexed at the interruption, as well as my nerves. "Please, get into the shadows." I looked back toward Palace Avenue and cursed under my breath. The shadowy figure with bouncy hair was gone, and the church bells were two chimes into counting out midnight.

"I was leaving OhLaLa late," Brigitte was saying. "And here you are, in the dark, by yourself. What are you doing, Rita?"

"You have to go," I told her, ignoring my vibrating phone. "I'm waiting for someone and . . ."

Brigitte was staring at me intently, her face serene yet with a hard, expectant edge.

"You are waiting?" she prompted. "You have an appointment? Here? At midnight?"

Why would she ask that? Adrenaline spiked through my brain. Brigitte had an alibi for Napoleon's death, didn't she? Jake and Cass both said so. She couldn't be the killer. Still, something nagged at my memory. Something about tamales. I attempted to cover my confusion by babbling. "It's Crystal. I may have seen her over by that streetlamp. I think she's the murderer. Like you said, she probably had an affair with Napoleon and he ditched her and she got mad. Then Don, he knew, didn't he? Bartenders—and hot dog guys— they know everything about everybody and he was here on the Plaza that night. He blackmailed her and she had to kill him. Probably she framed Linda because it was convenient or maybe she was jealous of Linda's fabulous tamales. All this could be about tamales. Tragic, isn't it?" I stopped to gulp air. Did she know all too well? She seemed to know what I was thinking.

"Tamales," she said, her tone flat. "Your friend Linda should be proud. Napoleon, he loved those *mole* tamales Linda made for Cinco de Mayo. He even wanted the recipe."

"Yep, she sure makes great tamales!" I said, inching away.

Brigitte stepped in front of me, blocking my path. "Do you know I begged to cook at Crepe Empire?" She waved a finger a fraction from my face. I leaned back until my back hit the bandstand.

She leaned closer. "Napoleon, he said no, I had no talent. The last we spoke, he crowed like a rooster. Even a tamale was a work of art compared to my cooking, he said. A tamale!"

"Horrible man," I said, trying to quell the tremble in my voice. "Your crepes are delicious. Perfect."

Brigitte stared at me. In a creepily steady but louder monotone, she said, "Of course they are. I am a Frenchwoman. Napoleon said I was a mere accountant, a number pusher. He never appreciated me."

"Awful!" I squeaked. "Well, it looks like Crystal's not showing. I better go get my backup." I emphasized *backup*.

Brigitte grabbed my coat sleeve. "Backup? But we are okay here together, *non*? We are friends, Rita?"

"Of course we're friends," I said, inching away. "And my other friends are waiting for me nearby, helping watch for Crystal."

She pulled me back into the shadows. "You will signal to your other friends that you're okay. Then, as you say, 'we make a deal.'"

Addie's words, the phrase she used on the phone to the spooky silent listener. A chill froze my body, and something sharp jabbed my ribs. I looked down. The knife Brigitte held could filet a side of beef, or me. Knees wobbling, I managed to whimper, "Brigitte, I need to go."

"*Désolé*, Rita. Identifying Don as my blackmailer, that was very helpful. But then you call and try to trap me?" She jabbed my ribs. "Wave to your friends."

Brigitte and I stepped out as one. I waved stiffly. Brigitte waved too, with the arm looped around my shoulders. Some boisterous college-boy types walked by. If they noticed us at all, they probably took us for revelers like themselves.

"Now for our deal," she said, drawing me back toward the bandstand.

A mouthful of Addie's salt cookies couldn't have dried my tongue more. "What kind of deal?"

"One where you go away and all is as it should be. Me, with my restaurant and crepes and Jake Strong. He loves me. I can tell. We are perfect together."

Fear tingled through every nerve, along with anger, mostly at myself. I should have told Celia where I kept my will. I should have taken tai chi with Flori or wrestling with Addie's cousin. I should have listened to Jake. I blinked hard, confused by what had to be a mirage formed from sheer terror. A cowboy was approaching across the Plaza, hands on his belt where six-shooters would be, boots clonking on the pavement.

"Ladies," Jake said, and tipped his hat.

Chapter 32

J ake sauntered closer, relaxed as if out for a
stroll with Winston. I tried to warn him without moving my body. Eyes wide, I stared in the
direction of the blade, which I feared was mostly
covered by the sleeve of Brigitte's coat.

"Well, I am a fortunate man tonight," Jake said
slowly, approaching within arm's reach. "It's not
often I happen across lovely ladies."

I willed him to yank me away. He, however, was
waxing folksy about the pale hazy ring around
the moon and some saying about cattle. *Cattle?*
Didn't he notice the tension? The knife? If nothing
else, couldn't he sense that Brigitte was way off
her rocker?

He caught my eye and nodded ever so slightly,
raising my spirits that he understood. To Brigitte,
he said, "Brigitte, I surely did enjoy our dance the
other night." He reached a hand toward her, as if
inviting her to two-step.

She loosened her hold on my arm and gushed that she'd enjoyed their dance too.

Jake continued, sounding like a lonely cowboy. "Here I was, out wandering, looking for a special lady to celebrate Cinco de Mayo with after Rita turned me down." He twisted his lips into a sad smile. "Seeing you, Brigitte, makes me yearn for a dance out here under the moonlight."

Brigitte jabbed me. "You turned him down?" she said, her low voice coming out as a hiss. "Fool."

"Stupid of me," I said, meaning it.

"Where?" she demanded, addressing Jake. "Where would we dance? It's past midnight. You know this town. No nightlife."

I'd had just about enough nightlife. I said I'd get out of their way.

"No you won't," she said in a hissing whisper. "You're still in my way. In everything!"

Holding out his hand, Jake moved closer. "I sure could use that dance, Brigitte. How about a waltz, right here on the Plaza, holding each other close." His brow wrinkled. "Rita, sorry, but I have a new leading lady."

Brigitte's loosening grasp suggested that she was tempted but not taking the bait completely. She stepped backward, dragging me with her. "Rita and I have some business first. A deal to make. Meet me up on this stage in fifteen minutes and I'm all yours, Jake."

And I'd be out of the way. How? Stabbed? Smacked on the back of the head? A quick poisoning? I decided I might as well clear up some questions. "Did you try to run me over?" I asked as she and I backed down the sidewalk. Jake followed, keeping a few steps back.

Brigitte kept moving. "Try?" she said in a harsh whisper. "It is not my fault that you fell off the street. I am glad, however. You were correct to direct my attention from the health inspector to Don Busco. Very clever. Too clever."

Not that clever or I wouldn't be in this mess. To keep her talking, I said, "What about Napoleon? How did you kill him when everyone thought you were dancing with Jake?"

Brigitte's face was so close to mine, I could feel the heat of her cheek and breath. "People are foolish about numbers," she said, voice dripping disdain. "Idiots. Everyone believed that broken watch on his wrist. Did you never think that the time could easily be changed before smashing it? Napoleon called me, like I always told you. What I didn't say was how cruel he was, insulting me."

"Terrible," I said shakily.

"It was unforgivable," she agreed. "I realized then, why do I have to endure such a man, holding me back? Less than twenty minutes, that is all I needed, and then I returned to dance with Jake . . ." She sighed. "He is so kind. We are meant for each other. I saw that immediately. Then I learn that you are in the way." She loosened her grip slightly to wave her fingers at the man of her psychotic dreams. Jake, still a few steps away, reached out his hand again.

"No!" Brigitte snapped. "You must wait, Jake. By the statue."

Jake wasn't following her instructions. In fact,

his pace was increasing, bringing him closer to us with each step. I tore my eyes from his seemingly calm face and scanned the Plaza. In an inky shadow along the Palace of the Governors, I thought I saw a movement. Addie? Cass? Somewhere behind me, I heard a soft gobble.

Brigitte and I reached a truck parked near the northeast corner of the Plaza. The vehicle was red with vintage curves and the silver grill of my nightmarish flashbacks, as well as something else. I'd seen this truck even before on Napoleon's office wall of hubris, in the photo of him and comedian Jay Leno. I mentally kicked myself. Brigitte had access to Napoleon's keys. We'd driven to Don's in one of Napoleon's cars. Now she fumbled with the keys, holding the knife on me with one hand while inserting the key with the other.

"Stop that!" she demanded as I tried to pull away. She emphasized her point by pressing the knife harder into my side.

Jake stepped forward and in one swift movement reached out to Brigitte. "One dance before you go, Brigitte. I won't take no for an answer."

Brigitte tensed and yanked back from him. "Liar," she said, and I felt her trembling, not with fear like me, but a boiling rage. She seemed to hesitate before pushing me away, hard. My hand scraped pavement, and when I scrambled to my feet my first thought was to sprint for Flori's car and safety. But I couldn't. Brigitte wasn't dancing with Jake. She thrust the knife at him, slashing. "You are no better than the rest. Trying to trick me? Trap me! For her? You'll both pay!" She swung the knife wildly.

Jake tore off his jacket and swung it at the knife,

tangling the blade, but only momentarily. Brigitte yanked it back and lunged again.

"Run, Rita!" he yelled.

I ran. Charging at Brigitte's back, I tried desperately to pin her flailing arms. Her strength, fueled by fury, almost overwhelmed me, but I wasn't alone. Jake grabbed her stabbing arm. I clutched a leg, and Flori coming around the bandstand landed a fast-motion tai-chi kick to her shin. Brigitte cursed in French, English, and guttural gibberish as Addie and Cass joined in and managed to wrestle her to the ground. In the distance, I heard the beautiful sound of sirens.

"About time," Flori said. "Cass and I called 911 as soon as we saw you wave."

"I caught that too," Addie said. "You were waving like a beauty queen, Rita, or the Queen Mum herself. Cupped palm, stiff, unnatural for you. I sneaked over to Miss Flori, and she said we should wait to pounce until Jake gave us the sign." Beneath her, Brigitte squirmed and cursed. Flori, threatening more tai chi, pulled out her pink, fluffy handcuffs.

I turned to Jake, who stood a few steps back, wrapping his right arm in his torn coat.

"Are you okay?" I asked. My voice was as shaky as my legs and hands.

"Fine," he said. "A little scratch."

The way he clutched his wounded arm suggested more than a scratch. "What were you doing here?" I asked.

His laugh lines, the ones that made my knees wobbly for much nicer reasons, fanned upward. "You ask me that a lot, don't you?"

I grinned back. "Well, you keep showing up to rescue me."

He looked over at my team guarding Brigitte. "Those are your real rescuers. I was almost too late, as usual. I confess, I was worried about you so I did a little tailing of my own. Guess I wasn't very good because Flori spotted me and sent Cass over to let me know you might be in trouble. When I saw you and Brigitte, I knew Flori was right."

Flori joined us and said with a chuckle, "You did pretty good with your tailing, Mr. Strong, although I made you back on Galisteo Street. I'm still giving you free meals for the rest of the month for your bravery. Just say 'hot pursuit' and we'll know."

Jake made a scoffing sound and lifted his wounded arm. "Some bravery. I'm the only one who couldn't fend her off."

"Yes, you did," I said, and leaned in to kiss him. The kiss was sweet and all too brief, interrupted by Manny's police car, skidding to a stop beside us.

That Friday, Flori, Addie, Cass, and I were again on the Plaza, this time in a line a dozen people deep. The female mariachis harmonized in the background, and red and yellow balloons floated on the park benches and trees. Crystal, apologetic, was throwing Linda a welcome back party, and every tamale-lover in town was invited. The other food cart operators had all joined in.

"I hope she'll still have some of those *mole* tamales by the time we get to the front," Cass said. "I never did get any of those."

"*Mole* tamales. That was a clue. I should have figured it out earlier," I said, moving another inch forward in line. "Brigitte practically gave herself away, and I let it slip right past."

"I should have questioned her alibi too," Flori said. She shook her head. "How easily she tricked us with that watch. And we call ourselves masters of the art of spying."

Cass grinned. "I thought it was the *Art of War* and tai chi, and I'd say you two solved the case. If it hadn't been for your persistence, we wouldn't be standing in this endless line." My crowdphobic friend added a groan I knew she didn't mean. We were all overjoyed to have Linda exonerated and back at her cart.

After a moment, Cass turned to us again. "Wait . . . why were *mole* tamales a clue?"

Flori bowed her head, graciously indicating that I could explain.

"It was right here on the Plaza," I said, setting the stage. "I was with Celia and Linda, and Brigitte was pretending to be my friend."

Cass snorted. "A friend until she stabs you in the back!" Seeing me flinch, she said, "Oops, sorry, that was a bit too real, wasn't it?"

It certainly was. "She was pretending to be Linda's friend too," I said. "All while using her as the scapegoat. But here's what we—I—missed. Brigitte told Linda that even Napoleon loved her tamales. Her *mole* tamales, which Linda only began serving the day of the cockroach incident. Napoleon planted that cockroach, so he knew that Linda's tamales were safe to eat. I'm guessing he went to Linda's cart late that night and tried one. Linda had left the warmer on, so the tamales would still have been good. That tamale was Napoleon's last meal."

"But why did Brigitte kill him right then?" Cass asked. "I mean, that benefit we were at was dull, but it didn't make me want to rush out and stab someone."

"Napoleon loved those tamales. Being a mean bully, he turned that on Brigitte. He called and told her how great they were—how much better than anything she could cook. It must have been one of many insults. She slipped away from the benefit. When they met, I bet he insulted her some more and that was that. The creepiest thing is that she had the presence of mind to cover up her crime by changing his watch, turning it to a later time when she knew she'd be back at the benefit and have an alibi."

"Definitely creepy," Cass said. "To think she was dancing and making small talk immediately after stabbing her boss. But what about Don's murder and the paint from Linda's truck on his wall?"

"The paint was luck," Flori said. "Lucky for Brigitte because it threw more suspicion on Linda. Like Linda said, she scraped Don's wall a while back while helping Don."

Despite the festive mood, and Linda's vindication, a cloud hung over me. "Brigitte befriended me to get close to the investigation," I said. "She knew someone had spotted her the night of the murder and was blackmailing her. She initially thought it was Jenkins the food inspector. That's why she poisoned him. Word is, she slipped the poison into his coffee thermos when he wasn't looking, just like Jenkins Senior thought, only he suspected Don. She probably would have tried again, but then I convinced her that Don was involved. When we broke into his house and she found that voice distorter—like the one on the blackmail calls she'd been getting—she knew for sure. I feel bad about that."

"Don knew the hornet's nest he was poking," Flori said. "I do feel a little sorry for him too, though. I think he would have told the police about Brigitte, eventually, if he had to save Linda from jail."

We had finally made it to the front of the line. "*Mole* tamales, please," Cass said.

Our order came with hugs from a grateful Linda.

Cass took her tamales back to her studio. Flori headed toward Tres Amigas to clean up the lunch dishes we'd left to come see Linda. I started to go with her until she ordered me home. "Don't you have a date to get ready for? Be sure to bat your eyelashes."

I was several yards away when I heard, "And pinch that handsome lawyer on the tush, Rita!"

"I made magic chocoflan," I called back to her and laughed as her "Woohoo!" echoed across the Plaza.

That evening, the doorbell rang minutes after Celia left for a film night with Sky and some other friends. My hair was still damp and butterflies swarmed my stomach, but at least I was mostly bandage-free to greet Jake. He, however, had one arm in a sling. In the other he balanced a box of chocolates and a bottle of wine.

"A happy Friday," he announced.

I took charge of uncorking the wine and urged him to take a seat. He hung his hat on the chair before sitting and leaning back. "It was a good day around the courthouse. Gerald Jenkins Senior is about to face charges for extortion, so no more worrying about that dirty food inspector. Even better, Brigitte won't be getting out on bail. Turns out she had a more than *petite* record back in France. It was expunged because she was a teenager at the time, but the prosecutor pulled some strings and dug up records for stalking and stabbing a classmate. Seems she was named in a few restraining orders too."

I shuddered hard enough to dislodge the cork. "How did no one know any of this?"

The defense attorney at my kitchen table smiled. "Brigitte moved a lot. Some past employers gave her great references, probably to be rid of her. We both dodged a bullet." He looked down at his arm. "Well, mostly."

I poured us extra-large glasses of zinfandel.

"To good news," I said, raising my glass.

Jake seconded my toast, adding, "Our friend Georgio has good news too. I got his latest case dismissed for lack of evidence. I think the judge felt sorry for me, waving my bum arm around."

"I feel sorry for you," I said. I did. His so-called flesh wound had required twenty stitches and a trip to the emergency room. I'd had to force him to go. He'd wanted to storm the jail and free Linda immediately.

"I don't feel sorry for myself," Jake said. He smiled up at me. "I'm a lucky man. I didn't realize how lucky until I thought I might lose you, Rita."

The butterflies migrated to my head. I covered by peering through the oven door. Inside, a cheese and chile soufflé rose to spectacular heights. Almost too high. I stirred the vibrant green cilantro vinaigrette and drizzled some over the asparagus and generally delayed. Jake rose and came over to peek in at the soufflé. When he straightened, he moved closer to me. I felt the bristles on his chin as he leaned in close to my cheek. "Beautiful," he said quietly, his steel-blue eyes focused on me. I took a leap and kissed him.

Rita's Cinco de Mayo Green Chile and Cheese Soufflé

Serves 4 to 6

INGREDIENTS

- 3 T Parmesan, freshly and finely grated
- 3 T unsalted butter
- 3 T flour
- 1 c whole milk
- 1½ c extra-sharp cheddar (4 oz.)
- ½ t salt
- ¼ t freshly ground black pepper
- ¼ t ground cumin
- ¼ t New Mexican dried red chile powder or cayenne pepper
- 4 large egg yolks, room temperature
- 5 large egg whites, room temperature
- ½ c roasted green chiles, mild or medium heat, chopped, preferably New Mexican. Freshly roasted or frozen are best, but canned (well-drained) are also delicious. If using whole roasted chiles, remove any charred skin, seeds, and the stalk.
- ⅛ t cream of tartar

DIRECTIONS

Adjust your oven racks so that you have a lower-to-middle rack available with about a foot of space above it. Preheat oven to 400°F.

Prepare the baking dish. Thoroughly butter the inside of an 8-cup soufflé dish (use a straight-sided dish, about 3½ inches high x 7 inches wide). Add the grated Parmesan to the dish and turn to coat the sides and bottom. The cheese will help the soufflé rise. Set aside.

Make the cheese sauce. In a small sauce pan, heat the milk over medium heat until scalding. Just before boiling, remove the pan from the heat. In a medium sauce pan, melt the butter. Whisk in flour. Continue whisking for about 2 minutes. Gradually pour the hot milk into the flour mixture, whisking until smooth. Stir in the salt, pepper, cumin, and red pepper/cayenne and continue to cook on low for 2 to 3 minutes. The sauce should be quite thick. Remove from the heat.

Place egg yolks in small bowl and mix lightly. Rapidly whisk a few tablespoons of the hot milk sauce into the yolks to temper them. Then, add the yolks, approximately one-fourth at a time, to the sauce, whisking well with each addition. Next, add the grated cheese and chiles and whisk well.

Prepare the egg whites. Add egg whites, cream of tartar, and pinch of salt to a spotlessly clean and dry mixing bowl. Using a stand or handheld mixer, beat until stiff, glossy peaks form. Note: be careful not to overbeat the whites. Overbeaten whites will lose their glossiness. Test the egg whites occasionally by stopping and raising your beaters. The whites will form thick, pretty ripples and peaks. The peaks should remain standing, with slightly drooping, glossy tops. Perfect!

Combine the egg whites and sauce. First, lighten the cheese sauce by folding in about one-quarter of the egg whites. Then add the lightened cheese mixture to the rest of the egg whites, carefully folding them together until mostly blended. It's okay if a few white spots remain, but try to blend in any sauce that might have sunk to the bottom of the bowl. Gently scrape the fluffy mixture into the prepared soufflé dish. Smooth out the top, ensuring that there are no gaps between the soufflé mixture and the bowl. Using a clean knife or your finger, create a thin line around the border of the bowl. This will help the top of the soufflé rise evenly and not catch on the sides of the bowl.

Bake. Set the soufflé dish in the center of the oven and immediately turn the heat down to 375° F. Bake for 35 minutes or until puffy, with a rich golden brown top. The center should still move slightly but not be runny. A skewer, inserted in the center, should come out mostly clean.

Important: Call your guests to the kitchen for the grand moment the soufflé emerges, as it will begin to deflate within minutes.

TIPS:

Don't mess with the soufflé when it's in the oven. No turning is required, and try to resist opening the oven door and peeking inside, especially during the first 20 minutes.

Room-temperature eggs really are helpful in this recipe. They'll whip up quicker and with more lift.

Have fun with different sizes of soufflés. In individual ramekins, check for doneness after 20 minutes.

Calculate your timing. Since soufflé is best straight out of the oven, estimate how long you'll need to prepare and bake your soufflé. After getting all your ingredients and the pan prepped, estimate about 15 minutes to make the cheese sauce, 5 to 10 more minutes to whip the whites, and another 10 minutes to fold together the sauce and whites and smooth the mixture into the bowl. So, together with baking time, give yourself about 1½ hours before your meal.

Roasted Asparagus with a French-Mex Vinaigrette

4 to 5 servings

INGREDIENTS
   1 bundle of asparagus
   ¼ c New Mexican pine nuts
   1 flour tortilla, cut into thin strips, plus cumin,
      red chile powder, and salt on hand to season

VINAIGRETTE INGREDIENTS
   1 c cilantro leaves (packed)
   3 T fresh lime juice
   2 T sherry, white, or red wine vinegar
   1 T shallot, minced
   1 t sugar
   1 t Dijon mustard
   ¼ t salt
   ½ c olive oil
   pepper to taste

DIRECTIONS
   Preheat oven to 400° F

   Prepare the toppings. Cut tortilla into thin strips. Heat a few tablespoons of oil in a frying pan. Add tortilla strips and stir-fry for a few minutes until almost crispy. Season with a pinch each of cumin, salt, and red pepper. Stir-fry a minute or so more. Move to a plate or bowl. Heat a bit more oil in the pan and gently brown the pine nuts, taking care not to burn. Warning: pine nuts brown very quickly. Keep a close eye on them.

Prepare the vinaigrette. Place all ingredients except olive oil in a food processor and whirl a few times. Drizzle in olive oil, blending until emulsified.

Prepare asparagus. Wash the asparagus and break off the tough bottoms. Dry with a paper towel. Place asparagus on a cookie sheet. Drizzle a few tablespoons of oil over asparagus. Sprinkle on a little kosher salt. Toss to coat and arrange asparagus as a single layer. Roast for about 15 minutes, depending on the thickness of your asparagus. Asparagus should be lightly browned on the bottom and tender. Arrange on a platter and cover with tin foil. Immediately before serving, spoon some dressing over the asparagus. Then top with the toasted pine nuts and tortilla strips. This dish is tasty at room temperature, so you can make it before you put in your soufflé. Or heat the asparagus in the microwave or quickly in the broiler if you would like to serve the dish warm. After rewarming, proceed with the dressing and toppings.

Date-Night Cherry Tomato Gratin

Serves 4 to 6

INGREDIENTS

  4 c of day-old or relatively dry French baguette,
    cut into 1-inch cubes
  1 lb cherry tomatoes
  ⅓ c freshly grated Parmesan cheese
  ¼ c extra-virgin olive oil
  ¼ c flat-leaf parsley, chopped
  2 garlic cloves, minced
  ½ t kosher salt
  ½ t cumin
  ½ t coriander
  ½ t dried or fresh oregano
  ¼ t freshly ground pepper

DIRECTIONS

Preheat oven to 375° F. Lightly oil a 9-inch ceramic casserole dish. In a large bowl, mix olive oil, salt, pepper, spices, grated Parmesan, parsley, and garlic. Add bread and tomatoes and toss thoroughly. Scrape into the baking dish and bake in the center of the oven for 35 minutes or until the bread is golden brown and the tomatoes are tender. Serve warm or at room temperature. This dish can be baked alongside your soufflé, since both require the same time and oven temperature.

Note: You can mix all the ingredients and place in the prepared baking dish a few hours ahead of time. Cover with cling wrap and refrigerate until ready to bake.

Flori's Magic Chocoflan

Servings: 12

EQUIPMENT

Bundt pan (straight-sided or classic rounded shapes will be easiest for unmolding) and a roasting pan large enough to hold the Bundt pan and a water bath.

INGREDIENTS

CARAMEL

½ c *cajeta quemada* (goat's milk caramel; can be found in Mexican groceries, online, or in some large supermarkets) or other prepared caramel sauce (salted caramel is particularly yummy)

FOR THE FLAN

3 eggs
1 can sweetened condensed milk (14 oz.)
1 can evaporated milk (12 oz.)
1 t vanilla
¼ t table salt

FOR THE CAKE

¾ c sugar
¾ c all-purpose flour
½ c unsweetened cocoa powder
½ t baking soda
¼ t baking powder
pinch of salt
½ c buttermilk (or use a scant cup of milk with
    approximately 1 T of lemon juice added)

3 T olive or canola oil
1 egg, at room temperature
½ t pure vanilla extract

Prepare your oven, pan, and bain-marie (water bath). Set a rack in the middle of your oven, with space for a Bundt pan above. Spray oil or bakers' oil plus flour on the bottom and sides of the Bundt pan. Add hot water to the bain-marie pan, enough so the water will come about 2 inches up the sides of your filled Bundt pan (press down on the empty Bundt pan to test the water level). Set the pan in the oven and preheat to 375° F.

Pour the caramel into the bottom of your Bundt pan, tipping the pan for even coverage. If your caramel is too thick to pour, heat slightly in the microwave.

Make the cake. Combine the sugar, flour, cocoa powder, baking soda, baking powder, and salt in a large bowl and whisk until well blended. In a separate bowl, whisk together the buttermilk, vegetable oil, egg, and vanilla. Add to the flour mixture, mixing until thoroughly combined. Pour the cake batter into the pan, spread to make the top even, and set aside.

Make the flan. Whisk the eggs, vanilla, and salt in large bowl. Add evaporated milk and condensed milk and whisk again. Gently ladle the flan liquid over the cake batter.

Wearing oven mitts, carefully pull out the oven rack with the bain-marie. Place the Bundt pan in the water bath and (again, carefully!) push the rack back into place. During the baking, the flan and cake batters will magically trade places, with the cake rising to the top. Bake until a toothpick inserted into the center of the cake comes out clean, about 40 to 45 minutes.

Remove the Bundt pan from the bain-marie dish, place on a rack, and allow to cool for at least 2 hours. To unmold, soften the caramel by placing the pan in a hot-water bath for a few minutes. Check the sides of the cake. If any parts of the cake seem to be stuck to the pan, loosen with a spatula or knife. Now, to flip. Hold a plate firmly over the top of the Bundt pan and flip quickly and boldly. If all goes right, you'll have a beautiful caramel-draped flan on top and moist chocolate cake on the bottom. Magic!

Note: For a super-quick chocoflan, use any store-bought chocolate cake mix in place of the cake recipe above. Mix the cake as directed on the box, and proceed with the caramel and flan steps above.

Crystal's Springtime Strawberry-Mint
Agua Fresca

Makes about five cups

INGREDIENTS

- 2 c cold water
- 2 c fresh strawberries, washed and destemmed
  (one or two reserved for garnish)
- ¼ c sugar
- 1 T fresh lime juice
- 1 t fresh mint or peppermint, plus a few leaves
  set aside for garnish

DIRECTIONS

Combine all ingredients in a blender and blend until smooth. Pour through a fine-mesh strainer into a pitcher. If not drinking right away, chill and stir before serving. Garnish with mint, a thin slice of lime, and a few strawberry slices.

AGATHA AWARD WINNER
KATHERINE HALL PAGE

THE BODY IN THE BOUDOIR
978-0-06-206855-2

Flashback to 1990: Faith Sibley is a young single woman leading a glamorous life in New York City. Then she meets handsome, charming Reverend Thomas Fairchild—and it's love at first sight. But a series of baffling mysteries is making her path to the altar rocky as someone seems determined to sabotage Faith's special day.

THE BODY IN THE GAZEBO
978-0-06-147428-6

A bizarre account of an unsolved crime dating back to the Great Depression piques caterer-turned-sleuth Faith Fairchild's interest. Now she's determined to solve a mystery more than eight decades old—while at the same time trying to clear the name of her husband, Reverend Thomas Fairchild, who's been falsely accused of pilfering church funds.

THE BODY IN THE SLEIGH
978-0-06-147427-9

All the Fairchilds are spending the Christmas holidays on idyllic Sanpere Island. While her husband, Thomas, recuperates from surgery, his caterer wife, Faith, rejoices in the rare family-time together. But Faith's high spirits are dampened when she discovers the body of a young woman in an antique sleigh in front of the Historical Society.